the
Onion
girl

Also by Tina Reilly

Flipside
Is This Love?

the Onion girl

TINA REILLY

POOLBEG

This novel is entirely a work of fiction. The names,
characters and incidents portrayed in it are the work of the
author's imagination. Any resemblance to actual persons,
living or dead, events or localities is entirely coincidental.

Published 2000
by Poolbeg Press Ltd,
123 Baldoyle Industrial Estate,
Dublin 13, Ireland
Email: poolbeg@poolbeg.com
www.poolbeg.com

Typesetting, layout, design © Poolbeg Press Ltd.

3 5 7 9 10 8 6 4

A catalogue record for this book is available from the British Library.

ISBN 1 84223 046 8

Set in Agaramond 11.5/13.9 by Patricia Hope
Printed by Litografia Rosés S.A., Spain

www.poolbeg.com

Acknowledgements

Thanks as always to Colm and Conor and Caoimhe.

Thanks also to the best family anyone could have – Mam, Dad, Claire, Seamus, Eithne, Treasa and Aoife. And new brother Tony!!!

Thanks to Margaret and Michael, Frances, Eamonn and the lads, Tom, Pat and Marie and the girls, Mark, Jim and Una (Irish spelling!!!), Deirdre and Michael and family. Also to Pat and Jack, Mary, Dermot and kids, Suzanne, Raymond, Esther and Brian and Louise.

Also to Kathleen, Niamh, Eimear, Betty, Kerry, Margaret (for the babysitting and coffee), Imelda (for reading and the coffee) and everyone in South Dublin who knows me.

Thanks to all my neighbours who've read my books.

Thanks to all the staff in Poolbeg, especially Gaye for all her hard work.

Special thanks to Aware for sending me out information so promptly.

And, finally, thanks to Joe for sharing his knowledge and experience with me – I couldn't have done it without you.

For Caoimhe – the other good luck charm.
And for Tom – for letting me make all his
fantasies come true!!

The Onion Girl speech from *Naked*

"*. . . being abandoned is worse than someone telling you you're worthless.*

At least if someone says you're worthless, they're still there, beside you, talking."

FROM ACT THREE *NAKED* BY ALFONSO MORELLI

Meg

The last time she'd seen him had been when he'd held a massive party in Danny McCarthy's field. Everyone had been there and, though she hated parties, she'd gone because he'd asked her to.

"So will you come?" he said.

"Not in public," she replied.

And they laughed. It was their stupid joke.

She went to the party because he was her best friend in the whole world, her only friend in the whole world and he was leaving. She wondered if he'd miss her like she'd miss him.

That night, the night of the party, everyone got drunk, the way you do when you're seventeen. But she hadn't.

She'd made her way towards him somewhere in the early hours of the morning and sat beside him on the grass. He started talking about the sky and the stars and then he took her face in his hands and kissed her. Not just a small kiss but the whole works. Afterwards, he said, without looking at her, "I'll write."

And because he wasn't looking at her, she knew he didn't mean it. So she said, really casually, "If you want."

Afterwards she was glad because he never did write.

Jack

The last time he'd seen her was at the mad party he'd had in the field down home. The night before his stupid crazy family moved from Wexford to Dublin. And it wasn't as if anything changed in Dublin. In fact, things got worse.

Anyhow, that night, he'd been drinking and drinking and he hated it because he couldn't get drunk and then she had come and sat beside him. He wanted to tell her all sorts of stuff. Stuff about how things were changing but they wouldn't change inside him. And he tried to tell her by talking about the sky and mountains. He thought somehow that life should be like that, get a battering but always still just be. But of course, he was crap with words so he'd kissed her instead. And it had been the best part of the whole bloody night.

So he'd told her he'd write but she hadn't seem bothered. It was just as well because he never did write.

TEN YEARS LATER

December 27th

Instead of one ancient Johnny Logan poster she could see two. Sort of mixed in together. Half a face superimposed on half a face.

He looked sort of funny like that.

She slugged back the last remains of the whiskey and giggled. Drunk. That's why she was seeing double. Blind drunk probably.

Well, she grinned, not blind *drunk, just, just . . . she searched the fog that was her mind for the right phrase . . . super-seeing* drunk.

"Cheers," she gave Johnny a wink. Both of them. So that neither one would be insulted.

She didn't like to insult people.

He knew one thing for sure. He knew that Shane was very rarely wrong. If Shane said it was a sure thing, it was a sure thing.

A hundred to one. Long shot.

There was no going back. Heart thumping, pulse pounding, head spinning like a top, he dumped a monkey on Athleague Guest in the Paddy Powers Steeplechase.

The buzz was mental.

AUGUST

Chapter One

"I – am – knackered!" Linda flung herself into her chair and gave a huge sigh. "Ab-so-lut-e-ly shagged."

Meg said nothing, just continued typing. If anyone should be knackered it was her. She'd spent all day inputting the new student files. All Linda had done was usher the job applicants to the interview room.

"I swear," Linda went on, wriggling her feet out of her narrow stilettos, "the *state* of some of the lads. Like I know an Art teacher is supposed to look arty but, God," she gave a shudder, "one fella had the most awful BO. I don't think he ever had a bath in his life. And like," she leaned toward Meg, "did Aidan actually ask for 'ugly' in his advertisement? Some of the guys could have got lead roles in *Star Trek.*"

"Yeah well . . ."

"Anyway, only one more left. But he's not due until four thirty. I think I'll have a cuppa. Make us some there, will you, Meg?"

"I'm sort of busy, Linda."

"My arse you are. Typing, huh, bloody doddle compared to what I was doing."

"Yeah well . . ."

"Two sugars, hold the milk."

What was the point? Meg got up and flicked on the kettle. She might as well get herself a cup too. It looked like she'd be there until six, which was probably just as well because it'd delay the start of her night out with her flatmate, Ciara. A wild night is what Ciara had said. Meg wasn't into wild nights. Well, not the wild nights Ciara liked, anyhow.

Linda had launched into a diatribe on her husband. Holding her nails up to the light she said, "He fell off the wagon again this weekend – well," she made a face, "'fell' probably isn't the word. Leapt off in bloody glee, more like. Made a holy show of himself singing up and down the street, and Clive and me looking out the window at him. Poor Clive was mortified. I was –"

Someone knocked on the door.

"Jaysus, who the hell is that?"

"Probably the guy for the interview," Meg said mildly. She handed Linda her tea.

"Come in," Linda snarled at the door. "What's he doing arriving early?" she hissed as Meg scurried back to her desk.

"Eh, sorry," a fella poked his head in the door, "I'm looking for the interview room. I'm here for the Art teacher job."

There was something very familiar about that voice. Meg glanced up quickly. The guy had come further into the room, but the sun was shining across his face and she couldn't see him properly.

Linda looked happy though. She gave the guy a big smile and Meg saw her hastily shove her feet back into her shoes. "The Art teacher job," she said, "Well of *course*, now you just hang on a sec and let me locate the file."

"No rush."

His accent wasn't all Dublin. Meg tried to place it. It almost sounded Wexford . . .

"And you are?" Linda bent over the desk, showing plenty of straining buttocks as she looked for the interview list.

"Jack," the guy said, "Jack Daly."

"Oh, I like the name Jack, very manly."

He grinned.

Jack Daly? Naw, it couldn't be. But suddenly Meg's heart began to thump. Big heavy thumps. Her fingers slipped on the keyboard. It couldn't be . . .

"Nice school you have here," Jack said. "Bit of a maze though."

"Isn't it?" Linda giggled.

It *was* him. He'd moved towards Linda's desk and Meg could see his face. The face that she'd thought about for years and then blanked from her mind. Thinking about him hurt, so she hadn't thought about him.

"I have your application here," Linda said. She eyed Jack up and down, "I must say you're keen; you're twenty minutes early."

"Aw, well, you know what they say, the early worm catches the bird."

He was *flirting* with Linda. On the day of an interview. And Linda was giggling like the eejit she was. And he *was* a worm, sure he'd never even written . . .

Smash!

Her mug hit the ground and coffee went everywhere. All the new student files were drenched.

"Shit!" Jumping up, she pulled the files out of the way of the dripping coffee. They were going to be ruined.

"Here." Her mug was shoved under her nose. "Lucky it didn't break."

"Thanks." She looked up and her eyes met Jack's.

They both recoiled at the same instant.

"Meg?" He sounded disbelieving. His eyes widened, "Meg Knott?"

Typical. Her face flamed red. "Yeah." There was a lump in her throat.

"It's me," a delighted smile, "Jack. Jack Daly!"

All the times she'd fantasised about meeting him, all the things she thought she'd say and all she managed was, "Ha."

She stood up. He stood up. He handed her the mug. She took it. "Ha," she said again, only this time it sounded even more of a crap thing to say. She focused on her mug, on the way the handle . . . oh God, she looked *awful*.

Jack was shaking his head and grinning. "Jesus, Meg," he said.

"Are you ready or what?" Linda, sounding disgruntled, spoke. "Like twenty minutes doesn't last forever."

"Meg's an old friend of mine," Jack turned to face Linda. "Jesus, we haven't seen each other in, what, how long?"

"I dunno," Meg managed a weak smile. She wished she'd got her hair cut instead of cancelling her appointment. "Ten years?"

"Must be." Another grin.

She thought of the last time she had seen him. And the way he was meant to write to her and he hadn't. The hurt flared up raw again. She gulped and made a big deal of putting the mug on her desk.

"It's half four now," Linda said. "You coming or wha'?"

"Eh, yeah." Jack seemed reluctant to leave. "Eh, Meg, how about a drink after?"

A drink? What would they say to each other? She could hardly ask him why he hadn't written, could she? That'd be a *real* case of 'get-a-life'.

"Well?" Jack pressed. He looked sort of anxious. Embarrassed too.

"Well, I'd really like to," she said, "but, I'm already going somewhere."

"Oh," he shrugged, disappointed. He gave a little laugh. "Right."

"Best of luck with the interview."

"Yeah. OK." He didn't move.

"Come on, willya," Linda snapped.

"How about lunch sometime? Maybe if I get the job or something?"

He'd probably forget that too. Meg shrugged. "Sure."

"Good." He wished she'd look at him. "Bye now."

"Bye." She watched as he followed Linda from the room.

She stood looking at the door for what seemed like ages. What an anticlimax that had been! For some reason whenever she'd thought about Jack, she had visions of him saying how much he'd missed her and how sorry he was not to have written. But it hadn't happened. Maybe to him it didn't matter as much as it did to her.

She wondered what he was like now. Different anyhow, that was for sure. He looked more together than before. Not the wild guy she'd known. And cared about.

But her? Huh! She was the same hopeless idiot he'd always known.

Mentally she went over everything she'd done.

She'd spilt her coffee.

She'd gone red.

She'd got tongue-tied.

Yep, same hopeless basket case.

❧

Chapter Two

Jack arrived back at the flat he shared with Peadar around six. After the interview, he'd driven out to Malahide. He had thought of calling in to Meg, but that ould wan with the short skirts had frightened the life out of him. Talk about laying it on. He grinned at the memory. He grinned at the thought of seeing Meg again.

And she looked kinda the same. All that mad red hair and those massive brown eyes. Her eyes hadn't changed. And her voice was still soft, the way he remembered. And even if he didn't get the job, he was going to call in to her.

In a few weeks.

Well, maybe.

He sketched the sea as he sat in his car. He liked the way it moved, a slow heave far out in the water, which in turn made a wave, which gained rapid pace before washing up onto the sand. He liked the noise of the sea and he liked trying to capture it on paper.

It passed the time.

The summer days were awful slow. As he sketched, he listened to the racing results on his crappy car radio. Another reason for parking out at Malahide, it was the only place he could get a half-decent reception.

His car was a banger. An old Volkswagen, falling apart because he never seemed to have the money to do it up. Bright yellow flaking paintwork, laryngitis in the engine and, boy, did it guzzle petrol. His brother-in-law, a mechanic, had told him not to buy it. So, him being him, he'd bought it. Feck it, he'd thought, it's my money.

At five thirty, he'd driven back to the flat. Peadar's shiny car was in the car park. His was like the poor relation beside it. Stepping out, he locked it.

"Hi," a cheery voice greeted him.

Looking up, he saw Vanessa, one of the girls in the flat on the second floor. She was getting out of her car – a shiny Astra with alloy wheels. Vanessa was a babe. Peadar was mad about her but Peadar was spoken for. Jack liked her car but he'd always been a little afraid of her, she seemed so . . . so . . . he tried to think of the word – the best he could come up with was *womanish*, which didn't describe her at all really.

"How's it going?" he grinned.

She walked towards him, long legs and blonde hair. "You're looking smart," she said, in her perfect, husky voice, coming up really close so that he could smell her perfume. "Nice tie." She touched it briefly and smiled.

"Thanks." Jack grinned again. He didn't know what

to say to her. It was one thing fantasising about her, quite another actually having a conversation with her. "I'd a job interview today. Bloody shirt had me murdered."

Vanessa leaned against the bumper of his car. "A new job – hey?" She sounded impressed.

He wanted to tell her not to lean on the car bumper too much or she'd knock it off, but he hadn't the nerve.

"So what's the job you'll be leaving?"

"I'm a teacher." He wasn't going to say any more. Maybe if he told her he had no job, this interest she seemed to have in him would wane. "I, eh, teach."

She giggled. "Naw!"

He wanted to kick himself. "Yeah," he stuttered. "I like moving from one job to the next, place to place."

A look of alarm crossed her beautiful features. She had huge hazel eyes, he noticed with a jolt. Really nice face. "You're not leaving here?" she asked.

"Naw," Jack shook his head. "Not unless Peadar throws me out." He hadn't meant to say that.

He was relieved when she seemed to think he was joking.

"Good," she beamed. "'Cause we're having a party and you and Peadar are invited."

This was great. "Great."

"Tonight. Around eleven or so. Be there or be square." With that she gave him another thousand-watt smile, tweaked his tie and walked away.

This day was getting better and better. Meeting

Meg, doing a good interview, and now, Vanessa asking him to a party.

Life was definitely on the up.

At last.

Six o'clock, Meg switched off her computer. She had to hurry to catch the six twenty bus into the city centre. All week she'd been dreading this night out. But at least by tomorrow it'd be over.

The phone rang.

Typical.

Still, it meant she'd be late for meeting Ciara.

"Hello, Yellow Halls?"

"Meg Knott, please."

She recognised Dominic's voice immediately. Her heart lurched. She felt sick. "Yeah. Yeah. Speaking. Is that – is that Dominic?"

"The very man." Dominic paused. "I'm ringing about your audition for the play."

Her heart went mental. She tried to sound normal and failed. Her voice went all fluttery, "Have I – is there – am I a part in it?"

A ponderous Dominic pause. "We'd like you to do the Onion Girl."

She couldn't have heard right.

The main part?

The *main* part?

The main *part*?

Her?

"The main part? Me?"

Dominic chuckled. "Well, yes. Alfonso thought you were perfect for his vision."

Alfonso, a real 'hey-chill-out-everything's-cool' friend of Dominic's had written the play and though it reminded Meg of a skewered version of Friel's *Philadelphia Here I Come* she'd liked it.

She gulped, speechless. To think that they all thought she was good enough for a main part. *The* main part.

"I suppose you want to know who else is in it?" Dominic asked.

She didn't care. She was in it.

"Sylvia is the nanny." Dominic snorted a bit. "She'll be over the moon about that. Johnny's playing the alter-ego and Tony and Avril are the lovers."

She hadn't a clue who Avril was.

"Avril's the new girl. She was there the other night," Dominic explained as if reading her mind. "I felt it was my duty to encourage her, you know."

"Right." Dominic was an asshole. Still he'd given her the main part. If he'd wanted her to kiss his feet, she would have.

Well, provided he'd washed them first.

"Rehearsals will start the last week of August – is that OK?"

"Fine."

"I'll drop you a note to remind you. Every Monday and Thursday at eight from then on."

"Great."

"So we'll see you then."

"Count on it."

Dominic hung up.

She put the phone down.

Imagine, *her*, the main part. It was brill. Totally great. The best thing she'd ever done.

Imagine, *her*, the main part. With everyone depending on her.

God.

With Dominic directing her.

Double God.

But wasn't it great she'd been offered the part?

Yep. She was good enough for that.

But maybe, the thought crept up on her, maybe she'd be *crap*.

But if she refused the part they'd all hate her.

What would be worse, to be hated or to be crap?

Maybe she should wait and see.

Expect the worst and anything that happened would be a bonus.

And for the first time in ages, she felt happy. Happy enough to suffer a night out with the girls at least.

But, Meg thought, it wasn't just getting the main part that had made her happy. She'd been sort of happy since seeing Jack. It was like finding something she'd lost.

Maybe life was on the up?

At last.

∽∾

22

Chapter Three

The Orange Tree was a pub in Temple Bar. It was usually jammed and that Friday night was no exception. Music boomed out onto the street and people stood, drinks in hand, outside. Meg scanned the crowd for Ciara. There was no sign of her. Normally, Ciara's shrieking laugh could be heard miles away.

She sighed. Why the hell had she bothered? Because Ciara had spent the last few weeks nagging at her to go out, that's why. And if she hadn't come, Ciara would spend the next few weeks nagging her and making her feel like a freak. I mean, thought Meg, as she pushed her way into the overcrowded, smoky pub, there have to be other people in the world who dread socialising with mad, drunk women.

There *had* to be.

"How's it goin', gorgeous?" a big fella leered down at her.

She smiled politely and tried to push past him.

23

"I assed you a question," he said. "How's it goin'?"

"I just want to find my friend."

His face grew cross. He stood back a bit from her. "How's it going?" he repeated belligerently.

"It's not fucking going your way, that's for sure," one of his mates chortled, slapping him on the back. "I don't think she's into ya."

"Aw, well, fuck off so!" The big fella waved his arm and glared at her. "Don't waste my time, baby."

His mates laughed. The one who had slapped him on the back winked at Meg. "Don't mind him. He's out of it."

She wished *she* was out of it. She smiled in what she hoped was an inoffensive way, muttered, "Excuse me," and finally got away from them. Please let me find Ciara, she prayed. *Please.* She suddenly thought that maybe Ciara hadn't come here in the end. Or maybe she'd arrived and gone somewhere else. That would be typical. Still, Meg thought, she'd made the effort. Maybe she should just go home. It was amazing the great feeling that gave her. She could just leave and go back to the flat and have a quiet night in and –

"Meg – you came!" Ciara's voice shrieked across the room.

Meg and the rest of the room glanced across. Ciara was standing on a table and waving frantically. *"Over here! Over here!"*

Meg pretended not to see her.

"Meg!" Ciara yelled even louder and waved more vigorously.

God, she was going to die. She put her head down and pretended to look towards the bar.

"OY!" A fella beside her gave her a shove. "Yer wan over there seems to be calling you."

"Pardon? What? Sorry?"

"That girl over there is calling you," the guy pointed towards Ciara who was nodding encouragingly.

"Hi – Meg?" Ciara did a sort of dance. *"It's meeee!"*

"Do you know her?" the guy asked. He was grinning, his face turned towards her flatmate.

"Oh, yeah." She tried to make it seem as if she'd just noticed Ciara. "I was, eh, looking for her."

"Well, looks like you've found her," the fella laughed.

Ciara, satisfied that Meg was on her way over, was busy climbing down from the table. A couple of lads were making a big deal of helping her.

"Thank you," Meg said to the guy who'd pointed Ciara out.

He took no notice. He was still busy staring over at Ciara. "She looks a good laugh," he said. Running his hand through his hair, he asked, "D'you fancy giving me an intro?"

"What? You want to meet her?"

"Well, if that's all right." He slicked his hair back again.

"Oooh, I dunno."

"Is there a problem?" The guy asked. He was quite good-looking. "Well?"

"Oooh, I dunno." Ciara would kill her for bringing a fella over on a girls' night out. Kill her.

"Meg, will you stop chatting that fella up and get over here!" This was followed by a shriek of laughter.

"I'd, eh, better go."

"Fine," the guy shrugged, lifting his pint to his lips. "Whatever."

As she moved away, he said, "Tell your friend, Greg says 'hi'."

Eileen, Peadar's girlfriend, arrived over at the flat around ten that night. Dressed in green sprayed-on hipsters and a green sparkly top, she reminded Jack of a Christmas tree. Massive dangly earrings added to the overall effect.

"Hiya." Pushing past Jack, she entered the small flat. Standing, hands on hips, she looked around. "Where is he?"

Her brown frizzy hair was bigger than her face – she'd enough make-up on to do a makeover of the whole American continent. Jack wondered again what Peadar saw in her.

"Well?" Eileen demanded.

Jack shrugged. "He's, eh, in there." He nodded at Peadar's bedroom. "He's getting dressed. Go on in if you want – I'll turn the telly up."

Eileen threw him a contemptuous look. "Juvenile sense of humour."

"Ah, but at least I *have* a sense of humour." Jack

plonked himself down on the sofa and put his feet up. "Not like some people."

"And at least I have a job," Eileen shot back, "not like some people."

"Ouch," Jack half-grinned, "that hurt."

Eileen didn't reply. She perched herself on the arm of the sofa and began looking at her watch.

"It bruised my ego," Jack went on in a deadpan voice. "I really need someone to come and massage it better."

Eileen began to go red.

"Will you stroke my ego, Eileen?"

"Shut up, Jack." It was the best she could do. The guy mortified her. Peadar had told her to ignore him, but she couldn't. Every time she met him, there he'd be, laughing at her with those lazy eyes.

"Aw," he said, "I'm –"

She faced him, full on. "Shut up."

To her surprise, he shrugged. "Yeah, right." And then, as a reluctant afterthought, he added, "Sorry."

She didn't bother to acknowledge his apology. Jumping up from the chair, she went to Peadar's door and hammered on it. "Are you nearly ready in there?"

Jack watched amused. He couldn't understand why on the earth the girl wouldn't just go into Peadar's room. She was calling through the door to him now, asking him to hurry up. She only wanted Peadar to hurry up because she didn't want to be left alone with Jack. Jack knew she hated being left alone with him –

she was petrified of what he'd say. He didn't know what made him be so horrible to her – he guessed it was because he didn't know what else to say to her. What would a sacked teacher and a genetic engineer have in common? Not a bleeding lot.

"I'm ready. I'm ready." Peadar emerged from his room and planted a kiss on Eileen's lips. "I couldn't find me shoe was all."

Eileen began to pat him down, smoothing his hair, straightening his collar and smiling up into his face. "I like those jeans on you," she said. "Very nice."

Peadar began to nuzzle the side of her neck and she pushed him off.

She looked so different when she was with him, Jack thought. A lot nicer. He watched as Peadar pushed her hair from her face and said something to her. She gave a giggle. They did look well together. Still, he thought, as he heaved himself from the sofa and stood up, it'd be fecking boring being with the one person all the time. Even worse if you couldn't be guaranteed a bit of action at the end of the night. And with Eileen, a lack of action seemed to be guaranteed as far as he could tell. "We ready to go?" he asked, getting a small thrill out of butting in.

Peadar waved him away. "You go on. We'll join you later." He didn't take his eyes from Eileen.

"Aw, no, it's cool. I can wait." He didn't know what made him say that.

"No," Peadar said. "You can't."

28

"But we're heading to a party and –"

"I'm not going to a party with him," Eileen said. "No way, Peadar. If I wanted to go out with Jack, I'd go out with Jack. But I don't."

"If I wanted to go out with you, I'd slit me wrists," Jack said.

"See? See? That's why I can't stand being –"

"OK." Peadar rolled his eyes and said affectionately, "We'll do what you want." He said to Jack, "You don't need me anyhow, do you?"

"Guess not." Jack wanted to kill Eileen. "But Eileen might get a few hints on how to, you know, how to –"

"Shut up, you," Eileen shrieked at him.

Jack grinned and decided to exit. As he climbed the stairs to the next floor, all he could hear was Peadar saying, "Don't be minding him, for Jaysus' sake."

"Wow," Ciara moved up a bit on the seat to let Meg in. "We're all mad jealous here." She looked around at her mates. "Aren't we?"

"Yep." That was Laura, Ciara's friend from work.

"Yeah." That was someone Meg didn't know.

"Lucky wagon." That was another girl from Ciara's work, whose name she couldn't remember.

"Imagine arriving in," Ciara went on, "and getting to chat up the nicest-looking fella in the place." She gave her an elbow in the ribs. "Wagon," she teased.

"What?" Meg began to take off her jacket. It was awful the way all the girls were looking at her.

"That fella you were talking to," Ciara said. "Nice or what?"

"More shag in him than a carpet," Laura agreed.

There was laughter and Meg joined in. She would have found it funny if she'd heard the line on the telly, but in a pub, tension invading every muscle of her body, it was like she was laughing outside but not laughing inside.

"I wasn't chatting him up," she said eventually. "In fact –"

"Course you were," Laura gave her a dig that nearly shattered her ribcage. "I mean," she waved her drink about and some of it slopped over her hand, "the only people that wouldn't chat him up would have to be *blind.*"

"Or lesbian," the other girl said.

"Naw," Ciara shook her head. "I betcha they use him to *convert* lesbians."

This comment was taken very seriously before they all burst out laughing again.

Meg sat uneasily between them. She wished she had a drink in her hand. It would give her something to do. Taking some money from her purse, she stood up. "I'm just heading to the bar," she said. "Does anyone want anything?"

"Yeah, get us some nuts," Laura said.

More sniggering.

"His preferably," Ciara pointed to where the guy was standing.

He waved over and raised his drink.

A stunned silence ensued.

"Did you see that?" Ciara whispered delightedly, tugging Meg back down. "He *waved.*"

"That's 'cause he thought you looked nice," Meg answered. "He wanted to meet you."

"No way!"

"Feck off!"

"You're joking, right?"

She shook her head. "Nope. He said he thought you looked a laugh." Once again she was the centre of attention. "He, eh, well, that's what he said."

Ciara gave her a push. "Tell him to come over."

"I *can't.* Don't make me do that."

Laura rolled her eyes. "What's the big deal? Just tell him to come over." She half-sneered. "You *were* the one he was talking to."

"I know but –"

"Just say we'd like to meet him," one of the other girls said.

"I *can't.*"

Ciara stood up alongside her. "Nope," she said. "Meg's right."

Meg managed a smile. Thank God. Ciara mustn't be as drunk as she looked.

"Nope," Ciara said, "if the mountain won't come to me, I'll have to go to the mountain." She draped her arm across Meg's shoulder. "Come on, flatmate."

The three girls cheered and began banging their glasses on the table. *"Go. Go. Go. Go."*

People at other tables turned and looked.

Meg wondered miserably why things like this *always* seemed to happen to her.

Jack stood in the corridor outside apartment 4b. The thump of party music could be heard from behind the door. Head-pounding stuff, it sounded as if things were in full swing. He loved a party, getting legless, getting laid. Mostly in that order.

He wished Peadar had come with him. Peadar was brilliant craic. Naw, he corrected himself, Peadar *used* to be brilliant craic. Ever since he'd met Eileen, he'd become a right fecking mammy. And such a bleedin' moan. All he ever seemed to go on about was cash. It was doing his head in.

Still, he consoled himself with the thought that maybe Vanessa would get off with him. She had certainly seemed interested when he'd met her in the car park. Well, sort of interested. She'd asked him to the party, hadn't she?

Taking a deep breath, he knocked on the door.

It was opened before he'd even finished his second rap. He had to catch his breath sharply at the state of the wan that answered it. She hardly had a thing on. Holding onto the doorknob, she eyed him up and down. "Hi," she said, batting her foot-long eyelashes at him. "I betcha you're the yella fella we keep hearing about."

Jack gave an uncomfortable grin. "Really?"

"Oh yeah," the girl gave an exaggerated nod. "The famous yella fella." Her voice seemed to rise. Suddenly she staggered a bit as someone pushed her out of the way.

The someone was stunning. Vanessa, aka The Blonde from Beyond, dressed in a short skirt and flimsy top. She flashed Jack a smile and took him by the arm. "Don't mind her," she tossed a half-amused glance at the other girl, who was staggering away. "She's one of my flatmate's friends. A headcase." Giving him another smile, she said, "It's great you could come."

"Isn't it?" Jack grinned.

She laughed. "Come on and I'll get you something to drink."

"Great." He allowed her to lead him into the party, past people in various stages of drunkenness. The apartment was bigger than his and Peadar's. And nicer.

They went past the television room where some people were dancing. One girl, who looked totally locked, was lying splayed out on the floor, comatose. A fella was standing over her, trying to wake her.

"It's all right, Dan," the girl with hardly any clothes on was saying. "She always gets like that. She'll wake up in a bit."

Dan wasn't convinced. Picking the girl up, he began to make his way toward the window. "Gonna give her some air," he said.

"More of my flatmate's lovely friends," Vanessa said. Jack grinned.

"And here we are." She took her arm from his and indicated the drinks table. "Have what you like. We've loads."

They had. Every type of booze was there. They had really splashed out. Jack took a can of lager and pulled off the ring-tab. "What's the occasion?" he asked. "Someone's birthday or something?"

Vanessa shrugged. "No reason. Just felt like a party." She avoided his eye and went a bit red.

The fact that she blushed made Jack feel more confident. "Do you always do what you feel like?" he asked. He tried for a casual tone, in case she'd take offence. His eyes drank her in. She was gorgeous. The nicest-looking girl in the place. Nicest-looking *woman* in the place, he amended.

"Most of the time," she answered softly. There was nothing casual in her voice or in the way her eyes gave him the once-over.

The thrill of it made him swallow the wrong way. He began to cough and his drink began to come down his nose. He had to place the can on the table as he hacked his guts up. In between spluttering and coughing he tried to apologise.

She observed him coolly, an amused look on her face. "Whatever did I say?" she asked innocently. Tipping her glass on his can, she said, "Cheers. See you later."

And she was gone.

Jack wanted to kill himself. What a moron!

Morosely, he picked up his can and, leaning back against the table, he began to drink.

The only solution, Meg decided, was to get drunk. She only ever got drunk in social situations. And this was one desperate social situation.

Gorgeous Greg had jumped at the chance to join their table. He'd even dragged two passable mates along with him. Now there was a whole heap of people she didn't know. She'd been introduced but two seconds after she'd been told people's names, she'd forgotten them. And it was impossible to hold a conversation with someone whose name you couldn't remember. It was impossible to hold a conversation anyhow.

Ciara had temporarily abandoned her and was giving all her attention to Greg. Laura and the rest were having a laugh over something that had happened to Laura at work. Meg tried to laugh too, but she couldn't. Or at least her laugh sounded sort of fake. All she wanted was to go home. But if she went home they'd all think she was a dry shite. So she had to get drunk.

She'd just stood up from the table when a huge groan went up. "Oh noooo!" Laura leaned across the table and tugged at Ciara. "Look who's here!"

Ciara looked up. And shrieked. *"Aw, Jesus, don't let him see me!"*

"What's the matter?" Meg asked.

"It's Danny," Ciara hissed. She pulled Meg down. "Here, sit down in front of me, so he doesn't see me."

"What's the matter?" Greg asked.

"It's this guy from work," Laura explained. "He fancies Ciara."

"Does he now?" Greg grinned at Ciara. "Well, good for him."

"Oooh, he's coming, he's coming." Ciara tried to hide behind Meg.

"He did say that he might drop in later," Laura suddenly remembered. "He said it just as you left the office today."

"Great." Ciara, sounding really pissed off, tried even harder to hide behind Meg.

Meg felt awfully sorry for Danny. It wasn't as if the guy was horrible or anything. Tall, brown-haired, slim. He even wore nice clothes. In fact, the only thing wrong with him was that he made it clear that he was nuts about Ciara and she hated that.

"How ye?" Danny smiled brightly around. "Out for the night, hey?"

"Yep," one of the girls answered.

"Hello there, Ciara." Danny gave a tentative wave in her direction.

The three girls began to grin.

"Danny." Ciara gave a curt nod.

"I'm just getting a pint, I'll join ye in a sec." He shoved his hand into his pocket and pulled out a tenner. "Anyone else?"

They all refused. Meg decided to wait until he came back down from the bar before getting her own drink.

He arrived back ten minutes later, a pint of Guinness in his hand. The only space available was beside Meg. Sitting in beside her he smiled, "You're Meg, right?"

She was surprised that he knew her name. "Yeah."

"You're Ciara's flatmate, right?"

"I am."

There was a pause. Meg didn't know what she was supposed to say. Danny was staring hard into his pint of Guinness.

"I'm Danny," he muttered.

"Yeah, I know."

"So you know me," Danny's voice lifted. "You've heard of me?"

"Oh yeah."

"From Ciara, like?"

"Who else?" She gave a bit of a laugh and a shrug. Conversation was flowing. Danny wasn't that hard to talk to.

"So she's mentioned me, like?"

"Loads of times."

"Oh," Danny sat up straight. "And here was I thinking she hated my guts."

Something jarred in her head. Had she just said the completely wrong thing? Desperately she tried to backtrack. "Well, she doesn't hate your *guts*," she began.

"No," Danny took a deep drink from his pint. "I know that now."

Meg knew she had to get drunk. "Excuse me," she said, standing up. "I, eh, just want to go to the bar."

Danny gleefully let her past and then plonked himself in beside Ciara.

A little while later, after Jack had polished off his second can, Jean, Vanessa's flatmate, came over. She wasn't half-bad, but compared to the opportunity he'd flunked just a while ago, she didn't even come close.

"So you came," Jean snapped out, making him jump.

"What?" Jack decided to have a fag to calm himself down. This had to be the crummiest party he'd ever been at. He'd arrived too late, everyone was locked and he still felt sober. He really needed a smoke. Digging his hand into the pocket of his jeans, he pulled out his fags.

"I said, so you came," Jean answered, pouring herself a large drink. "Vanessa was planking in case you'd forget." She threw the drink into her mouth. "It was great to see her like that," she added.

"Vanessa?" Jack said. He wondered absently if he was drunk or something. He couldn't seem to follow a thing the girl was saying.

Jean nodded. "We call you the yella fella," she confided. "And Van keeps saying that you're the shag to bag." She leaned in nearer. "She fancies the arse offa you – well, that and other things."

"Yeah?" Jack wondered if she was making this up.

"Absolutely," Jean shook her head. Then nodded it.

The girl was seriously drunk, Jack decided.

"I mean," Jean went on, "you are the star guest tonight. You are the reason for this." She indicated the room. "You are," she leaned up against Jack in an attempt to point at him, "dee main man. You know what I'm saying?"

Jack nodded. "Yeah," he said weakly. He held out the packet of cigarettes to Jean. "D'you smoke?" Even though she was drunk and rambling, he liked what she was saying.

Jean shook her head. "Gave them up," she said.

"Right." Jack shoved the fag between his lips and flicked on his lighter. With a smoke in his hand he felt calmer, more relaxed. Leaning back against the table, he inhaled deeply and blew the smoke upwards.

"Vanny hates fags," Jean said idly. "She says it's a filthy habit." She couldn't suppress her smile at the alarmed look on Jack's face. But he recovered quickly.

"Couldn't agree more," he nodded. "Fuckin' awful habit." Then he took another drag and grinned at her. He wished he could put the damn thing out but it was too late now.

"Woah, here she is, our gracious hostess," Jean said sardonically, raising her glass as Vanessa came into view. "Hi, Vanny, just keeping him warmed up for you."

Vanny ignored her. "Come on," she said gaily, taking Jack's hand, "Gimme a dance. You're the only fella I haven't had a dance with."

"His name's Jack," Jean said. "And you haven't danced with everyone – Dan said you refused to dance with him."

"You invited him. You dance with him."

The two girls glared at each other. Jack tried not to look at either of them. Instead he pretended to gaze about the place. He didn't know what was going on and he didn't much care – all he wanted was to dance with Vanessa. He wouldn't fuck up a second time, that was for sure.

"Come on, Jack, let's go." Still glaring at Jean, Vanessa pulled at his sleeve.

Jack stubbed out his fag on a saucer and putting down his drink said, "Ready whenever you are."

"Enjoy," Jean raised her glass and nodded. "I would." She smirked at the look her flatmate gave her.

"Why is she talking all the time to that Greg fella?" Danny asked.

It was about the thousandth time he'd asked her. Meg gritted her teeth. "Because she wants to," she answered for the thousandth time. Taking a massive gulp of cider she prayed for it to kick in. Four pints and *nada*.

"That girl," Danny waved his hand about, "is breaking my heart."

"Is she?" Another mouthful. Maybe if she drank it quickly, she'd fall asleep or something.

"I love her, I do." Danny put his hand on his heart and gazed mournfully at Meg. "I keep telling her, but will she listen?"

Meg couldn't imagine anyone not listening to Danny, especially as he repeated everything about a million times. Trust her to get landed with the person no one else wanted to talk to.

"I love her." He dropped his head. "I really do."

She tried to detach herself by gazing past him to the others. Ciara, who was doing a great job of totally ignoring Danny, was holding court at the table. She was telling them all about James, their landlord, and of how he had promised faithfully to fix their shower in the coming weeks. Doing a brilliant take-off of his slimy accent, she was making everyone laugh. "And," Ciara threw a glance in Meg's direction, "he fancies the knickers off Meg."

Everyone roared.

"No, he doesn't –" The rest of Meg's sentence was drowned out in laughter. Ciara was doing an impression of James' 'leer'.

Meg noticed the way Greg kept sneaking looks at Ciara. Glumly she wondered how Ciara managed it. She'd only just met him and, without even trying, she had him on a leash.

No one had ever treated her like that. Or looked at her like that.

"She's gorgeous, isn't she," Danny said. "Beaut-i-ful."

That was it. She had to ignore him. She had to be rude. Otherwise she'd be up for murder.

The music was really slow. Sexily slow. Dr Hook's *Sharing the Night Together* was playing when Jack took her in his arms. She entwined her hands about his neck and closing her eyes, she lay her head on his chest. He hoped she couldn't hear the way his heart had begun to thump. The smell of her hair and her perfume and the feel of her body in his arms began to intoxicate him. Slowly he began rubbing his hands up and down her back.

Vanessa shivered as his hands made small circles on her back. She was glad she'd worn the light top, that way she could feel the heat of his palms through her blouse. This guy had got to be the most beautiful fella she'd ever set eyes on, and she'd seen quite a few. She wanted to kill Jean for daring to talk to him. Basically she just wanted to kill Jean full stop. How had she chosen such a dire person to share her flat with? She was usually such a good judge of character. The girl, with her common, loud-mouthed, drunken, puking friends, just got on her wick and –

"Sorry, have I done something wrong?" Jack's voice, low and husky, asked.

Vanessa looked up. She tried for a heavy-lidded, drowsy, sexual glance. "Nothing," she answered. "Why?"

Jack shrugged. "You stiffened, I thought . . ."

Vanessa wished he'd stiffen. She'd done all the running so far – it was about time he made some sort of a move. "I was enjoying your hands on my back," she said coquettishly. "Don't stop."

Jack's eyes crinkled in a smile. Slowly, without saying anything, he started again to caress her back. "You liked that?" he asked, his lips brushing her ear.

"Mmm," she snuggled against him. He was in

control. This was his language. He was good at this. He slowly began to massage the back of her neck. She moved her head against his palm – it was like stroking a cat. "And that?" he asked.

"Lovely," she whispered.

He tilted her face towards him and ran his thumb down her cheek. "How 'bout if I kiss you?" He kept his voice calm, his eyes pinned on her face – women went mad when he did that.

"That'd be nice." Her voice was barely audible.

"What?" he quirked his eyebrows. "Didn't hear you."

"I said," Vanessa began to push herself against him, "that'd be nice."

And so, he bent his head and kissed her softly on the lips, all the time keeping his eyes open.

She put her hand up and pulled him back down.

Suddenly he knew this was going to be his kind of party.

43

Chapter Four

Bleep.

Bleep.

Bleep.

What the hell was that noise? And where was all that pain coming from?

Bleep.

Bleep.

Bleep.

Oh *God*, she wished she was dead. It was her alarm clock. Time to get up, pack her weekend bag and head home. She didn't think she'd be able to get up. The pain in her head was unreal. Last night was a complete blur. Just as well. The memory would be even worse.

She managed to prop herself up on one elbow. Then she made some more progress by pushing the bedclothes down.

And then it hit.

Stomach lurch, mad dash to the bathroom. Followed

by the promise that she was never going to drink again.

Jack awoke in a strange room. Strange, because it was neat and tidy and smelt of flowers. He sat up in the bed and stared wildly around. He saw his clothes thrown over a wicker chair in the corner of the room and it was only then that he remembered. Gradually his heart resumed its normal beat and a slow grin spread itself over his face. He'd spent the night with Vanessa.

And what a night it had been.

Jack lay back down, his hands behind his head, and replayed the night in his mind. Slow sexy kisses, her pulling at his arm, whispering for him to follow her. He, kissing the back of her neck all the way to the bedroom. The click of the key in the lock, her face in the half-light. The feel of her body, the way she knew what she wanted. Drinking wine, laughing. Sex.

Waking up, slightly hung-over, wondering what the hell came next.

Jack groaned and turned over. This was the part he hated. The morning after. Normally he just sneaked off, pulling his clothes on as he made his way across the bedroom, but that morning, it was too late for that. Vanessa was already up. He could hear voices coming from the kitchen as if she was talking to someone. He wondered if he could get out of bed and dressed before she came back into the room. It wasn't that he wouldn't like to see her again; it was just that he wouldn't know what the hell to say to her that morning. Sleeping with her was fine, but conversation, now, that was something else altogether.

Slowly, trying not to make too much noise and attract attention to himself, Jack pushed the duvet cover off. His feet touched the carpet and very softly he began to tiptoe across the room to the chair where his clothes were. He got dressed at rapid speed, almost ripping his shirt apart in his eagerness to do up the buttons. In the end, he buttoned it all wrong but he pulled his jumper over his head so that it wasn't noticeable. He completed the job with the lacing up of his Doc Martens. Pulling his fingers through his hair to flatten it down, he happened to glance at himself in the mirror.

Love-bites adorned his chin.

Jack balked. "Jaysus," he muttered.

He stood a bit back from the mirror. Maybe they wouldn't be so noticeable then.

Nope, they were just as noticeable.

Wild, panicked thoughts flittered rapidly through his brain. Could he cover his chin with his hand and talk that way? Nope, he looked stupid. Could he keep his head down and hope they'd be in shadow? Yeah, right, Jack, he thought miserably.

How could he face the world with bruises all over his chin?

He'd have to stay in.

He gawked at himself again in the mirror.

"Someone's up early."

Vanessa's voice made him jump. Turning around, he smiled weakly. "Eh, yeah," he said. "I figured I'd better be heading off now."

Vanessa, dressed very becomingly, thank you, in just a flimsy nightdress, draped herself across the bed. "Don't go on my account," she said. Her eyes looked him up and down.

Jack gulped. She was lovely, but sort of suffocating. And anyhow, he didn't know what she wanted.

"I was hoping to bring you in some breakfast," she said, patting the bed for him to sit down.

Jack shrugged. "I'm not a breakfast eater," he muttered. "And anyhow, I've a bit of a head on me."

"Nice one," Vanessa smiled. "In that case . . ." She tugged at the narrow bit of lace that was holding her nightdress together and it opened.

Jack, hardly able to believe his luck, came over to the bed. If this was breakfast, then he was starving.

She couldn't face breakfast. In fact, the thoughts of the coming day, the four-hour-long drive in Mikey's fume-filled minibus, the lunch her mother had promised her, the whole idea of the weekend at home made her wish that she could crawl back into bed and never surface. It'd be bliss. Just to turn off life for a while.

Meg stared despondently into her glass of water. An image began to solidify. She tried to switch it off but it was too late. Like a kind of developing photograph, it took on substance and colour. Last night, everyone having a great time, even Danny. And her, sitting on the edge of things, not able to talk to any of them. Slowly getting more and more jarred. The puking up on the floor of the loo, Ciara bringing her home in a taxi. Her embarrassing tearful apologies.

Jesus.

She cupped her head in her hands and groaned.

"So you're back?" Peadar was eating a massive triple-decker sambo and watching Italian football on the telly when Jack got in.

"Just about," Jack grinned and plonked down beside him on the sofa.

"Good night?"

"Great." Jack took a bit of ham that had fallen from Peadar's sandwich and popped it in his mouth. "Your woman Vanesssa is some woman," he said. "Look at me face."

Peadar peered at him. He could just about make out bruising. "Bruises?" he asked. "What happened? She beat you up or what?"

"More of the 'or what'," Jack said. "See me chin. Feckin' love-bites all over it. She ended up covering me in make-up to hide them."

Peadar laughed. "Make-up? You're wearing make-up?"

"No bleedin' choice, had I? Me face is wrecked." Jack made a face as Peadar coiled up laughing. "It's not that funny," he said.

Peadar grinned. Winking he said, "Aw, you're gorgeous altogether."

"Feck off. Right? Feck off."

"What kind is it? Self-renewing or what?"

"Pead —"

"Or is it the stuff that hides the wrinkles?"

"Fun-ny." Jack gave him a shove.

Peadar shoved him back.

They began to mock-wrestle until they both slid off the sofa and landed with a bang on the floor. The telly shook and Peadar jumped up to steady it. He looked down at his flatmate and they grinned at each other. "So, what happened?" he asked. "You sleep with her or what?"

Jack nodded. "Brilliant night. She's all right."

"You seeing her again?"

Jack stood up from the floor and brushed himself down. "Yep." He couldn't meet Peadar's eye. "She's a bit, you know, forceful. I told her, like, I'd see her next weekend, but she said she'll call me during the week. Probably on Wednesday."

"Yeah?"

"Yep." Jack shrugged. "I hope she's not going to get all heavy on me."

"The girl has a great body. She won't be that heavy on you."

"Fu-nny," Jack smiled. Changing the subject, he asked, "So how was last night for you then? Thanks for not turning up at the party, ya bastard."

Peadar grinned. "Yeah, sorry 'bout that." Then shrugging he added, "It went all right."

"Did she stay?"

"Nope." Now it was Peadar's turn to avoid eye-contact. "That's just the way she is," he mumbled.

Jack began humming *Come on, Eileen.*

Peadar whirled on him. "Now don't," he jabbed his finger in Jack's direction. "Just don't. She's my girlfriend, right? And what we do is none of your business."

"What you *don't* do, you mean."

"Jack, I'm warning –"

Jack nodded. "Yeah, right. Sorry."

"She's my girlfriend, you know. A bit of respect."

"Absolutely." Jack rolled his eyes.

Peadar stared hard at him. Then in a half-mumble, he said, "She doesn't believe in sex before marriage."

Jack stopped grinning. Totally stunned, he stared at his mate. "Come again?"

"You heard." Peadar made his way back to the sofa and picked up his sambo. "That's the way she is. Sort of old-fashioned."

"Jurassic more like." Jack shook his head. "So, like, you'll have to marry her to get some action going?" He started to laugh. "That's a bit drastic, isn't it? Even for you."

"Fuck off."

"I bet you wish you could, hey?"

Peadar didn't laugh. Instead he glared at Jack and said evenly, "I've told you what the story is, right? Now back off."

Peadar was not in good form. Not at all. Jack shrugged. "Fine. Whatever you want." The best thing to do would be to say nothing, just watch the soccer and keep stumm. But wow! What a bummer! Still, Jack thought, at least now he might dump Eileen and get someone with a bit more fun in them.

And things would get back to normal.

"How are ya? Heading home again?"

Mikey always asked her that, despite the fact that she went home every weekend. She smiled at him and paid her fare.

Mikey spent ages counting out the money and then, handing her a ticket, he said, "I shouldn't be saying this, but, there's great news awaiting you at home, so there is."

"News?"

"Oh, now, mum's the word." Mikey tapped the side of his nose and chuckled. "Suffice to say," he pursed his lips, "I've had three husbands, Bert, Ernie and Jim, and I must confess I haven't had an orgasm."

Meg gawked at him. He smiled cryptically back. She had to be hallucinating.

"And that's all I'm saying." Mikey chuckled again before he fired his bus into life. It shuddered violently. "And that's all I'm saying."

Well, thank God for that, Meg thought.

"I'll have you home in a jiffy."

"Great." The lump in her throat was back. For some

reason, she always got a lump in her throat whenever she went home. She swallowed hard. The lump hurt as forced itself down into her chest where it settled like a stone.

She felt caught between a rock and a hard place.

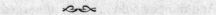

Chapter Five

It was funny the feeling of sadness that seemed to wash over her every time she came home. It had to be homesickness.

She loved anything on the telly to do with people returning home. She was the only person she knew that cried at the ESB ad. The ad where the boy was coming home and his mother was rushing about preparing for his arrival. The bit that touched her most was the way the boy's mother took her apron off before answering the door to him. As if everything, including her, had to be perfect.

It was a nice ad.

The 'blip' of Mikey's horn cut through her thoughts.

Meg shook her head. What was she like? A right eejit.

She waved 'goodbye' to Mikey. He waved back and then, still waving, he reversed onto the main road and almost collided with a car.

Meg hoisted her bag onto her shoulder and began to trudge toward the house. Behind her, she heard Mikey shouting at the car driver to 'effing watch out'.

Her mother opened the door before she'd even had a chance to get her keys from her bag. As usual she looked great. Hair perfect, make-up perfect, slim perfect figure. "Meg," she nodded, "you're back."

"Yeah," Meg smiled, "hi."

"It's 'yes' not 'yeah'." Her mother strode away leaving her standing on the doorstep. "I don't know," she called, "five years spent in Speech and Drama and all you can say is 'yeah' – I don't know."

Meg picked up her bag and hurried into the kitchen after her mother. Something was wrong. The 'speech and drama' attack was always brought out in times of extreme stress. She felt sick.

"Tea?" her mother asked. She was rummaging about in the press, slamming cups and saucers about.

"Eh, no, no thanks, Mam. I, eh, think I might, eh . . ."

"What?" her mother glared at her. "You might what?"

She *had* been going to say that she'd like a lie down to try and ease her hangover – not that she'd tell her mother she had a hangover – but she couldn't. If her mother wanted her to have tea then that's what she'd do. "Nothing," she muttered, putting her bag down. "Tea is fine."

"Well, thank *you*." Her mother sniffed a bit. A cup and saucer were crashed down in front of her. "I'm *honoured*."

"Oh, Mam, don't."

"Don't what?"

Meg shrugged. Gulped. Decided to change the subject. In a bright voice, she said, "It was a long trip down. Mikey's bus gets worse every week. D'you know what's happening now?" She stopped, wondered if her mother would react and when she didn't, Meg went on, "The exhaust fumes keep pouring into the bus. I'm as high as a kite now."

No reaction. Instead, her mother turned and began to fill the kettle.

"And Mikey drives so *slowly* – he's mad." Meg gave a bit of a laugh. Maybe if she kept talking, her mother would smile back. "The other drivers on the road keep –"

The kettle was slammed down. Water splashed everywhere.

Meg jumped.

"Do – you – think I give a *toss* about Mikey and his stupid bus? Do you?"

"I'm only –"

"Things are falling apart here and all you can do is yabber on about Mikey!"

Meg stared at the table. The scorn on her mother's face made her cringe. She supposed it *was* stupid. Mikey wasn't exactly a great conversation piece. "Sorry," she muttered.

"Do you want to *know* what's wrong?"

Nope, she wanted to say. No, I do not. "What's wrong?"

"Your Nan," her mother spoke slowly, spitting out each word, "has only gone and made a show of all of us."

"What? Sorry?"

"She went on radio yesterday, *national* radio and said a *filthy* poem."

"She what?"

"*Apparently* her and Daisy Donnelly concocted this poem between them and in return for making a *show* of themselves, they won a cruise."

"Nan won a cruise?"

"Are you a parrot? Didn't I just say they'd won a cruise? Huh," her mother sniffed, "it's saying their rosaries they ought to be instead of going on the radio. And now," biscuits were thrown onto a plate, "now they'll be chasing men on a ship. That Daisy is a man-eater. The black widow, that's what we call her in the bridge club. And off they'll go, leaving me on my own." She put her hands on the table and leaned toward Meg. "I don't know – my *only* daughter's in Dublin getting up to God knows what and my mother's saying horrible poems and winning holidays and I'll be left here on my own. I don't know."

"I'll be down to visit you."

"Wonderful." Her mother rolled her eyes. Turning back again to the kettle, she snapped, "Now, do you want tea or coffee?"

She knew her mother didn't mean to sound so sarcastic. She was just upset over her Nan, but the 'wonderful' hurt. "Coffee. Please."

"I only have tea."

"Tea so."

"Right."

More banging and slamming.

Her head throbbed.

She managed to escape for a walk. Danny McCarthy, her mother's bridge partner had rung and while her mother laughed into the phone, making plans for a bridge game the following night, Meg slipped out the kitchen door.

She decided to head for the hill behind the harbour, the place where she could gaze down on the cars as they came off the ferry. She loved Rosslare in the late summer. The smell of the sea, the sound of the sea. Jack used to sit on one of the benches and paint the ships. The sudden thought startled her. She remembered how he'd sketch and she'd sit beside him and watch. He'd been good. Jack had always liked the sea, she remembered then.

He had a favourite seat too.

She found it and sat down.

For the first time in years she thought about him and the way they used to be.

He'd had a bad time.

She'd had a bad time.

Still, somehow they'd coped because they'd had each other.

They used to be able to make each other laugh.

She rubbed her hand along the seat wishing she

could turn back the clock, just once, and see him the way he used to be.

He was the best friend she'd ever had.

When she got in her mother was sitting at the table reading the newspaper and her Nan was bent over the cooker frying.

The atmosphere was strained.

"Something smells good."

Her Nan smiled across at her. "Well, hello there! How's things? How was the trip down?"

"Fine, thanks, Nan."

"Will you have a sausage?"

"Yep. Thanks."

"Why did I spend money on Speech and Drama?" Her mother threw her arms skyward. "I don't know. Can't even say 'yes' properly."

"Would you like one sausage or two?" her Nan asked swiftly.

"Just one." Meg slid into a seat.

"A rasher?"

"Eh – yeah."

Another dramatic sigh from her mother.

"Yes," Meg corrected.

"Egg?"

"OK, so."

Her Nan began taking the sausages and rashers from the pan and dumping them on a plate under the grill. Then she cracked a couple of eggs and began to fry them. "Meg, will you put on the kettle for me, luv?"

"Sure."

The tea made, her Nan began setting the table. She set for four. "Daisy Donnelly is coming over," she said as she put out the knives and forks. "We're discussing our holiday plans."

Meg winced. Decided she had to say something. "That's right!" she mumbled, almost dropping the teapot. "You won a holiday!"

"Indeed I did."

"Well," Meg gulped, "well done."

"Daisy wrote a poem and I performed it," her Nan said proudly.

"A *filthy* poem," her mother clarified looking up from her paper.

"Daisy was too scared to go," her Nan lowered her voice and said, knowledgeably, *"on air."*

"Oh, for God's sake!" Mrs Knott snapped, standing up from the table. "Call me when tea's ready." She left the kitchen.

"She's been like a bitch since I won the thing," her Nan said, whispering. "She just doesn't seem to understand that Daisy and I won it together. And that she can't come with us."

Meg nodded uneasily. She had to change the subject, the weekend wouldn't be worth a toss if her mother stayed in bad form.

"D'you want to hear the poem?" her Nan interrupted her thoughts.

"Eh . . . maybe –"

"I can't remember it all, mind, but I'll give you the gist of it. Hang on till I think. Now what was the first line . . . oh yes. . . yes, I have it." She took a breath and stood to attention, *"I've had three husbands, Bert, Ernie and Jim. But I'm awful sorry to report, I've never had an or-gas-im."*

Her Nan had said that on air! No wonder her mother was freaking.

"Hang on now, there's more." Her Nan bit her lip. "Yeah – *What does it feel like, what can I do? 'Cause to be perfectly honest, I'd like a good screw.*"

"You didn't?" Despite herself, Meg giggled.

"And," her Nan was into her stride now, *"I dress really sexy, I move with such grace. I go about with a sex-starved face. Then . . . something, something, something."* She frowned. "And the end went . . . *'Cause you know what they say, and you know that it's true, out there there's a man that's a right fit for you.*"

"You're fecking mad," Meg grinned at her. Punching her lightly, she added, "Fair play to you. I'd never have the nerve to go on radio."

"Well, to be honest, I was a bit embarrassed meself, saying the poem but sure, what harm? Didn't we win? And wasn't it worth it?"

"Oh, worth being the laughing-stock of the place, all right," Mrs Knott said from the doorway. To Meg, she added, "Do you know, she's had every dirty ould fella in the place making a pass at her these past few weeks. My own mother."

"Aw sure, aren't you easily offended!" Her Nan flapped her away. "'Tis only a laugh."

"Oh, a right laugh, talking about organisms on air."

"Orgasms, child."

"Orgasms, my backside!"

"An interesting place to have an orgasm all right."

"Oh, you make me sick, Mother!"

Someone began tapping on the glass of the back door and the bickering stopped.

"That'll be Daisy," said her Nan. "Let her in, will you, Meg?"

Meg opened the door and Daisy bounced in. All twenty-odd stone of her in a big flouncy flowery dress. Her hair was long and curly and her make-up consisted of a slash of violently red lipstick. "Hello, hello, hello," she boomed. "And how's Megan? Home for the weekend?"

"Yeah."

"How's the job going? Your mother tells me you're loving it and having a wonderful time up there? And that you've a very responsible job no less."

Responsible. Her job? She shot a glance at her mother.

"Well, isn't it?" her mother said defensively. "Running a school?"

"It's grand," Meg smiled at Daisy.

"Modest as well as beautiful," Daisy chortled. "You've a lovely girl there, Maureen."

"Mmm. Be nicer if she stayed at home, instead of abandoning me."

Meg blushed but Daisy and her Nan ignored her mother.

Daisy sat at the table. "So how's the form?" She rubbed her big fleshy hands together. "All set for our trip?"

"As set as a piece of dried dung."

"Mother!"

Daisy and her Nan laughed. Meg tried not to.

"We're having our tea. There's a time and a place."

"The child corrects the parent," Daisy said. "Well, well."

"Someone has to." Mrs Knott stabbed the sausage she'd been given. "Someone has to," she muttered again.

"Oh, it's like that, is it?" Daisy winked at her friend. "Well, now, bad atmospheres don't suit my creative streak." She flexed her fingers. "Poets don't like that kind of thing."

"Poet my arse," Meg's mother snapped.

Everyone ignored her. Meg, glancing over, felt sorry for her. She guessed it must be terrible not to be included in their plans. Still, who the hell would want to go on holiday with two oldies? She knew she wouldn't.

The tea was eaten with sullen silence from her mother, and laughter and slagging from the other two. Meg didn't say much and she wasn't able to eat at all. It was awful, not being able to talk to one without offending the other.

That kind of thing made her feel sick.

In the middle of the tea, she decided to say something to cheer her mother up. She hadn't intended telling her at all, because the pressure to do well would be too great, but feck it, she couldn't stand a whole weekend of mournful silence and bitching.

"I got the main part in my drama group's play." All attention riveted on her. She gulped and blushed and knew she sounded bigheaded. "Just thought you'd like to know."

"Isn't that wonderful?" her mother was beaming now. "Wonderful." Her voice dipped. "Well, if it's a *suitable* part."

Meg flushed. "It's fine." There was no point in telling her mother the play was called *Naked*. It'd only give her the wrong idea.

"When will you be on?" her mother asked. "I'll have to come and see that." She turned to Nan. "Maybe she'll be performing when you're on holiday and you'll miss her – wouldn't that just be awful now?"

"That won't happen," Daisy said. "We can take the holiday when we like. Once we go by the end of the year, it's fine." She turned to Nan. "She must get her dramatic talent from you."

"And her mother," Nan said slyly. "She's big into dramatics."

"Funny, ha, ha," Mrs Knott spat.

"And sure if we miss it, you can video it for us."

"Video my arse!"

"No, not your arse, darling daughter, the play!"

Daisy screeched with laugher and Meg managed a small grin.

Mrs Knott slammed down her knife and fork and stormed from the room. They heard her upstairs slamming about her bedroom.

Meg wanted to vomit.

Daisy and Nan continued laughing.

Meg knew that things could only get worse.

Chapter Six

The weekend at home had been so bad that it was a relief to go to work Monday morning.

Meg dumped her bag on her desk and flicked on the kettle. Might as well relax before Linda arrived.

Saturday had been bad but Mass on Sunday had been the cruncher.

Her Nan had been propositioned by every fella, old and young, in the place. The priest had even winked at her outside Mass and said that he wouldn't mind a sabbatical on board a cruise ship. Her mother had been mortified when her Nan had winked back and said that if sabbaticals meant he could abandon his vows for a few weeks then she'd drop Daisy like a bucket of slurry.

"Jesus, Mother," her mother had said. "Do you have to?"

"'Tis only a laugh – will you ever laugh, Maureen?"

"How can I laugh? What's there to laugh at?"

"Your ould face for one. 'Tis like a cross between a crab apple and a crab."

"People say I look like you."

"Not at the moment, you don't."

And that had set the tone for the whole of Sunday.

Meg grinned ruefully as she remembered.

Still, her mother had come back from her bridge competition happy – she and Danny had won all about them. And Danny had stayed for supper. It had been nice to hear her mother laugh, Meg thought, even if she was only being polite laughing at Danny's stupid tales.

The kettle snapped off and Meg made tea. Carrying her mug to the window she looked out onto the car park. She liked the view. Behind the car park, green playing pitches spread out, and beyond that, the mountains.

It was nice and quiet first thing in the morning.

This time of the year in the school was usually a doddle. Once all the new students had been keyed in, there was nothing to do except wait for the new school year to start. In another two weeks, the rest would be over and the place would be filled with noise again. One or two of the teachers had popped in within the last couple of weeks looking for their timetables. Meg envied them – they had a brilliant life.

Hearing footsteps outside, she scurried to her chair and flicked on her computer. Linda'd have a face on her if she caught her doing nothing.

Linda had a face on her anyway.

Meg sighed. Another brilliant day ahead.

"Little bollix," Linda muttered as she stomped into the room. "I'll get him. By Jesus, I'll get him."

She'd changed the colour of her hair. It was roaring red.

"Your hairdresser?" Meg asked.

Linda's eyes narrowed. "Are you being funny?"

Meg shrunk. "Funny? No."

"What did you just say?"

"I, eh, well, I said, your hair's dressy." It didn't sound convincing. She wasn't good at lying. Her voice always dropped at the end of sentences.

"Why, thank you," Linda said graciously. She fluffed it up. "Red is in." She shot a glance at Meg's hair. "Well . . . this shade is in. I don't know about yours."

"Oh . . . right."

"I got it done on Saturday," Linda said, settling herself in at her desk.

"Where?" Meg asked. There was no way she was ever going there.

"Blaire's," Linda said. "You probably don't know it. It's an exclusive place in Grafton Street. Blaire himself did it."

Blaire of the nightmare hair. "Well, it's gorgeous." She got a sick pleasure out of being insincere.

"I know." Linda gave a gratified smile. Turning to the phone, her smile faded. "I just want to ring home," she said. "Make sure Clive is up."

That must have been who the bollix was, Meg

realised. Clive was Linda's eighteen-year-old son. He was the big black cloud of her life. The only time she got on with him was when they sided against Linda's husband, Leo. Clive had dropped out of school when he was fifteen. He'd lost jobs left right and centre. He didn't give a damn what Linda said to him. He'd even told her to fuck off over the phone once.

"Clive," Linda barked into the phone, "are you up?"

Meg tried her best not to listen in but Linda was the sort of person who made her phone calls public property.

"That's not a stupid question," Linda snapped. "I meant – were you up *before* I rang? Now, I'm warning you. Don't be cheeky." Linda began to drum the desk with her four-inch fingernails. "That's not good enough. It's not what I asked you to do. Did you put out the bins? When? That's no good – sure the binmen come at *eight!* What's the point of putting the fucking things out at *nine?* I'll curse if I want. Now listen, get out two pieces of fish from the freezer. Yes, two pieces. Leave them out and let them defrost. *Fish.* Well, I'm very sorry, that's all there is. If you want chips, get a job and buy some. And after that, you better hang out the washing . . ."

"Hello?" Aidan, the principal, poked his head in the door. "Any chance of one of you doing something for me?"

Linda's face dropped. Her mouth opened and closed like a goldfish. "Well, that's when we're re-opening," she said cheerily into the phone. "Thank you for calling." Slamming the receiver down and blushing like mad, she turned to Aidan. "Yes? What can we do?"

Aidan paused. He frowned. "Your *hair*," he said.

"Yes?" Linda shifted about in her chair, preening herself for his compliment.

"It's *red*."

"Sorry?"

"Very red," Aidan nodded, looking puzzled. "Is it like that for a reason?"

Meg closed her eyes. She wished she was deaf because if she heard any more she was going to laugh and that would ruin her whole life.

"It's like that," Linda said evenly, her smile fixed in place, "because my husband paid for it to be like that. And I like it."

"Ohhh." Aidan looked as if she'd just announced that she was going to bite his testicles off. "Well . . . yes . . . I can understand that."

"So, what can we do for you?"

"Well . . . it's this," Aidan waved a sheet of paper in the air. "It's the references for the new teacher we want to hire." He smiled at his secretary. Assuming his most placating voice he said, "I'd be delighted if either you or Meg could check them out?"

"Of course," Linda did her best to smile back. "No problem." She took them from him. "Who's the lucky person?"

Lick-arse Linda. Meg rolled her eyes.

"We settled for a guy called Jack Daly."

Linda almost had an orgasm.

Meg was numb. She wasn't sure if seeing Jack every day was what she wanted – just knowing he was out there, alive, was enough. Maybe her memories would be spoilt if she got to know him. He could be Mr Sensible Teacher now and it would jar . . .

"He was the last guy in on Friday," Aidan continued. "He came in just as we were giving up hope. Young enough fella." Aidan tapped the references. "Anyhow, just check them out and then one of you can give the lad a call and tell him he's got the job. You know the usual: tell him when we start, that sort of stuff. He can ring me with any questions."

"Fine." Linda gave another smile and Aidan left.

"Asshole," Linda flounced over to Meg's desk. "Here, Meg," she threw the papers down in front of Meg, "will you ever give those schools a buzz and check it."

"But you –"

"After what he said about my hair? You're joking, aren't you? Anyhow," she walked across the office and took a file from her drawer, "when you're finished checking out the references, I'm going to have the pleasure of calling Jack."

Meg made a face at her and scanned the letters for the phone numbers. St Enda's was the first school. She dialled the number at the bottom of the page.

"That kinda fella would make you cream in your knickers," Linda sighed.

The phone rang at the other end.

"I'm pretty sure I read that in Jackie Collins," Linda continued. "Good description, innit?"

"Wonderful," Meg said dryly.

"I just can't believe you knew him," Linda began backcombing her hair while observing Meg. "But I suppose he was just a kid when you knew him, probably all spotty and fat."

The King of Cool, that's what he called himself. Meg grinned at the sudden memory.

"You just make sure they back up what they say in those references," Linda said sharply. "Don't get them to say anything negative. Not that they would anyhow. References are a load of crap."

"Uh-huh."

The phone was picked up at the other end. "Hello, St Enda's?"

"Hi," Meg said. "May I speak to Principal Sean Duffy, please?"

"He's not in today. Can I help?"

"It's about an ex-teacher you had there, a Mr Jack Daly. I'm just ringing to check out a reference."

"I'll get the file."

She heard the girl pulling open filing cabinets. Eventually the girl came back. "I've the reference file in my hand," she said. "I'm just flicking through it now. Hang on. Eh, Jack. Jack Daly?"

"That's the one."

The girl began to read out the copy of the letter Meg

had in front of her. "That's fine." Meg stopped her midway. "That's all I need."

"It says at the end refer to personal file," the girl sounded puzzled. "Do you want me to do that?" She gave an embarrassed laugh. "I'm only new here. I haven't a clue how things are done."

"No. It sounds fine. Thanks for your help."

"Bye."

She checked out the other reference and it too was legit.

"What do I do now?" she called over to Linda who had her head buried in a book. "D'you want me to ring Jack and tell him he's got the job?"

"No, I already said I'd do that." Linda picked up her phone. "That's a job for the senior secretary, don't you think?"

The horniest secretary more like, Meg fumed.

She pretended to work as Linda punched in Jack's phone number.

She felt miffed as Linda giggled at something Jack said.

"We'll see you soon," Linda finished, putting down the phone. "Such a nice guy," she sighed.

Meg bit her lip. She wished she'd talked to him. Still, she'd see him soon enough.

Meeting someone after ten years, it had to be fate.

She hoped it was.

Well, sort of.

❧

Chapter Seven

YH Theatre Group, established five years, held their rehearsals in a room in Yellow Halls Community School. Aidan, a theatre lover, gave it to them for free. The only condition he imposed on the group was that he be given tickets to their performances.

It was exciting being chosen for the lead, Meg thought, as she made her way to the rehearsal room, but being directed by Dominic would be a bit of a nightmare. Dominic wasn't capable of directing traffic, much less a play. And yet, confidence poured out of him in greater quantities than blood would from a slashed wrist.

Amazing.

She was five minutes early so she bought a cup of coffee and sat down to wait. Bright and airy, the room faced onto the playing pitches. She tried to ignore the posters of actors and film stars which adorned the walls. Aidan's idea. It was supposed to inspire the group, but pictures of Laurence Olivier, James Dean and Meryl Streep totally intimidated her. It was like they were glaring down and sniggering at her attempts. Meryl Streep in particular looked spectacularly unimpressed.

Meg took off her jacket and hung it on the back of her chair.

There was the sound of footsteps along the corridor. She straightened up. No, relax, she told herself. Try and look casual. Drape yourself across the chair. Cross your legs. Don't look as if you think you're great just because you're the main part. Maybe sip the coffee. That'll make –

Sylvia and Tony came in.

"Hiya, Meg," Tony grinned. He ambled over to the coffee machine. "Sylvia," he called to the woman, who was currently giving Meg dirty looks, "d'you want a coffee?"

"I suppose." Sylvia sat down opposite Meg. "I'll need something to keep me awake when Dominic comes in."

Tony chortled and began putting coins into the machine.

Meg smiled at the two of them. And stopped. And started again. And drank some coffee.

She didn't want to look at Sylvia. Sylvia had wanted the part of the Onion Girl, had made it quite plain in fact that she was well able to play it. But she was too old. The Onion Girl was young, in her twenties. Sylvia was in her fifties *at least* and despite the fact that she wore a belly-top and hipsters she still looked fifty.

Tony was young, in his twenties, had every inch of

his face pierced. Eyebrows, lips, tongue, nose, earlobes. He reminded Meg of a sieve.

He put the coffees on the table and sat down. "Is our brill director not here yet?"

Sylvia made a big deal of sniffing the air. "Can't smell his particular brand of BO," she announced. "He can't be."

More sniggering and Meg smiled too.

"What's this shagging play about anyhow?" Tony asked her. "I couldn't understand the frigging thing at all last week."

"Oh, it's, well, sort of about –"

"I don't anticipate that there'll be a lot of shagging in it, man."

The three looked towards the door as the owner of the phoney American accent sashayed into the room. He stopped, did a gyrating motion with his hand on hip and drawled, "No shagging at all, in fact."

"Is that 'cause you wrote it from experience?" Tony asked.

Sylvia snorted and tried to cough.

"Writin' from the heart, man. From the soul, you know." He held a clenched fist to his chest, looked soulfully at them and nodded. "Don't mock." Alfonso continued his snake-like stroll across the room toward them. "It'll be a cool play, wait an' see." He winked at Meg. "How's my Onion Girl?"

"Oh, fine." She couldn't look at Sylvia. Thank God for the coffee.

"This play," Alfonso sat in beside Sylvia, "is about

peeling away the surface character of a person – leaving them in a mentally and emotionally naked state."

"Oooh," Sylvia did a big wide-eyed suggestive leer. "Sounds wild."

Alfonso leaned towards her. "Wild," he confirmed. "You know the way everyone wears masks to hide who they really are?"

"Well, I wish you'd put one on," Tony commented. "Or else, the one you have on is faulty."

Sylvia tittered.

"Not *physical* masks, man," Alfonso exclaimed, totally missing the sarcasm. "Psychological masks."

"Oh *them*," Tony shrugged nonchalantly, "They cost a fortune."

Sylvia began to laugh. Meg felt a bit sorry for Alfonso who was looking confused.

"Anyhow," he continued, "the whole plays starts off with the Onion Girl," he bowed toward Meg, who flushed, "and she's seeing this dead cool guy," he bowed toward Tony.

"I'm being typecast again," he moaned.

Sylvia sniggered.

"And the Onion Girl has this Alter Ego who keeps warning her about –"

The new girl that Dominic had mentioned arrived cutting Alfonso off mid-flow. "Hi," she stammered. She looked around nervously and sat down beside Tony. Meg felt sorry for her. Maybe she should say something to her. But, God, what would she say? And how long would she be expected to talk to her for? And what if –

"You're . . ." Sylvia turned to the new girl, "Oh, dear, what's your name again? I can't remember."

"Avril."

Sylvia began to introduce Avril to everyone.

Meg wondered why she hadn't thought of that. That would have been a great thing to do. Conversations buzzed around her. Tony was talking to Avril and then Sylvia joined in and then Sylvia talked to Alfonso and Avril butted in and Alfonso turned to Sylvia and . . . she began to wish for Dominic to arrive so that she wouldn't have to sit on her own with no one to talk to and pretend she was enjoying herself.

The coffee was great. OK, it was cold but she could still look into it and smile and look as if she was thinking. Thinking deep thoughts about her character or something. She even smiled a bit as if some brilliant idea had struck her. But the longer it went on, the more her face hurt from smiling and the faster her heart raced.

She looked stupid. She knew she did.

Stupid and committable. She'd be committed for smiling at a cold cup of coffee. She was. . .

Dominic arrived.

Everyone stopped talking. She wasn't a freak any more. She was just like the others.

Dominic was wearing his director's cravat and his orange trousers. "Hello, people," he said in a cheery upbeat voice.

Everyone mumbled a greeting.

Dominic's eyes swept the table. "Where's Johnny?" he asked. "Is he late?"

"Lateness is a human concept, time has yet to be defined." Johnny's rich baritone voice spoke from the top of the room. "To say I'm late wouldn't really make sense. Defining time as a three-dimensional force is idiotic. Only an imbecile would attempt to do it."

Dominic looked confused.

"I'm here now," Johnny said, as he strode into the room. He picked up a chair and, turning it backwards, sat astride it. "That's of course if 'now' actually exists."

"Quite," Dominic gave a nervous smile.

"So proceed," Johnny rested his elbows on the table and looked expectantly at him.

Dominic gave Johnny a distinctly sour look before turning from him. Indicating Alfonso, he said, "This is Alfonso. He's written a marvellous play for us, one that I'm sure will be a great success. And if it is, we might bring it on tour next year."

"Yeah, a tour de farce," Sylvia said dryly.

A few people laughed.

Dominic ignored the barb. Instead, he beamed at Alfonso who nodded amicably around.

"And now, Alfonso," Dominic went on, his voice rising as his arm swept the room, "meet my actors."

Meg saw Johnny bristle when Dominic said that. She prayed he wouldn't say anything and start a row.

"One cannot own another human being," Johnny said ponderously.

Meg gulped but Dominic ignored Johnny. Instead, he said, "Oh by the way, Alfonso is sharing the director's role with me. He's second in command."

Tony gave a bark of laughter. "Sounds like fun," he chortled.

"Sounds like suicide," Johnny said casually.

Dominic chose to ignore them again. He distributed the scripts. "Right so," he said when everyone had a script, "let's get rehearsing this baby."

Meg knew that the play was doomed. Most writers were hopeless when it came to directing their own work. Plus how could a play have *two* directors?

The whole project was doomed.

Jack had twenty quid left. The bloody dogs were gone to the dogs.

Twenty shagging quid, and he'd had nearly two hundred when he'd arrived. It was the weather. The bloody dogs hated weather like this.

He'd only managed to hang onto his last twenty because he hadn't known it was even in his pocket. It must have been left over from the last time he'd worn his jeans.

He decided to spend it on some booze. Maybe head home and drop up to see Vanny – she'd told him to call whenever he liked.

He joined the crowd filing out of the gates. He liked the buzz of the place, the excitement. It filled him up, made him go crazy. But in a nice way. And it was the best way of celebrating the fact that he'd just landed himself another job.

"Any luck?" Shane asked. Shane was a regular at the track.

"Naw," Jack shook his head. "You?"

"Yep. Had two come in. Won three hundred."

"Great stuff." Jack felt the tiny flutter of anxiety within him. What had happened to him since last Sunday? Where had his touch gone? Maybe with Shane around he could get close to it. "You going for a pint?" he asked.

Shane laughed. "You buying?"

"With what?" Jack asked laughing.

"Then I'm heading – see you around." Shane patted him on the shoulder and sauntered off.

They read the whole script through. Alfonso led a discussion on the complexities of the play while Dominic nodded. Meg didn't think Dominic had a clue as to what the whole thing was about. In the end, he wrapped up the discussion with, "Well, I think it's brilliant. Now, who's heading down for a pint?"

Everyone agreed that a pint was just what they needed. Meg put her coat on and began to make her way from the room. No one had asked her to go – well, she supposed she didn't need an invitation but, God, if she couldn't talk to them in rehearsals how would she manage in the local pub? No, better just leave. She paused at the door and wondered if she should say 'goodbye'. "Bye." she said, heart hammering in case no one replied.

A couple of people looked up and waved.

She waved back. At least they'd noticed her. The new girl was chatting away to Sylvia. Both of them were laughing and it looked as if the girl was heading down to the pub with the crowd. Meg had sort of hoped that the two of them would be outsiders together but that didn't look likely now. She wondered how Avril had found it so easy to fit in. She, Meg, had been with the group for the past three years and they still seemed like strangers to her.

It was just the way she was, she guessed. She wasn't good with people.

It was like they were on one side of the road and she was on the other.

She didn't know what they wanted and even if she did, she'd make a mess of it.

Just like she'd done all her life.

By the time he got back to the flat, he had it sorted out. For feck's sake, he told himself, if Shane could win, anybody could. There was absolutely nothing special about Shane. Nothing special at all. Well, maybe except for the fact that he was the only living brain donor. The guy was a moron, for Christ's sake.

Yep, Jack had a good feeling that next time he'd do it. Hadn't he won on Sunday? Hadn't he won a monkey on Sunday?

He stopped at the off-licence to grab a six-pack. He

bought a few fags as well to keep him going for the next couple of days. Lastly he bought some chips. He'd forgotten to eat that day. It was feckin' amazing what twenty quid could buy.

If only he'd bet it on Lucky Dancer in the sixth, he'd have bought even more.

He drove back to the apartments and made his way to Vanny's flat. He wasn't yet sure what to make of her, but he knew some things for definite: she was generous with cash, great in bed and she liked him.

He felt he could put up with her for a while at least.

"It's me," he said, banging on her door. "Gotcha some chips and some booze."

She opened it. "Chips and booze, now there's an offer to tempt any girl."

Even though she smiled, Jack felt stupid. Vanny wasn't a chips and booze sort of girl. More a strawberry and champagne woman. "There's me too," he quirked his eyebrows and gave her the smile she'd liked so much over the weekend. "I'm on offer."

She grabbed him by the shirt and pulled him in.

The chip-bag fell to the floor.

That was one thing he was good at, Jack thought, as Vanny began unbuttoning his jeans – he was *bloody brilliant* with people.

SEPTEMBER

Chapter Eight

Wednesday morning. September seventh. First day of the new school year.

Jack had a bad case of the shakes, but he couldn't let Peadar see it.

"Good luck now," Peadar said as he picked up his bag and coat from the chair. "I'll see you later."

"Yeah," Jack flashed him a smile. "Thanks." He shoved a spoonful of flakes into his mouth so that Peadar would think he felt like eating. He really felt like puking. A new job in a new school, meeting new people. Scary. Still, at least Meg'd be there and he had promised her lunch.

He hoped she remembered.

But maybe she didn't hold on to things the way he seemed to.

He couldn't explain why he was so thrilled to be seeing her. Maybe it was because she was easy to be with.

He'd gone over and over the day he'd met her in his head. His brain was twisted wondering what sort of an impression he'd made on her. At least he had his good suit on – that had probably worked in his favour. For some reason he hadn't told anyone about meeting her. He supposed that maybe it wasn't a big deal. She was just someone he used to know.

Picking up his bowl, Jack dumped the flakes into the bin. He rinsed the bowl under the tap and left it in the sink to drain off. He'd ten minutes to kill so he flicked on the telly. Turning to the Aertel page, he checked the racing results.

Before he'd a chance to study it properly, someone knocked on the door.

"Jack, Jack, it's me."

Vanny! What the hell did she want at this time of the morning? He opened the door. "Yeah?"

"Well, isn't that a nice way to greet me?" Vanny, looking great as usual, dangled a yellow envelope under his nose. "Just a good luck card."

"Oh, right, ta." He grinned and took it from her. "I'll hang it up with the millions of others I got."

"Nervous?"

"Me? Naw."

"Good, 'cause you'll be great. Tell you what," she rubbed his cheek, "I wouldn't have minded you being my teacher."

He gave a bit of a laugh. Jesus, he'd wished she'd go. He didn't feel like talking to anyone.

"Here's a kiss for luck."

Big smoochy kiss.

Someone passing by wolf-whistled.

Jack pulled away. The girl was suffocating him. He couldn't go anywhere but she was there.

Still, she was good to him, lending him money and stuff.

She looked a bit offended at the way he'd cut the kiss short.

"Hey," he gave her his sexy grin, "thanks for the card."

"Yeah." Still looking put out, she murmured, "Gimme a call and let me know how you get on."

"Sure." He grinned again.

She smiled back. "Bye now."

"See ya." He closed the door and legged it to the telly. It was nearly time to go. He didn't want to be late on his first day. He glanced quickly over the racing results.

Nothing major. No big wins.

He decided to put a bet on a football match. Maybe United midweek.

It was the last time he was doing this. This job was a new beginning.

There was no way he was going to fuck it up.

When he arrived in the staffroom at nine o'clock, he was met by a sea of strange faces. "How's it going?" he smiled around. He hoped his terror didn't show on his face. Blindly, his eyes swept the room, seeking out Meg. His heart dropped as he realised that she wasn't there.

"Hello, Jack." It was John, head of the Art department that he'd met at the interview. "Come here and I'll introduce you around." John was dressed in jeans and a white grandfather shirt.

Jack felt a bit ridiculous in his good suit trousers. He hadn't the nerve to dress casually on his first day. Tomorrow though, he would.

He let John lead him around the staffroom and tell him who everyone was. Most of the staff were young enough, in their thirties or forties. Jack guessed that he was probably the youngest staff member. A small group of about five oldies were whispering in a corner together.

Jack, after being introduced to everyone, soon found himself standing on his own with a cup of coffee in his hand.

"So, Jack," a teacher asked him, coming over, "what classes have you got?"

Jack tried to remember who this guy was. He thought it was Damien Walsh, an English teacher. "Mostly First Year," he answered. "A few Second Years as well."

"Aw, you're in for a smooth ride this year so," Damien grinned. "First Years are grand. Frighten the shite out of them on the first day and when they're sufficiently cowed, ease off. That's the way to go with them."

A few people nearby laughed.

"That's one way of putting it," someone else grinned.

Aidan came over to them. Slapping Jack on the back he wished him the best of luck. "Now, you know how to find your way about, don't you?" he asked. "Not that you've a lot of rooms to remember, it's mostly the Art department you'll be in."

Jack pulled a ragged map from his pocket. "I've been studying it," he smiled. "I reckon I know the place backward at this stage."

"Good man." Aidan moved on to another group.

"He's a nice boss to have," Damien said. "Since he's been here the school has improved so much. The last fella didn't give a shit."

"Yeah?" The door had opened again and Jack's interest wandered. Some stupid part of him hoped it'd be Meg coming in, but it wasn't. It was the ould wan she worked with. Disappointed, he turned his attention back to Damien.

Meg glanced at her watch. It was just gone ten o'clock. Tea-break time. Only Linda was giving out so much, she hadn't the nerve to interrupt.

" . . . and Leo brought me away for the weekend."

"That's nice." Maybe now she could –

"Nice?" Linda almost spat the word out. "It woulda been nice if I didn't have my period for the whole of it, doubled up I was." She rolled her eyes. "You'd swear he did it on purpose."

"Oh, I wouldn't say –"

"But would Leo check before booking this holiday?" Linda shook her head. "Oh *no*. That'd be the sensible thing to do, wouldn't it? Huh?" She glared at Meg.

"Eh . . . well . . . maybe he just didn't think –"

"No. He did not think! He never thinks! And guess what else?"

It was five past ten now. Meg rose slightly from her desk.

"Guess!" Linda ordered.

"Eh –"

"My little bastard of a son only threw a party for everyone while we were away," Linda said. "And I mean, literally *everyone*. Little bollix. And when I arrive home, what do I find?" She stabbed with her finger in Meg's direction. "What – do – I – find?"

Meg shrugged.

"Him, sprawled out on the kitchen floor and some young wan, barely dressed, alongside him. Oh, like father like son, that's what I say."

"Eh, Linda –"

"And do you know how much it'll cost to get the smell of puke out of my carpet?"

"Eh –"

"Do you?"

"Nope."

"Fifty shagging quid. *Fifty quid.* And I said to the guy, 'That's daylight robbery' and do you know what he said?"

"Eh –"

"Do you?"

"No."

"The smart-arsed little prick said he'd do it at night. *At night!* I'm making a formal complaint about him."

"You should," Meg nodded. "Right now, before you forget."

"I will. I will." Linda turned to the phone.

Meg got up from her desk. "I might as well go on tea break so."

Linda ignored her so she legged it out as quickly as she could.

Despite Linda, she normally enjoyed the first day of the new school year. There was such a buzz about the place what with the noise of the kids and the way the teachers dropped into the office to ask her and Linda how they'd enjoyed the summer. Of course it was normally Linda who monopolised the conversations but Meg didn't care. It was enough to know that for the next few months it would never be just her and Linda alone.

She had twenty minutes for her tea break. Enough to grab a coffee in the staffroom. She hated the staffroom, all the hassle of trying to engage people in conversation for a few minutes. And anyhow, most of the teachers only wanted to talk about their classes which made her feel like an outsider. Still, it was either that or drink coffee in the office with Linda moaning on.

There was no comparison.

Opening the door of the staffroom, she cringed as five ancient faces turned towards her. Typical. Linda had put her on the 'Toffs' tea break. The 'Toffs' didn't talk to anyone except each other.

"Hello, Meg," the five chorused together, before turning away.

She smiled politely and decided that in future she'd buy a paper and read it. There was nothing worse than sitting alone and being ignored.

It was a nice day so she decided to have her coffee outside, sitting in the sunshine. Filling her cup to the brim, she carried it towards the door. Just as she was about to open the door, someone shoved it inwards. Coffee splashed onto her shirt and jeans and all over the floor. *"Oooww!"*

"Christ, sorry!" Jack stood in the doorway with a semi-grin on his face.

"It's fine. It's OK!" Meg pulled her shirt away from her skin and hopped about a bit.

"You sure?" He was still grinning.

She nodded, not able to speak. The *pain.* And her good clothes were ruined. She'd never get the stains out.

"Here, I'll get you a cloth," one of the oldies said, hobbling towards the sink. "That's the best thing."

"The best thing," the other four chorused.

"You seem to do that a lot," Jack remarked, sounding amused, "spill coffee."

"Ha!" Embarrassment made her sound sharp.

Jack flinched.

She wished Jack would go away. She knew how stupid and clumsy she looked. Taking the cloth proffered by the 'Toff' she started to wipe down her clothes.

"D'you want another cup?" Jack asked meekly. "I'm getting one for myself."

"Please." She followed him to the sink and rinsed out the cloth. She tried not to stare at him as he made the coffee. But she couldn't help it. He sort of shone, all yellow hair and white teeth. And he hadn't changed much – if anything, he'd only got better looking.

The coffee made, Jack carried both cups to a table. "No point in making it third time unlucky," he joked.

She tried to smile. "Yeah."

She sat down and Jack sat in beside her. He smelt nice, sort of after-shavy and boozy. She'd forgotten that new teachers were invariably put on the worst tea breaks. Their free classes were always worked around the ten o'clock break. At least now she'd have someone to talk to.

So she'd better start.

She tried desperately to think of what to say. "So how's your first day been so far?" That was a good question. Something most people would ask.

"Great," he said, "the kids are great." He nudged her gently. "Sorry again."

"Forget it."

There was a small silence before Jack asked, "D'you come at this time for tea break every day?"

"Yeah."

"Great. At least I'll have someone to talk to, huh?"

Someone to talk to? *Her?* She felt sorry for him.

"I mean," Jack lowered his voice, "I'd say the geriatrics convention in the corner would be riveting stuff but like, I don't need that kind of excitement in work."

She giggled. "Linda calls them the Toffs," she whispered.

"Yeah?"

"The Old Fuckin' Farts Society."

Jack's roar of laughter caused one of the oldies to slop his tea all over himself. The other four all tut-tutted simultaneously.

"Sorry," Jack spluttered. He turned laughing eyes on Meg. "The Toffs. That's brilliant."

His smile was like sunshine on her.

"My good tie ruined," one of the Toffs said loudly.

Jack ignored him. Looking at his watch, he stood up. "I gotta go," he said. "I've a Second Year class in five minutes." Still smiling down on her, he said, "Eh, will I see you lunchtime?"

"Sorry?"

"Remember? I said I'd bring you to lunch –"

"Oh." She had wondered if he'd remember. It was flattering that he did, but terrifying too. She'd be expected to really *talk* to him, to tell him about herself. "You don't have to, you know. I know you only asked me because . . ." her voice trailed off. Why had he asked her?

94

Jack smiled at her, said softly, "I asked you because, well, I just think," he shrugged, "well, it'd be nice – yeah?"

"Mmm," she smiled slightly, feeling shy, "suppose."

"See you at one."

"Yeah . . .yeah . . .OK."

"Great," he grinned. Winking at her, he left.

It was the wink that did it. Thrilled her and scared her all at the one time.

The Second Year class were jumping about and firing pens around the room when he arrived in. For a second, Jack stood in the doorway watching them. It reminded him of when he was in school, the chaos before the teacher arrived. Or in his case, the chaos that still went on even after the teacher had arrived. He'd been every teacher's nightmare.

"Quieten down," he shouted as he entered the room, slamming the door after him. "Let's just all settle down."

Some kid wolf-whistled up at him. "Hello, sir," she said.

Jack ignored her. Taking the register out, he said, "Now, I'm Mr Daly and I'm new here this year. I'd like you all to sit in alphabetical order so I can get to know your names."

No one listened to him.

Jack began roll call. "Brendan Byrne."

"Here." Brendan said, his feet plonked up on the table.

"Up here," Jack pointed to the first seat, "and keep your feet off the tables."

Brendan didn't move.

"Get up here," Jack said.

The rest of the class, sensing a conflict, began to quieten down.

Brendan shook his head. "I sit at the back in every class," he eyeballed Jack, *"Mr Daly."*

Jack eyeballed him back. "Not in my class you don't," he said firmly. "Now you've a choice. You either sit where I put you or I report you."

Brendan shrugged. "Report me."

Jack nodded. "Fine." Amid the laughter Brendan's response generated, he turned over the register to write his complaint. There was no free space. Every teacher, it seemed, had some complaint about Brendan's behaviour.

He looked up to see Brendan grinning cockily at him. Something in the way the kid looked made Jack's heart twist. It was like looking down through time and seeing himself all over again.

Putting down his pen, Jack shrugged. "I guess you're in a whole heap of trouble already, Brendan," he said loudly. "I don't think there's much point in me adding my complaint."

"I don't care."

"But I do," Jack stood up. "At least it'll look good. The only teacher who had no complaint about you was me. Shows what a brilliant teacher I am. I reckon I'll get kept on."

Some of the kids laughed, others applauded. Even Brendan sneered a bit.

Jack continued to roll-call, wondering if he'd won the kid over.

The trick had worked on him many moons ago.

There were ten topics on her card. Meg studied them hard before shoving it into her bag. Top of the list was the weather. That was a sure-fire icebreaker. Something everybody talked about. Then a what-have-you-done-since-I-last-saw-you question. She reckoned she'd get at least ten minutes out of that. *At least.* That would be followed by what she'd done, which definitely wouldn't last too long. After which she'd ask a how-is-everybody-in-your-house type of question. Just leave it pretty much open-ended. He wouldn't have to talk about stuff that he didn't want to. Then a have-you-been-on-holidays-this-year. Hopefully he had. And hopefully – though it was a long shot – he'd have the photographs with him so that he could spend ages explaining just who everybody in the pictures were. That should take forever.

Why had she agreed to go? This whole conversation thing was a nightmare. Ten years was a long time . . . she longed to go into the ladies', just to give her hair a brush, but then Linda would want to know what she was at and then she'd start slagging her. The best way was to play it cool. Not let Linda know just how she was feeling.

She racked her brains to think of what came after the holiday question. Family? No. Career? No. Best to get it out of her bag and have a look. She was just about to pull the card from her bag when the office door opened and Jack strode in.

"It's lunchtime now," Linda snapped. Then seeing it was Jack, she giggled and amended, "But seeing as you're new, you mightn't know that." She flashed him a smile, "So, Jack, what can I do for you?"

"Actually, it's more Meg I'm after," Jack smiled. "You ready to go, Meg?"

He still had the same smile, Meg noticed with a pang. Sort of sudden and surprising.

"Meg?" Linda snapped. "Why do you want her? I'm senior secretary."

"He's bringing me to lunch, Linda," Meg said.

Linda's face flushed. "Well, I hope you've all your typing done." She turned to Jack. "She has piles of typing to get through – she might be held up."

"I'll wait."

"For ages," Linda finished firmly. "In fact, it might be another hour before she can make it."

"Oh." Jack couldn't explain the disappointment he felt. "Right so." He shoved his hands in his pockets and made for the door.

"I can type after lunch." The words were out so quickly that Meg blushed. What the hell was she doing? She sounded desperate. But wasn't it better to sound desperate than let him down? That would be awful.

"*Sure* you can," Linda smiled sarcastically.

The way Linda was looking at her, Meg knew that if she went with Jack her life in the office wouldn't be worth living. But it wasn't worth living anyhow so maybe she should just get up and go. She'd just tell her out straight –

"That's great," Jack smiled at Linda and turned to Meg. "Are you right so?"

"What?" That was Linda, stupefied.

"What?" That was her.

"Well, you said she could do the typing after lunch, didn't you?" Jack looked innocently at Linda.

"I said –"

"You said, *sure* you can." He gave her a huge smile. "That's really nice of you. Most bosses wouldn't be like that."

"Oh," Linda said.

Meg looked from one to the other. Linda had a puzzled expression on her face and Jack, he was just like she remembered. Calm and laid-back, hands in his pockets, eyebrows quirked, the innocent expression that he always used when he was about to make a fool out of someone. Slowly she began to smile. "So can I go?" she asked timidly.

"I said it was fine, didn't I?" Linda didn't look at her. She kept her gaze riveted on Jack.

"You're dead on," Jack said sincerely. He glanced over at Meg. "You right?"

"Sure." She grabbed her bag and made a dash for the door.

"See you," Jack smiled amicably at Linda and ushered Meg in front of him from the room.

Closing the door, he turned and looked down on her. She looked up at him. They began to grin at each other.

"Nice one," she said.

He felt great.

Chapter Nine

"So where to?" Jack asked once they'd left the school building. "Any nice places around here?"

"I usually bring my lunch in with me, so I'm no expert." She found it hard to meet his gaze. She'd made a big effort to look nice that morning in case she met him, but now, with her clothes all coffee stains, she looked horrible. She figured that if she kept her gaze on the ground, he wouldn't notice.

"So it'll be pot luck – huh?" Jack wished she'd look at him. He couldn't be that bad, could he? Maybe she didn't want to be there? "Are you sure you want to come?" he asked. "You don't have to, you know. I just thought it might be nice to catch up and all." He tried to smile, "Like, I'm not going to kidnap you or anything."

Her head jerked up. "No. Yes." She blushed. "Sorry." She looked down again. "It's just, well, it must be at least ten years and, like, it's a long time. And anyhow," she gulped, "I don't know what to say."

He liked the way she blushed. He took the risk of gently shoving her with his elbow. "It's only me."

He was rewarded with a shrug and a half smile. "I guess."

Her smile gave him the courage to say, "It's nice to see you again, you know." He stared ahead and didn't look at her. He didn't want her to think he'd missed her or anything stupid like that. "I used to wonder what you'd done with your life," he added.

"Yeah?" For some reason she was touched. And flattered.

"I think about the whole class in fact." Turning to her, he grinned, "And now you can fill me in."

"Oh, right." He could have written if he'd *really* wanted to know.

Jack stopped in front of a gleaming car. He was half-hoping she'd think it was his. Taking his keys from his pocket, he asked, "Will I drive or is there a place local?" He prayed she wouldn't want him to drive.

"You'd better drive. It takes about twenty minutes to walk."

She was looking expectantly at him. As casually as he could, he pointed in the direction of his VW. "Right so, let's go." Without looking at her, he strode over to his car, opened the door, hopped inside and leaned over and opened the passenger door.

Meg hopped in beside him and slammed her door closed. The car shuddered. "Eh, sorry," she gulped.

He pretended not to notice. Shoving the key in the

ignition, he tried to start her up. *Start, you bitch*, he prayed as the engine grudgingly fired into life. At least that was something. Trying to look as if it was what he'd expected, he turned to Meg. "So, tell me where to go." He flicked on the radio just as she began to speak. He wanted to hear the sports results.

They drove into the village and found a small café. It was waitress service at lunchtime.

"Yeah?" a young wan asked, pen poised. She chewed some gum. "What yez want?"

"I'll have . . ." Jack studied the menu. It was shite. He was starving. "Any chance of giving me a sambo with just about every bloody thing in your kitchen on it?"

"Wha'?"

"You know – basically all the stuff you guys put on sambos in one sambo."

The girl stopped chewing. "Didn't you read the menu?" She picked it up and pointed to the sandwich section. "Them's the stuff we do – on the menu."

"Yeah, but like, I'm starving. I just want a huge sambo."

She narrowed her eyes. "Mmm." She bit the top of her pen. "I'll have to ask about it."

"No probs," Jack said.

"And you?" The girl fired the question at Meg.

"Just a coffee."

"Right." She wrote it down and walked away.

"A coffee?" Jack stared at her. "That's all?"

"I'm not hungry," Meg lied. She was famished, but there was no way she was going to eat in front of him. She'd end up choking on her food or putting crumbs all over the place or something. She'd just have to eat when she got back to the office.

"Right." Jack didn't know what to say. His order made him sound like a savage.

"We can do dat for you," the waitress reappeared as if by magic at their table. She eyed Jack sternly. "But Louis, de boss, says it'll cost."

"Fine," he agreed.

The waitress nodded and left.

Jack looked over at Meg. She was fiddling with her paper napkin. She folded it over and over until she began to tear it apart. "So," arms flat on the table, he leaned toward her. "How's life then? Jesus, it's been a long time."

"Yeah, hasn't it?"

"The last time I saw you was when I had that mad going-away party. D'you remember, in the big field opposite Danny McCarthy's place?"

Of course she remembered. How could she forget? "Yeah, I remember."

"You got a load of booze from your house and the rest of the lads bought cans and we had a wild night."

"Danny McCarthy wasn't too pleased though," Meg said softly. "His good grazing pasture all puked on."

Jack laughed. "And then, d'you remember, you came

over to me at the end? I was lying on me back, thinking all sorts of weird shit and you came and sat beside me." He shrugged. "D'you remember?"

She nodded. He'd kissed her and told her he'd write. She felt herself going red. "Sort of, vaguely," she muttered.

"Oh," he said. "Yeah, it was all a bit of a blur. I got in shit trouble from me Ma afterwards."

"So what was new?"

He laughed and Meg felt pleased. At least she could still make him laugh. He was the only person bar Ciara that she'd ever felt comfortable enough to joke with.

"So, what've you been doing with yourself since that famous night?"

"Not a lot – just, working and stuff, you know."

"So how come you work in Dublin? I always had you figured to stay at home."

He looked so interested that Meg cringed inwardly. This was going to be awful. "Well, I did work at home for a while," she said, hating all this talking about herself, "but then, well, my Nan saw an ad in the paper for the job I have now and I went for interview and got the job. So I took it. My Nan kept telling me that it was nice to work in different places." She shrugged. "See the world or something like that."

Jack laughed. "So in order to see the world you moved to Dublin, yeah?"

She bit her lip. He was laughing at her. "Yeah," she agreed lamely.

"Big move," he slagged.

He saw the way her shoulders hunched, like as if she was protecting herself. Hastily he changed the subject. He didn't want to know what he'd said wrong. "And, so, where do you live now?"

"In a flat with another girl. Ciara. She's a granddaughter of a friend of my Nan's."

Silence. Jack looked at her encouragingly.

"It's OK of a place," she went on, "nice enough." Stop. "For the two of us." Stop. Gulp. "So . . . well."

"Yeah?"

Oh God, was he going to keep looking at her? "Yeah. So, any nice holidays booked?"

"No. I started work today. In *your* school – remember?"

He was grinning at her, looking amused. What a stupid question to ask! She wanted to kick herself. Best thing was to keep talking about the flat. "The only thing not nice about where I live is the landlord. Like, he's, you know, *awful* . . . basically."

"Yeah?"

"Yeah." Maybe he'd be interested in hearing about the shower? Ciara made people laugh when she told that story. "Our shower is broke and he won't fix it." No. No she couldn't tell him the story, he wouldn't laugh and then she'd feel stupid. She settled for what had happened the previous night, "Ciara, that's my flatmate, had a big run in with him last night so he's sending someone out very soon to fix it."

"Oh, good."

"Well, it is. He's tight. Tight as a drum. 'Water's a precious commodity, girls. It's not meant to be splashed on willy-nilly'."

Jack's laugh startled her. She hadn't meant to be funny, but she'd done James' voice without thinking. Jack had his chin cupped in his hands and he was all sparkly eyes as he looked at her.

What to say now? His smily face was unnerving her. "He was lucky last night though. Ciara was set to tear him limb from limb and I was terrified about a whole big scene happening but Ciara got a call from this guy, Greg. She met him a few weeks ago in a pub and now she's going out with him and the call put her in good form and so last night she was nice enough to James." She couldn't breathe fast enough. Her voice was speeding up and her words were tumbling over themselves. But if she stopped talking now, when she was babbling away, it would seem a bit sus so she had to keep going. "Greg is a –"

Slam!

A plate was slapped in front of Jack.

She could stop and pretend interest in his lunch.

"Big enuff for ya?" the waitress asked, indicating the plate. On it was the most enormous sandwich Meg had ever seen. It was struggling to stay upright.

"I've seen bigger," Jack replied nonchalantly.

The girl made a sneering face at him and then slammed Meg's coffee in front of her. Some of it slopped over the sides and onto the saucer.

"Thanks," she said.

"Yeah," the girl answered. She shoved her notebook into her pocket and walked back up the length of the café

"Classy joint – what?" Jack grinned. "So what were you saying?"

Oh no.

But before she could start, Jack picked up the sambo and the middle part of it began to plop onto his plate. "Shit." Putting it gently back down again, he attempted to squeeze the bread between his hands to stop it leaking. Bits squished everywhere. "It's bigger than I thought," he said amused. "Probably cost me a bleeding fortune."

She smiled at him.

Jack picked up a knife and fork. "Right, you fecker," he said, poking the bread with the knife, "I mean business."

Meg didn't know whether to be embarrassed or to giggle while bits of mayonnaise and other things she couldn't identify squirted across the table as Jack attacked the two slices of bread. She'd have been mortified.

"Bastard of a thing," Jack grinned ruefully. "D'you know what it reminds me of?"

"Nope."

"That big fish from that shite book we read in sixth year – what the hell was it called?"

"*The Old Man and The Sea*?"

"Yeah, that's it." Once again he attempted to do battle with the bread.

"I liked that story," Meg said, smiling at the analogy.

"Aw, yeah, well, you were a swot." He spoke through a mouthful of meat.

"*I wasn't.*"

"Knott the swot, that's what I used to say."

"Get lost!"

Jack grinned. "Only messing." He managed to cut the sandwich in two. "D'you want some?" He held it the plate towards her. "I don't think I'll eat the whole thing. It's bigger than I thought."

"Oh –"

"It'll only go to waste," Jack said. "And besides, I hate eating on me own."

She decided to go for it, Jack was making so much of a mess she didn't think he'd notice any mess she made. And besides, she was starving. And maybe with food in her mouth she'd stop herself from saying more stupid things. "Gimme half of that half."

Jack threw her a mock-anguished look. "You want me to bleeding cut it again?" he asked.

She giggled. "Please."

Jack made a big deal of hacking the bread again. "You're as bad as Vanny," he said. "Taking her out for a meal is a waste. She never finishes anything. I end up eating all her food." He held out the quarter sandwich to Meg.

It looked like a car crash.

"Thanks," Meg put it on her saucer. Sensing an opportunity to let him talk, she asked, "Vanny?"

"Yeah. Short for Vanessa. She's a girl I see now and again."

So he had a girlfriend. She didn't know whether to be disappointed or relieved. She settled for relief. "Vanessa is a nice name," she said.

"D'you think so?" Jack looked surprised. "I think it's shite."

The way he said it made her laugh.

"What?" Jack looked confused.

"Nothing." Meg took a bite of bread. It tasted lovely.

"And you?" Jack asked. "Are you seeing anyone?" Jesus, he hoped she wasn't.

"Well, not right now." Meg blushed. She should have lied. He'd think she was desperate.

"Good," Jack said and then he began to cough. "Sorry," he winced, "that's not what I meant. I meant, good you told me not good you weren't seeing anyone."

"Oh, right."

Jack wanted to kick himself. Jesus. What a moron! "So," he said hastily, "tell us about everyone. Tell us about that girl I went out with in fifth year. You know, yer one with the huge boobs?"

"Celia?"

"Yeah, her. What's she doing now?"

It wasn't so bad when she talked about other people. She sounded normal when she wasn't discussing herself. In fact, she talked for about a half an hour without a break. And he listened to her. And she didn't get embarrassed. And, when she told him about Jimmy working on the missions in Africa, he'd cracked up laughing. And so had she. But eventually she ran out of stories and totally dried up.

So she did what it advised in all her self-help shyness books, she focused on him. At least she tried to. She couldn't think of what to ask. In the end she opted for, "And you?"

"Me?"

"Yeah."

Jack shifted in his seat. He shrugged. "Not much to tell. I had to repeat me Leaving. I failed it first time around." His eyes dropped to the table and his grin faltered.

Meg felt her heart lurch. Jack used to always look like that when something upset him. She felt all the feelings she used to have for him literally rush up through her.

"The second time I did it," Jack continued, his eyes still downcast, "I got into Art college, then I drifted around Europe for a year or so. Eventually I came back and did a H.Dip." He wiped his hand across his mouth to get rid of the mayonnaise, "And that's it," he finished. He gave her a small smile. "The end."

"Europe?"

"Yeah, you know the big place near England where all the countries are stuck together."

"Never heard of it."

He laughed again.

Meg marvelled at her wit. It relaxed her enough to ask, "So what made you want to be a teacher?"

"Nothing." Jack shrugged, "I had fuck all else to do. Nothing interested me, so I said I'd give teaching a go."

"And you like it?"

"Yeah." He didn't really want to talk about himself any more. Instead he looked at his watch. "It's ten to two," he said.

"Jesus," she jumped up. "Is it that time already? Linda'll be going mad if I'm late."

"Sure, I'll drive you back. Relax." Jack shoved his hand in his pocket. "Just hang on till I pay."

She couldn't let him pay. She rooted around in her bag for change. "Here." She held out the money for the coffee.

"Feck off," Jack waved her away. "I asked you out, I'll buy. And anyhow, what's a bleeding coffee?"

"Oh, I can't –"

"Yeah – you can." It made him feel good to pay.

"Well, let me get it for you next time," Meg said.

"The next time, that sounds good." He winked at her and walked over to the cash desk.

Meg wanted to die. What had possessed her to say that? The guy had a girlfriend, for God's sake.

Still, when people made promises about next times, they never materialised.

∞

She felt an ache start somewhere in her chest. Deep. It was heavier than anything she'd ever known and it dragged out of her and pulled her hard.

No booze left to numb the hurt.

And not even two Johnny Logans could make the lump in her throat disappear.

She couldn't cry, there was no point or reason to that. She couldn't cry even if she wanted to. Tears were for real people who lived on the outside and held their faces up to the sun.

People like Jack.

She'd been conned. She'd been stupid.

Everything was her fault. Somehow, it all made its way back to her.

He'd shown her how things should be, and when she'd made a grasp for them, she'd fallen.

Really fallen.

Down to where she was now.

To where she'd always been before only she hadn't known it.

It was better than E. Better than sex. The rush to his head, the way his thoughts tumbled over and over themselves. The intensity, the intimacy.

Shane was beside him and he knew Shane was feeling the same way.

Bound together by the high vibrancy of the moment.

They waited, not speaking, as the horses were led into the enclosure.

There he was, number three, gold with purple stars.

"Let's go for the stars," Shane whispered.

Jack felt his mind narrow, only one pure adrenaline rush beginning to build.

Inside there was no room for anyone else.

Chapter Ten

Ciara was on a high. Meg had never seen her so excited about meeting a fella before. "You must really be into this Greg fella."

"Aw, I dunno. It's early days, but at least it gets Danny off my back for a while. Honestly, he's been following me around like some kind of pathetic creature ever since that night in The Orange Tree. I think he thinks I *like* him."

Meg gulped. She hoped it wasn't anything *she'd* said.

"I mean, telling him to fuck off is like an invitation," Ciara went on. "So I just tell him out straight now that he hasn't a hope. But he says," Ciara stopped brushing her hair, "he says – and this'll show you what a nut he is – he says that I'm just playing hard to get."

"Really?" Meg said faintly. Ciara would kill her. *It was definitely something she'd said.*

"And I told him, I told him, right, that I'm not playing, that I'm just hard. But," Ciara rolled her eyes

115

and resumed her brushing, "it's like talking to a brick wall. The guy is a moron."

"Love is blind," Meg said. "Maybe –"

"And in his case it's deaf and stupid as well. I mean how many hints does he need, how many –"

Buzz.

Buzz.

Buzz.

"Shit!" Ciara made a dash for her room. "If that's Greg, let him up. Tell him I'll be ready in a few minutes. I don't want him to think that I've been ready for ages."

"Aw, Ciara," Meg pleaded desperately, "don't do this. What'll I say to him?"

"I dunno," Ciara waved her hand about. "Offer him tea or something." She grinned. "Use your imagination."

"But . . . but, I've got . . ." Meg floundered. "Well, I've rehearsals in an hour."

Ciara grinned. "Don't worry, I won't leave you talking to him for an hour." She gazed appealingly at Meg. *"Please?* I just want you to drop the hint that I've come in the door this second."

Ciara *always* did this. It was her tiny effort at playing hard to get. And it normally worked.

"All right," Meg nodded, "but you owe me one."

"No probs." Ciara disappeared into her room.

Meg buzzed Greg up. "Hiya," she smiled. "Ciara'll be ready in a sec. She's just got in from work about ten minutes ago. Eh, take a seat."

"Right, thanks, Peig," Greg nodded.

Did he just call her Peig? Meg decided to say nothing. Maybe she had heard wrong.

Greg sort of ambled toward the sofa, hands half in and half out of his pockets. His jeans were so tight, he had a jock line. Meg thought she could even see the V part of them in the front. Greg sat down, tossed his hair back from his forehead and smiled. "So, Peig, how's life?"

He definitely did call her the wrong name. But, sure, there was no point in embarrassing him. She hated when she couldn't remember someone's name. "Life is great." Where the hell was Ciara? What was she supposed to say to this guy? "Want a cuppa?"

"Naw, I'm hoping for something a bit stronger when I hit the pub, you know."

"Right." She made sure to sit as far away as she could from him. Maybe if she sat too near, Ciara would think she fancied him. Not that Ciara would care, but she would.

"It must be awful being called after the greatest moan in history, huh?" Greg laughed heartily.

"Sorry?"

"Peig. You know, yer woman who wrote the book we were all tortured with in school."

"Oh yeah," she gave a pretend laugh. "I never thought of that." Maybe because my bloody name is Meg, she felt like saying.

"There you are now," Greg said. "Something for you to think about."

"Yeah, yeah, I will certainly."

Silence.

Greg shifted. Then he stood up. Slow, lazy walk. Sort of angled toward the mirror. Flick of the head, grin and a little wink.

He'd just admired himself in the mirror, Meg thought in amusement.

"I sure hated that book," Greg said.

"Did you?"

"She never stopped moaning. It was unreal."

He spoke whilst admiring his reflection. He was going to have an orgasm if he stared at himself any longer.

"So," Ciara bounced into the room, "we ready to go?"

Greg turned around and whistled softly. "Hey, Ciara, you look great." He eyed her up and down. "I like those slacks."

Slacks! Meg stifled a giggle. It was years since she heard someone say that. It was almost as bad as calling them pants.

"Thank you," Ciara beamed. Indicating the door, she said, "We ready to head?"

"Sure are."

Meg watched as they left.

As usual she was on her own while Ciara had company.

She was late for rehearsal. The others were all in the classroom sitting around and chatting when she arrived.

"Sorry," she said as she burst in the door, breathless

from having run all the way from the flat. "I lost track of the time."

Everyone smiled at her except Dominic. He tapped his watch. "Ten minutes late," he reprimanded. "If we were all ten minutes late all the time, where would that leave us – hmmmm?"

"We'd all get here at the same time, Dominic," Sylvia sniggered.

"Very droll." Dominic wasn't impressed. "Meg, just be more punctual in future?"

"Yeah," she muttered. Huh – it wasn't as if she'd been late before. Johnny was late all the time.

Johnny pointed his finger toward Dominic. "Time is only a human con –"

"Concept," Dominic finished for him. "Yeah, yeah, Johnny, I know."

"Well then, don't be getting your knickers or whatever it is you wear underneath those garish trousers in a twist."

Dominic flushed. Deciding to ignore Johnny, he beckoned Avril up.

"Oooh," she giggled. "It's my go. I was dying for this."

"I'd die for a go of *you*," Tony joked poking her as she went by him.

Avril honked with laughter. *Arf. Arf. Arf.*

She sounded like a sea lion, Meg thought in amusement.

Dominic regarded the honking Avril with a mixture

of awe and distaste. He let her laugh for a few more seconds before saying to her, "Now, you are going to open up the play. And so you have to have a great big voice, get people's attention."

Avril nodded.

"I can think of better ways to get their attention," Tony said.

Avril started laughing again.

Dominic glared at her. "So we'll spotlight you," he spoke loudly, trying to get her to shut up, "and you say your lines."

"Right," Avril nodded.

Silence.

"Well, off you go," Dominic nodded encouragingly.

"Well, I just have to get my script."

"You're supposed to have learnt your lines by now," Dominic said sternly. "This is real life, you know. We have been at this the last few weeks, you know."

Avril blushed. "I'll know them next week, I promise."

"Mmm."

Meg felt sorry for Avril as she ran down to retrieve her script.

Avril stood in the place where Dominic indicated. Once again, in between giggles, she attempted to explain, "It's just *hard* to remember the lines." Her voice sounded vaguely amused, as if she couldn't quite understand what Dominic was getting so annoyed about. "It's really weird," she went on. "I sit down and read the script and like, I *know* them. I know every single word. And then," she gave a nervous giggle, "I come here and I just, well, I just forget everything."

"Aw," Tony said soothingly, "it's only your first big play. Don't worry."

Avril turned and smiled gratefully at him. He gave her the thumbs up.

"Oh," Dominic strode ponderously down toward Tony. "That's fine then. We'll just stick a notice in the programme beside Avril's name, will we? We'll say, don't mind if Avril forgets her lines, it's her first big play." He banged his head with his fist and did a whirl. "Well, why didn't I think of that? Oh, silly stupid me!"

"Hit the nail on the head there," Sylvia remarked.

Meg giggled but stopped dead when Dominic glared hard at her.

"Begin," Dominic ordered crossly.

"Let me tell a tale of a girl," Avril read hesitantly. She gulped. "God, it's very different reading the lines standing up to sitting down, isn't it?"

"Vertical as opposed to semi-vertical," Johnny said.

Avril nodded. "Yeah, I mean Meg makes it look so *easy,*" she smiled at Meg who blushed with pleasure. "I mean, up she gets and she's like *brilliant.* The lines just pour out of her as natural as anything but I –"

"Sorry, is this a Meg appreciation night?" Dominic scowled.

"Well, no, all I'm saying –"

"Just *read* the script," Dominic said.

"Oh, right," Avril gave a little cough. "Let me tell

121

the tale of a girl, a tale as common in the world as –"

Alfonso stood up. "Naw, you gotta get it right. See, 'girl' and 'world' have a sort of internal rhyme, you gotta bring it out?"

"Oh," Avril looked bewildered.

Alfonso took the script from her and began to read. He read the whole first paragraph. "See?" he handed the script back to Avril

"Now," Dominic said. "See?"

Avril didn't see at all. She read again.

"Good," Dominic said.

"Oh man," Alfonso said and put his head in his hands.

It took until half ten to get the first page done. Sylvia had brought along a deck of cards and she and Johnny and Tony were playing Snap. Meg hadn't the nerve. She kept thinking that as soon as she started to play the game, her part would come.

But it didn't.

At ten thirty, Dominic decided to call it a night. "Let's wrap it up now," he said, rubbing his hands together. Looking pointedly at Sylvia, he said, "And no card-playing on Thursday. All of you have to know what is happening on-stage, so please try and take an interest."

"I would if it was interesting," Sylvia gathered her cards together and eyeballed her director.

"Are you saying I'm not interesting?" Avril asked, beginning to laugh. *Arf! Arf! Arf!*

"*I* think you're interesting," Tony remarked.

Avril shrieked even louder.

"So who's heading to the pub?" Sylvia talked over Avril. "Anyone driving?"

"Yep, Dominic is," Johnny said. "Driving us all round the bend."

"*Very good,*" Avril clapped her hands together and stamped her foot. "Very witty."

Meg slipped out while the going was good. She didn't think anyone even noticed she'd gone.

Hopelessness combined itself with relief.

Ciara and Greg were in when she got home. Lying side by side on the sofa. Greg was nuzzling into the side of Ciara's neck and she was making some very half-hearted attempts to push him away.

Meg could only conclude that the night out had been successful.

Strangely enough, she felt a stab of envy go through her. Not that she would have fancied Greg if he was the last man on the planet.

Well, maybe if he was the *very* last man on the planet.

"Oh," she said. "Hi yez. Good night?"

They grinned at her.

Focusing her eyes on a picture of a flower that hung over the telly, she said, "Well, don't mind me. I'll just, eh," she flapped her hand in the direction of her room, "eh, go to bed."

"Wish I could," Greg said.

"You can." Ciara stood up and taking his jacket

from the back of the sofa handed it to him. "Off you go now and nighty-night."

Greg looked sadly at her. "You're a hard woman."

"And I'm just getting rid of you before you become a hard man," Ciara chortled.

Meg laughed and Greg smirked.

"Come on," Ciara took him by the arm. "I'll see you out."

"Night," Meg said going to her room.

Neither of them answered her.

Glumly she wondered how on earth Ciara could manage guys so well. It was like the way some people were good with animals, the way she was with fellas. She could bring them so far and then make them jump through hoops for her.

And Ciara made it look so *easy*.

Only Meg knew it wasn't easy. Even if she could get as far as having a guy she fancied *like* her back she'd feel she'd achieved something.

Some kind of worth.

Anything else would be a major bonus.

Looking at Ciara and Greg made her feel . . . she didn't know . . . hopeless or something.

OCTOBER

Chapter Eleven

"Oy! Meg!"

She jumped. Even though she had her Walkman on, the yell penetrated the headphones.

"Oy! Meg!" The shout came again, followed by the blast of a car horn. Not a normal horn, it sort of played a tune. *"Meg!"*

Turning, Meg saw Jack pulling his car up alongside her. He rolled down the passenger window and grinned out at her. "Hiya, stranger. D'you want a lift?"

"Oh, no –"

"Hop in and I'll drive you."

"No, it's all right – it's just around the corner."

Jack bit his lip. For some reason that he didn't understand, Meg seemed to be avoiding him. He hadn't really seen her since his first day in the school when they'd had lunch together.

And it hurt him.

"You sure?" he asked.

"Positive." Meg forced a smile on her face.

"I don't mind."

She wished he'd go. He made her uneasy. "Look," she said, trying to sound as if she was doing him a favour, "I don't want to put you out."

To her surprise, Jack's grin broadened. "Don't be a feckin' thick – I offered, didn't I?" He opened the door. "Hop in."

Looked as if she'd no choice. She sat in beside him and closed the door.

"So," Jack asked, "you on a half-day or what?"

"Yeah. There's a plumber coming to fix our shower. He's due at three."

"Oh, your landlord finally caved in, did he?"

Jack had a good memory. Meg smiled. "Yeah. He'd no choice. Ciara terrified him into it."

Jack indicated and pulled out from the kerb. "Just tell me where to go," he said as the car shuddered violently.

She clutched the sides of her seat. "Straight on and take the first left," she stammered. As the car began to speed up and the shaking subsided, she added, "It's the tenth door down."

"Grand."

They didn't speak as Jack drove. He kept glancing at her out of the corner of his eye when he thought she wasn't looking. She interested him. There was something about her that made him want to get to know her all over again. If only he could get back just a little of the friendship they'd had, he'd feel happy. If only there was something he could say to slot the past back into place . . .

"Turn left here," Meg interrupted his thoughts. "And it's the tenth door." She wished he'd stop glancing at her. What was she supposed to say? She'd known that the minute she sat beside him, she'd become tongue-tied. That was just her way. He probably thought she was dull. Well, he'd be right, wouldn't he? No life in you at all, her mother was always saying. And she did want to talk to him 'cause she liked him. Well, if she was honest about it, she sort of fancied him, and it wasn't his looks. Even when he'd been sixteen, it hadn't been his looks. It was *him*. She couldn't understand it.

"So," Jack asked, "you been avoiding me or what?"

The question startled her. "No." She knew she sounded defensive. "Why?"

"I just haven't seen you around." He braked as the traffic lights in front turned red. "I was beginning to think you were afraid I'd make you spill more coffee and wreck more of your clothes."

"Don't be stupid." She elbowed him and then blushed. It was a very *familiar* thing to do to someone she hardly knew. So she started to rub her elbow so he'd think she'd just hit it off him by accident.

"I never see you around," Jack said. "You never seem to be in the staffroom for lunch or anything."

"I, eh, well, I never really have lunch in the staffroom." She gave an embarrassed smile. "I normally have it in the office. I'm not much good at talking to all the teachers, I mean, they spend the whole break talking about their classes and stuff."

Jack laughed. "Yeah, boring load of ould shites."

"Oh, no, I didn't mean you –"

"Yeah. Yeah. I know." He continued to smile.

"And, well, I do see you. I see you on tea break."

"Yeah, for about two minutes."

His smile disappeared and he sounded glum. And hurt. It surprised her.

"Only 'cause I've piles of work to do," she explained. "The start of the year is always a bit mental."

The smile again. Her heart twisted. That smile could always do that to her.

"So it's nothing personal then?"

"Nope."

"Good."

The way he held her gaze when he said that made her flush, because all sorts of mad stupid thoughts started churning in her head. She knew if she looked at him for much longer she'd probably do something mad and stupid. Like leg it out of the car in case she did something mad and stupid.

The sound of a car horn made both of them jump. Jack tore his eyes away from Meg and muttered a 'fuck' under his breath. He gave a wave of apology to the driver behind and took off just as the lights once again turned red.

"That driver's giving you the two fingers now," Meg exclaimed, mortified. The car behind had been forced to stop once more at the lights.

"Anyone that gives me anything is all right by me."

She laughed. If that had been her she would have probably crashed the car worrying about what everyone else on the road was saying about her. But it was typical of Jack, from what she could remember he'd never given a toss what anyone had thought about him.

She liked that.

He pulled up outside a yellow-painted door. "Here?"

"Yeah, thanks."

"I'll have to call in to you some lunchtime, seeing as you spend your lunches in your office – yeah?"

Her hand on the door-lock, she turned to him. He was staring out the window, his hands resting on the steering wheel. He had the same expression on his face as the time he'd told her he'd write but then he hadn't. So she made the same reply. "If you want to."

She saw his shoulders tense, then slacken, almost as if he was deliberately relaxing them. He continued to stare out the window as she opened the car door. "Thanks again," she said, just as she was slamming it shut.

"No probs," he turned to face her and the grin was back on his face. "Any time I'm going your way and it's raining or whatever, just ask me and I'll give you a lift."

"That's very kind of you – thanks."

"It's not kind – it's 'cause I want to." The words came of their own accord. Unable to take them back, Jack's hand clenched the steering wheel while he waited to see what effect they had on her.

Meg flinched. That had been a weird thing to say. Or had it? Maybe it was just something he meant and it had come out sounding weird. "Great." She closed the door and raised her hand to wave, but the car took off before she'd got her hand halfway up. Bouncing along whilst blowing white smoke out its exhaust, it virtually tore down the street.

She didn't care about him. That was the bottom line. Everything he remembered about her was just that, a memory. Time changed; things changed. He hated that, but it was true. Since he'd met her again, he'd started to feel the same way about her as when they were kids. But it was too late. She'd moved on. And so had he, he supposed. But it didn't mean that he forgot people he'd liked.

He wished he could turn the clock back.

Turn it back to before everything became so fucked up.

Nothing to do and all afternoon to do it. Story of her life. She couldn't even be bothered learning the lines for the play and anyhow, her concentration had gone AWOL lately.

Still, the plumber would be arriving soon. Not that that was exactly Richter-scale excitement. But it was about as exciting as her life would get.

She picked up her latest Mills and Boon novel and tried to imagine herself into the part of the heroine. But the heroine in the book was witty and funny and beautiful. She had men falling over her. Meg's imagination wasn't *that* good.

But still, the book passed the time.

Escapism, the best thing ever invented as far as she was concerned.

He was bored. All alone in the flat and going mental. He'd prepared all his classes and he felt apeshit. Totally restless. He couldn't stop prowling around the dog-box of a flat. Time to kill and no cash to kill it with. How come life was so incredibly dull?

He flicked on the television. Nothing.

Maybe he could head out for a drive, take his pencils and art paper with him. He wondered how much petrol he had in the car. Not much. And anyhow, for some reason, though he'd always loved art and drawing and stuff, he couldn't concentrate as well any more.

Well, he reasoned, it wasn't the concentration. He could concentrate if he found something interesting to draw, but there was nothing. Nothing.

It was kinda frustrating.

Jesus, he had to get out. His head was going to boil over if he didn't. Edgy. That's what it was. Itching for something to do.

Then he saw the jar. The one where they kept the money for food. Taking it down he counted out forty quid. He grinned as he shoved the money into the pocket of his jeans. Suddenly some of the edginess went. It seeped away and his head became focused. He'd sworn he wouldn't bet when he'd got the new job, but what was the harm? A little here, a little there, it made him feel good, cheered him up, so what was the fucking harm? Only Peadar nagging on, that was all.

He could cope with Peadar.

He'd bought a paper on the way home from the school. Somehow, when he'd bought the paper, he'd known that this is what it was all leading up to. Fate. That's what it was. He was fated to win.

Jack opened the newspaper to the racing page and pored over it. His head raced, his palms shook. This was it, baby.

There was racing on in England that day. He'd studied form. He knew his stuff. Watch out, lads, Jack is going to clean yez out. Maybe make a hundred quid or so.

That'd be grand.

If the knocking hadn't come, Meg would have had a drink. Or maybe two drinks. But the knocking came. It couldn't be the plumber. He wouldn't have been able to get into the building without buzzing up first. "Who is it?" she called.

"It's me. Hello?"

It was James. Meg bit her lip. "I don't know anyone called me," she said, hoping to sound sarcastic. Hoping he'd think it was Ciara and do a runner.

He cackled with laughter. "It's James. Your landlord. That's who."

She got up from the sofa and padded to the door. "What do you want?"

"Well, 'twould be nice if you opened the door for starters."

Meg undid the locks and opened the door a tiny fraction. She pulled back as James' moon-like face peered in through the crack.

Holding up a battered brown leather bag, James announced loudly, "I've come to fix your shower!"

"What? You? But, but you said a plumber!"

"Yes. Yes. I know. And aren't you looking at him?" James flapped his arm about and smiled. "Fixing an ould shower is no problem to me. *And* I've a little friend with me. A little helper." He pulled a kid of about six in front of him. "This Meg, is my nephew, James Junior. Say hello, James Junior."

James Junior stuck out his tongue.

Meg opened the door wider. She supposed she'd better be nice to the kid. "Hello," she bent down and put on a high voice she knew kids liked, "Aren't you a big boy?"

"Piss off."

Meg recoiled and then attempted a laugh.

"His poor mammy is very sick today so I said, well, I'll take him. Sure Meg and Ciara won't mind at all. Meg and Ciara, they're the tops when it comes to tenants, I said." Turning to James Junior, James said, "He's going to be helping me out, aren't you, James Junior?"

"No."

James laughed. "Oh, now, that's a terrible way to be answering your favourite uncle." He gave him an affectionate clout.

"Fuck off," James Junior said.

James laughed louder. "Well, isn't that terrible?" he tittered.

"Awful," Meg agreed, smiling weakly.

"So, are you going to let me in?" James looked hopefully at her and rubbed his hands together.

Meg gulped. She kept her hand on the door. "You mean, it's *just* you? You're repairing our shower on your own?" She looked at James, dressed in his usual brown cords and check shirt. "But . . . I didn't know. . . I mean . . . you're not a plumber, are you?"

"Haven't I my bag of tools?" James patted the brown bag. "And," opening the bag he fished out a well-thumbed DIY manual, "haven't I my book?"

"But James," she gulped, wishing Ciara was there, "I don't think . . . well, you're still not a plumber and you told Ciara . . ."

"With this book," James interrupted her as he waved the book about, "I could plumb to the depths of despair if I wanted."

"Aw, I dunno . . ."

"Well, I do. Come on there now, girl, and let us into your flat."

Oh God, he was being a bit forceful. What was the best thing to do? She couldn't tell him to get lost or they mightn't see him for years and, sure, maybe he *was* able to fix things. And if he could and she let him go, Ciara would freak.

Ciara would freak anyhow.

She stood aside and James entered. He looked around and in a lowered tone, he asked, "Is the other wan around? The Ciara wan?"

"No."

"Ah," he rubbed his hands together. "That's great so. We'll have a nice cup of coffee before I start."

"This place is a kip," James Junior said loudly. "Isn't it, James?"

James' only response was to begin to cough.

Meg wondered what she should do.

Tell him to start work? Yeah, that was *definitely* what she should do.

"Coffee?" James said again.

"Eh . . . d'you not think . . . maybe?"

"Yes?"

She sighed. One cup wouldn't hurt. "Black or white?"

James beamed. Rubbed his hands together. "Aw, you're a great woman. A great woman. A *lovely* woman."

There were a few people he recognised in Byrne's that afternoon. Leonard was there, lounging up against number two window – he thought Jane, one of the girls that took the bets, was gorgeous, so he spent his time at her booth and no one else got a look in. Shane was there as well.

Most times, they never really acknowledged each other.

"Hey, Jack," Shane surprised him by greeting him as he walked in, "how's the form? Haven't seen you in here in a few weeks."

Jack shrugged. "I'm great. Not a bother. Here, give us one of those slips, will ya?"

Shane handed him a betting slip and Jack studied the board on the wall. He was tempted to bet the whole forty quid on Celtic Queen but she didn't race well on hard ground.

"Got a tip for that race," Shane said. "Go for number six – Dancer. I've fifty on her."

The odds were good. Twenty to one. Jack bet the whole lot on a win. He handed his slip to the young wan behind the counter and she stamped it and gave him back his half. The race was to start in five minutes. The telly on the wall showed the horses being paraded around the enclosure. Number six was in yellow and green.

Jack took out his fags and offered one to Shane.

"Ta."

They lit up and sat in silence as the horses were put into their boxes. Jack felt the familiar rush in his head. The way the smoke of the cigarette plunged down deeper inside him with each inhalation. The way his heart began the slow rhythmic pound, the tension, the murmur of voices behind him as punters discussed form. The talking, the shouting, the slamming of hand into fist as the horses shot out of the starting gates. The yelling, the noise filling up his head, blotting everything out except the race, the race, the race. Shane howling for Dancer who was leading by a length. His own voice, screaming at the telly, yelling at the jockey to use the whip. The thud of the feet, the blur of colour, the scream of joy at the end.

Shane was slapping him on the back. "What did I tell ya? What did I tell ya?" he kept repeating over and over. "Jaysus, we'll have a great day."

They cashed in their slips. The girl handed Jack eight hundred and forty quid. Shane made over a grand.

"What now?" Shane began studying the board again. "Let's see . . ."

Jack lit up another fag and decided to go with number four. Eight hundred on a win. The adrenaline was flowing, his brain was jumping. No way could number four lose.

Shane peered over his shoulder. "Number four?" he said. "I dunno."

Jack shrugged. He didn't give a fuck if Shane didn't know. "Eight hundred to win," he said, passing the cash across the counter. He liked the way the girl looked half-impressed, half-shocked at the same time.

Once again she took his bet and once again he lit up and waited for the race to start. A few more lads that he recognised arrived in.

There was nothing to do between races except get psyched up. All that money, hanging on one race.

Totally mental. He wished he was in a pub. He could get a drink, watch the race, enjoy himself.

"Sorry, sir," there was a tap on his back. "Could I bother you for a second?"

His mind jumping, Jack jerked around. He hated being disturbed. He hated talking to people when his mind was floating so far above everything. "What?" he snapped. His fag trembled in his hand.

"The manager'd like a quick word, if you don't mind."

"Yeah, well, I do mind," Jack said. "Can't it wait?"

"Sure," the girl smiled apologetically at him and backed away.

Jack turned back to the screen.

James Junior was eating all the biscuits. He'd taken the packet and had begun to munch his way steadily through them as he watched some violent film on the telly. James had asked for one and been told to 'fuck off'.

"Now you know I don't like you using that word," James had said, rolling his eyes at Meg and grinning fit to split his face.

"Uh-huh," his nephew had replied, spraying biscuit crumbs all over the place.

Meg gazed at the two of them in bewilderment. As far as she was concerned the kid needed a good thump. But then again, what did she know about kids?

Nothing, thank God.

"Another cup'd go down nicely," James shoved his mug towards her.

She stared at it. It was now after six and nothing had been done on the shower. In a shaky voice she said, "Well, only one more and then, well, wouldn't it be nice to start on the shower?"

James chuckled. "Nice? Whoever thought work was nice? Anyhow, I like talking to you." He smiled a black-toothed smile at her. "You're much nicer than that sharp-tongued Ciara one. Oh, now, she's funny, mind, and you're not. You're quiet, but I like you. I like you, so I do."

There was a look of semi-tenderness on his face.

She was glad she hadn't eaten lunch. It'd have come up all over the floor.

Later, later after the race had finished, he went to see the manager. Things were on the up. He was on the up. The manager smiled at him. Told him to take a seat.

"We'd like you to open an account with us." The manager looked at Jack across his desk. "You can phone in your bet, we'll bill you by the month and pay out by the month."

"Right," Jack grinned. He was in the big time now. He was a valued customer, the manager had told him so. He won big and they wanted more of his business. "That sounds great."

The manager smiled. Passing some forms across his desk, he said, "Well, all you have to do is sign these and we'll issue you with your account number. Is that OK?"

"Yeah. "Jack bent his head and scanned the forms.

Taking the pen the manager offered, he signed his name at the end.

"Look forward to doing business with you," the manager said.

"Yep," Jack nodded. "Me too."

"And well," James began to noisily slurp the remainder of his coffee. "To be honest, 'twasn't just to fix the shower I came about." He went red. "I've a bit of a favour to ask you, as it happens."

He went Very Red.

Alarm bells began clanging in her head. "Yeah?"

"There's a bit of a hooley in December. A Landlords' Ball. Sort of a Christmas party type of thing – only it's on after Christmas."

"Oh." What had that to do with her?

"I'd like if you'd," James coughed, "do me the honour like . . . of . . . accompanying me."

"Accompanying you?" This wasn't happening. Why of all the people in the world did James pick on her? Probably because he knew no one else would entertain the idea. Not that she would either. No, she had to refuse. Politely but firmly.

"Yes. Come with me. We'll have great craic."

Jesus.

"You want *me* to go with *you* to a dance?" She could barely get the words out.

"Aye."

"Oh . . . I'm hopeless. I can't dance. I'd stand on your

feet. God, imagine asking me to a dance." She gave a slightly hysterical laugh. "And it was so nice of you to ask me but I'm rubbish. I just . . ."

"Well, I'm getting dancing lessons. You could come to them with me." James' face had taken on a celestial radiance. "And as it happens I need a partner for the dancing too."

"You do." She felt sick.

"Begod, I do. And you're just the girl."

"I'm very busy. I do lots of stuff after work. I just wouldn't . . ."

"But you'll come to the dance?"

"Eh . . .well . . ."

There was a sound of footsteps clattering along the hallway.

Ciara's voice telling someone to 'fuck off and die'.

James heard her too. He paled.

"That's Ciara," Meg said, trying to keep the relief from her voice. "She'll want to know what you're doing here."

James gave a shaky smile. "There's a hint if ever I heard one."

He'd heard about a million.

He winked at her as if they were conspirators in doing nothing. "Well, off to work I go." He stood up and she willed him to make it to the bathroom without saying anything more about the dance. She just couldn't go. There was no way . . .

"I'll put you down for that other thing," James

gave her a broad wink before scuttling off into the bathroom.

She pretended not to hear. She settled herself alongside a very pale-looking James Junior and tried to look as if she was concentrating on the telly.

"I swear, I'm going to kill that bastard Greg . . ." Ciara slammed the door closed. Then, hearing noise from the bathroom, she looked in. Her voice hostile, she snapped out "And what are you doing here?"

"Plumbing."

A big forced belly-laugh from Ciara. She was in a foul mood. Meg didn't envy James one bit. In fact, she almost, but not quite, felt sorry for him.

"You? Plumbing?" Ciara snorted. "Where's the *plumber?*"

"Right here, in front of your eyes."

Ciara walked into the bathroom. "I see no one in front of my eyes except a tight-fisted landlord." She pretended to peer into the toilet. "Nope. No one down there."

James sniggered. "You're a terrible woman," he tittered. "Amn't I going to repair your shower? It'll take a bit of time, mind, but I'll do it. I fix everything for James Junior's mammy." He raised his voice and yelled, "Don't I, James Junior?"

James Junior didn't reply.

Meg tried not to wince as Ciara asked, "So what exactly have you done?"

"I've assessed the situation," James replied smoothly.

"I can't just go knocking plasterboard out willy-nilly, you know."

"And?"

"And I'll be knocking out the plasterboard after I take off the tiles."

"Well, don't let me stop you," Ciara said, "unless you want to be knocked out yourself."

James laughed. "Begod, that's a good one," he cackled.

Meg marvelled at her flatmate's nerve.

"And who is this?" Ciara had come into the sitting-room and was staring at James Junior sprawled out across the sofa. "And why is he lying on our sofa?"

"It's James' nephew," Meg whispered. "He had to mind him today."

"So he's a landlord, plumber *and* a baby-sitter, is he?" Ciara hissed. "Is there no end to the man's talents?" She poked James Junior in the ribs. "Get your feet off our sofa."

"Can't," James Junior moaned. "I feel sick."

"Well, you'll feel even sicker if I drag you off," Ciara said. "It's your choice, mate."

"Ciara!"

"What?" Ciara looked innocently at Meg. "I don't mind him being here, but, Christ, look at the muck on his shoes. The least he could do is take them off him." Once again she thumbed for James Junior to move himself.

Meg watched as he did. Holding his stomach and groaning, he slowly dragged himself over to the edge. "I feel sick," he moaned.

"Well, maybe you should go into the bathroom," Meg suggested.

The kid gave her a despairing look. "Can't move, feel sick."

She was just about to lift him up when Ciara yelled, "James, your nephew is sick out here."

The sound of tools being dropped onto the floor was earth-shattering. James whizzed out of the bathroom as if a cup of coffee was on offer. Standing over his nephew, he said breathlessly, "What's the matter?"

"Uuuhhhhgggg."

"He's going to get sick," Ciara said. "I think you should take him inside."

"Oh dear, oh dear." Hoisting him up out of the sofa, James half-dragged, half-carried him into the bathroom. Very soon the noise of violent puking could be heard.

"He ate too many biscuits," Meg said idly as she turned up the volume on the telly to block out the sound of the kid being sick.

Ciara looked at her incredulously, "Not our biscuits?"

"Yep."

"You let him eat our stuff?"

"I didn't *let* him. He just did."

"Right."

Ciara sounded really mad.

Meg gulped.

"He ate too many biscuits," James yelled from the bathroom. "Brown chocolate puke, that's what's coming up."

"I don't believe this," Ciara muttered furiously.

"Well, how could I stop him?"

Ciara threw her an irritated look and didn't answer.

"The sister is going to go mental," James yelled. "She can't bear for him to be sick." More puking sounds before James re-emerged. "Listen girls, I'll have to go. I can't be expected to work with this fella sick. I'll be in touch." Very gently he led James Junior out into the sitting-room. "Now," he said, "one of the nice ladies will get you your coat."

Meg jumped up. Any excuse to get away from Ciara. She handed James Junior's jacket to James. Gently, James put it around his nephew's shoulders. Hoisting his bag onto his back, he led James Junior from the flat.

"Bye now," Meg said.

"Bye," James said. Winking at her, he added, "I'll talk to you again."

Then they were gone.

For some funny reason, the sight of James leading his nephew down the hallway made Meg sad. James had his arm around him and was ruffling his hair. She had to close the door really quickly before she saw any more.

When she got back inside, Ciara kept staring at her. "What?" she asked uncomfortably.

"I'll just bet James was drinking all our coffee too," Ciara said.

"No, no he wasn't." As Ciara continued to stare at her, she added defensively, "Anyhow, what's the big deal?"

Ciara made a scoffing noise. "Meg," she said, "he

was here to fix the shower. Now, personally I would have run him on first sight, but, still, if he fixes it, it's fine. I don't mind him having a cup of tea, but don't let him take complete advantage."

"I didn't." Ciara was patronising her. As usual.

"Right."

The way Ciara said 'right' pissed Meg off. She said it as if she thought she, Meg, was a fool. And she wasn't. "Just – just – just because you're in a bad mood, don't take it out on me."

"What?"

"And, and also, if you're so worried, you take the half-day next time."

The words came out in a rush and before Ciara could retaliate, she said hastily, "I've lines to learn for my play. I'm going into my room." Without looking at her flatmate, she made a bolt for the bedroom door.

She sat on her bed and hummed as she learnt her lines.

In the pub, Jack bought all the rounds for everybody. At least he must have 'cause he'd no money left by the time he left. Zigzagging out the door at closing time, he waved at everybody and everybody waved back.

What a brilliant night it had been.

He was a hundred feet tall.

"I've given you all I have to give, I've, I've . . ." she stopped. "Shit." Glancing at the script again, she mumbled, "I've given you all I have to give. I've given it so that I can live. I've given my heart, my thoughts, my soul. I've given it to you to make me whole."

Meg closed her eyes. Tried to remember the lines again. "I've given . . . God!"

It was hopeless. She couldn't concentrate. The row with Ciara kept playing on her mind. Normally, if both she and Ciara were home, they'd have supper together. Only, Meg didn't know, after what had happened, if Ciara would speak to her.

And she didn't want to make a fool of herself by trying to talk to Ciara and getting ignored.

That sort of thing hurt her.

So she'd just stay in her room until Ciara went to bed. Then maybe, she'd grab a cup of tea or a can and get her book which she'd left outside on the table.

Anything rather than learn her lines.

Eleven fifteen. She heard Ciara filling the kettle.

"Meg?" Ciara's voice.

She jumped. "What? Yes?"

"Are you all right in there? It's after eleven. D'you want a cuppa? I've got the kettle on."

Ciara was talking to her. She'd put the kettle on. It was a nice feeling. "Oh, oh right, sorry. I didn't realise . . ." Meg jumped off the bed. "Just a sec . . . I'm coming."

Poking her head around the door Ciara grinned, "Betcha you got stuck into one of those shit-arse books and lost track of the time."

Normally the reference to her Mills and Boon books

as 'shit-arse' would offend Meg a lot, but the relief that Ciara seemed to have forgotten about earlier made up for it. "Hit the nail on the head," she smiled.

"I wish I could hit you on the head," Ciara grumbled, good-naturedly, "and stop you from reading all that crap."

"Ha, ha."

"Oh, yeah, and by the way, I was thinking about what you said earlier –"

Oh God, now she felt sick.

" . . . time."

"What?" She tried to focus her mind on what Ciara was saying.

"I said I'm sorry – I was in bad mood. I had a row with Greg. And I will take the day off next time."

"Oh, right. Right. That's OK."

"But you still shouldn't have let James take advantage."

"Yeah. I know." How the hell could she have *stopped* him?

"And if toerag James calls around and I'm not here, you ring me on my mobile. I'll sort him out."

"You will?"

"Bloody sure I will."

Ciara was great. Meg smiled ruefully. "That'd be great 'cause maybe then he won't think I'm going to a dance with him."

"What?"

Oh shit. She shouldn't have said that. Ciara would go on and on about it now. "Forget it."

"A dance?"

"Yeah." She gave a nervous laugh. "He said it was a Landlords' Ball. For landlords, I suppose. It's on at Christmas."

"What? Celebrating the fact they have balls or something?"

"I dunno. And Ciara, I don't know what to do. It's not like I said I'd go, I think he just sort of assumed it."

"He *couldn't* have assumed it." Ciara rolled her eyes. "Listen, you better put him straight. Tell him you're not a masochist."

"Oh, stop, I couldn't."

"Well, which'd be harder?" Ciara grinned a bit. "Saying that or actually going?"

Meg smiled, though it wasn't funny. "I get your point."

"Swear that you won't go?" Ciara looked anxiously at her. "No matter what happens, say no – right?"

"Oh, Ciara, don't start. Of *course* I'll say no."

Ciara looked doubtfully at her. "Well, you didn't say no the time that fella kept calling around to the flat selling his encyclopaedias."

"That was different. He was a salesman. He didn't want a relationship."

"No, just four hundred quid of your money for a bunch of crappy books."

She knew this would happen. Ciara was going to drag everything up now. The time she'd had the Hoover salesman in and they couldn't get rid of him, the

Mormons that had kept calling. She bit her lip, "I didn't think they were crappy books and that salesman, well, he was good at his job."

Ciara gave her an exasperated look. Then she started to laugh. "Well, good or not, I swear, if you go out with James, you deserve no sympathy."

"No, but I'd deserve a medal for bravery."

It was nice to laugh at her own joke. And it was nice to see Ciara laugh.

But she sort of felt a bit sorry for James.

It wasn't nice to be laughed at and anyhow, who was she to be laughing at anyone?

He was flying. The room spun around like crazy as he lay in bed. But this was it. Pure adrenaline-driven happiness.

He laughed.

He could do anything now.

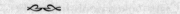

James.

He'd *liked her. Well, she supposed he had. She couldn't count on anything any more. Everything was crumbling.*

. . . she couldn't remember leaving her room and entering the bathroom. She wondered when she'd done it. The first she knew of it was when she stood on a shard of a tile. It cut her foot and made it bleed.

The blood looked funny, strangely real, dripping onto the white cement floor.

Drop after drop, plop after plop.

It fascinated her the way the blood trickled.

It didn't hurt.

She was so far inside herself that nothing hurt any more. So far floating above herself that nothing mattered any more.

Nothing.

That was good.

The sound of the horses' hooves thudding across the ground as they were moving to the starting line filled his head. The smell of the freshly cut grass, mingling with the aroma of chips and burgers and over it all the sound of chat and laughter. And him, just being somewhere in the middle of it all, above it all, carried along by it all.

Athleague Guest thudded by and he raised his fist and gave a shout. "Come on, ya beauty!"

The sound of his voice startled him.

Excited him.

Not long now.

≈≈≈

Chapter Twelve

His head was splitting. He knew he looked really bad as he stumbled out into the kitchen the next morning. He'd fallen asleep in his clothes and, as he had nothing else to wear, he'd have to make do with the stuff he had on. Well, maybe when Peadar left, he could sneak into his room and nick a loan of a shirt or something. There was no way he could turn up at the school reeking of sweat and stale beer and fags.

"Good night?" Peadar asked.

Jack noticed that he was smiling, so he couldn't be ready to give him an earful.

"Yep." He began to root around in the fridge for a Lucozade. The best cure in the world for hangovers. He twisted the top off and, closing his eyes, he began to drink it down. The fizz hit his stomach and for a minute he thought he'd be sick, but he knew, from vast experience, that it would only be a matter of time before he began to feel better.

"So where'd you go?" Peadar was stuffing papers into his briefcase and not looking at him. "I thought you'd no money."

Jack's hand froze on the Lucozade bottle. Was this some ploy to catch him out? "I, eh," he coughed a bit, pretending that some drink had gone down the wrong way while he searched his mind for an excuse, "I met some lads I know. They were celebrating something or other, I dunno what, and they just kept buying me drinks." Shrugging and grinning he added, "I tried to stop them, but, nah, it was impossible."

Peadar clicked his briefcase shut. "I only asked 'cause Vanny came haring around last night wondering where you were."

The whole of Jack froze. "Oh shit," he mumbled.

"She was bringing you out to the pictures or something."

Vanny in a bad mood. It didn't bear thinking about. He suddenly really did feel sick.

"I wouldn't like to be you when she meets you." Peadar wasn't smiling. "In fact, I'd rather be chief witness in a Mafia trial."

"Ha-Ha!" He had to sit down.

"I felt a bit sorry for her," Peadar went on. "Look, it's none of my business, but you keep standing the girl up. If you're not into her, why the hell don't you just call it a day? Huh?"

Jack bristled. There Peadar went again! Trying to tell him how to run his life. Anyway, it wasn't that simple. He owed Vanessa at least eighty quid and, if he broke it off with her, she'd want paying, and he hadn't got any money. Maybe when he got his next pay from the school he'd dump her but for the moment it wasn't an option. And besides, Vanny didn't seem to mind bringing him out or driving him places and it saved him money. So, glaring at Peadar, he said, "I just forgot I was meant to be seeing her. It wasn't a deliberate thing. And anyhow, the bleedin' film she was dragging me to was one of those arty subtitled things that she's big into. I'm glad I wasn't around."

He didn't like the look Peadar gave him. Or the way he said, "Suit yourself," before self-righteously exiting the apartment.

"Fuck off," Jack spat. Trust Peadar to try and spoil his morning. It was probably all down to Eileen anyhow. She had to have something to do with it, Peadar never used to be such a tight-arse. She probably had the guy totally frustrated the way she wouldn't sleep with him.

Draining the last of his Lucozade, Jack swore that the rest of the day was going to improve.

He concentrated on how he'd felt the night before and some of the good feeling he'd woken up with that morning began to trickle back into his head.

He was in control. If he wanted to feel good, he could. No one else could spoil it, least of all Vanny and Peadar.

He arrived at work just as classes were starting. He missed his kick-start cuppa in the staffroom, but he didn't care. Just like in the last job, he found the teachers all right but not exactly stimulating. Everything they did seemed so low-key and sort of flat. The only person in the whole place that even half-interested him was Meg and he hardly ever saw her.

Well maybe, his good feeling told him, you should change that. If you want to see her, go for it. After last night, when he'd proved to everyone what he could achieve, he knew that anything was possible. Meg had been his friend once and she would be again.

Some part of him balked at the idea; it told him that maybe he should leave her alone.

The other part said that if it was what he wanted he should go for it. Besides, she was gentle, not like Vanny, and she used to understand him, definitely not like Vanny.

And he wasn't afraid of her.

But you like her, the part that balked whispered. It's not fair.

Exactly, the other part of him said. If you like her, go for it.

He had the Second Year class first thing that morning. Brendan sat at the back of the room, chewing gum with his feet plonked on top of the desktop. Jack ignored him. Instead, he said. "Right lads, today we're going to work on what in my opinion is the most boring discipline within Art. Still life."

"Boring," Brendan shouted up from the back of the class.

Again Jack took no notice. "Normally," he continued, "I'd plonk a bowl of fruit on the table with an empty bottle of wine or something and get yez to draw it, but today, walking into this class, inspiration struck."

He had their attention now. The chattering abated as they looked at him.

"We are going to draw Brendan. He's gotta be the most inactive still-life study going."

The kids laughed as Brendan scowled.

"Yeah," someone shouted, "an' drawing vegetables is a lot more interesting than drawing fruit and wine."

More loud laughter.

"No way are you gonna talk like that!" Brendan startled the whole room by pouncing on the fella that had spoken. He grabbed him by the scruff of the neck. "No fucking way."

"Brendan, sit down," Jack ordered.

Brendan dragged the fella over toward the wall and pinned him up against it, yelling into his face, "You take that back or I'll burst ya."

Jack jumped across tables to get to the end of the room, his head jarring with each leap he took. "Oy, lads, stop," he shouted.

The two lads were nose to nose, one terrified, the other murderous. "You take that back," Brendan yelled. "Take it back or else . . ."

One of the girls had her hand on Brendan's arm and was tearfully telling him to stop. The rest of the room had fallen silent.

Jack wished he'd kept his mouth shut now. It was all his fault. Some teacher he was. And the last thing he needed with a hangover headache was aggro in the classroom. "Look, Brendan," he said, "what I said was only a joke. Let's forget about it, all right?"

"Brendan?" the girl asked.

Brendan shook the guy he was holding. "Yeah, well, what Fitzer said wasn't even close to a joke, so he's gotta say sorry."

Fitzer gulped. "I didn't mean anything horrible by it. I just said it. Honest," he said softly, "I wasn't meaning anything about your bro —"

Brendan shook him again before letting him go. "Shut up," he snapped. Ignoring Jack he sloped back down to his seat.

Fitzer, white-faced, stayed where he was.

The girl went and sat in beside Brendan, whispering to him.

The room was still.

Looking around, Jack said, "Can someone tell me what all that was about?"

No one answered.

"Well?" Jack asked.

Still silence.

"Sit down," Jack said. He watched as Fitzer scurried to his seat. Glancing about the room one more time, he saw that no one was going to volunteer any information. The best thing to do was to get the class back to normal. "Fine," he walked back up the room.

"So can we get started?" Giving a small grin, he added, "Maybe we will stick to the fruit and wine after all."

A few kids grinned back.

Jack took out the fruit and the wine, arranged them at the window, so that the light could reflect off them. Giving a commentary as he did so about shape, texture and colour, he decided that after class he'd call into the secretary's office and get the file out on Brendan Byrne.

It'd give him an excuse to see Meg too.

What was he like?

While the kids were painting, Jack took out a requisitions form for the Art Department and began to fill it in.

Eleven o'clock, not feeling as high as he had earlier, he made his way to the secretaries' office. Loud voices emanated from behind the closed door. Knocking loudly, to warn whoever was doing all the shouting that he was on his way in, he opened the door.

"Yeah?" Linda's voice snapped as he entered the room.

Jack glanced hastily around. To his disappointment, the only other person in the office was a small fat teenager with an acne-covered face. He was lounging casually against Meg's desk, chewing gum and looking for all the world as if he'd rather be anywhere else.

"Well?" Linda demanded.

"Listen, Ma, I'll head off." The teenager lifted himself from the desk.

"You will not!" Linda snapped.

Rolling his eyes and making a face, the lad slumped back down.

Linda smiled, "And what can I do for you, Jack?"

He gulped. Maybe it wasn't the best time. "I, eh, I'm looking for the student files."

"They're all on computer. Everything was scanned in during the summer. I can do a printout for you if you like, but you'll have to wait a while. And anything you get, you can't take it out of this office."

"Fine," Jack said. He gave her Brendan's name and his class. "I'll pick it up at lunchtime." Another excuse to see Meg, he thought. God, what was he like? Like some oversexed teenager. Then, handing her the requisitions book, he said, "Here, John Dunne said to pass this on to you."

She barely glanced at it, just nodded and turned her attention back to the young lad in the office.

Chapter Thirteen

"Fat lot of use that shagger is," Linda spat, slamming the phone down on Leo. "I tell him his son is up for shoplifting and all he can shagging do is laugh."

Meg didn't know if an answer was expected of her. So, she just said, "Laugh?"

"Yeah, shagging laugh." Linda yanked open the drawer of her desk and pulled her lunch box from it. "Toerag. He thought it was funny that Clive was caught nicking twenty packets of Pretty Polly tights." Slamming the drawer closed, she added, "All he can say is why didn't he take some booze or something decent."

"Oh." She stared fixedly at the computer. The thoughts of fat, spotty Clive with packets of tights hidden under his jacket made her want to laugh too.

"I mean, booze – honestly," Linda shook her head. "Huh, pity he didn't take some hair colour. All me roots are showing."

"Mmm."

Linda glared over at her. "Do they look bad?"

"Huh?"

"Me roots. You said, *mmm.*"

"Oh, I didn't mean anything by it."

Linda came toward her, head down, exposing black roots in violently red hair.

"Your hair looks fab, Linda. Fab."

"Yeah. Right." Standing upright once more, Linda shook her hair. "I'm getting it done next week anyhow. For me birthday." She stressed the word *birthday*. "I'm thirty-five," she added.

"Oh, great." Thirty-five my arse, Meg thought. "Happy birthday for then," she said. Huh, she thought, it was more like thirty-five multiplied by two.

"Anyway, I'm heading on lunch break. Coming?"

"Nah. I'll eat it here." With Linda gone, she felt she could breathe again. There was only so much complaining a person should have to listen to every day. There was only so much work a person should have to do every day too, she thought as she took her lunch from her desk. What exactly Linda did in the office, she wasn't quite sure, but one thing she knew was that it was feck all. "Feck bloody all," she muttered as she plugged in the kettle for a cuppa.

Someone rapped on the door.

"Eh, we're on lunch," she said. It was best to be assertive, so she repeated, "It's lunchtime."

"Yeah, sorry 'bout that." Jack strode into the office, his face a huge smile. "Hiya."

"Oh, hi." She wondered what he wanted.

"I've just to pick up a file from the other girl that works here – eh, what's her name?"

"Linda?"

"Yeah. Her."

It was disappointing because for some stupid reason, Meg had hoped that he'd wanted to talk to her.

"She promised to have a student file for me this lunchtime." Jack tossed his lunch box from one hand to the other as he spoke.

"Well, that's Linda's desk – have a look there."

His back to her, he began to search the desk.

Meg stared at the bum of his jeans. Nice. What was it Ciara said about guys like that? Something about hoping their morals were in indirect proportion to their gorgeous tight arses.

Jack turned about to find her grinning. "What?"

Jesus, what had she been thinking? Flustered, she dropped her lunch box onto the floor and felt her face heat up. Diving under the desk, she stammered, "Eh, did you find it – the file?"

"Nope."

"Then it's probably not ready." Back up into her seat. The best thing now was to try and save some face. "Do you want me to print it out for you?"

"Nah. You're on your lunch break. Just ask yer wan, what's her name again?"

"Linda."

"Yeah, ask her to get it for me, will you?"

"Write her a note and leave it on her desk." She held up a pad and a pen to him. "She'll do it quicker if you write it down."

As he reached for the pen and paper his hand brushed hers. Pulling away quickly, she found she suddenly couldn't look at him.

"So do I write a nice polite letter or wha'?"

"A grovelling letter."

Jack laughed. "Fine."

He thought she was joking and she wasn't. Grovelling was the only way to get Linda to do anything. His blond head came into her field of vision as he bent over the desk and began to write. She had this mad urge to reach out and touch his hair. It looked so soft and shiny. She remembered a time when she'd held him, really tight, and of how she'd rested her head on top of his and smelt the clean smell of his hair. It made her heart twist a bit to think of it.

"Finished." He held out her notebook.

"Eh, just leave it down there." She didn't want to touch him again. She'd only go red and it wasn't as if she had anything to go red about. It wasn't as if . . .

"So, I'll just leave the note on, on," he couldn't remember her name again, "on yer wan's desk, will I?"

"Yeah, I'll tell her you were in."

"Thanks," he said.

He didn't move. He just stood smiling at her.

She started to blush again. In desperation, she began to fiddle with the lid on her lunch box. But all she could do was fiddle with it. She couldn't open it. That would be suicide. Egg and onion sambos were not exactly the image she wanted him to have of her.

"Your kettle's boiled," Jack said, interrupting her thoughts.

"Oh, yeah, yeah." It was a relief to be able to turn away from him to make the tea. Maybe now he'd leave. Trying to give him the hint to go, she said, "Just pop the note on Linda's desk."

"Right."

As she took her mug from the shelf and began to spoon coffee into it, she heard him walking up the office. Pouring the boiling water into her mug, she heard him walking back down. *He wasn't going to go.* The water slopped out of her mug all over her hand. Biting her lip, so she wouldn't cry out, she carried on.

"Ouch," Jack remarked.

"It's fine." She waved her hand about in the air. "Just a bit burnt, but fine." If she kept moving it, he'd never see how purple it had gone. "So – anything else you want?"

"Cup of coffee'd be nice." Then, he joked, "Unspilled."

The joke went over her head. "Now?" she asked, "Here? From me?"

"Yeah." To her horror, he pulled up Linda's chair and sat down opposite her at her desk. "If that's all right?" He shrugged, "I did say I'd call in to you for lunch, didn't I?"

It was all she needed. It was bad enough that he expected her to talk to him but having to eat egg and onion sambos in front of him was another thing entirely. Well, not that she could now.

"Sure," she muttered, "if you want."

"I do." He gave her a smile. "Sure the staffroom will be black by now, I'd have no chance of a quiet cuppa."

Meg didn't think in a million years that something Jack Daly ever craved was quietness, but she didn't want to say that. Instead, she took Linda's mug from the shelf and began to spoon in some coffee. "One spoon or two?"

"Three," he said.

"Black or white?"

"Sort of brown."

Despite her unease, she laughed. Handing him his cup, she sat down in her chair.

He began to unwrap a tinfoil package. "Me lunch," he said unnecessarily. There were about twenty digestive biscuits inside. "Want one?"

"Thanks." She took one because otherwise she was going to starve and then her stomach would start rumbling and she'd be mortified and he would too, probably. And he'd go right off her, not that he was interested anyhow, but still . . .

"So what have you got?" Jack nodded toward her lunch box. "Something mad healthy, I bet."

Healthy being his word for boring probably, she thought. "Oh, nothing much." She tried to shove her box back into her drawer. "I'm not very hungry now anyway."

"Oh, right."

"Had a big breakfast."

"Did you?"

"Bran Flakes. Orange." She stopped. "Toast," she added.

Jack was grinning. She felt she had to go on. "Cup of tea. Two cups actually."

Now he was giving her a weird look. "It was just this morning," she explained. "I don't have that every morning."

"Thanks for telling me that," he nodded gravely. "I really needed to know."

"Huh?"

"Joke."

"Oh, right." Doing her best to smile, she began to nibble at the biscuit he had given her. God, she was *so* hungry.

"I couldn't eat at all this morning," he said, "so I'm starving now." He shoved a biscuit into his mouth. "Digestive biscuits are lovely, aren't they?"

"Lovely." She wished she had about twenty more. "So were you sick this morning?" He did look a bit pale.

"Hung-over, big time."

"Ouch."

"Yeah," he gave a rueful smile. "I've been chewing mints and eating chewing-gum to get the smell outa me breath. You know the way kids would notice stuff like that."

"And do you feel OK now?"

"Not too bad." He grinned at her. "Not too great either."

"There's some Disprin in the press." She indicated the big wooden press that stood against the wall. "D'you want a couple?"

The way his expression softened caught her by surprise. He didn't answer for a second, then he nodded. "Great, yeah."

As she tried to locate the First Aid box, he said, "D'you remember the time we bunked school and drove up the mountains in me Da's car?"

That was a hard one to forget. In a glum voice she muttered, "Yeah." She spotted the box at the back of the shelf and, standing on her toes, she managed to get the very tips of her fingers to it. Gently she began to ease it forward.

"And I got locked outa me head and you had to drive the car home and try and sober me up."

"Yeah, some job that was." She wished he'd stop.

"And you wrecked me Da's car."

She didn't want to talk about it. Or think about it. Her fingers shook as she opened the box of tablets. Taking two out, she handed them to him, "Hang onto them until you're feeling better."

"Thanks."

Another brilliant smile.

A lurch of her stomach.

He took the tablets and washed them down with a gulp of coffee.

"That's what this reminds me of," he said as he put his mug back down on the table. "You minding me."

"I always minded you." It just popped out. She hadn't meant to say it.

"You did."

Pause.

"Still," Jack smiled at her, "at least you won't get grounded for a month this time. Jesus, your Ma went really mental, didn't she?"

"Locked me up. Told me you were a bad influence and that I wasn't to see you any more."

"She was probably right."

"Probably?"

"OK – she was dead right."

"Like she always is." She didn't mean it to come out sounding so hard.

Just as she was about to add a nice sentence about her mother, Jack asked, "How is your Ma? Does she still –" He stopped. That wasn't exactly a tactful question. He started again. "Is she still . . ."

Meg jumped in before he could finish. "Strict?" she offered. "Oh no, she's not strict. Just, you know, over-protective."

"Like the bodyguard you didn't order?"

He had a funny way with words. "Like the dozen bodyguards I didn't order." His laughter made her feel guilty. It wasn't very nice talking about her mother like that. Still, *he knew* it was only a joke. "It's only a joke."

Jack didn't seem to hear. Instead, gazing into his now empty coffee cup, he muttered, "They were good days."

Good days? Was he mental? "Good days?" she gulped. "They were *terrible* days. Don't you –" She stopped. "Well, I didn't enjoy them," she finished up.

"But we were good," he said, bringing his gaze up until it was level with hers. "We had a laugh."

He sounded sort of sad. "Yeah, I suppose we did." She drained the last of her coffee, suddenly wanting him to go.

"I was thinking," he said, "that maybe we should go out together sometime."

"Why?"

The question hurt him. Hurt him more than he'd have thought possible. It was like he really didn't matter to her any more. "Just for old times' sake." He attempted a grin. "I'd, well, I'd like to get to know you again, Meg."

Silence.

"Well?" he asked. "How 'bout it?" He tried to look as if he didn't mind if she said no.

A small thrill ran through her. "Serious?"

"Yep," Jack nodded. "'Course I am."

But thrill or not, why would he want to get to know her again? Sure, he probably had loads of friends. And what would they talk about? And where would they go?

"Oh, I dunno . . ."

"It's OK," he said swiftly. "Don't worry about it. It's cool."

She'd hurt his feelings. She *had*. And she hadn't meant to. "Where would we go?" she blurted out.

"Anywhere you like," he said softly.

Oh God. "Well, I don't mind." Gathering up her courage, she half-muttered, "I suppose it would be nice to get to know you too."

"Thanks – I needed that ego boost."

"Oh, no, I didn't mean to insult –"

"Joke?" He quirked his eyebrows.

"Oh, yeah, right." She wanted to go through the floor. She tried to laugh but failed. "Ha," she said weakly.

Jack didn't seem to notice her embarrassment. Instead, he said, "So how about we meet sometime next week?"

Next week?

"Eh – just you and me?"

"Yeah."

"But, but won't your girlfriend mind?"

"Nah," Jack shook his head. "It's not serious between us."

"Oh, right." She smiled slightly. *Next week.* "Well, sure," she gulped. "If you've nothing else better to do and you're sure . . ."

"Yeah, I'm sure." Jack stood up. Smiling down on her, wondering if he looked as weirdly happy as he felt, he tried to say casually, "Let's head out somewhere next – next Monday night?"

"OK." She felt a mixture of terror and delight. Mostly terror. But, he wanted her company. *Her* company. But then again, he hadn't a clue about how boring she was. Maybe he'd go out with her once and decide he didn't want to see her again. That would hurt. But she had until Monday to change her . . . Monday. It was like a blessing. "Oh, I can't make it Monday. I'm in a play and we've rehearsals."

"What time do they finish?"

"Ten."

"Pick you up afterwards and we can head out for a drink?"

He *really* sounded as if he wanted to. It was a bit hard to take in. "Are you sure? Like I bet you'll be doing other stuff that night."

"No." Hands in his pockets, he gave a wry smile.

It was the way he said it, the way he looked. It made her heart feel like melting ice cream. And she hadn't felt like that since . . . well, ages.

Scrunching up his tinfoil wrapper and firing it at the bin, he nodded, "See you then. And sure, maybe if you're on tea break I'll see you before then." He winked. "Bye."

There had to be a catch. Why would a guy like him be bothered with her? No one had bothered much before.

One thing was for sure. She wasn't going to dive in all pally with him.

But he was awful cute, and he'd a nice bum, and he made her feel . . . she sought for how he made her feel, and with a jolt she realised that he made her feel happy.

At least, she was *pretty* sure it was happiness.

Chapter Fourteen

The poor kid. That was all Jack could think of as he drove home the following evening. He'd eventually wrangled Brendan's student file from Linda. The girl had pressed all sorts of buttons and muttered all sorts of colourful expletives as she'd tried to gain access into the student records.

Eventually, she'd managed it. Brendan's file, complete with letters, had been almost flung at him. "And you can't leave the office while you're reading it," she'd snapped. "It's all confidential information. We can't have you carrying it about under your arm all day, can we?"

So he had his ten o'clock tea break sitting beside Meg and reading Brendan's file. Even the closeness of Meg and the gorgeous smell of whatever stuff she sprayed on herself hadn't impinged much on his thoughts as he'd read about Brendan.

He'd carried it around in his head all day.

The poor kid.

He knew there was feck all he could do to help him, like, he was a teacher, not a social worker, but, still, it made him feel powerless. He felt there had to be something he could do. Just something small.

The boy reminded him of himself. Maybe that was it.

He drove into the car park, still thinking. There had to be something he could do. He slammed his car door closed and began to lock it.

"Well, the magical disappearing man returns."

Jack closed his eyes despairingly. *Shit!*

"Or should I say, the shitty, cowardly, mouse of a man returns."

Vanny was either getting closer to him or her voice was getting louder. Either way, he felt he should at least turn around and face her. "Vanny," he said turning. "I've been meaning to call in to you." His pathetic smile withered under her gaze. "I honestly have."

"And I've been meaning to bawl into you."

"Ha, ha – very good."

"I honestly have."

He gulped. "Yeah, well, not here, huh?" He tried to get past her. "How 'bout you come into my place and –"

"What happened the other night?" She stood in front of him, arms folded. She no longer looked like a gorgeous Blonde from Beyond. She was more like the Banshee from 4B.

"Inside, yeah?" He looked desperately about.

Vanny stood her ground.

There was no way he could get past her. She was standing in the space between two parked cars and the only way he could get out was to get back into his car and climb out the passenger side. But that would look stupid. And he'd feel stupid.

"So," Vanny asked, "enlighten me. What happened Wednesday? Any babies had to be delivered? Any people needed rescuing from the canal? What?"

He shifted uncomfortably. "Don't exaggerate."

Vanny gave a swooping laugh. "Exaggerate," she pointed to herself. "Me?"

Jack was aware of other people in the car park looking in their direction. Vanny obviously wasn't or else she didn't give a shit. "Van –" he began.

"What was the excuse you gave me the last time you stood me up?" she frowned as she tried to remember. "Oh, yeah, some woman started to have a baby two cars in front of you – remember?"

"Yeah." He glared at her. "That was true."

"And then there was the one about the fight in the hotel. And then there was one about the major car accident you witnessed. You lead a dramatic life, Jack."

"I know I do." He shoved his hands in his pockets and scowled. There was no way she was going to start poking fun at him.

"So what happened Wednesday?" she asked.

He shrugged. "I met some guys after work and ended up having a few jars with them." Meeting her gaze, he said levelly, "I forgot I was going out with you, right?"

"You forgot?"

"Yeah."

"So where did you go for your drinks?"

"Does it matter?"

"As a matter of fact it does."

"Doyle's."

To his surprise, Vanessa began to smile. He couldn't understand it. He thought she'd yell and scream and call him all sorts of terrible names and then dump him. But no, she was smiling away.

"What?" he asked. "Why are you smiling?"

"Because that's where Jean saw you," Vanny said, still smiling. "She came back to the flat around ten on Wednesday and I was going mental saying you'd stood me up and she said that she'd seen you in Doyle's and that you were making a show of yourself, ordering drinks and being really loud."

"I wasn't being loud."

"Whatever," Vanny tossed her head. "So you forgot about me. Simple as that."

"Look, Van, can we go inside?"

"Why didn't you call up and just tell me that?"

He didn't answer.

"Well?"

"Dunno."

"What did you think I was going to do? Eat you for breakfast?"

More like crush him to death with the massive heels she wore.

"If you forgot, you forgot."

She was being awful nice. Jack couldn't understand it. He'd thought she would throw a wobbler. Truth was he'd been too scared to face her. He'd hoped she'd break it off with him, that way it wouldn't look as if he'd broken it off with her because he couldn't afford to pay her her money back. Looked like he was stuck with her for another while. Maybe when he got paid, with his next pay packet, he'd give her her money and then call it a day. She was still smiling at him and so he smiled back.

"So, d'you fancy going for a drink tonight?" she asked.

His grin faltered. "Huh?"

"To make up for Wednesday."

"Oh, eh, yeah," he nodded. "I'd love to like, but, well, I'm smashed."

"Oh." She didn't look too impressed. "My place so?"

Why couldn't she have paid for the drinks? But he guessed that beggars couldn't be choosers. "Yeah, great. Later."

She smiled at him. "Sorry for yelling at you."

"Sorry for forgetting about you."

"Kiss."

The sight of her upturned face made him feel trapped. Hesitantly he bent his head and brushed his lips over hers. He couldn't understand it. She was lovely, loaded and longing to be kissed and all he wanted to do was run. And he hadn't the nerve. He tried to grin as she linked her arm in his and began to walk into the apartment block with him.

He knew there was something wrong the minute he walked in the flat door. Instead of the flat being empty, like it should have been, Peadar and Eileen were there.

"Are you two not meant to be having some sorta cutesy, cosy, pukingly couply day together?" Jack asked, taking his jacket off and dumping it on the sofa.

Neither of them answered him. He saw Eileen give Peadar an elbow.

"Speak Peadar or Eileen'll give you the elbow," he winked over at them and chortled at his wit. It was amazing how funny he could be when he wanted to annoy someone. He shoved his mouth under the kitchen tap and turned it on. "Vanny almost burnt me alive out in that car-park," he said after he'd had a drink. "I'm as thirsty as hell now."

"Well, get used to it," Peadar said sombrely, "'cause it's all you'll be drinking from now until next month."

"What?" Jack looked from one to the other. Nodding at Eileen, he asked, "Is she doing that purifying yoke she did before, where all she drank was water and some pissy-looking soup?"

"Celery soup," Eileen sneered. "And no, that's not what Peadar is talking about." Another elbow, "Say it, Peadar, go on."

"Spit it out there, Pad," Jack grinned.

To his surprise, Peadar didn't grin back, or even tell him to lay off Eileen. Instead, he coughed and shuffled and said haltingly, "Did, eh, did, well, do you know what happened to forty quid of our food money?"

"Of course he does," Eileen said smugly.

"Well?" Peadar asked, looking miserable. "Do you, Jack?"

Jack shrugged. Eyeballing Peadar so that he'd look away, he asked, "Are you saying I took it?"

"No." Peadar went red.

"Oh for God's sake," Eileen snapped. "Of *course* he took it." She glared at him. "Peadar didn't spend it, so it has to be you."

"Eileen –" Peadar held up his hand.

"Maybe it was you, Eileen," Jack said calmly.

"Right. Sure." Eileen made a face.

"See, she's admitted it," Jack gave a mock bow and turned away. "Case closed."

"She didn't take it," Peadar's voice stopped him in his tracks. "We know it was you, Jack, so don't try and get out of it."

"Is this some kind of gang-up-on-Jack routine?" He didn't turn around. Calmly he began to make himself something to eat. If he concentrated on that, he wouldn't get annoyed.

"And I know why you took it, too."

"Really." He began to butter some bread he'd taken from the press.

"I mean it's nothing you haven't done before."

"Yeah, yeah."

"And Eileen and I were talking . . ."

That did it. "What the fuck has she to do with me?" He glared at the two of them and pointed his knife at Eileen. "What I do is none of her fucking business." Turning back to his bread, he snapped out, "Anyhow, I only took the money to pay for someone to look at the telly."

"What?"

"Yeah," he nodded. "It broke on Wednesday and I had to pay a guy to fix it."

"Peadar, for God's sake don't believe him." Eileen advanced toward Jack. "Well," she asked, "If that's all it was, how come you didn't tell us?"

"Forgot."

"And who was the guy that fixed it?"

"Forget."

"And why –"

"Eileen, leave it." Peadar grabbed her by the arm and pulled her back. As she was about to say something, he just said again, "Leave it."

"Yeah, leave it," Jack sneered.

"But –"

"I know you're lying," Peadar interrupted her by talking directly to Jack. "I know you are."

He shrugged. "Suit yourself."

Peadar dug his hand into his pocket. "I got you these today. Maybe you should take a look at them." He threw a handful of leaflets down on the table. "I think you should."

Jack took a step toward the table and almost, but not quite, laughed. "Gamblers fucking Anonymous," he sneered. "Yeah, right. What the hell am I supposed to do with all that crap?"

"Read it," Peadar said. "Go to a meeting – whatever."

"This is a joke, right?" He couldn't believe this. What sort of a thing were they trying to lay on him. "I take forty shagging quid and suddenly you start making out I'm some sort of a freak? Get a grip." He looked toward Eileen. "It's just her. She's trying to cause trouble between us."

"Oh *please,*" Eileen rolled her eyes.

Peadar bit his lip. "Look, Jack. This is hard on me too, you know. You're a friend, right, and, like, I'm only trying to help."

"Well, don't."

"Look, if you don't read that stuff," Peadar pointed to the leaflets, "I'm moving out, and who'll you get to sub your rent the next time you can't pay, huh?"

"I'll be able to pay next time."

"Fine." Peadar nodded. "So when are you going to pay me back the money you owe me for entertaining Vanny? I'll want it before I go."

Jack stared open-mouthed at him. "I get paid next week."

"And, eh, how are you going to manage to pay the

next month's rent on your own? I'll be getting my share back from the landlord."

Silence.

Peadar knew he had to keep going, but he felt awful. "Well?"

"Bastard." Jack stared at him through narrowed eyes. "I'm not a fucking head case."

"No, you've just got a gambling problem."

"I don't. It's all in *her* head."

"Well, if you don't have a problem, you'll soon find out when you go to a meeting." Peadar knew Jack had no choice now. "Just one meeting, that's all."

He hated Peadar. Hated him so hard it hurt. But he'd no choice. He'd probably end up homeless otherwise. But he wasn't going to make it easy. "I'm heading over to Vanny's," he spat. "Nicer company over there."

Slamming the door hard, he left.

Chapter Fifteen

They'd arranged to meet on the ground floor of the airport, beside the escalators. Her Nan and Daisy were catching the plane to London and from there they were being brought to the ship for the start of the cruise.

Meg knew she'd be glad when the holiday was over. Never in the history of the world had a holiday caused so much friction in a person's life. Her mother bitched about it every weekend.

She looked around but couldn't see any sign of her mother or her Nan. It was ten past twelve now and the place was jammed. A woman of about fifty came and stood beside her. In her hand she held a huge placard that read, *I'm here to pick up Dee Clap*.

Meg moved slightly away, trying not to *look* as if she was moving away. There was no way she wanted to be associated with a sign like that.

A load of Irish football fans with massive green hats went by singing *Molly Malone*. Then, one of them stopped and stood in front of the woman's sign. "Here, lads," he bellowed, "anyone here want to oblige this ould wan?"

"I beg your pardon?" the woman said, flushing.

"Aw, ya can beg all ya like, missus, but like, yer a bit old for us, isn't she, lads?"

Roars of laughter followed this comment.

Meg tried not to smile.

"I'd have *her* though," one of the fellas pointed at Meg. "She's not bad."

The smile slid from her face. That was all she needed, to be harassed by a load of drunken guys making fun of her.

"Cute," another one pronounced.

"So, you looking for Dee Clap too, are you?"

"No. I'm waiting on my Mam actually."

"Ooooh, her *Mammy.*"

"Aw, dat's nice, luv. Very devoted," a big red-headed freckly guy said.

"Yeah." She tried to smile.

"Is she nice, your mother? Is she as nice as you now?"

"A bit older," she muttered. She wished they'd leave. The last thing she needed was for her mother to come along now. She looked beyond the lads to show she wasn't interested in talking.

"Older? You don't say? I like an experienced woman, I do."

"You'd like any woman. You're desperate."

"Fuck off."

Meg flinched. The 'fuck off' was yelled really loudly and people had turned to see where it had come from. Everyone was staring at her. And now, here was her mother, striding along, her Nan following in her wake.

Oh Christ, she muttered, don't let her think I'm with these guys. *Please*.

"We're off to," big belch, dangerous sway, "Austria."

"That's nice." There was one good thing. Her mother seemed to be arguing with her Nan over something and they hadn't noticed her yet.

"Ireland are playing a match and we're off to it. They've kangaroos over there, you know."

"That's fucking *Australia*, you moron," someone else said. "They have snow in Austria, not kangaroos."

More laughter.

The guys didn't look like they were ever going to leave. In fact, one of them had plonked himself on the ground beside her and seemed to be sleeping.

"Wake up, Nailer." Someone started kicking Nailer with his boot. "Wake up, ya wanker!"

Her mother and her Nan were almost on top of her now. She braced herself for her mother's withering look of disapproval. To her astonishment, neither of them looked in her direction. They stood on the opposite side of the placard woman and continued with their argument. Bits of it floated in her direction. She decided to stay where she was until they'd finished. It was too embarrassing being with people who were arguing. If they spotted her first, she'd say she hadn't seen them.

"I wish I wasn't going now," her Nan was saying loudly. "I don't trust you to tell her."

"Well don't go, Mother – stay. I'll go instead."

"If you don't tell her, I'll put it on a postcard."

"It's none of your business. And anyhow, it's not the sort of thing you put on a postcard and well you know it!"

"It is my business when my own . . ."

Her words were drowned out by a howl of pain from Nailer. Holding his head, he stumbled up from the ground and began shouting at his mates who'd kicked him awake.

Once again everyone was looking.

Meg took the opportunity to look towards her mother and Nan. "Mam, Nan," she exclaimed. "There you are."

They both smiled. She knew those kinds of smiles, the ones people used when they hoped she hadn't overheard what they'd said. She was an expert in ignoring them. "So," she breezed, joining them and dissociating herself as quickly as possible from the football fans, "did you just get here?"

"See ya, luv," one of the lads called.

Meg ignored him.

"Yes," her mother said. Giving a sour look, she said, "Daisy's with us. She's gone to the toilet. Again," she added pointedly.

"The woman has weak kidneys," her Nan said.

"Four times on the way up," her mother griped. "I'd have been mortified."

"You'd be mortified if anyone even thought you ever went to the toilet, so you would."

"Don't be ridiculous!"

"SEE YA, LUV!"

"So, how'd you come?" Meg chatted on. Oh God, she hoped the guys weren't yelling at her. "Did you drive?"

"No," her mother answered. A small smile. "Danny drove us up. He's very obliging. He's driving me back afterwards."

"Danny?"

"Yes – Danny McCarthy."

"Danny McCarthy from down home? The guy with the rug on his head?"

Her Nan laughed and her mother's face shrivelled up. "A toupee, Meg," she snapped. "And yes, it's that Danny."

"And he's driving you back after?"

"That's what I said."

"Sure, your mother and Danny are very friendly now, aren't ye?" her Nan gave her mother a big elbow which her mother ignored.

"He's my bridge partner," she replied frostily.

"And sure it makes no odds who you see now, isn't that right, Maureen?"

"Shut up, Mother."

"But," Meg stuttered, "I thought you were staying with me tonight and heading down home in the morning."

"I never said that."

"But it's what you always do when you come to Dublin." She sounded like a child. And a pathetic one at that.

"Well, this time I'm heading home," her mother said firmly. "I hate this ould place anyhow. Full of stabbings and smoke."

She should have been thrilled. Over the moon. She *hated* her mother staying in her flat. Her mother *hated* her flat. It was too small, too poky, too dirty, too expensive. And now, when her mother *was* going home, she was upset. She couldn't explain it. "So where is the knight in shining armour now?" she asked. The bitterness in her voice belied the smile on her face.

"Waiting on Daisy to get off the toilet," her mother answered. "He said he'd wait as Daisy was petrified of losing her way in the airport."

"He's loo-seful like that!" her Nan cackled.

"Shut up, Mother!"

They glared and then turned away from each other.

The placard woman was staring at them, her mouth open. Then, noticing that she'd been spotted ear-wigging, gave them all a smile before beginning a hum.

"Eh – see ya, luv," one of the football guys tugged Meg's hair. "Bye now."

Without looking at him, Meg muttered a 'goodbye'.

"Nice-looking but a bit snobby," she heard one of the lads say.

"A bit fuckin' snobby? I betcha she bleedin' luvs herself."

At last they were gone. She could breathe easy now. Still, she felt sorry for whatever girl they were talking about.

"Do you *know* those boys?" her mother asked aghast. "They're all drunk!"

She couldn't look her mother in the face. "Not really. They just stopped for a chat. They're going to a football match."

"I don't know," her mother shook her head and spoke in a very sombre voice. "No wonder I worry so much about you when you're up here. If those," she pointed towards the lads who were now busy chatting up someone else, "are examples of the men you attract."

"I didn't –"

"But then," a dramatic sigh, "when you put out manure you're not going to attract butterflies, are you?"

"Huh?"

"It's 'pardon', Meg, not," her mother put on a thick Dublin accent, "'huh?'." Shaking her head. "Five years in Speech and Drama and all you can say is 'huh?'. I don't know."

"What did you mean about putting out manure?" Meg asked.

"Don't be minding her," her Nan flapped. "Just –"

"I meant," her mother overrode her Nan, "that in order to attract the right sort of man, a woman must look her best, otherwise, well . . ." her voice trailed off and her eyes looked Meg up and down and then turned towards the lads.

"Well, *you* haven't been too lucky, Maureen," her Nan said sharply. "Your man left."

Meg cringed.

Her mother shot her Nan a withering look. "John leaving wasn't my fault," her mother said. "At least I always looked well when he was around. Not like Meg here."

Meg didn't think she looked *that* bad. OK, so she had a pair of jeans and an old *Nike* sweatshirt on, but they were clean and the green sweatshirt suited her. Or so she'd thought.

"Ah, sure, who'd be bothered dressing up coming to an ould airport anyhow?" her Nan said softly. She ruffled Meg's hair and gave her a smile.

Meg tried to smile back. But suddenly she felt dirty. As if she badly needed a bath and a hair wash.

"Oh, here they are," Mrs Knott said. "At long last."

"Here we are," Daisy gave a huge wave, almost knocking Danny's eye out, as half-running she waddled toward the threesome. "And how's Meg?" she beamed.

"Grand."

"Good, good," Daisy said, slightly breathless. "That's what I like to hear." She was dressed in an orange check dress that screamed 'loud'.

"Hello, Megeen," Danny said. "You're looking mighty."

Meg nodded. She didn't want to talk to him.

"Gets more like her mother every day," Daisy said. "'Tis the spit of her you are."

"Isn't she?" her Nan said, winking at Meg.

Meg just wanted the day to be over. Trapped in the airport between them all, it was a nightmare. And as for Danny McCarthy being Mr Compliment Lick-Arse, it made her sick.

"So what now?" her Nan asked. "Will we check in?"

"Begod we will." Daisy rubbed her hands in eager anticipation. "And then it's the Duty Free for us, a few drinks and we won't need a plane to get us anywhere. We'll be flying, so we will."

Meg laughed and then wished she hadn't, as her mother rolled her eyes and gave Daisy a contemptuous look. "There'll be no getting you off the toilet then," she snapped.

"Small price to pay," Daisy chortled. "You have to live, isn't that right, Anna?"

"Piss to live and get pissed to live, huh?"

"Mother!"

Danny chortled.

Her mother's lips thinned out to almost nothing. It was a bad sign. Meg almost felt sorry for Danny having to drive her home. Then another part of her said that it served Danny right. If he couldn't stand the heat, he should do a runner as fast as he could. And something told her that he wouldn't last, the way her dad hadn't lasted.

Men were like that.

They came to the arrival gates. Meg walked in front with her Nan, the other three followed behind.

Danny was solicitously helping Daisy walk in the new white trainers she'd bought for herself.

"Fecking things have the ankles cut offa me," Daisy complained loudly as Danny caught her by the elbow and attempted to support her.

"The man will collapse," her Nan whispered. "Daisy's an awful weight."

"Serve him right. I hope he does."

"Aw, now Meg, don't be like that," her Nan said, surprised. "Isn't he making your mother happy, and isn't that nice to see?"

She shrugged. "Suppose."

There was a second's silence before her Nan spoke again. "Meg, just a word of advice."

"What?" Danny had his hand in her mother's now. It made her sick. The man was a total eejit.

"Don't be rushing home every weekend. I think maybe being with Danny will stop your mother clinging on to you so much."

Pause.

"What?" Astonished, Meg turned to face her Nan. "Mam doesn't cling – how does she cling?"

"Just, just let her be on her own the odd weekend.

It'll do her good." Then, her Nan added, "Danny's great company for her."

Huh, there was no way Danny McCarthy was going to slither into *her* place, that was for sure. "If Mam wants me, I'll go down."

"Right so," her Nan nodded, sounding sort of resigned. She reached out and squeezed her arm. "Take care."

"I will." Meg placed her hand over her Nan's. She didn't want to hug her; she hated hugging people, especially in public. And anyhow, she never knew quite how long or how hard to hug for. So it was better not to bother. "Have a great time, Nan."

"With Daisy how could I have anything else?"

Daisy caught up with them. "Are we ready to rock?" she yelled, startling them all.

"Yeah!" her Nan laughed.

"Are we ready to roll?"

"Yeah!"

"Oh Jesus!" Mrs Knott rolled her eyes as the two women, to the tune of 'I wanna be old before I die', began to sing 'You gotta be old before you fly'."

Meg and Danny both laughed and some others around grinned at them.

The song over, Daisy grabbed Nan and began to pull her into the tunnel.

"Mother, Mother, hang on a second!" Mrs Knott, wobbling in her shoes, ran towards her mother.

Meg wondered if she was going to wish her Nan well. It'd be a nice end to the day.

But from what she could see, it didn't look like her mother was. Her Nan was shaking her head and her mother looked half-angry. Then without so much as a wave, she strode back to where she and Danny were standing.

"Let's go," she said.

Meg wanted to stay and watch the two as they walked away, but she hadn't much choice. With a final look back, she ran to catch up with Danny and her mother.

"What did my mother say to you just now?" Mrs Knott demanded, startling her.

She blushed. There was no way she could tell her mother *that*. "She just said to take care, that's all."

"I hope that's all," her mother glared at her. "I hope you're not hiding anything from me."

"Now what could the girl possibly be hiding?" Danny asked good-naturedly.

"Did I ask you?" Mrs Knott whirled on him. "Did I?"

"Well, no, but –"

"Then keep out of it."

Meg smirked. That'd show him.

"Fine so." Danny hoisted himself up to his five foot five and stalked off. "If that's the way you want it."

Meg was about to console her mother with smooth words when her mother pushed her, snapping, "Now see what you've done."

"Me?"

"Yes!"

"Sorry."

Her mother ignored her, instead shrieking, "DAAAANNNNEY!"

People looked.

"COME BACK!"

She wished her mother wouldn't make such a fool out of herself. "Mam –"

"PLEEASE!"

Her mother had said please! Gobsmacked, Meg gawked at her.

"SORRY, DANNY!"

Her mother had said sorry. She didn't know how that made her feel.

Danny stopped walking. Cocking his hand to his ear, he yelled over, "What was that you said, you mad cow?"

Danny had called her mother a mad cow.

"I said sorry."

Her mother and Danny walked towards each other and began to laugh.

And it was Danny who beckoned her to join them.

Not her mother.

He'd woken up in Vanny's bed at midday, She'd already left for work but she'd left a note telling him to grab himself some breakfast when he got up. So he'd eaten with her gobsmacked, totally incredulous flatmate, Jean. She couldn't believe Vanny had taken him back. "I reckon our Vanny has big plans for you," she chortled, making him feel distinctly uneasy. He couldn't get out of the place fast enough. He abandoned his grub and drove out to the beach at Malahide.

He was low on petrol so, parking the car by a roadside, he got out, and began to walk toward the sea front.

There was a time when walking and listening to the sea used to quieten his head. A time when he could stand on the rocky beach and enjoy listening to the waves. Later on he'd sketched them and painted them. There was something about nature, the way it never changed yet always looked different that attracted him.

Nothing did that for him any more. He didn't like quiet; it got boring. His head was always buzzing. Demanding to be eased and listened to.

Only thoughts of Meg could push the noise away and, even then, the noise would come back. Meg could maybe make the silence interesting again.

Sometimes he thought his brain was moving so fast he'd crash.

"Come on now, Megeen, and let me drive you home?" Danny looked hopefully at her. "'Tis no bother at all."

"I'd be quicker on the bus." She meant it as an insult.

"Not at all." Danny leaned over and shoved open the passenger door. "Hop in there now."

She didn't want to. The man annoyed her, smiling

and chortling like some kind of hyperactive Brendan O'Carroll. And the way her mother laughed at everything he said. She hoped her mother'd still be laughing when he bunked off.

"Meg?" Her mother arched her eyebrows. "Will you ever get in and not be holding us up. We've a bridge game on tonight."

"I'll get the bus." She did her best to glare at the two of them. "I'd hate yous to miss your game."

"Yous?" Her mother nudged Danny. "Did you ever hear of such a word?"

Meg flushed and began to fidget.

"Suit yourself so." Her mother banged the door. "I hope you're in better form the next time we see you."

"Bye now," Danny called as he started up the engine. "Safe home."

She managed a feeble wave as the car drove off.

She watched as it rounded the corner and disappeared from sight.

Her mother and Danny. Danny and her mother.

It didn't feel right. It didn't look right. It wasn't fair.

It just wasn't fair. It wasn't fair. Her heart began to beat it out. Getting faster and faster and faster. It's not fair. It's not fair. Her heart was pumping very fast. So fast that her chest seemed very tight and the lump that always seemed to be there was growing bigger. And filling up and making her empty. And it was hard to breathe. And her head was pounding and she was going to faint . . .

"Are you all righ'?"

"What?"

A young fella was staring at her.

"Are you all righ'? You look sorta pale?"

Breathe. Breathe. She put her arms around herself to hold it all together. If she didn't get away she was going to . . . going to . . .

She turned and fled.

Later, as she found her way back to the bus stop, she wondered if she was going mad.

Chapter Sixteen

Monday night.

Rehearsals moving at a contentious pace. Johnny sat, legs crossed, making sarcastic comments every few minutes and causing Sylvia to crease up with laughter.

"Is it a play or a pantomime we're putting on here?" he asked laconically.

"It's a fiasco, that's all I know," she chortled back.

Meg couldn't pretend to laugh along with them. Her stomach was in bits and her head was booming. She must have got the headache from the sound of James working on the shower. He'd arrived at the flat that evening, without warning. James Junior had come along too. Luckily enough, Ciara had been in when they'd arrived and she'd appointed herself director of operations.

Meg had slipped out while Ciara was ordering him about.

"Hey, hey, Meg," he'd shouted after her, but she'd

slammed the door in his face and sprinted down the stairs, almost colliding with one of the other tenants.

"Meg!" Dominic's voice made her jump. "Up!"

"Oh, eh, yeah, right." Scurrying to the middle of the floor, she suddenly realised that she hadn't a clue where they were. "Eh, what, what's going on?"

Avril dissolved in giggles beside her. "That's what *I* normally say!"

Dominic threw her a sour look. Turning to Meg, he said ponderously, "I don't think that's the attitude to have coming to rehearsals, do you?"

"Well, it's not that I have that attitude," she stammered. "It's just a —"

"We're at the part where your lover is dumping you."

"Oh, eloquently put," Johnny shouted up. "I like it."

"Yeah, and he's just about to tell you he's shagged me," Avril giggled.

Johnny gave a roar of approval.

Tony applauded.

"Page seventy-eight," Dominic snapped.

Hurriedly she found page seventy-eight. She said her lines like a zombie. There was no way she could concentrate. Luckily she hadn't told anyone about meeting Jack that night. Especially as there was every chance he'd forget. Yesterday she'd seen him leave with a blonde girl. The girl had been waiting for him outside the school when he'd finished work. And he'd walked off with her, his hand in hers. And if Jack was seeing someone that looked like that, why on *earth* would he bother wanting to meet her? In fact, she'd understand perfectly if he forgot.

"Meg?"

"Huh?"

Dominic sounded pissed off. "Your line?" He raised his eyebrows. "Like if you don't *mind* saying it?"

"Oh, sorry." Flustered, she stared at the script. "Eh, which line is it?"

"I don't believe this." Dominic turned on his heel and walked away.

"Top of page eighty," Alfonso called out. "Hey, chill out, man," he said over to Dominic.

"Chill out?" Dominic scoffed. "Huh, if I heat up any more I'll . . ." he shoved his arms into his coat, "I'll explode."

"Ugh!" Sylvia said.

"Gross," Avril nodded.

"Oh, go to hell." Dominic stormed toward the door. As it swung closed behind him he called out, "Ammm-a-fucking-teurs!"

Silence.

Avril giggled.

Meg wished the ground would open up. "Sorry," she said, looking around at the others. "It's all my fault."

"Yeah," Johnny nodded. "Any chance you could do it on a regular basis?"

"Like every fuckin' rehearsal?" Tony asked.

They were only being nice. "Ohhh," she blushed. "Ha."

Alfonso rubbed his hands together and looked hopefully around. "So," he said, "will we head on down for a jar or what?"

It was only nine thirty. She'd have to wait for Jack to show all on her own in the dark. And then she'd feel stupid if he didn't turn up. She hoped the others would want to continue with the rehearsal.

"Well?" Alfonso asked.

"I'm on."

"Me too."

They all began shoving on their coats and jackets and debating which pub to go to.

"Are you coming, Meg," Johnny asked. "We'll all stand you a round to show our appreciation."

The others laughed.

"I'm, eh . . ." Now they'd think she was awful if she said no. "Well, I'm meeting someone," she said. "At ten."

"Here?" Avril asked.

"Mmm."

"D'you want me to wait with you?"

"No!"

Avril gave her a funny look. "Suit yourself," she said, sounding a bit insulted.

"Thanks anyway." There was no way she wanted to be stood up with an audience in tow.

Pulling on her good jacket, the one she wore for special occasions, which meant that it hadn't been worn much at all, she wondered if she should wait for the others to be ready or just walk on ahead of them to the front door. If she didn't wait, they might think she was anti-social and if she did wait, they might think she had a nerve. Maybe they'd want to talk about her messing up the whole rehearsal. Despite Johnny's jokes, she was sure they were all a bit angry with her. The play was due to go on just after Christmas and it hadn't even begun to take shape. Maybe if she zipped her jacket up really slowly, she'd be ready to go just as they were and it wouldn't look as if she'd waited on them.

It worked. They all exited the room together.

As they left the school, Johnny, who'd been elected to drive, was working out how to fit them all into his mini.

"See you, Meg," Avril shouted.

"Bye." Meg smiled at her. Avril was nice. A hopeless actress but nice.

The others said their goodbyes before leaving her standing alone on the school steps. It was beginning to drizzle, so she stood inside the porch. She couldn't let her hair get wet. She'd put intensive conditioner, shine boost *and* hairspray into it. It looked nice. Not that she wanted to impress Jack or anything but just looking well gave her a little bit more confidence.

At nine forty-five, the rain started to come down in bucket-loads. Huge drops, blown by the wind, bounced off her face. She pulled her jacket up on her head to keep her hair dry. If it got wet, it'd frizz. She'd look like a troll.

Five minutes later, just as she was seriously

considering entering a wet T-shirt competition, Jack arrived. She didn't know whether to be glad that he'd come or horrified that she was going to look awful in front of him.

He didn't see her standing in the shadows. He pulled his car up about as far away from her as he possibly could have.

She waved.

He didn't notice her.

There was nothing for it. Taking a deep breath, hoping she didn't look as bad as she knew she must, she began a sprint over to his car. She could feel the rain stinging the mascara on her eyes. Her mind began to slow-tumble in panic. Was it waterproof? What had it said on the barrel? She'd bought it so long ago that she couldn't remember. But she wouldn't have bought cheap stuff, would she?

Would she?

Jack was lying back with his eyes closed. He had the radio on and was listening to music.

She felt the breath catch in her throat as she gazed in at him through the fogged-up window. He was going out with *her*. This lovely fella, with the big grin, wanted to get to know her . . . oh God.

She'd be expected to make *conversation*.

How on earth could she hold his interest?

It took all her willpower not to do a runner. Instead, she hesitantly knocked on the car window.

Knock. Knock. Knock.

His eyes opened and, looking surprised but smiling at the same time, he leaned over and opened the passenger door for her.

"It's not ten, is it?" he asked as she sat in beside him. "I was going to drive up to the door to pick you up." He was gazing at her in amusement.

"Eh, we got out early." She wished she'd the nerve to look in the rear-view mirror. But if she did, she'd probably die.

"You're soaking." He bit his lip.

"I'm not too bad." She attempted a smile.

He began to rummage about in the glove compartment. Eventually he located a tissue. It looked a bit grubby. "Eh, your, eh, eyes are all sort of black," he said. "Maybe . . ." He held out the tissue.

She knew she'd gone red. If not purple. "Oh God." Taking the tissue from him, she lifted herself up to look in the mirror. *Jesus. Oh God.* Ten rounds with Steve Collins and she would've looked better. "I looked nice when I came out." She had to say it. He had to know she wasn't normally this ugly. "It's just, with the rain my hair has sort of gone all bushy and the make-up wasn't waterproof. And I suppose I'm just red because –"

"You look lovely."

Silence.

Jack was gazing at her. His elbow rested on the steering-wheel and his other arm was slung across the back of his seat. His eyes didn't waver. "I think so anyhow," he half-smiled.

She knew he didn't. He was only being nice. "But my hair –"

"Forget about your hair," he grinned. He couldn't help himself. Reaching out he tossed it with his hand. "Just wipe your face and say the word and we'll go somewhere."

He'd messed her hair up. He still wanted to be seen with her. It didn't make sense. "I don't mind where we go," she said, flattening her hair back down. Rubbing the tissue vigorously over her eyes, she added, "once it has a massive open fire."

"What? You planning on hanging your clothes out to dry or something?"

"No." More blushes.

"Pity." He gave her a wink that made her feel weak before starting the car up.

He brought her to a pub in Palmerstown. It was about a half-hour drive from the school and during the drive she spent the whole time trying to look nice again. It didn't work. There was no way she could possibly regain how she looked earlier on.

Confidence nose-dived.

Dutch courage was on the agenda.

What was new?

"So," Jack asked, as they entered the pub, "what are you having?"

"Pint of cider." She wondered what the strongest was. "Bulmers."

"No probs," Jack took some money out of his pocket and began to sort it out. "Find a seat and I'll get it in."

The pub wasn't crowded. In fact there were only about twenty people in the place. They were all gathered around a big log fire up at the top of the bar. She found a window seat beside a radiator and sat down. Taking off her coat, she hung it over the rad to dry. It was nice to be inside in the warmth listening to the rain pelting off the walls. Of course, everything would've been so much better if she didn't look so awful. She fantasised about the witty conversation she would've had with Jack had she looked lovely. But as it was, she just had to get drunk and hope he did the same.

As she fiddled with her hair, trying to hammer it into place, she watched Jack making his way towards her. He was one of those lucky people who looked gorgeous no matter what. A real Ciara. Even though his hair had got wet walking from the car to the pub, it didn't stick out all over the place like hers. And she'd just bet her life that he didn't get spotty from eating chocolate. And even if he did, they wouldn't go yellow on the top the way hers did.

"Here you are." He sat down and put her pint in front of her. "I haveta say," he grinned, as she lifted it to her lips, "I didn't have you down for a cider drinker."

"Life's full of surprises, huh?" Even the smell of the alcohol made her brave.

"Yeah," he tilted his glass against hers. "Cheers."

"Cheers."

They drank in silence for a few minutes. She, wondering about the state of her hair, and him, wondering what to say now he had her all on her own. He desperately wanted to impress her but he hadn't a clue how to. He didn't think she'd go for all the mad stuff he normally said to girls. And besides, he had to be drunk to carry on like that. And tonight, just for once in his pathetic life, he was not going to get plastered. He was going to be himself.

Whatever that was.

"It's mad," he muttered eventually. "I was looking forward to meeting you tonight and now . . ." he shrugged and grinned ruefully, "I dunno what to say."

She tried not to cough as some of the cider found its way back up her throat. "Right!"

"Naw, serious, I don't." He paused, considering. He wondered if being totally honest would mean she'd think he was sad. "It's like," he bit his lip, "I want to talk to you – ask you things – but, I dunno where to start."

"Start anywhere." She stared into her pint, wondering if he was having her on. "There's not much to know."

"Yeah, there is." The certainty in his voice surprised her. "Like, I dunno, what do you do with yourself?"

Now that was a tough one. She hoped he wouldn't want an answer to that.

"Well?"

"Oh," her mind blanked. "This and that."

"Yeah?"

There was an expectancy in his voice that made her shudder. "Yeah." Why hadn't she drunk something before she'd met him? "Nothing major," she added.

"Oh, so d'you go out much," Jack's voice had a smile in it, "where you're doing nothing major?"

"Mmm." She nodded. Took a slug of cider. "I go here and there." Oh God, she sounded so inane. "Around and about, you know."

"Right."

Silence.

Please don't ask me any more, Meg pleaded silently.

Jack searched his mind. "Still into the ould Chris DeBurgh, are you?" He had a grin in his voice that made her cringe. "Or like," he gave a gulp of laughter, "d'you still fantasise about Johnny Logan?"

Shit! What a thing for him to remember. Street Cred zero, Meg.

"Get real," she gave a semi-indignant laugh. "All that stuff was years ago."

"Yeah," Jack nodded solemnly, "but scary stuff like that sticks in your head."

"Get lost!" Mortified, she lied, "And I was *never* into Johnny Logan."

"You were. Sure you even went to a gig of his one year."

"I was only a *little* bit into him."

"Still scary stuff."

"I wasn't into Chris De Burgh either for that matter."

"Liar." He dipped his finger into his pint and flicked it at her. "D'you remember you went out and bought two copies of *Lady in Red* in case one got scratched?"

"Nope." She did, but cringed at the memory. She'd fancied him at that stage. "I liked," she pretended to consider, "I liked all the sixties music."

"My arse." Jack shook his head. "I liked that. You always said the lyrics of the Beatles music was crap."

"Ha!"

"You did." He grinned at her. "In fact you thought 'Penny Lane' was about a girl, d'you remember?"

"Isn't it?"

They both started to laugh.

She'd made him laugh! She found she could do that. He laughed at a lot of stuff she said.

Then they both stopped laughing.

So she took another gulp of cider.

If she drank it too quickly, it not only numbed the part of her brain that made her herself, it also numbed her whole face. She felt the side of her cheek begin to dull up and decided to slow down a bit. Anyhow, she'd enough good feeling to get her through the next little while. Jack was still looking at her. "So," he said, sort of jokingly, "what else are you into now, besides," he paused and grinned slightly, "sixties music?"

She could answer that one! "Drama."

"Yeah? Who with?"

"The local group."

"Right." He nodded. Maybe he could keep this going for a bit. Her eyes had sort of lit up. "How'd you get involved with them?"

"Well, it's funny really. Well, not *very* funny, I mean you won't laugh out loud or anything. But, well, Aidan, Aidan Gibbons, the principal, you know? Well, he found me reading a play one day, I dunno, one of the students left it behind and he said why was I reading a play and I said that I liked drama and he told me about the drama group and he kept telling me to join." Meg took a breath. She was talking too fast again. Way too fast. "So, eh, he seemed so interested in me that I felt I had to join."

"No way! You joined 'cause Aidan wanted you to?"

He thought she was stupid. She took a long slug of cider. Her head spun nicely. "Yeah. But I always liked drama. I missed it a lot when I didn't do it. And I'd never have had the nerve to join the group off my own bat so he did me a favour really."

"I see." Jack looked amused. "So are you doing a play soon?"

"After Christmas. *Naked,* it's called."

"Now that sounds like my kinda play."

"What?" She raised her eyes. She felt witty. Amazing what half a glass of cider drunk at speed could accomplish. "You're into deep and meaningful plays, are you?"

"Oh yeah. Especially ones called *Naked* or *Starkers* or *Full Frontal Nudity* or anything along those lines." He was delighted to see her smile. "I could even go as far as *Bare Assed* at a push."

"Stop!"

"So," he pulled his leg up onto the seat so that he could turn towards her. "You got a big part in this play or what?"

The smell of his aftershave did funny things with her head. She took another swig of cider before nodding.

"Yeah. What part?"

She hoped it didn't sound like she was boasting. "The main part," she said. She didn't want to look at him in case he'd think she was showing off.

"Good for you."

"Mmm." More cider was needed, especially as he as now looking really impressed with her. "It's not a big deal," she hastened to explain. "It's only amateur drama."

"Well, I remember you were brill in school. D'you remember you played Rosie Redmond in *The Plough and the Stars*?"

"Yeah." She didn't want to remember that.

"I mean, no one could believe it was you. You were so quiet in school and there you were playing a slapper," he gave her a puck, "and we all slagged you saying that it was the quiet ones that were the worst – d'you remember?"

She gave a brief smile and wished he'd stop.

"But I didn't think, after that . . ." his voice trailed

off. He'd said the wrong thing. Trying to change the subject subtly, he asked quickly, "D'you remember the way the set fell down on top of Peter Whelan in rehearsal?" He laughed and leaned in towards her, "Jesus, the guy was so big, every time he came onstage the set shook like mad."

"Yeah. Poor Peter."

"The poor set more like. I had to re-paint the whole frigging thing the next day."

"Awww."

"Awwww," he said back.

She was suddenly aware that his face was only inches from hers. Pulling back, she slopped some of her pint over her clothes. "Amn't I awful clumsy," she muttered. "I'm soaking now." It was a relief not to have to look at him.

"Sure you're soaking anyhow," Jack said amused.

"Yeah, yeah, I am, amn't I?" She giggled. Cringed. Drank a lot more. Then, "I went out with Peter, you know." At least he'd know that she wasn't too much of a social outcast. At least she could tell him that she'd had a boyfriend. And there were a couple of others she could name if she wanted to. There was no way he was going to think she was a social pariah.

To her horror, he laughed. Bits of his drink sprayed everywhere. "Fuck off!"

"What?"

"No way you went out with him, no way!"

"I did. In sixth year." She didn't like the way he was

trying not to laugh and looking shocked all at the same time. "For ages actually."

"But he was *huge!*" Jack looked stunned. "And, like, he wasn't your type."

"He was all right." She drained the last of her cider. "And anyhow, I didn't have a type." She wished she hadn't told him now. He was acting as if she was a real freak. She felt she'd just shot herself in the foot. Scored an own goal. Hung herself by her own rope. Drowned by. . .

"You and Peter Whelan!"

The way he said it annoyed her. As if he was laughing at her. Which, all things considered, wasn't surprising. "Yeah," she snapped out.

"Jaysus," Jack gave a rueful grin, "if I'd have known you'd go out with him, I'd have chanced me arm myself."

The words made her think she was *really* drunk. "Pardon?"

"Nothing." He nodded to her glass. "Another?"

"Sure, yeah."

She watched him stand up. Long legs and narrow hips. God, if only he had chanced his arm, he'd never have gotten away. His arm wasn't the only thing she was interested in. His arse now . . . the thought made her realise that she was drinking too quickly. Sexy ideas and drinking usually equalled disaster. She'd have to slow down.

"Back in a sec." He flashed her a smile and walked off.

It wasn't working. His being sober and responsible was not doing it for Meg. Glancing across at her as he stood at the bar waiting to be served, he just knew by the way she was unable to sit still that she couldn't wait for the night to be over. And she kept fiddling with her hair. He'd read somewhere that when people did that it was a sign that they were bored.

He'd have to do something to impress her.

Maybe if he got some real Dutch courage inside him, he could tell her how he felt? And if she was shocked, well, he'd always be able to blame the booze.

And maybe he could make her laugh and then she'd really go for him.

"Shot of whiskey to go with the pint," he shoved some change across the counter.

The barman poured him a measure and he downed it in one gulp.

Then taking his pint and Meg's Bulmers he made his way back to the table.

Chapter Seventeen

Jack was totally legless. The relief she felt was amazing. It was as if every part of her was going into spasm from being tensed up for so long. She didn't have to get too drunk. She didn't even have to puke up – Jack was drunk instead.

She loved when people got like this. They laughed at everything and, even if she said something stupid, it didn't matter.

Jack was gazing at her with half-focused eyes and a sleepy smile on his face. "You are some woman, d'you know that, Meg?" He moved towards her. "I've always had a soft spot for you."

"Yeah," she nodded. "Right there." She touched his forehead. "Soft in the head, you must be."

She marvelled at her nerve. But, just like she'd anticipated, he gave a low rumble of laughter.

"Yeah," he nodded. "But you make me hard in the head somewhere else."

She didn't know if he meant what she thought he meant.

She hoped he did.

She hoped he didn't.

Oh, she hoped he *sort of* did.

She took a slug of cider.

"You're dead on, d'you know that?"

"Thanks, Jack." She smiled and then gulped as he moved nearer her on the seat. His leg was touching hers.

"I mean it. I really, *really,* mean it." His voice was slurred. "It was so nice to see you after all the long time apart."

"Right." He couldn't have given a shit. Sure he'd never even written.

"I wished I'd kept in contact." He gazed mournfully at the table. "But, well, it's half your fault, you didn't – didn't – enc . . . enc . . ." he shook his head, as if searching for the word.

"Encourage?"

"Uh-huh. You didn't do that for me."

"I didn't encourage you?" Indignation and drink made her voice louder than she'd intended. She lowered it. "What are you on about?"

"I wanted to write at the time." Jack sighed. "But when I said it to you, you didn't care." He shook his head and raised his eyes to look at her. "It hurt me."

"I did care, I told you to write."

"You said to write if I could." He stopped. Looked

confused. Drank a bit. "Nope. If I *wanted* to, you said I could."

"Yeah, and obviously you didn't want to write because you never did." She tried to say it in an off-hand manner. As if she hadn't spent months checking the post for his letter. "No harm done."

"Suppose not." He moved nearer to her. "Would you have *liked* me to write?"

"Sure."

"Good." He gave a bleary smile and drained the remainder of his glass. Banging it down on the table, he asked, "Want another?"

She didn't think she'd need one. Her head was nice and floaty and besides, Jack would need someone to get him home. "I'll pass."

His face dropped. "You don't like drinking with me." He sounded sulky.

"I do."

"So you'll come again." He staggered to his feet and, swaying slightly, he looked anxiously at her.

"Sure." It was best to keep him happy. He'd hardly want to go out with her again.

Even though she knew he was drunk, the way he smiled at her made her heart lurch about so much she was convinced she'd be sick.

It was twelve by the time they left the pub. She hauled Jack up from the seat and, staggering under his weight, she began to manoeuvre him to the door. His head rested on top of hers and she could feel his breath as it blew down over her face. It was the most beautiful feeling.

He kept apologising for not being able to walk.

"It's fine."

"I just wanted you to like me," he muttered.

"I do like you, Jack." That was safe to admit. She was the one in control.

"And I really like you." He tried to lift himself away from her and he fell on top of a couple that were behind them. The woman went crashing into a table and the man landed on top of her.

"Hey, watch it," the man said, annoyed as he helped his girlfriend up. "You could have caused an accident."

"Eejit," the girl with him looked on in disgust, as Jack, with Meg's help, tried to right himself.

"Sorry." Meg gave the two a placatory smile. "He's just had a bit too much to drink."

"A bit?" The man shook his head. "There's an understatement if ever I heard one." Putting his arm around the woman, he ushered her in front of him.

"Thanks." Jack winked at her. "Only for you, I think the guy would have floored me." He wrapped his arm about her and once again she felt him nuzzling into the side of her neck.

It made her feel the best she had in ages.

He wanted to drive.

"I think we're better off getting a taxi." Meg gently

took his keys from him and put them in her pocket. "Honest, Jack, you'll thank me in the morning."

"You drive." He slurred, waving his arm at his car. "She's not fussy about who takes her for a spin. Look at her. She's grateful to be taken anywhere, the state of her."

Meg felt sorry for the car. She could empathise with it even. "I, eh, can't drive," she mumbled. "So I think we'll take a taxi."

"Whatever." He brought his forehead down so that it was touching hers. "Whatever you want, I'll do."

She couldn't help it. And the fact that he was so drunk and wouldn't even remember in the morning made her braver. She reached up and touched his hair. It was just as soft as she remembered. It curled just behind his ear, the way she remembered.

"I like that," he whispered.

She couldn't take her hand away. This memory would have to do her forever and she was going to make the most of it. She let her hand wander to the base of his neck and she ran her thumb across his smooth skin and her fingers knotted themselves in his hair. He pressed his forehead harder against hers and she felt his arm encircling her waist and pulling her towards him. His chin rested on her shoulder and the length of his body pressed against hers.

He began to gently kiss her ear, running his tongue across it. One hand snaked up her back and began to stroke her hair.

Meg gasped. Shoving him from her, she tried to say brightly, "Jack, it's me – Meg."

He stumbled, "Huh?"

"I'm not your girlfriend." Giggly laugh that sounded mortified. "I'm sorry I touched your hair and I'm sorry for all this mess. But you're drunk and I'm sort of drunk and it's the stupid thing –"

"I like you, Meg." He tried to walk in a straight line towards her. "Kiss me."

"Jack!"

"Please."

"You've a girlfriend."

"No." Very definitely, he shook his head. The world spun. He felt Meg rushing to hold him upright. She was great. "That's only a casual thing. Not like you and me could be."

"That's the drink talking."

Silence.

Jack made a big deal of looking all around the place.

"What?" Meg said uneasily.

"What drink? Where?" He gave a gulp of laughter and punched her. "Don't look so confused. You said, that's . . ." he swayed a bit, "that's the drink talking so I'm looking for it. Must be strong stuff."

It took a second for the joke to register and it took another second before she could muster up a smile.

"Not funny – huh?" Jack quirked his eyebrows.

"No, it's funny." The end of her sentence came out in a breathless rush because he'd started to look at her in a weird way. His eyes went all cloudy and thoughtful.

"I like you a lot, Meg," he said. Then he belched.

"Good." He was definitely drunker than she'd thought.

"I would like to, eh, you know, see more of you." He held up his hand to stop her from saying anything. "As in a bloke-woman kind of way, you know."

She gulped. It was like all her fantasies coming true. OK, so the guy of her dreams hadn't been swaying on his feet, or belching, or even been a tiny bit drunk, but then again, he hadn't been Jack Daly either. "Tell you what," she said, her heart hammering, knowing she was going to regret saying it, "if you're sober tomorrow, say it to me then." She wondered about his girlfriend, but then again, Jack *had* said it was just a casual thing and she believed him.

"I've to wait until then to get a snog offa you?"

It was unreal. He actually wanted to *kiss* her. But then again, people always looked nicer through drunken eyes. And he was so far gone, he probably thought she looked like Julia Roberts. It was a nice feeling. "'Fraid so," she replied, enjoying the temporary sensation of being desirable.

And, as Jack gave another alarming stagger backwards before she steadied him, she enjoyed the sensation of him clinging on to her, the way he used to.

∾∾∾

Chapter Eighteen

He should've been in bad form. He'd a hangover so bad he thought he'd died during the night. And then, when he found out that he hadn't died and, in fact, that he had to head into work he'd wished he *was* dead. But then, he remembered Meg. And he remembered vaguely something about kissing her. And the way she'd responded. The rest was a blur but he knew that if he wanted to, maybe now he could have her.

And he did want her. He wanted her very much.

Walking into the kitchen at breakfast, he managed a sort of half-smile-cum-grimace at Peadar.

Peadar remained funeral-faced. Instead of a cheery 'good morning' he'd stared into his porridge, or whatever horrible slop he ate in the morning, and asked, "Are you going to that meeting tonight, the GA one?"

"Aw Peadar," Jack smiled and shrugged. "Gimme a break, yeah?"

Peadar stared at him. Then in a very hard voice, he snapped, "No – you gimme a break and go to the shagging meeting."

"Did you have a row with Eileen?" Jack asked hopefully.

For some reason, the remark seemed to annoy his flatmate. Slamming down his spoon and pushing his chair back from the table, he stood up. "Don't," he said, pointing his finger at him, "don't dare bring Eileen into this."

"I only asked –"

Peadar began to advance on him. "I meant what I said, Jack. No meeting, no flatmate. Take it or leave it."

He didn't want to have to give in. So he just walked past Peadar on his way to get some Flakes from the press.

Still, that hadn't been *too* bad.

Nothing that morning would be too bad.

In fact, he felt so confident that he bet his last fifty quid on number six in the four fifteen at York.

He had to ring in his bet, which wasn't the same as placing it in person, but still, the anticipation was nice.

The power was nice.

He felt ready to face anything. Even a bunch of weirdos at a GA meeting.

She should've been in great form. Last night had been brilliant. Better than she'd hoped. But now, she had to face today.

Which couldn't possibly live up to expectations.

Firstly, she had a headache which, in normal circumstances she could've coped with except for the fact that she had to face Jack.

Jack.

She felt sick.

Did he remember anything at all about the night before? And if he did, would he be as mortified as she was?

But still, it wasn't as if she'd done anything *too* bad, except maybe touch his hair. He'd been the one that had said all the stupid things people say when they drink too much. If she'd said half of what he'd said there was no way she'd ever be able to face him again. In fact, handing in her resignation at work would have been preferable.

And, just as she was contemplating how he'd face her, the telephone in the flat had rung.

It was her mother to tell her that there was no point in her coming down that weekend.

For the first time since coming to Dublin, she'd have a free weekend.

Her mother had sounded all businesslike. "Danny and I will be going to a tournament on Saturday."

"What, like a jousting competition?" She knew she sounded bitter.

"Don't be so facetious, Megan," her mother laughed tolerantly. "Humour isn't your forte."

Meg wondered what was.

"Danny and I are competing in a bridge competition – it'll be very exciting."

"Great."

"The prize money is well over a hundred pounds."

"So you stand to win fifty quid. That sounds marvellous."

Silence.

"I don't know what's got into you."

Meg didn't either.

"Well," her mother said frostily, "I'll ring you back when you're in better form."

"Sorry!" she blurted out. "Sorry, Mam. It's just, that, well, I'm not a morning person."

"Huh, it's no wonder you've no friends except that weirdo you share the flat with if that's the way you treat people."

"Mam –"

The phone went dead.

He was late for class. Arriving into the horrible Second Years, Jack cursed the fact that he hadn't been able to talk to Meg. It looked like he'd have to wait until the ten o'clock break. Flinging his jacket onto the chair and yelling at the kids to calm down, he took up the register and began to call out names.

When he came to Brendan, there was a silence. "Brendan?" he asked, looking up. "Anyone know where he is?"

No one said anything.

"Well," Jack placed his hands on his desk and leaned towards the class.

Eventually one of the kids muttered, "No, sir."

"He was in first thing this morning for registration." Jack said, scanning the register. "Is it just my class he's avoiding?"

Silence.

"Should I begin to take it personally?"

"He's just not feeling well," one of his mates spoke up from the back of the class. "He, eh, went home."

"With his girlfriend?" He had just noticed that she seemed to be missing too.

"Eh, yeah, she brought him home."

"Must be love," he commented wryly. A few of the kids laughed. Making a note on the register that Brendan was missing he began his class.

"Clive's solicitor says that if Clive says that he's from a dysfucktional family, he'll probably get a vote of sympathy from the judge," Linda said.

"Dysfunctional," Meg corrected absently. She hated herself. Was she a thick or what?

"It's dys-fuck-tional," Linda repeated, sounding irritated. "Means your family is all fucked-up – right?"

"Right." *Jack hadn't called in to her. He hadn't even been in the staffroom before classes started.* She knew that because Aidan had come into the office wondering if either she or Linda had seen him. The guy was avoiding her. And who could blame him? He obviously thought that she was the sort of girl who snogged just about anyone once she'd a few jars on her. After all, hadn't she done it before? And had it got her anywhere? He hadn't even written to her after it, not even to *thank* her.

"And there's a no more fucked-up family than mine," Linda said matter-of-factly as she took out a huge bottle of scarlet nail varnish and began to unscrew it. "For one thing, Leo has gone on a bender again. Haven't seen him since last Saturday night." She blew a large chewing-gum bubble. "Fucker."

Looked like Linda was being avoided too. But then again, Meg thought, if she could avoid Linda she would.

"*And* he's only staying away because he knows I'll kill him when I see him. He thinks the longer he stays away the more I'll worry." Linda began to chew her gum again. "Fat bloody chance."

It was five to ten. She should go on her tea break. She wondered if Jack was in. Glancing out the window, she tried to see if his car was in the car park.

But sure, there was no way it'd be there. She still had his car keys in her pocket.

One way or the other she was going to have to face him.

Oh God.

"Still," Linda said, waving her nails about to get them dry, "this only makes it better for Clive, the fact that his dad's such a bastard." She beamed at Meg. "Isn't that right?"

"Yeah." There was nothing else for it. The sooner she gave back the keys the better. That way she could get him out of her head. "I'm going on tea, Linda."

"Charming. You go on tea while I deal with my family cri –"

She didn't wait to hear the rest.

She hoped she could hold it together until after she'd seen him.

Ten o'clock.

The bell rang for the end of class and Jack made the kids wait until he'd left the room. There was no way he was hanging around while they jostled and shoved their way out. Precious minutes from his tea break would be missed otherwise. He needed to catch Meg before she got into the staffroom.

Head hammering, he sprinted down the corridor.

"Caught short again, sir?" one young fella shouted after him.

Normally he would've pretended to be annoyed at such a lack of respect, but that day he hadn't the time.

He caught up with Meg just as she was opening the door to go into the staffroom. "Meg, hang on!" he yelled out.

She jumped.

"Sorry," he gave her an apologetic shrug. "I, eh, had to see you."

"Oh . . . right."

"Eh, it's about last night. I eh –"

Meg couldn't bring herself to look at him. Instead, she picked a point over his shoulder and studied a spot on the far wall. Her heart was hammering but she knew, by the way he was tripping over his words, that he didn't sound as if he was going to beg her to go out with him. More than likely, he'd probably forgotten all about what had happened. "We were both drunk," she said attempting to cut him short before he started to embarrass them both with excuses.

His bumbling speech came to an abrupt halt. "I was anyhow," he said, sounding ashamed. "Sorry about that."

"It's fine." Only it wasn't. She wanted to cry with disappointment. But she had *known* that this would happen. In an attempt to change the subject, she handed him his car keys, "I, eh, here."

"Ta." Jack took them from her and jingled them in his hands. He smiled tentatively, "You probably saved me life by not letting me drive."

"Probably saved someone else's life more like." It was the only dig she could give.

"Yeah." Jack bit his lip. "Sorry for being such a thick."

If he didn't go she was going to cry. This was not what was meant to happen. But still, it was the story of her life. "Doesn't matter. Forget it."

He took a deep breath. Somehow he had to make her like him again. He hated feeling like this – wide open. Sober and very much open. "I liked when we kissed," he said softly. "I don't want to forget that."

That made her look at him. Her eyes rested on his face and flitted away and then came back. Only he was looking at the floor and shuffling his feet and all she could see was the very top of his head and the way his finger kept tapping his leg.

"Just wanted to say that," he mumbled.

She didn't know what to say. He'd never struck her as the shy type ever before. It was appealing in a strange sort of way.

"It's just," he lifted his eyes to meet hers, "I can't remember much else."

There was no boast in the remark, just an uncomfortable, sheepish glance. She felt sorry for him. "It *was* nice," she admitted shyly. "I liked it too."

"So, like, what else did I do?" He shoved his hands into his jeans and hopped from one foot to the next. "Did I, you know, say I fancied you or anything?"

"Ohhh," she forced herself to smile, "it's all a bit of a blur to me too. I can't remember the finer details, all I can remember is that –"

"'Cause I do, you know," he cut her short and gave an awkward laugh, "fancy you, that is."

Silence.

"It's not a big deal between Vanny and me. I won't see her any more if you'll have me."

To her horror, the words made her eyes water. Tears virtually leap-frogged into them out of nowhere.

Jack started. "Sorry." He felt such a thick. "Sorry."

Meg shook her head. "No, it's," she gulped, "it's lovely, you saying that to me." She ran her hands over her eyes and sniffed.

"Yeah?" Jack didn't look too convinced.

"Yeah."

They both jumped as the intercom in the hallway blared, "MR DALY TO MR GIBBONS' OFFICE! MR DALY TO MR GIBBONS' OFFICE!"

"That's you," Meg said, disappointed. "You'd better go."

"Yeah." Jack took the chance of reaching out and touching her arm. "I'll talk to you lunchtime – right?"

It was like her legs turned to jelly. "Sure." Hardly able to believe her luck, she watched him turn and walk away from her. Halfway down the corridor, he turned back and winked.

It was stupid but the tears started to run out of her eyes and down over her face. She spent tea break in the loo shoving tissues filled with cold water on her face.

The boss was not in good form. Jack could tell the minute he walked into Aidan Gibbons' office. Only thing was, he couldn't keep the grin off his face or out of his voice. Things with Meg were picking up and it was great. "You wanted to see me?" he asked pleasantly.

"Not particularly." Aidan indicated a chair. "Only it couldn't be helped."

"Oh." Jack sat down and wondered what he'd done. He knew from past experience that something was up.

"What happened to you this morning, Jack?"

The question was fired at him. "Sorry?"

"You were late for class. It's the third time this term. What happened?"

"Me car broke down and I missed the bus." He couldn't help the insolent tone. He hated this, when people bossed him about.

"Fine." Aidan nodded.

He said nothing for a few minutes and Jack didn't know whether to leave or not. But somehow he got the impression that Aidan wasn't finished.

He was right.

Tapping a biro on his desk, Aidan said, "Look Jack, you're a good teacher and to be honest what you do in your own time is your own business." He spoke very carefully as if he was treading a minefield.

Jack stiffened. He wondered uneasily what was coming. All his happy thoughts began to evaporate and, to his shame, his hands began to shake slightly. He wished he could have a fag.

"And I know you're young and you're probably out most nights," Aidan continued, "but to be honest, Jack, I've had a number of complaints from some of the other teachers about the constant smell of alcohol on your breath. It's not on."

"What?" Jack jumped up. "Who's been complaining?"

Aidan held up his hand. "It doesn't matter."

"It bloody well does!"

"Jack," Aidan's voice was sharp again, "can I remind

you who's the boss here?" He waited until Jack had sat back down again before continuing, "The problem is, it's not a good example for the kids, is it? And say something happened in your class, where would that leave you? The smell off your breath wouldn't do you any favours."

Jack glared at him.

"So in future, be more careful, all right?"

It took all his willpower to nod. His hands were shaking so badly now that he had to sit on them.

"And eh, go get yourself a packet of mints or something at lunchtime, all right?"

"Yeah."

Aidan nodded. "Fine. That's it." He looked at his watch. "You'd better go – you've a class now, haven't you?"

Without saying anything, Jack left the office.

Linda was gawping at her. "Well, something musta happened. You look horrible. Your eyes are all swollen and red. And your *nose.*"

"My nose what?" Meg knew she wouldn't be able to face Jack looking horrible. He'd regret saying he fancied her.

"Weeeell," Linda began to cackle, "put it like this. If you were around at Christmas time, Santa'd have no problem ditching Rudolph."

"It's not that bad."

"Mmmm."

Linda continued to study her so she put her head

down and pretended the she was writing something.

"So what happened? Did one of the Toffs make a pass at you or what?" More cackling.

"No," Meg shook her head. "All of them did."

It was a relief when Linda laughed because, after she'd done that, the subject of Meg's grief was forgotten and she began to speculate on what the male Toffs would be like in bed. "Better than Leo anyhow," she pronounced bitterly. "D'you you know it takes him only two minutes to come?"

Meg felt sick.

He had to get away. The lunchtime bell was a relief. His head was bursting. Unless he calmed down, he was going to kill one of the kids. He'd lifted a First Year out of it for spilling some water over the floor. She'd ended up crying. And after she'd mopped it up and a quiet had descended on his class, he'd read *The Racing Post* while they painted.

She waited all lunchtime and he hadn't shown. She wondered what he was playing at. When the bell had rung for the last class of the day, she'd seen him heading out of the school grounds towards the bus stop. She wondered what she'd done wrong.

After school, he picked his car up in Palmerstown and tuned in to the sports results. One of his horses had come in at five to one. He'd made six hundred quid.

It was a dark evening as he manoeuvred his car through the traffic in Yellow Halls village. He had the radio blaring and his fingers tapped the steering-wheel, keeping time with the rhythm of the music. It was a summer tune, wrong for the time of year, but totally great for the way he was feeling.

Five to one, she'd come in, the beauty. Six hundred quid into his hand.

He'd have loved to shove Peadar's nose in it. Six hundred quid would have Peadar slaving for a week at least. And that'd be before tax.

And even Aidan Gibbons would hardly earn that much in a week.

"Up yours, assholes," he said.

The car in front of him braked suddenly and he slammed his foot down, narrowly missing it. He was just about to roll down his window and ask what the hell the guy was playing at when he saw why he'd braked.

A young fella had stumbled out into the road. He was weaving his way through the traffic totally oblivious to the danger.

A girl was attempting to pull him back onto the path but with a vicious wrench of his hand, he loudly told her to "fuck off".

The girl stood stunned on the path and Jack looked at her. She seemed to look at him in the same instant, then she turned away quickly and ran off down the street.

But he'd seen who it was. Jane. Brendan's girlfriend.

With a sort of a hopeless feeling, he watched Brendan stumble onto the opposite path. Suddenly, his win went sour. He couldn't explain why.

Brendan put his two hands against the wall and bowed his head. By the looks on the faces of people passing, Jack guessed the kid was getting sick.

He wondered if he should get out and bring him home but the lights in front went green and the traffic began moving again.

His chance was gone.

And then, he remembered Meg.

"Shit!"

238

Chapter Nineteen

"Are you going to that meeting?" Peadar asked, lifting his head from the *Farmers' Journal*. He looked pointedly at his watch. "It's on in fifteen minutes."

Jack tensed. "It's only down the road," he muttered. "D'you think I'm a fucking cripple as well as a chronic gambler?" When Peadar made no response, he looked up at him, "Why do I have to go?" he asked. "This is *madness*, Pead."

Peadar flushed. He rattled his paper about a bit. "I don't think so," he said softly.

"Yeah," Jack said bitterly, "'cause Eileen has you brainwashed."

Peadar gritted his teeth and, keeping his voice remarkably even, said, "Just go to the meeting, Jack. Maybe you'll learn something."

Jack wondered if he could get away with pretending to go. Maybe walk around for a couple of hours and come back and say it was a load of crap.

"I'll meet you afterward," Peadar said then. "Maybe we could even go for a pint?"

Fecker! Jack stood up and grabbing his jacket form the back of the chair said, "More like you want to spy on me. Make sure I go."

Peadar shrugged. "That too."

Jack froze, his jacket half-on, half-off. "I wouldn't drink with you if we were stranded in the desert."

"Fine."

He hated the calm way Peadar said 'fine'. Nothing was 'fine'. His best mate had changed and Jack felt as if he didn't know him any more. He'd fucked things up with Meg just when he'd been getting somewhere. He opened his mouth to speak but closed it when he realised he hadn't a clue what to say.

"I'll still be waiting outside for you though," Peadar said, his eyes not leaving the paper.

"You bollix," Jack said softly. "Some mate you are."

Peadar didn't reply.

Christ, Jack thought as he slammed the flat door closed. Sometimes he hated Peadar.

"Ciara?"

"Mmm?" Absently Ciara looked up from some horrific pottery thing she was painting.

Meg slid into the seat opposite her. She had to ask someone's advice. Normally she kept things pretty much to herself, but to go from being outrageously happy to seriously depressed in one day made her desperately want to talk to someone. Even if it was only Ciara whose sole piece of advice was telling her to tell everyone to 'fuck off'.

"Can I ask you something?"

"If it's about Greg, don't bother."

"Huh?"

"Jesus, Meg," Ciara snapped as she slammed her paintbrush on the table, "do you *know* what he kept doing the other night in the restaurant?"

"Sunday night?" As Ciara nodded, she remembered that Ciara had come home in foul humour, slammed the door on Greg and stormed into her bedroom. Meg hadn't had the nerve to ask her what was wrong. "Eh, no, what did he do?" She wondered when she would be able to ask about Jack.

"He kept looking at his reflection in the knives and stuff on the table."

"He didn't!"

"Oh, go on," Ciara spat, *"laugh."* She viciously dipped her paintbrush into some blue paint and began to attack her pottery piece again. "Laura laughed when I told her."

"Oh, I won't laugh."

"And on the way there, right," Ciara stabbed the brush in her direction, "he nearly crashed his car three times because he kept glancing at himself in the rear-view mirror."

"God!"

"That's who he thinks he is all right," Ciara spat, "God's fucking gift."

Meg tittered nervously, not sure if Ciara was joking or not.

Ciara glared at her and then her whole body seemed to sag. Glumly she asked, "Do you know what it's like to go out with a guy that fancies himself more than he fancies you?"

"Nope." Meg paused. "Well, I haven't known what it's like to go out with *any* sort of a guy in *absolute* ages."

"Mmm," Ciara nodded. "Suppose." She stopped painting again. "I mean," she said in a puzzled voice, "I like him. He's a laugh."

"And he's nice-looking."

"So why does something *always* have to spoil it? I mean, things start off great and then, the horrible thing happens – you get to know him."

Meg smiled.

"I mean," Ciara went on, smiling a bit too, "why isn't it possible to have a purely superficial, surface relationship with a guy?"

"I dunno."

"Anyway, that's it."

"Oh." Silence. "So . . . is it over?"

"We-ell," Ciara shrugged, "he's off in York this week, doing bookie for his Dad, but if he rings me when he gets back, I might give him another chance."

"Well, good. I'm sure he didn't mean to look at himself in the forks and stuff."

"Yeah," Ciara said nonchalantly, "he's probably cross-eyed or something!"

Meg doubted it. But she nodded. "Well, maybe. Maybe he could be."

"That was a *joke*, Meg."

"Oh. Right. Well, I *knew* that. I knew it was a joke."

"So, was that what you wanted to ask?" Ciara giggled a bit and reaching across the table gave her a dig. "I was wondering when you'd pluck up the nerve."

There was no way she could ask about Jack now. Ciara would think she didn't care about *her* problems. "That was it, yeah." She smiled slightly and got up from the table.

She would just have to cope on her own.

Like she'd always done.

Only she didn't know if she had the energy.

The GA meeting was to be held in the local leisure centre. Jack walked as slowly as he could, hoping he'd be late and they wouldn't let him in. That'd be great.

Lighting a fag, he took his time walking down the road. It was sort of relaxing, just inhaling and exhaling and walking really slowly.

It was five past eight when he arrived at the leisure centre. The place was busy, shapely girls walking in and out, carrying sports bag and wearing lycra. Jack wondered why the hell he'd never come here before. The sights were great. He hung about in the foyer for a few minutes pretending to read the notices pinned to the wall but really eyeing the stairway to where the meeting was being held. There was no way he was walking up those stairs with everybody looking at him.

Eventually the foyer was deserted and when the receptionist turned her back to answer the phone, he bolted across the lobby and took the steps two at a time.

There were a lot of them.

And his shoes just weren't cut out for running up slippery steps. He stumbled on the final one and clattered his shin off its edge.

"Jaysus!" he couldn't help yelling out as he collapsed onto the floor. The pain was unreal. He sat for a while waiting for the throbbing to ease.

"Here for the meeting, are you?"

Jack jumped at the voice. A guy of about fifty stood above him.

"Meeting?" Jack gulped. "Huh?"

"GA meeting?"

"Oh, eh, well, yeah." He attempted to stand up. "Just, you know, just to see, you know . . ."

The guy smiled. "I'm Paul," he held out his hand. "I heard you shout and I figured you were a first-timer."

Jack took the guy's hand. "First-timer?"

"Yeah, you ran up the stairs and slipped."

"Huh?"

"Most first-timers run and arrive in breathless. You were unfortunate."

Wasn't he just, Jack thought despondently. "I'm Jack, by the way."

"Nice to meet you, Jack."

Paul began to lead the way along the corridor. He

walked past two doors before entering a room. Jack winced at the big GA sign with an equally big arrow outside the door. This was great; now everybody passing would know what was going on. He vowed that he was going to find a seat that would have his back against the door, just in case someone walked in.

About five people, four men and a woman were sitting down, chatting quietly, as he entered.

"This is Jack," Paul announced.

The five smiled at him and Jack, feeling like a carrot at a veggie convention, smiled uneasily back.

"Sit down, Jack," another guy of about thirty said. "We've a small crowd tonight."

Thank fuck for that, Jack thought. He found himself a chair as far away as possible from the others. Sitting down, he found that he didn't know what to do with himself. Should he fold his arms, link his fingers, sit casually, put his legs together, smoke? Smoke.

He badly needed a fag.

"Can I light up?" he asked, interrupting someone talking.

They all looked at him.

"Not used to this, you know." God but he was jittery. His foot kept tapping up and down. He couldn't sit still. This just wasn't his scene. He needed a smoke and a pint.

Paul nodded. "Sure you can, but don't say we said so, right?"

"Yeah. Great." He almost ripped his jacket apart in

an attempt to find his fags. His hand shook as he tried to light the lighter. Eventually, he was sorted and his heart began to slow down.

"Jack?"

For some reason they were all looking at him.

"What?"

"Do you want to tell us why you came?"

Double take. "What?"

"Would you like to talk about what brought you here tonight?"

Me legs, he felt like saying, but he didn't think they'd find it funny. "Eh," he inhaled deeply. "Eh, do I have to?"

"No," the woman shook her head. "Of course you don't, but maybe later, at another time, you might want to talk about yourself."

There wasn't going to be another time. But he didn't say that.

"So, Paul," the woman turned to Paul, who was sitting directly across from Jack, "do you want to tell Jack a bit about your experiences." She turned to Jack. "It's just to give you an idea of what we're about." She raised her eyebrows, "You've never been to a GA meeting before, have you?"

"Nope." He couldn't help the insolence in his voice.

"Well, there's a questionnaire about your gambling habit you can fill out. It's a yes/no thing. It's just that most people who have an addiction answer yes to most of the questions on the questionnaire."

An addiction! Yeah, right, missus.

The woman turned back to Paul. "So, Paul, d'you want to get the ball rolling?"

"Sure."

To Jack's horror, Paul seemed to focus on him as he began to speak. Maybe it was just his imagination.

"Well, as Jack already knows, I'm Paul." He paused and said matter-of-factly, "And I'm a gambler." He stopped, as if to let the words sink in. Then, leaning forward in his chair and clasping his hands together, he said, "I suppose I might as well start at the very beginning." He spoke slowly, weighing up his words. "I had my first bet at twelve. An innocent bet. I was at the races with some relations and I stuck a few shillings on a horse called Dark Lady and she won." He screwed up his face. "I suppose in today's money it'd be worth about fifty quid. A lot for a twelve-year-old kid." He shook his head. "Anyhow, it wasn't the money that made me remember the day. It was the attention I got, just for winning. Everybody clapping me on the back and saying 'good man' and slagging me over being rich. It was great."

Jack forgot that Paul was looking at him. Instead he began to gawk at Paul with horrified fascination.

"I was a shy kid, a runt, my father used to say. The win made me feel different about myself, I don't know how. It was as if I was suddenly somebody. Somebody important. Anyhow," Paul gave a bit of a grin, "it set me mad. After that, I would've bet on two flies crawling up a wall. At first it was fun, but then, well, I grew up, got a job, got a wife, got kids." Paul paused and looking away from Jack and down into his hands, he said quietly, "I lost them all."

Jack wondered how in hell he'd lost his wife. Maybe she'd died.

"It was like," Paul frowned, "like I was two people. On one hand there was the nice ordinary me; on the other, there was a me that didn't give a toss about anything. My mind was a constant battlefield, the nice person always losing. I spent every penny I had, and even more that I didn't have. The wife left me when I lost the house in a bet over a photo finish."

Jack blinked. This guy, this normal-looking fella, had lost his house. And his wife. And his kids. In a bet over a photo finish. What a complete and utter tosser!

"That's when I knew I'd hit rock bottom. I couldn't go down any further. So I decided enough was enough." He pinned Jack with his stare.

Jack said nothing. There was no way he was even close to being as mental as that.

"So why'd you do it, Paul?" the woman, whose name Jack had been told, but had forgotten, asked. "Tell Jack why you did it."

"The buzz, the high, the rush, call it what you like. I felt I was in control."

Jack gulped. Placing a bet made him feel like that. "That's why people bet," he said belligerently. "It's fun. No one would do it if it wasn't good *craic.*"

"Yeah, but it was like," Paul bit his lip, "like sex for me. An urge. I had to do it. It was part of me, not just the – the bet, the whole ritual of the thing. Reading the papers, studying the odds, the whole anticipation of doing it, you know."

"Exactly." A youngish guy rubbed his hands down his jeans as he said nervously, "It changed me. I became someone else when I did it. You see," he turned to Jack, "it's not the winning. It's the way it completes you."

"Do you want to tell Jack your story?" the woman asked.

"Eh, well, all right."

Jack cringed inwardly. This was worse then he'd thought. He didn't know what he'd expected but it hadn't been *this*. People sitting around and telling other people about what losers they were. He knew the whole thing was going to do his head in.

"I'm Rudy and I'm a gambler." Rudy gave a bit of a laugh. "I hate saying my name 'cause it's what's caused me grief my whole life."

Jack smiled politely.

In contrast to Paul, Rudy's words tumbled from his mouth. It was like he was purging himself.

"I was bullied as a kid. I was small, weedy and unattractive. I hated myself. Typical gambler source material. If I hadn't gravitated to it, I probably would've been a junkie or something."

Jack tuned out when Rudy began describing how he'd skip work to shove a bet on a horse. He tuned out for the bit where Rudy had lost his job for stealing money from the till.

" . . . in the end I was just gambling to get back to where I'd always been. Back to normal." Rudy stopped and seemed to be thinking. "I ended up, like Paul, with nothing. Only I was lucky – I wasn't married and I didn't have kids. But I lost all my friends. I even have a brother now who still won't talk to me. It was only when I'd lost big time and I knew there was no way on this earth I was ever going to be able to make up the loss that I finally admitted I'd a problem." He stopped. "And it was the best thing I've ever done. Ever," he said emphatically.

Nobody said anything for a bit.

Jack wished like mad that Peadar was there to listen to these guys. Then he'd know that he, Jack, was normal. Didn't these guys say they lost money? And hadn't he, Jack just won six ton that afternoon? There was no way Paul and Rudy and the rest of them were anyway like him. No way.

The woman turned to someone else and he began to speak. Another lose-all-and-fuck-up-life story.

And another.

And another.

And then the woman spoke. All about the slots in Bray and the amount of money she'd spent. About how she'd left her kids on their own in the house when she gambled. Until one of them had fallen down the stairs and died of head injuries.

That was his least favourite story. It made him feel a bit sick.

Eventually the meeting ended.

Jack stood up the minute the woman said that they might as well finish up. He tried not to appear too eager as he made for the door.

"Do you want your questionnaire, Jack?" the woman called.

"Next week," he said, smiling amicably around. There was no way he was coming back. "See yez."

They smiled and bade him goodbye.

Bolting from the room, he wondered if Peadar was still on for that pint.

She immersed herself in her Mills and Boon novel. It was lovely, the way the two people found each other at the end. Everything had gone wrong, mistakes had been made, but in the end, they'd found out the truth. She went to bed crying.

But her mind was made up.

If Ciara was prepared to forgive and the heroine of her book was prepared to forgive, well, so should she.

She'd give Jack another chance.

It was scary how much she wanted him.

"They're all fecking headcases, Peadar," Jack said as Peadar put a pint in front of him. "Wasters."

"Yeah?"

"One guy actually gambled his gaff on a photo finish."

Peadar took a gulp of his pint. "Is this stuff not confidential?"

"I dunno," Jack shrugged. God, he felt great. Going to that meeting was the best thing he'd ever done. There was no way Peadar could call him a gambler now, not when he heard all the hairy stories he was going to tell him. "I'm telling you, Pead, they're all mental. I'm not like them."

It was one of the best nights him and Peadar had in ages. Well, he thought so anyhow, Peadar hadn't laughed as much as usual, but that was only because he was going to have to face Eileen with the truth that his best mate wasn't as bad as she'd thought.

Jack wished he could've seen her face.

Chapter Twenty

Chewing mints, parsley and whatever else he could get his hands on, he arrived into work half an hour before time. Another hangover, but because he'd been copped-on enough to drink piles of water before collapsing into bed the night before, he didn't feel at all bad.

Smelling of Peadar's best aftershave, reeking of Eileen's shampoo that she'd left behind in the flat and dressed in a really neat orange shirt Eileen had forced Peadar to buy the week before, he knew he looked good.

He only hoped Meg would think so too.

He parked his car opposite her window and casually sauntered over towards it and peered in. The office was deserted.

His heart lurched and began a sickeningly slow thudding.

Nothing for it but to hang around outside until he spotted her.

She didn't know if dressing up was worth the effort. On the one hand, if Jack didn't want her, maybe it would show him what he was missing, but on the other, dressing up took up so much energy. And if she did make the effort, well, it wasn't as if she'd look spectacular or anything.

Still, Ciara always tried to look well if she sensed a guy was going to break it off with her. It helped her get in there first, she said.

And Ciara knew about fellas.

So she'd done her best.

It was difficult walking to Yellow Halls in high platforms. She had already gone sideways onto her ankle twice. But, because she had her Walkman planted firmly in her ears, it made her almost oblivious to the sniggers of people that passed her.

The only thing was, it was a nice sunny day and the DJs on the radio kept harping on about it. And sunny days meant people would be in good form and she'd have to pretend to be the same or they'd all think she was weird.

She wished she'd stayed in bed.

He spotted her coming up the road. She was weaving about a bit, and for a second he wondered if she was drunk. Then his hopes were dashed when he saw that it was only the mad high shoes she was wearing that made her look that way.

Straightening himself up, he adjusted his face into

the hangdog expression that normally stopped women giving him an earbashing when he'd let them down.

"Hiya," he said softly as she came alongside him.

She walked past without even looking in his direction. For a second, he stood stunned, staring after her. Then he noticed the headphones and heard the faint tinkle of music. Relief washed over him and full of hope he ran to catch up with her. "Meg?" he tipped her on the arm.

She jumped and turned to face him. "God," she muttered, blushing and fumbling with her radio, "you shouldn't do that." Attempting to take her headphones off, she got them tangled up in her hair. She wondered if she should leave them dangling there or attempt to rip them out. Both choices were painful. But anything rather than look at *him*.

"About yesterday – I'm sorry."

Not as sorry as me, she wanted to say.

Jack braced himself for the lie. "I, eh, didn't call in to you at lunchtime because I wanted to tell Vanny first." He shrugged, did the sad-faced, rueful look. "I wanted to be honest with both of you."

She left her headphones dangling.

"I think I, eh, upset her a lot. But anyhow," he bit his lip, "it's over with her now. Sorry again."

He looked so sad that she longed to comfort him. Vaguely she wondered why he hadn't called in to her after classes, but maybe it was because he knew Linda'd be there. Or maybe he was upset about upsetting

Vanny. It was no joke breaking it off with someone. Well, she *guessed* it was no joke. "It's fine," she said.

Jack felt a tiny spark of guilt at the understanding way she said it. But, he reasoned, he *was* going to break it off with Vanny, so technically it wasn't lies he was telling her. And anyhow, after this, he'd never lie to her again. He decided to smile at her. But not too cocky, sort of as if he couldn't believe his luck. "So, does that mean, if I, eh, wanted to ask you out, I could?"

"Yeah – if you want."

He loved the coy way she lowered her eyes. And the way she blushed. And he loved the way her red hair covered her face. Putting his hand gently on her face he turned it up to his. To his surprise and horror, she looked weepy again. The last thing he needed was a weepy woman.

So, he kissed her. That way he wouldn't have to ask if she was all right.

It was the first time anything had ever been better than she hoped. The first thing she'd ever wanted that she'd actually got. His kiss was soft and tender and beautiful. He smelt a bit boozy but nice. And the taste of his mouth made her tremble.

But she couldn't keep kissing him in full view of anyone coming into the school. Especially not in front of the kids. So she'd led him into the office.

Jack closed the door and stood up against it. "In case your wan you work with walks in," he explained. He grasped her hands in his and pulled her towards him. "I can't believe me luck," he said earnestly.

His luck? Meg nearly laughed. Did he know how good-looking he was? He could have anyone. She wondered if she was dreaming. The desire she felt for him was lighting up the whole of her head, a brilliant light in the muddle of her crazy emotions. "I'm the lucky one," she said shyly.

Jack looked strange, sort of sad, for a second before squeezing her hands harder and saying, "I'll be the best I can for you."

The way he sounded nearly made her giggle. So sombre. All she wanted was for him to be him. "Just be you."

"Yeah." He pulled her against him, kissed the top of her head and asked, "So, d'you fancy heading out somewhere at the weekend?"

Disappointment shot through her. "I dunno about the weekend," she muttered. "I head home –" But then she remembered. Her Mam was heading out with Gammy Danny. "No. No. The weekend is fine." She smiled up at him, "I'd – I'd love to."

"Anywhere you fancy?"

"Naw."

"So you're not fussy? You'll come anywhere with me?"

Meg smiled, remembering the joke they used to have when they were kids. "Well, I don't normally come in public."

A delighted smile danced across his face. "You remembered!"

"Just now, this second."

"Real adolescent humour, what?" He laughed and then he kissed her again. Slow, easy, intimate.

"The bloody door won't open!"

Meg sprang away from Jack and almost broke her ankle on the shoes. Linda was muttering and cursing to herself outside and the handle of the door jerked up and down.

"Hello? Hello?" Linda began to hammer on the door. "Anyone in there?" Then she stopped. In a slightly shakier voice, she continued, "If you're a robber, there's nothing worth taking. Well, only the cash box in the press, but even that's not got much in it."

"What'll we do?" Meg began to smooth her hair down and wish like hell that she had a mirror.

"Open the door," Jack said easily, totally unflustered. Moving away, he opened the door and said pleasantly, "Sorry eh," he racked his brains to try and remember the woman's name, "eh, gorgeous. I, eh, must've been leaning against it."

Linda gave a gratified smile as she sailed past him. "Oh, all right so."

Meg felt slightly hurt but cheered up as Jack made puking motions behind Linda's back

"So," Linda put her bag on her desk and asked archly, "it's you again, is it?"

Jack made a big deal of looking at himself. "Yep," he eventually pronounced, "I think so anyhow."

More flirty giggles.

Meg gritted her teeth.

"What do you want anyhow?"

"Aw, I was just looking for, eh, a file from Meg, wasn't I, Meg?"

"Eh, yeah." He was such a *good* liar.

"Oh," Linda said dismissively, "Meg's just a typist. I handle most everything else. So what is it you want?"

"Naw, it's cool now – Meg's been *really* helpful." Turning away from Linda, he mouthed to Meg, "See you soon."

The look on his face made her feel warm. She couldn't help the huge smile she gave him.

"Bye now, ladies," Jack said, as he made his way to the door.

Linda waited until he'd left. Then swivelling around to face Meg, she said, "I dunno, I think that guy has a crush on me. I can't turn around but he's buzzing about like a fly on a cow's arse."

She had a face like a cow's arse all right, Meg thought.

"I wonder does he know I'm married?"

"I dunno. He never asks about you." She winced. It had come out all wrong.

"What? Are you trying to be smart or something?"

Huh, if she'd meant to be smart, she wouldn't have been able to think of something like that to say. "No."

Linda regarded her with narrowed eyes and then, obviously satisfied that Meg wasn't being smart, added, "Well, if he does ask, say I'm not – all right?"

"Yeah."

"Good." Linda turned back to her desk. "Oh, by the way," she said, over her shoulder, "I'm on a half-day today. Leo and I are meeting with Clive's solicitor."

"Oh right."

"He turned up last night, sick as a dog but begging forgiveness."

"Huh? Why did the solicitor want your forgiveness?"

"Leo."

"Leo's forgiveness?"

"Leo fucking turned up last night begging forgiveness. Honestly, Meg, are you thick or what?"

Meg said nothing.

"So I forgave him. He'd bought me a nice bunch of flowers and a . . ."

Meg tuned out. Instead she let the feeling of happiness inside her pour itself through her. It was weird. Suddenly she felt hungry and energetic and really really alive or something. It was funny how one guy could make her feel all that. Nothing, let alone Linda was going to spoil it.

Meg wondered if grasping the feeling hard enough would make it last.

All she knew was that she'd try her hardest.

～～

As she reached upwards towards the bathroom cabinet, she was forced to glimpse herself in the mirror. She turned and stared, studying hard the way she looked.

Dead flat hair. No frizz or bounce in it now.

Serve it right.

Dead flat eyes. Empty, like the rest of her.

Empty and stupid.

Dead flat mind.

Dead flat two-dimensional life.

Dead flat.

He pressed himself up against the fence, straining for a glimpse of the horses at the starting post. He didn't want to look at the big screen — he might as well be at the bookies if he did that.

He visualised it in his head. The giddy horses, the riders calming them, the snorting, the pawing the ground. Their breath, crystallising on the air.

The smell of excitement.

The tantalising whiff of victory only ten minutes away.

And that's what did it.

The head rush.

Everything in his life riding on ten minutes.

Mental.

❧

Chapter Twenty-one

Friday evening. There was a letter waiting for him when he got in. It was postmarked Dublin and for one horrible moment, he thought it was from one of his sisters or even his mother. But the way his address was typed on the front of the envelope dispelled those scary thoughts. The last people he wanted to get a letter from were his sisters. Still, he couldn't stop his hands from shaking as he tore it open.

It was a statement from the bookies. Before looking at it, Jack picked the discarded envelope from the floor and shook it. Funny, he thought, they hadn't enclosed a cheque for his winnings. Turning back to the statement, he glanced at the end figure to see exactly how much they owed him.

One thousand quid.

Jesus, had he really won that much? He'd have some blow-out with that cash. And, he thought with satisfaction, he wouldn't let Peadar see a penny of it.

One thousand quid.

He wanted to kiss the paper. He wanted . . .

Slowly his head began to spin as he once again studied the statement. Sweat beaded his upper lip. His winnings were set out in one column and his losses in another. It sorta looked like his winnings didn't amount to an awful lot. He'd placed a lot of bets though. Lots and lots. Some that he didn't even remember.

Euphoria vanished.

He fucking *owed* a grand.

Owed.

He clenched the paper hard so that it crumpled inside his fist.

Fuck.

Then just as he was smashing towards the bottom, he remembered that he'd a five-grand overdraft on the account. And there were other bets, other races.

He was Jack Daly for Christ's sake.

He knew about horses. And dogs.

And thinking of dogs, he remembered Vanny.

Once again, depression set in.

She was going to crucify him when he broke it off with her and, even worse, she'd want all the money she'd lent him back.

Jack had lost count of it, but he knew she wouldn't have.

"There's your ticket now for the ball." James slapped the ticket onto the table. "Deee-cember the twenty-seventh." Hitching up his cords, he beamed at Meg. "It's going to be a hoot of a night."

Dumbfounded, she gawped at him. "But I never . . ."

"If I ask a lady somewhere, I pay!" James sounded very proud of himself. "Never let it be said that James Meehan doesn't know how to treat a lady." He flapped his hand at her. "And don't be pulling all that women's libber stuff at me."

Meg was glad that Ciara wasn't there to witness this. "It's, eh, not that," she gulped. "It's just that, well . . ." Stopping, she wondered how she could let him down gently. Polite but firm. "I'm seeing someone," she muttered in a flash of inspiration. Thank God for Jack! Thank God for him anyhow, she thought with a grin. She'd spent the last day reliving the way he'd kissed her.

"Since when have you been dating someone?"

James's obvious surprise annoyed her a bit. "Since this week," she replied. She congratulated herself on sounding quite firm. "So I'm sorry, James, I'd love to go but . . ." she let the rest of the sentence trail off. If she said any more, she knew he wouldn't believe her.

"Ooohhh!" James nodded sagely. "That's a fine, fine, turn of events. You tell *me* you'll go out with *me* of an evening and then, and then," he picked her ticket from the table, "you get someone else to go out with and I'm dropped like a hot potato." He sniffed a bit and righted himself up. "I'd never have believed it. Just being dropped like that."

"It's not like . . . I never said . . ." she bit her lip. Why did she feel so guilty all of a sudden?

James waited on her to continue and when she didn't, he asked, "Is this fella you're seeing the possessive type? The sort that'd have a go at you for being friendly with another man?"

"No!"

"So what's the problem?" Once again he was beaming, his hands splayed. "All it is, is a night out."

"James . . ."

"Yes?"

The way he looked so eagerly at her made her hate herself. She hated herself even more as she held out her hand and muttered, "OK, fine."

"Wonderful." He did a sort of gleeful dance before handing her the ticket. "'Tis marvellous altogether. I'm telling you James Meehan knows how to give a girl a good time."

"That's what I'm afraid of."

"Huh?" He looked at her. As she shrugged and shook her head, he began to roll up his sleeves. "And d'you know something? The promise of your company puts me in the mood for working. I've only the last few tiles to knock off the bathroom wall and soon we'll get to the bottom of what's the matter with that ould shower."

"Great." She wanted to drown herself in it. What sort of a thick was she?

"Shove on the kettle for us, would you? There's a good girl."

She wanted to shove the kettle onto him.

Peadar was skulking about the flat and driving him mad. It was like neither of them knew what to say to each other any more.

Reluctantly, Jack decided that the time had come to face Vanny. Her throwing a wobbler was better than his having to endure this horrible frostiness from Peadar. Shoving his copy of *The Racing Post* underneath the seat, so that Peadar wouldn't find it, he stood up. "I'm off," he grinned. "See you later."

Peadar nodded. "Oh, by the way," he said, "I need next month's rent by tomorrow."

Jack stopped, hand on the door. "I get paid next week," he said. "I'll give it to you then?"

"Tomorrow," Peadar said.

"Yeah, but I don't have it on me."

"Look, Jack –"

"I'd sub *you*. You know I would." Jack felt hurt. What the hell was happening?

His words made Peadar turn away. It was true, he guessed. If Jack did have money, he'd never see him stuck. The problem was, Jack never seemed to have money any more. And neither did he, seeing as he was always lending to Jack who never seemed to pay him back.

"Next week so," Peadar spat. "I'm warning you, Jack. You'd better give it back."

Jack flinched. He wanted to thank him, but the way Peadar was looking at him made it impossible. "Don't do me any favours," he spat back.

They turned away from each other, Peadar to his paper and Jack to the door.

She thought James would never stop talking. It wasn't that he sat and drank tea all night. In fact, from the sound of smashing and hammering coming from the bathroom, he was working very hard. And the louder the noise he made, the louder he talked and the louder she had to turn up the volume on the television. He shouted all through *Coronation Street* and totally ruined *The Simpsons* on Sky. And then, just when *Brookside* was starting, he announced that he was whacked and would she ever make him a cup of tea like the grand woman she was.

"Isn't that awful loud?" he nodded towards the telly as he came out. "Take the eardrums outa your head."

Mutinously she lowered it.

"It's a grand television though," he glanced approvingly at it. "A real modern one. And you say it's yours?"

"Yep." She knew if she looked at him, she'd hate him even more than she did already.

"A woman with her own television, now that's my kind of woman." He poked his head in under hers and gave her the full benefit of his rotting teeth.

A man with his own teeth, now that was her kind of man.

Jack wondered if Vanny was just thick or totally insensitive. Or maybe it was he who was thick.

He'd gone into her flat and Jean had been sprawled out across the sofa, all legs and bare feet watching *The Simpsons*. As soon as he entered she started singing softly, under her breath, *Here comes the Sucker. Here comes the Sucker. Wait'll you see what Vanny has, You poor, poor fucker.* Then, hauling herself up, she gave him a grin and a wink and patted him on the back. "Vanny," she yelled, "Lover Boy is here."

And exit.

Jack stared after her, a cold sort of feeling creeping up his back. It was as if she'd abandoned him. Which, he guessed, is what he wanted. There was no way he could break it off with Vanny in front of a sniggering audience.

"Hi," Vanny startled him as she floated into the room. Dressed in Diesel jeans and a tight blue top, she looked gorgeous. Her blonde hair had just been washed and it gleamed like corn in the sunshine. "I've a surprise for you," she said gaily, waving some magazines about.

Despite acknowledging the fact that the girl was beautiful, the cold feeling spread out into his chest. This was going to be more difficult than he'd thought. He wanted to tell her that he'd a surprise for her too, but somehow, the choice of words seemed wrong. "Eh, Van," he gulped, "I've something to tell you."

"Me first." She waved for him to be quiet and, sitting on the sofa, she patted it for him to join her.

He'd no choice. Awkwardly, trying to keep some distance between them, he sat down.

She moved up beside him.

His heart started to hammer.

"Now," Vanny opened one of the magazines, "what's your favourite colour out of all these?"

Jack stared dumbly at the page. He flicked a quick glance at the magazine's title. *House & Home*. She was showing him an interior design magazine! "Why?" he asked faintly.

"Because, silly," Vanny nuzzled up to him, "I'm moving out into a place of my own." She lowered her voice. "I can't stand living with that bitch any more," she fired a look towards Jean's room and continued, "and she won't move out, so I'm leaving."

"Oh – right." His apprehension lifted. With Vanny moved out, he could break it off with her and not have to see her any more.

"And I'm moving into an apartment and I want to do it up and seeing as you're always giving out about Peadar, I was thinking . . ." She looked at him hopefully.

His mouth went dry. "What?"

"That we could get our own place!"

It was as if she'd belted him.

"Well?" she asked.

"Eh, no. No, I don't think so." He couldn't look at her. This was it. "I, eh, well, I don't think we should see each other any more."

To his surprise she laughed. God, he was glad she was taking it like that.

"That's a bit drastic, isn't it?" she giggled. "I didn't know you were so commitment phobic."

"Oh, yeah," he nodded vigorously, smiling back at

her, delighted she wasn't going to throw something at him, "that's me."

She pressed herself against him. Nuzzled into his neck. "Well, sorry, I didn't mean to frighten you. Tell you what, I'll move out and we'll just carry on as normal. You say when you want to move in with me."

"Eh . . ."

"I mean, you don't think I hurl myself at every guy I meet, do you?" She arched an eyebrow. "You, Jack Daly," she ran her finger down the front of his shirt and, finding a space, slid her palm in and began to pluck his nipple, "are very special to me."

Despite his horror at how everything was going wrong, he couldn't help gasping as she began to unbutton his shirt.

"And I loan you lots of money," Vanny whispered, as she began to cover his body with hers. "I don't do that for just anyone."

Jack gave a weak laugh. "Sixty quid is hardly lots," he muttered.

"Sixty quid!" Vanny had his shirt open to the waist now. She was busy running her fingers up and down his stomach. "More like three hundred, you chancer!" Her hand found its way inside the band of his jeans.

"Sure you'd hardly want that back!" Jack stopped her just before she went any further. He wouldn't be able to trust himself otherwise. He held her hand in his and grinned. "Sure, if you love me, you'd just gimme the money."

"If you loved me, you'd move in with me." She began to use her other hand to unbutton his fly. Teasingly, she looked at him, "Wouldn't you now?"

There was no mistaking what she meant. He despised himself as he let her touch him and kiss him.

Still, the next bet he won, he could get her out of his life.

All he needed was some cash.

"Any chance of another lend?" he asked. He began to unhook her bra and run his hand up and down her back. She loved that. "Just until next week?"

"How much?" she gasped.

He stopped and very slowly he lowered his lips to her breasts. "Just me rent, that's all." He made sure she agreed before he gave her the shag of her life.

"Is that slimy moron and his equally slimy nephew still here?" Ciara yelled loudly as she banged the door closed. She was feeling great. She'd had a few pints, a bit of a sing-song, Danny had boosted her ego by telling her how much he loved her and that he'd wait for her until she broke it off with the action-man she was currently seeing.

Life, despite the fact that it was Greg-less, wasn't too bad.

Until she saw the ticket on the table.

And the mortified, I've-dug-myself-into-shit-again-Ciara look on Meg's face.

"The slimy one is gone," Meg muttered, "and his nephew didn't show this evening. Apparently his mother

271

is out of hospital. She was really sick or something. James told me all about –"

Ciara held up her hand. "Did he leave this behind by accident?" She pointed to the ticket.

"No," Meg whispered in a small voice. "He thinks I'm going with him."

"And do you *want* to go with him?"

"No," Meg said in a smaller voice. "But, it's just, I felt sorry . . ."

"I've heard it before," Ciara said abruptly. "Meg, there is one simple word you have to learn to say and it's 'Fuck off'!"

"That's two." She was trying to make Ciara laugh.

"Not if you say it quickly." Ciara then began to say it a number of times very quickly. "Easy, see?"

"Can you not say it to James for me? Or tell him I've AIDS or something? Anything?"

The answer was a slam of Ciara's bedroom door.

She despised herself.

Jack despised himself. As he watched Vanny write out a cheque for his rent, he felt sickened at what he'd done.

But sex made him forget things.

And it got him money.

And it wasn't as if he'd even started going out with Meg *officially.*

It was just sex with Vanny.

It meant nothing.

❧

Chapter Twenty-two

He said he'd call for her at eight. It was half-past now and he still hadn't arrived.

"What time did he say he'd be here?" Ciara demanded.

"Eight," Meg mumbled. She wished she hadn't said anything to Ciara now because Ciara had abandoned her own plans in order to size Jack up.

But it wasn't as if she'd had much choice about telling her. When Ciara had discovered that she wasn't heading home that weekend an inquest was held. And Meg, unable to face telling Ciara about her mother's new man, had blabbed out all about Jack instead.

"Is he smelly?" was Ciara's first question.

"What?"

"The last fella was," Ciara reminded her. "And after it was off, I had to fumigate the flat."

Meg laughed uneasily. "Get lost!"

"Well, is he?"

"No, he's not! He's lovely."

"Fat?"

"Ciara!"

"Well?"

"*No.*"

"Let's see," Ciara bit her lip. "Has he, eh, severe gastric problems?"

Meg cringed. Her worst fella. Foul Bowel, Ciara had christened him. "No."

Then, giving a shy smile, she added, "Jack's lovely. I knew him years ago and we met up when he came to teach in Yellow Halls."

Ciara didn't look too convinced. "That's nice." Then, "Would you sleep with him if he hadn't showered in three days?"

It was the tester of love.

"I'd sleep with him if he hadn't showered in three years."

Ciara laughed. "Oh, ya girl ya!" Then, grinning and smirking, she added, "And just think, if it doesn't work out, you can always fall back on James."

"I wouldn't fall back on James if he was a safety net and I was a tightrope walker."

Ciara's giggles made her marvel at her wit. It was the thought of being with Jack that made her like that. Gave her confidence. She only wished he'd hurry up and arrive. The way the second hand ticked around her watch made her feel sick.

It hadn't been easy getting away. Vanny had arrived down and demanded to know why he wouldn't be seeing her that night and he'd told her a very convincing story about meeting up with some old schoolfriends. Which was true, as it happened.

Then, producing a stack of magazines from behind her back, she asked him if he'd thought about paint colours and he nodded and deliberately picked a horrible puky pink from the millions of colours on offer. He was hoping that she'd go off him because of his horrible taste.

But she loved it. Kissed him and told him that she couldn't believe that they actually agreed on the same colour. After all, she said, wasn't his bedroom a Picasso nightmare? He'd obviously come a long way from the juvenile days when he'd decorated it.

He'd only done it last year and he loved it.

Jack's hands clenched on the steering wheel as he thought of Vanny. Still, at least he'd managed to cash the cheque she'd written out for his rent in the bookies that afternoon. They trusted him and it was nice they felt like that.

He put a bet on a horse race in Newcastle the following Wednesday. He got great odds, fourteens. It had been strange placing the bet. Since he'd gone to that freaky GA meeting, it was like he'd developed a conscience about betting, but he knew it was just down to the scare stories they'd plied him with. They probably had a stack of tales they trotted out to unsuspecting members of the public. Dampening the voice of doom in his head had been easy and once the bet had been placed, the voices vanished. It was all down to willpower.

And he still had fifty quid left to take Meg out.

He hadn't felt so excited at seeing someone in years.

Ciara was seriously impressed. It gave Meg a warm glow to see the big smile Ciara bestowed on Jack as he came into the flat.

"Sorry I'm late. The car let me down."

"It's fine." She couldn't stop smiling at him. It was half-joy, half-relief. And he looked gorgeous. It was hard to believe he was calling for her and not Ciara. Though it had crossed her mind that once he met Ciara he might dump her. So, her priority was to get him out of the flat and onto the street asap. "Ciara," she said hurriedly, "this is Jack. Jack – my flatmate, Ciara."

"Hi."

"How's it going?"

Jack shook Ciara's hand and Meg hated the jealous feelings that coursed up through her. It was crazy but she couldn't help herself.

"So," Jack turned from Ciara and let his gaze rest on Meg. She looked great. Red hair tied back, white milky skin, big brown eyes. "Where to?" He hoped she wouldn't notice the slight tremor in his voice. It was her eyes that did it. Turned him on and made him feel like a heel all at the one time.

"Anywhere."

"Aw, that's very romantic." Ciara, now that she'd

seen what she'd stayed in to see, began to bunch her hair up in front of the mirror. "My recommendation would be somewhere quiet. "Like," she began to adjust her shirt, pulling it down and smoothing it out, "like somewhere you can talk. Don't go to a club or anything."

"Thanks." Meg wished she'd butt out. This was her night. Making her way towards the door, she called out a 'bye'. Then, ushering Jack before her, she closed the door.

She couldn't help it. It was like a scab she had to pick. The minute Jack joined her in the car, she blurted out, "So, what'd you think of Ciara?"

She was gratified to see him look a bit startled. "Huh?"

"My flatmate." Assuming a neutral voice, she said, "She's dead nice, isn't she?"

"Eh, yeah." He inserted the key into the ignition.

"She's good fun too. *And* she has piles of guys after her." Oh God, she wondered, why was she saying this? "Isn't she dead good-looking?"

"She's all right."

All right? That could mean *anything!* "In what way is she all right?"

Jack turned puzzled eyes on her. Letting the engine idle, he shrugged, "All right all right."

"Oh."

It wasn't the right answer. He knew by Meg's face.

"Well," he said, "you're gorgeous and she's all right."

That seemed to do the trick, because her face lit up. But then it darkened. "Sure," she smirked. "Right."

It was as if she didn't believe him. "Honest." He ran his thumb down the side of her downcast face. "I think so anyhow. I've always thought so."

She wanted desperately to believe him. And why would he say it if he didn't think so. No one had ever told her she was beautiful before. "Thanks."

The 'thanks' amused him. "Come here, you." He pulled her towards him and wrapped his arm about her shoulder. "I couldn't wait to see you tonight," he confided. He was glad she wasn't looking at him. It made telling the truth easier. "And I hope the way I feel now lasts. It's a good feeling."

His voice was warm. His arm was snug. He made her want to cry. But that'd be mental. Instead, she held her face towards his and he bent down and kissed her.

And he kissed her harder than he ever had before and she couldn't help responding. All she wanted was his lips on hers, his arms about her.

Making her feel loved.

❧

Chapter Twenty-three

Jack decided to take a risk and bring her to Malahide, his favourite haunt. He hoped she wouldn't think he was a cheapskate. Easing the car out onto the road, he asked, "How about the seafront in Malahide?"

"Fine." She'd never been there but she didn't care where they went. If he'd brought her to a tiphead she'd have been thrilled.

Jack hoped desperately she would think it was fine. When he'd first started dating Vanny, he'd driven her to Malahide. It hadn't gone well. She'd moaned about the suspension in his car, sneered at all his tapes, complained about the smell of fags, and finally, she'd declared that looking at stupid waves made her feel seasick and could they please go home before she died of hypothermia as the heating system in his car was crap. He wished he'd broken it off with her then. His head wouldn't be all over the place tonight if he had. Just being with Meg made him feel safe and . . .

"You're very quiet," Meg said, sounding nervous. "Are you sure you don't want to go somewhere else? Like a pub?"

"Nah." He turned to her and switched on a smile. "I don't think I could afford the taxi fare home again. Bleedin' thing cost me a fortune."

"Oh." She reddened. "Do you want me to pay half? The amount it took –"

"I was joking." The amused look in his eyes was affectionate. It made her legs feel a bit shaky. "Anyhow," he went on, "I want to remember everything about tonight."

Suddenly Meg wished they *were* in a pub. If Jack remembered everything, he'd probably get so bored he'd drift off into a coma. "I hope it's worth remembering," she tried to joke. Maybe that would give him advance warning that she wasn't *the* most stimulating companion on the planet.

His only response was a wink.

It was dark when Jack finally stopped the car. He'd parked it in a small car park that faced the beach. The tide was in and, rolling down the window, he said, "Hear that? Isn't it a great sound?"

"It's peaceful," Meg acknowledged. "I like the smell."

"Yeah." Full of enthusiasm, he turned to her. "I come here a lot."

"You do? Why?"

He cringed at the surprise in her voice. "To paint," he muttered. "I, eh, I like the colours and stuff." His voice trailed off. Idly he began to fiddle with the door-lock. He wished he'd kept his mouth shut now.

"D'you still paint ships?" Meg floundered for something to say. She knew she'd hurt him but couldn't quite figure out how. "You used to paint the ships in the harbour at home – d'you remember?"

"Yeah." He busied himself rolling up the window before asking, "Fancy going for a walk?"

The abrupt way he changed the subject caught her off balance. "Eh – sure." She'd freeze. She knew she would. All she was wearing was a light shirt and even lighter jacket. Her shoes were going to cripple her. But she couldn't say no. It'd be rude. And besides, she wanted to please him. Opening her own door, she joined him.

"We'll walk along the seafront?" It was a question more than a plan.

"Sure."

Together they headed out of the car park and over the wall. The wind, always colder and wilder on the coast, attacked her shirt. Meg was afraid all fifty quid's worth of it would end up in tatters. It was the most expensive thing she'd ever invested in. She tried not to shiver.

Side by side they walked. Jack was quieter than she'd thought he would be and she knew, just knew, that he was regretting this whole idea. Still, she'd a few hours to redeem herself. Maybe she should have had a drink or something to loosen her up. But she hadn't, so it was up to her very feeble personality to add some kind of sparkle once again to the night. But there wasn't a lot of sparkle in her. What could . . .

He slipped his hand into hers.

Her heart lifted. He wanted to hold her hand! To show people they were a couple! It was all very well kissing in private, but a public display . . . it made her feel important and warm. Without thinking, she gave his hand a gentle squeeze. He squeezed hers back. And looked at her. Smiling again.

Things were back on track.

She was turning blue.

Jack – who was stumbling through an awkward monologue, telling her about the way the sky and the sea never, ever, looked the same but yet they always *were* the same – hadn't noticed. She was just glad he was enjoying himself. What did it matter if she froze?

A particularly nasty blast of wind, as they rounded a corner, caught her by surprise. She shivered.

"Jesus," Jack exclaimed, "you're frozen!"

"No, no I'm not." Her teeth clattering gave her away.

"Here," he took off his green combat jacket and wrapped it around her. It was an excuse to put his arm around her shoulders and pull her nearer him.

"I can't take that," she exclaimed. "Now you'll get cold."

"Nah, I won't." He cuddled her to him. "I'll have you to keep me warm."

She didn't know what to say to that. But it was great. His arm around her as they walked. And his jacket was lovely. The smell off it was Jack's. Smoke mingled with drink mingled with aftershave. The odours of a man. She enjoyed the feel of it around her. It was as if she'd been transported into another life. She tried to envision what they looked like to the outsider. The way he was cuddling her to him might make it look as if they'd been together years, as if she was used to being with someone who looked like Jack. Wouldn't that be great? Getting *used* to him?

"So how about it?"

"Sorry?" His voice cut through her thoughts.

"Chips?"

In horror she realised that she hadn't listened to one word he'd said to her since he'd wrapped his arm around her shoulder. What did that say about being an interesting person? "Chips?" she said faintly. "Sure."

"So we'll head back to the car and over to McDonald's, yeah?"

She'd never been a fan of McD's since Peter had compared her to a Big Mac Meal all those years ago – good to look at, good to eat, but ultimately unsatisfying – but still, she wasn't with Peter any more. "Yeah. Great."

"Come on, so." Once again, he pulled her towards him.

The car felt warm when she got back into it. An igloo would have felt like the fires of hell, she was so cold.

When Jack had turned on the engine, he flicked the switch for the heater. "It's not brill," he said apologetically, "so just keep me jacket around you until you warm up."

"I think I will all right."

"Sorry."

"What?"

"For this." He indicated the car, the beach, everything. "It was a stupid place to bring you."

She was stunned. As if he should care where he brought her. "No," she shook her head, "I enjoyed myself."

He laughed slightly. Half-bitterly. "In the freezing cold? In the semi-darkness?"

"But I was with you." It was the most forward thing she'd said and she wanted to die. But he looked so mournful that she had to say something.

"But the bloody beach was sub-zero and I kinda forget that not everyone appreciates the stuff that I like." Jack smiled ruefully. "Please don't tell anyone where I brought you. They'd laugh."

"They wouldn't."

"And anyhow," he took a deep breath and said what he'd been trying to say all along, "you hardly said a word to me. I probably bored you stupid, going on and on about me art."

The glum, shy way he said it gave her the impetus she needed to touch him. "But it was just me," she said gently. "And I didn't say much, because . . . to be honest . . ." she took the plunge, "I wasn't listening." Then, ploughing on before he took offence, she said, "I was just thrilled to be with you." Embarrassed laughter. "Crap, isn't it?"

"Not half as crap as me talking for," he glanced at his watch, "ninety minutes about the colours of the sky."

She giggled and Jack smiled back.

"If I'd a load of booze in me – preferably a fuckin' brewery – I'd be a really fun guy."

Emboldened, Meg confided, "Even if a brewery the size of Guinness's took up residency in my stomach, I couldn't be funny."

"Yeah, but at least you'd *look* funny."

"Like you do, you mean."

"Ha." He tried to look offended. "That's very nice, so it is." He reached out and pulled her hair gently. The way she was bantering with him reminded him of the way they used to be. "So, will we get chips or not?"

He was looking at her in a way that suggested that if it was a choice of eating chips or just being together like this, he just wanted to be with her. The way he stared at her, his arm resting on the back of the seat and his body angled towards her made her long for him to kiss her and she wanted to transport herself months into the future when all this getting to know you stuff and the being wary of what you say stuff was totally in the past. "I don't mind if we don't get chips," she answered. "I'm not really hungry."

"I am." His voice was husky and if he hadn't looked so sexy, she would have groaned at the cliché

To her surprise however, he didn't kiss her. He just moved over to her seat and sat squashed in beside her, his arm about her shoulder. "I like just looking at you," he confessed. "When I kiss you, I can't see you right."

"Oh."

"You've nice hair, just the way I remember."

"No, it's –"

He kissed her head.

"Nice face, even *nicer* than I remember."

"I think it's spo –"

He planted a kiss on her face.

"Nice eyes." Gently, almost reverently, he planted a kiss on each of her eyelids.

She didn't feel she deserved this sort of attention. The embarrassment made her want to laugh. Or crack a joke. But that was the problem with being spectacularly boring; jokes took ages to think up. She squirmed a bit.

"Nice body." He paused and grinned mischievously.

Why wasn't there some kind of a guidebook for this sort of thing? There was no way she was letting him kiss her body. Not on a first date anyhow. She wondered what Ciara would do. "Which part in particular do you like?" she tried to sound flirty, but ended up sounding terrified.

"Can't see it all."

"Oh." *Jesus!*

"But . . . I like your neck." He trailed a finger along her neck.

It made her shiver and she couldn't get out the

words to tell him that her neck had lines on it already.

"And me?" he asked. "What's nice about me?"

Sparkling eyes looked hopefully at her and she blanched. She was hopeless at these games. Hopeless at giving flirty compliments. "Oh, everything," she said airily.

"So you want to kiss everything?"

A weak laugh escaped her. She wished she'd opted for chips. Maybe if she started to kiss him he'd shut up. But then he might get the wrong idea? And then where would she be?

"I'm tired of looking at you now," Jack whispered. "I think I want to play with you for a bit."

Play? "Oh, well, play away." She tried her best not to sound too excited. Or too apprehensive.

"You are beautiful." Both of his hands cupped each side of her head.

"No, I'm –"

"Sussh." He planted a tender kiss on her lips. "I'm a painter, right? I know a gorgeous girl when I see one." Solemn hazel eyes looked into hers. "You make me feel good, d'you know that?"

It was as if everything she'd been holding back burst out of her. He meant it. She could tell. Jack Daly always looked like that when he said something he meant. It was like the time he'd told her he hated his Dad. He'd really meant it. It was like the time he'd told her he was going to make her feel better when her own Dad had walked out. And he had. And so what if, in the dim light, he thought she looked nice? That was his problem, not hers.

"You do the same for me," she said awkwardly back, blushing. She was useless at giving compliments. It was as if she was losing part of herself in the process. But with Jack, it was different. And suddenly, she had her arms about him and he began to kiss her neck. It was the feel of his silky blond hair in her fingers that made her feel the bond they'd shared was reasserting itself.

Stronger than ever.

Chapter Twenty-four

"So," Ciara demanded the next morning, "what's the story?"

Meg glanced at her watch. It was after ten. Ciara normally never surfaced before midday on Sundays. "What's the story yourself?" she joked. "Up so early?"

Ciara gave a bright smile. "I'm romance-less at the moment. I need something to keep me going, even if it is only you."

"Thanks." Meg shoved some bread under the grill. Normally all she had for breakfast was a coffee but that morning she'd woken up and felt hungry. Trying to get out of what she knew would be ultra-probing questions from Ciara, she asked, "So Greg still hasn't phoned?"

"Probably can't tear himself away from the mirror to make it to the fucking phone." Ciara stabbed her fried egg making it run all over her plate. She studied it for a second or two, with a smirky smile. "Bastard," she said pleasantly.

Meg turned her toast over, glad for Greg's sake that he hadn't rung.

"So, what about you?" Ciara cupped her chin in her hands and looked expectantly at her flatmate. "It must've gone well – I didn't hear you puking down the jax like you normally do after a night out."

Meg flinched. "What does that mean?"

"Oh, you know," Ciara said airily. "Normally you hate going out so much that you end up getting plastered to try and enjoy it."

That wasn't why she got plastered, Meg thought mutinously.

"And the next day, you get too mortified to face anyone."

Meg wished she'd stop. She had a horrible feeling she knew what was coming.

Ciara giggled. "I mean," she said, "d'you remember about two years ago when you went to your work Christmas party and you were dead set to resign the next day?"

Her one and only Christmas bash. She remembered all right. Puking over two of the teachers. Falling down the stairs in the hotel. Being hospitalised with concussion and telling her mother she'd been mugged.

"It was the best laugh I ever had, especially as your mother actually *believed* you. And she tried to get you to come home and your Nan wouldn't hear of it and the two of them had a massive stand-up row in front of the whole hospital ward." Ciara grinned broadly. "Your Nan is a gas woman."

"Isn't she?" She hoped Ciara would stop.

"So, last night couldn't have been too bad if you managed to stay sober?" It was a question more than a statement.

She switched off the grill and without looking at Ciara, muttered, "Yeah, it went fine."

"So, what'd you do?"

"We just went for a drive in his car and that was it." After buttering her toast, she carried it over to the table and sat down.

"And – that – was – it." Ciara repeated, not sounding impressed. "Come on," she urged. "Spill the beans. Is this it? Are you mad about him? Is he mad about you? Did you shag him?" She grinned. "Answer the last question first."

"No, I didn't." Meg was a bit offended. She'd have never dared to ask Ciara anything about her love life. Anyhow, Ciara was good at evading things. If she didn't want to answer, she gave a smart reply and made people laugh. Meg was hopeless at that. She couldn't lie, she couldn't ever think up a lie on the spur of the moment and so, somehow, she always ended up making people uncomfortable when she wouldn't answer their questions. Or else she stammered and stuttered her way through a story no one could follow.

Ciara reached out and tore a piece of crust from Meg's toast. "He's gorgeous, Meg," she commented. "I'd have shagged him."

Meg glared at her. Felt like telling her she'd never get the chance. There was no way she was going to be hanging around with her and Jack.

"So," Ciara asked, her face a huge grin, "how far did it get?"

She didn't want to answer. He'd touched her breasts. Not in the flesh, but he'd slipped his hand up her shirt and rubbed them through her bra. She was glad she'd worn one with extra padding because it meant she didn't feel as much. And he'd basically let her do whatever she wanted to him. Which wasn't a lot because she was too terrified of sending out the wrong signals. So she'd just unbuttoned his shirt and felt his nipples. He liked that a lot.

"So?" Ciara asked, mashed-up toast displayed in an hopeful grin, "Was it a grade eighter?"

An eighter was everything bar penetration.

"No."

"Seven?"

Everything bar penetration and socks.

"No."

"Six?"

Lower part of the body clothed.

"Between a four and a five," she muttered.

"That's not bad," Ciara conceded. "Sort of like a test drive."

"Huh?"

"You know, showing your potential without taking it up all the way." She gazed dolefully at the table. "Doesn't always work though. I mean, look at Greg. I showed lots of potential, but it still didn't stop him from having a fatal attraction for anything shiny and reflective." She laughed slightly.

Meg smiled but soon realised that Ciara wasn't really laughing. Her eyes were too shiny and the way she couldn't look Meg in the eye was a dead giveaway. "You really liked him – huh?"

A nod.

She didn't know what to do. Obviously Ciara wasn't as tough as she made out. Shoving the rest of her toast towards her, she said shyly, "I vote we head out somewhere this afternoon. The pictures or something? How about it?"

"You feel sorry for me, don't you?" Ciara muttered.

"No!" Pause. Her scarlet face gave the game away. "Well . . . yeah, yeah I do." Taking the risk of touching Ciara on the hand, she stammered, "But . . ." it was hard to admit and the words rushed out of her, "but it's only because I've been where you are at least five times before. Just think yourself lucky it's your first time ever."

Ciara appreciated the confidence as Meg normally nursed her wounds in silence. "So can we go to the pictures and try to get drunk afterwards?"

"Sure."

"So," Peadar asked, in the new sneery voice he seemed to have adopted lately, "where *were* you last night?"

"Huh?" Jack lifted his head out of the Sunday paper.

Peadar stood beside him. "Oh, not that I care or anything, but I think Vanny deserves the truth."

Jack's heart jumped but he tried not to show it as he said, "What the hell are you on about now?"

"Out with some school pals," Peadar went on. "Huh, if you'd been out with some school pals, you'd have come home plastered like you always do. Plus," he stabbed his finger towards Jack, "you haven't any money to go out, have you? I mean, you can't pay the rent, can you?"

So that's what was eating him, Jack thought. "No, I can't pay the bloody rent," he spat. "So I didn't go out with the guys last night at all – satisfied?" He buried his head back in the paper. "I just couldn't face another night of Vanny and Vanny's new apartment. I swear, she makes me feel like nuking every paint shop from here to fucking Mars."

Peadar laughed slightly. "Yeah, I know what you mean. It is a bit much." He bent his head nearer to Jack. "How many shades of pink did she say there were?"

"Fuck off!" Jack laughed too. "I dunno, Pead," he said his voice more serious, "she's expecting me to move in with her at some stage."

"So?"

"Aw, come on . . ."

"It doesn't surprise me," Peadar said. "I mean, I can't ever remember you going out with a girl for as long as this, plus, you're sleeping with her. I mean, what else is she supposed to think?"

Jack bit his lip. "Yeah, well, she can think what she likes."

Peadar shrugged. "It's your funeral."

Jack didn't answer. Instead, he concentrated on

where the hell he'd bring Meg the next time. He'd spent the night cursing himself for bringing her to Malahide. OK, so they'd had a nice time in the car afterwards and OK, she'd said she'd enjoyed walking on the beach with him, but she couldn't have. He knew that now. The next time he'd bring her out, he was going to make it mad exciting. So that she'd see what a fun guy he was. And there was only a couple of places where he ever felt like that.

He'd bring her to Shelbourne Park.

To see the dogs.

Chapter Twenty-five

"Meg, is that you?"

Meg thanked God that Linda was out of the office for the week. Since that morning, she'd had three personal calls. The first had been from her Nan who'd phoned from some island whose name neither she nor Daisy could pronounce. Very cautiously, she'd asked Meg how she was.

"Fine," Meg said. "And yourselves?"

"Your mother hasn't been on to you by any chance?" She sounded weird. Sort of angry. "No."

Her Nan muttered something that she couldn't catch and finally, with a forced laugh, said, "Daisy's after being cornered by some funny-looking fella." The laugh turned to a genuine chortle. "Oh God, isn't she looking terrified!" Her voice dropped confidentially as she murmured, "She thinks they're all cannibals over here." More laughter. Her Nan yelling, "He's only chatting you up 'cause there's good ateing on you, Daisy!"

A shriek from Daisy before the line went dead.

The next call had been from Jack. He rang her because he'd thought Linda was there and when he found out that she wasn't in, he'd come over and they'd spent tea break and lunchtime together in the office. He left with a promise to pick her up after rehearsals that night.

Meg couldn't wait for all the lads in the play to see him. The thrill of being with him carried her through the day and, even when Aidan, who'd been in foul humour, had come into the office demanding to see all the bills paid that year it hadn't bothered her.

"Here," she said, digging them from the filing cabinet and smiling at him.

He just grabbed them from her and stormed from the room.

"Thank you," she mouthed, making a face as he slammed the door.

And now, at 4.50, just as she was about to pack up and leave for the day, her mother rang. "Yeah, it's me," she answered, hoping it'd be a quick call.

"Oh," her mother gave her habitual 'well-you-could-sound-a-bit-more-pleased-to-hear-from-me' sniff.

"It's great to hear from you," Meg said cheerily. Nothing, absolutely *nothing* was going to phase her.

"Well, I was hoping to hear from *you,*" Mrs Knott snapped. "I mean, you couldn't even be bothered to ring me and ask how my weekend went and you not even down for it."

"But you told me not –"

"It – was – *appalling.*"

"Really?"

"Yes 'really'! And you could sound a bit more upset about it."

"It couldn't have been that bad," Meg cajoled gently, not wanting to upset her already upset mother. "What happened?"

"Well," Mrs Knott said shakily, "it was all *his* fault."

"Who? Danny's?" It was awful, Meg knew, but for some reason she was glad.

"Yes." Big sniff. "He lost the bridge game for us."

"He *didn't.*"

"Yes, he did." Her mother's voice grew stronger, obviously taking comfort from Meg's support. "The cards he played were so bad they made . . . they made . . ." she floundered around looking for the right word, "well, they made us *lose,* didn't they?"

"And it was all *Danny's* fault."

"Yes! Yes it was. *And,* of course, like all men, he can't take a bit of constructive criticism. D'you know what he said to me? Do you?" Without waiting for a reply, she spat, "He said that I made Hitler look like a pussycat."

"Did he?" She tried to sound horrified.

"Now – isn't that hurtful? Wouldn't you be hurt if someone said that to you?"

"Yeah."

"It's 'yes', Meg."

The criticism stung.

"Well, I told him I didn't want to partner him any more," Mrs Knott continued. "Wasn't I right?"

"Yes."

"Really?"

The unsure way her mother asked the question made Meg's heart go cold. It was as if she was regretting it. As if she wanted to phone Danny and was looking for permission to do so. As if she, Meg, was being used in a funny way that she couldn't explain. "If you're happy, then that's it," she managed to babble out. Her knuckles grew white from holding the receiver.

"Mmm." Her mother's voice seemed to float down the line from somewhere far away. "Oh, and there's, eh, something else you should know."

The wary way her mother spoke made her heart skip in her chest. "Yeah? Yes?" Hearing her own voice sounding so normal steadied her.

"Your father is divorcing me." The words rushed out of her mother. "Bastard hasn't been in contact for years and suddenly I get divorce papers in the post."

The world started to float.

"Of course, I wasn't going to tell you," her mother went on. "I mean, what difference does it make? But my mother insisted you should know. Rings me today from some godforsaken island with some crude-sounding name to tell me that if I didn't let you know, then she would. Even from thousands of miles away she's still trying to run the show."

Meg couldn't focus on what her mother was saying. All she knew was that her Dad had contacted them. He'd been in touch. "And where is he?" she asked, hating the way her voice sounded so eager. "Dad – where is he?"

"Where – is – he?" Scorn poured down the line towards her. "Well, how the hell would I know? Or even care for that matter. It's not as if he even asked after *you* when he got his solicitor to send the papers. He just sent them, that's all."

"Oh." It was all she could say. She felt as if the whole room was closing in.

"He's getting married again. Apparently he has a child by some trollop and the fool wants to marry him."

She couldn't take any more. The weird feeling she'd had at the airport was back.

"I mean your father seems to make a speciality out of having children and then getting married. Look at me, there I was, nineteen, totally . . ."

Gently, Meg replaced the receiver. She'd heard it before.

She just made it to the ladies' before she vomited.

∽∾

Chapter Twenty-six

He had the tickets for Shelbourne in his pocket. He was going to surprise her with them.

He'd bought them after work with what little remained of his salary. It had been a bad week. Since Saturday last, he'd watched the odds on his horse in Newcastle narrow down from fourteens to fives. Full of self-congratulation, he'd grown steadily more cocky.

Until the shagging animal had come in second.

So he'd had to give Peadar most of his salary to pay the rent and all he had left was sixty quid. Still, Saturday night in Shelbourne Park should have him back in the black again. He *knew* dogs. Knew how to pick them. He knew he'd impress Meg big-time.

It was raining slightly as he parked his car outside the school. It had just gone ten and, putting on the radio, he watched people coming out of the building. Yellow Halls looked different at night. Dingier or something. He spotted Meg's flatmate, Ciara, coming out accompanied by two or three other girls. They were laughing over something and showing grotesque-looking pottery pieces to one another. Meg had told him that Ciara was doing a nightclass on Thursdays and always came home with weird stuff she'd made. Other people began to pour out of the building. Obviously other nightclass people.

A guy with a luminous green shirt and yellow trousers caught his attention. He seemed to be arguing with a girl over something. Pointing to a sheet of paper, he kept shaking his head and eventually ended up shoving the paper at the girl and storming off. The girl gave him the two fingers and turned towards some others behind her. A communal 'he's-such-a-bastard' conversation began to take place. Jack couldn't hear them but he knew the signs.

Three lads joined the group and eventually they wandered off and began to pile into a car.

No sign of Meg.

He waited ten minutes more until he was sure that no one else was coming out.

Then the lights were switched off and he saw someone come to the front door and lock up.

"Hey," Jack rolled down his window and yelled across at the caretaker, "is everyone gone? Is the drama group not still in there?"

The caretaker looked ever so slightly pissed off. "Oh yeah," he nodded vigorously, "it's just my job to lock them in for the night, you know?"

"Fuck you too," Jack muttered rolling up his window.

He couldn't believe that she'd stood him up. There was no way . . . they'd been getting on great together.

Maybe she'd found out about Vanny? His stomach heaved.

Naw. Not possible.

Maybe she was sick or something? He decided that that was much more likely.

Trying to push the hurt he felt to the back of his mind, he reversed and drove over to Yellow Hall apartments.

A half-read Mills and Boon lay on the kitchen table. The telly blared MTV all over the flat. Meg furiously began cleaning the bathroom, picking up the broken tiles from the floor. Washing and scrubbing the remaining tiles on the wall. Ajaxing the bath. Parazoning the loo. Dusting the window-sill.

And still the place looked dirty.

Just like the kitchen presses had.

And the cooker.

But they were clean now and soon the bathroom would be clean.

Until James came.

But she could clean it again after he left.

Humming along to the music on the telly, Picture House's 'Fear of Flying'.

Scrub. Scrub. Scrub.

Jack buzzed the door.

Meg's apartment was at the front of the building.

One of the rooms had the curtains drawn and he wondered if it was hers. He hoped that she wasn't asleep. Still, the sound of the buzzer would waken the comatose at Sunday mass.

"Please fucking answer," he muttered as he pressed the bell for the third time.

The sound of the buzzer made her freeze. But just for a second.

As she began hoisting herself onto the side of the bath to clean the massive cobwebs from the bathroom ceiling, she decided that she wasn't going to answer the door. If she answered, it would mean talking to someone and talking to someone meant pretending that she was fine, when she wasn't. Which was too much of an effort. At least tonight it was.

Dominic hadn't been too pleased when she'd rung him and told him that she couldn't make it to rehearsals. In fact, he slammed down the phone on her after telling her she was letting everyone down, especially herself. And *most* especially Dymphna, who was coming to explain the set design she envisioned for the production. And even *more especially* the other cast members. And *even more importantly and especially* himself and Alfonso who had so much faith in her commitment.

"Sorry," she said meekly before the dial tone had kicked in.

There was no way she was going through that again.

The buzzer rang for the fifth or sixth time.

A huge spider scurried down the wall. Homeless. She felt sorry for it.

Buzzzz.

Maybe it was Ciara? Maybe she'd left her key behind?

Shit! Why did that thought have to creep up on her?

Annoyed, she jumped down from the bath and padded out into the kitchen. "Yeah?" She pressed the intercom.

"Meg? Is that you?"

Jack! She'd forgotten about meeting him! How could she forget? And she couldn't meet him now. She looked a state.

"Eh, yeah," she stammered. "Is that you," she said his name warily, "Jack?"

"Yeah." Pause. "I, eh, went to meet you at the school and you weren't there, so I kinda wondered if maybe you were sick or something."

"Oh."

"So are you? Sick, I mean?"

"Eh, well . . . not really." She stood rigidly beside the intercom, unsure of what to do. Maybe she should have said she *was* sick and sent him away. But she'd stood him up and that was bad. She felt really bad about that. "I, eh, I just didn't go to rehearsals tonight. Sorry for not telling you."

"Oh. Right."

God, this was awful. "I, eh, I don't have your flat phone number."

"You have my mobile."

"Oh, yeah, yeah I do."

"So why didn't you ring me?"

"I just forgot – sorry," she said weakly.

"Have I done something?" He sounded wary.

"No!" She didn't want him to think like that. "It's nothing like that."

"'Cause if I have –"

"No. No, you haven't."

"So, like, are you going to let me up?"

"I, eh . . ." She couldn't face anyone.

"Or are you just going to talk to me like this all night?"

"Well no, but . . ."

"So?"

She couldn't think of any reason not to see him. And if she told him she wanted to be on her own, he'd think she was a weirdo.

Buzzz.

She had to get it together before he arrived. Before he copped on to what a loser she was.

Plastering a smile on her face, she waited for his tap on the door.

Meg looked wrecked, as if she *was* sick, Jack thought. She opened the door only wide enough for him to squeeze through before slamming it hastily behind him. Then, her back pressed against it, her hands clenched together in front of her, she gave him a smile. Slightly too bright, but a smile nonetheless.

He gave her one back. Only his was pure relief. He'd been frightened, really badly. He'd been scared that she'd dumped him. The thoughts of her finding out about Vanny had bothered him. He'd even invented a story for her in case she *had* found out. But from the smile, he knew that she was the one feeling bad about things. It gave him confidence. "Hiya."

"Hi, Jack." Another high-voltage beam.

Her smile was too bright. Too bright.

And the way the telly was turned up full blast was weird.

The whole scene began to make him uneasy.

"I've been cleaning," she said then, indicating her clothes. "This place is a mess."

"My place is worse."

She laughed heartily. Jack felt embarrassed.

"You wouldn't *believe* the cobwebs I've found since I began." She passed him by on her way to the kitchen. "I even found a cup under the sofa with all stuff growing in it. I dunno, I guess it's been there years. Imagine." She began to fill the kettle. "Tea?"

The last thing he wanted was tea. The way she was chattering on troubled him. It reminded him of years ago. The time in his house when no one would talk about things that mattered.

"Well?" Her smile didn't quite reach her eyes. "Tea?"

He wanted to ask her what was wrong. He knew something was but he was scared to ask.

"I'll make some anyhow." She brushed down her

clothes. "I'm a mess, amn't I? But sure, what of it? Aren't you supposed to get dirty when you're cleaning up? I dunno, I got so caught up in cleaning that I forgot about rehearsals. That's never happened to me . . . ."

And she was talking too much. It was a bit freaky. He wanted her to stop. His heart hammered as he walked towards her. As he reached out and put his hands on her arms, she stopped. Almost like turning a switch on a battery-operated toy. Slowly, he began to rub his hands up and down her arms. It was hard to get the words out. It was like he was dragging them back up through time. "What's wrong?" he asked. "Just fucking tell me, for Christ's sake."

How did he know something was wrong? Her body jerked slightly at the question. How could he tell? Wasn't she talking, being good company, making him tea? Wasn't she trying her very best to let him know that she didn't want to fall out with him? "Wrong?" she attempted to push him away. "Nothing's wrong."

"Don't keep talking on and on like that so," he said. He kept hold of her arms. "It's wrecking me head."

"On and on like what?" The kettle was boiling. She desperately, more than anything, wanted to make tea. But he was still holding her and his hands were hurting her a bit.

"Like me . . . like the way you are." Abruptly he let her go. "Don't do that." She pretended not to see him rub his arm across his eyes. He turned away and began to make for the television room. With shock, she saw that he was going to leave.

She followed him out.

"I'll see you tomorrow," he said.

He couldn't just go.

He had his hand on the front door handle.

"You get on with your cleaning."

He was pressing down the handle. The door began to open.

He couldn't just *go*.

But he *was* going.

She couldn't let that happen. Deliberately flat, she said, "My Dad is divorcing my mother." She turned away and stared fixedly at the telly. "My Dad is divorcing my mother," she repeated.

Jack said nothing.

"And I know it's stupid, especially after all this time, but it shook me." She didn't want to cry, not in front of him, not about something that was dead and buried years ago. Her hands clenched themselves into fists and she took deep breaths so that her voice wouldn't shake. "And I only found out today and I wanted to be on my own and I didn't go to rehearsals. And I forgot to ring you and I'm sorry." Her voice faltered as she heard the apartment door close. She didn't know if he had left or not. But she kept going. Maybe if she said what she felt aloud it wouldn't seem so bad. "And, d'you know, he never – even – asked – how I was. He's been gone years and I haven't seen him in ages, but still . . ." She stopped.

Hiccuped. Regained control. "He could've asked how I was and he didn't." It had been a bad idea. It sounded worse said aloud. Humiliating. She hoped Jack had left. What must he think of her? Who'd want her when her own Dad didn't? Facing the thought was like standing on the very edge of a pit.

She was vaguely aware of Jack's arms as they encircled her from behind. It felt suffocating. As if he was only doing it out of pity.

"Well, your Dad is a fucking eejit," he muttered into her hair. "Wasn't I always telling you that?"

The words made her laugh a bit. "You said that about everyone."

"I know." He turned her towards him. "Mostly I was right." He sounded bitter and he looked bitter. But he pulled her to him and planted a soft kiss on her forehead. Awkwardly, he asked her if she wanted a cup of tea.

"OK."

He pulled her toward the sofa and made her sit down.

He was so glad she hadn't cried. He was useless at dealing with tears. But still, it felt good to be able to cheer her up. He hadn't been able to do that for someone in ages. And because of what she'd told him, she seemed to be opening up. Telling him stuff about herself.

"I used to envy you," she said. "When my Dad took off and disappeared, it was horrible. And there you were giving out yards about your folks." She looked sadly at him. "At least they didn't dump you."

"Suppose." There was no way he agreed with that one.

"So how do you get on with them now?" Meg looked at him. "How is your Dad?"

"Dead."

She spluttered with laughter. "Jack!"

"Naw, it's true. He died about a year after we came to Dublin."

"Oh, I'm sorry."

"Are you?"

Meg gulped. Jack actually looked amused. It was weird.

"Well, you didn't know him," he said offhandedly. "So why be sorry?"

"I'm sorry for you," Meg said. "And for your Mam. It must've been awful when that happened."

"It was a relief."

"Jesus, Jack . . ."

"What?" He looked cold. His eyes narrowed and he turned away from her. "It was. I'm only being honest."

"But you must've been sad."

"Nope," he muttered. It was the way he dipped his head. The way his hair fell across his forehead. Meg knew he was lying.

She put down her tea and moved up beside him. Thoughts of her Dad dimmed slightly as she put her hand on his arm.

He didn't want to think about his Dad. He very rarely ever did anyhow. The feel of Meg's hand on his arm made him long for some way of escaping the subject of parents and families and shit. He couldn't help it. He pulled her towards him and ignoring her startled look he began to kiss her. Long and hard and furious.

He wanted her. He didn't care that her Dad had left. He didn't care that she was dusty and dirty and had her hair covered in cobwebs. He made her feel desirable and needed. And she needed to feel that way. So she kissed him back. His hands seemed to burn their way across her face and into her hair. He pushed her down onto the sofa and still kissing her he positioned his body on top of hers. Instinctively, she spread her legs and he began to move up and down on top of her. Arching her back, she felt his erection through his jeans and he held her against him.

She loved the look on his face, the way his mouth opened slightly as he gasped. But most especially, she loved the way he had his eyes closed. As if he didn't care that she should see him so turned on. She was always far too tense to do that.

"Oh, Meg," his eyelids flickered. "Oh God." He stopped holding her and looked down into her face. "Touch me."

She knew what he meant. And she wanted to. Her hand shaking slightly, she unbuttoned his jeans. She slid her hand into his boxer shorts. He moaned as she took his penis in her hand and she gasped.

"Can I?" he whispered, indicating her sweatshirt.

She nodded.

She held him as he manoeuvred her sweatshirt over her head. All she was wearing underneath was a bra. He took that off too. She felt embarrassed as he stared down at her.

"Can we go somewhere?" he whispered. "It's just I'd like to see a bit more of you."

She wanted to. Badly. But at the same time . . .

"If you want to," he added, his voice uncertain. "Only if you want."

She had to tell him. "I'm not very, eh, eh, you know . . ." She couldn't say it. She was hopeless in bed. Hopeless with a capital Really Crap in front of it.

"Experienced?" Jack asked. He flicked his tongue over her breasts making her tremble. "Jesus, Meg, I don't care. Don't go all the way if you don't want."

"And you won't mind?" She knew it was a crap question. It should be her choice.

"I just want to be with you, you know. I'm just planking it in case your flatmate walks in." Once more he kissed her.

"Come on so." Meg, barely able to get the words out, took his hand and led him toward her room.

Meg's room was a bit mental-looking, Jack thought through the fuzz of his thoughts. Beside her bed, she had a pencil drawing of a ship. A really nice picture. Good artist. She had a few other nice pictures on her walls too. There were books everywhere. But the thing that jarred with everything else was the huge tattered poster of Johnny Logan that hung proudly over her bed. He tried not to smile as he noticed it.

"It's just covering over a stain." Meg's voice broke into his thoughts.

"Must be a pretty bad stain if that," he jerked his head at the poster, "looks better than it." Sexy smile.

Meg felt self-conscious. Here she was, standing in a pair of jeans, her breasts exposed, trying to explain to a guy in a pair of boxer shorts with the biggest erection she'd ever seen as to why she'd a JL poster on her wall. She wished they'd never come in here. The atmosphere was spoilt.

Jack looked faintly ridiculous. If anyone should feel self-conscious, he should've. "Can we pick up where we left off?" His eyes sparkled and Meg's heart lurched. He pushed himself against her and wrapped big arms around her body. Together they fell onto the bed.

She didn't know how it happened. One minute she had her jeans on and the next she hadn't. One second he had his shirt on and the next he hadn't. Tanned limbs, exposing a six-pack chest appeared above her. He was beautiful.

She felt his hand slide down her body, into her briefs.

She wanted to respond but she was mortified. "Jack . . ."

"Mmm." His finger was doing something to her.

"Please . . ." She arched her back toward him. She wanted him to stop.

He pulled down his shorts. "D'you want to?"

She couldn't say anything. Never in her life had she felt like this. It was like an ache for him. But it was terrifying. What if she disappointed him?

He took her silence as assent. Taking his hand out of her pants, he began to kiss her. And he kissed her until she didn't know if he'd been inside her or not. And she closed her eyes and gave herself up to the sensations that flooded through her.

And suddenly she felt him enter her. Painlessly, effortlessly, their two bodies merged and she clung to him. And closed her eyes and called out his name.

And he felt sweaty and smelt of salt. And he told her that he loved her.

And when it was over, she lay awake, feeling connected to someone for the first time in her life.

Chapter Twenty-seven

Vanny was in a huff. He'd told her that he wasn't going to be able to see her Saturday night and arctic conditions had set in. She studied him mutinously as he shaved.

"I never knew any other teachers that socialised like the ones in your school," she pouted. "Every Thursday and every Saturday. And why can't I come with you?"

Jack jumped as Peadar came into the room. There was no way he wanted this conversation to take place in front of him. Peadar would only scoff and wreck everything.

"You just can't," he said, trying not to sound impatient. "It's called making contacts."

"I never heard it called that before," Peadar said airily.

Jack kept shaving, aware that Vanny was looking suspiciously at both of them.

"Never heard *what* called *it* before?" she asked Peadar.

"Sorry, Vanessa, what was that?"

"Jack said he was making contacts and you said," she glared at Peadar, "that you never heard it called that before. What's 'it'?"

"Sorry, not my business."

"Jack?" She barked. "What's not Peadar's business?"

"My *life* isn't Peadar's business."

Vanny stood up. She looked from one to the other. Every time she came in here lately, the two lads were at each other's throats. The sooner Jack decided that he was moving in with her the better. And he would, sooner or later. There was no way a guy like Jack could live with a waster like Peadar indefinitely. According to Jack, Peadar was always looking for loans off him and Jack, big softie that he was, kept giving money to him. And as for Eileen . . . Vanny shuddered. Such a common-looking yoke: tight clothes, gaudy make-up and hair that looked as if a poodle lived on her head. Jack didn't fit in with people like that. Even if he sometimes did weird things and got drunk and drove a car that literally farted every time it went somewhere. He was still better than the others.

"Well, I'm off," she said. "I've contacts of my own to make." She kissed Jack briefly on the cheek. "Enjoy yourself."

"Yeah." He kissed her back. "You too."

Peadar threw him such a look of disgust that he felt

ashamed. So he kissed her harder, just so that Peadar would think he really liked her.

She felt guilty going out. Ciara was looking mournfully at her and telling her how much she envied her. "Even Danny's lost interest in me now," she said glumly. "He's plaguing some young wan that started work just last week. And I wouldn't mind if she looked like me, then I'd know he's just trying to replace me with a lookalike, but she *doesn't*. In fact, she's the complete *opposite*. And she's a mouth like a sewer and a laugh like a foghorn. She drinks like a fish too, or so Laura said."

"Mmm," Meg pulled on her boots. The least said the better.

"So, where's he taking you?"

It was awful. Since Greg had disappeared, Ciara seemed to have developed a fascination with her life. She thought Jack was a ride and Meg was terrified she'd make a play for him, though really, it wasn't Ciara's style. Still, you could never trust anyone. She of all people knew that. "He's bringing me to Shelbourne Park."

"To the dogs?"

"Yeah."

"Ooohhh." Ciara sat up straight. "Arsehole Greg works there. He does the bookies some nights."

"Does he?"

"Yeah." Stop. "Bastard." Stop. "If you meet him, tell him I'm seeing someone else." Stop. "Make sure you do now."

"I will."

"And tell him I'm having a brilliant life."

"Sure."

"And that I've lost weight and look fab." She paused. "And that I've dyed my hair blonde. Greg likes blondes."

"Sure."

"And that –"

"Look, if you want, I won't bother placing any bets or even bother talking to Jack. I'll just seek out Greg and spend the night talking to him about you. I mean, it's no problem."

Ciara giggled slightly. "I dunno," she teased, "since you've been seeing that fine hunk of testosterone, you've gone very cheeky. Lost the run of yourself. Staying up in the vice capital two weeks running, your poor mother must have her heart scalded."

"My mother hasn't got a heart." She tried to make it sound flippant but failed.

Ciara laughed. "So what did she say when you told her you weren't heading home?"

Buzzz.

"I'll get it. It's probably Jack." It was a relief not to have to answer Ciara's question. She didn't want to let Ciara know that her mother had told her not to bother coming down the weekend. Apparently, Danny had arrived with a huge bunch of lilies on Wednesday night and communications had been restored. Huh, her mother hated lilies. Funeral flowers she called them.

And yet she'd started on about how beautiful these ones were. "He grew them himself, Meg," she cooed.

"Where?" Meg had muttered. "In his ears?"

Shocked. That was the way that comment had affected her mother and though Meg tried desperately to backtrack, the damage had been done. "Don't bother coming down the weekend if you feel like that," her mother sniped. "I was going to bring you to a show but I'll just go with Danny instead."

"Mam –"

"And I signed the divorce papers, by the way. Just to let you know."

Gutted. That's how she felt. Her Dad was finally gone. Exorcised. But not by her. And he'd a new child. She'd a half-sister or – half-brother somewhere. And that person had *her* Dad.

If it wasn't for Jack she didn't know how she'd get by. He'd called in to her at lunchtime on Friday, full of the joys of living. Full of his plans for Saturday night. And he'd made her forget all about her mother. And her father.

The doorbell rang again.

"He's impatient," Ciara sang.

"Come in," Meg said, opening the door. Jack looked fab, she thought.

"How're ya?" He winked at her as he entered. "You're looking great."

"Excuse *me* while I puke!" Ciara called from the living-room.

Jack laughed.

"Come on," Meg pulled his arm, anxious to get him away from Ciara.

"See ya, Ciara," he called out. "I'm just heading out with your gorgeous flatmate."

They exited to the sound of Ciara's *'uuugghhh'*.

It was the first time they'd been on their own since Thursday. Jack caught her hand as she closed the door behind them. "I've been living for tonight," he said quietly, his grin fading slightly. "You?"

"Yeah, me too."

He bestowed a big sunny smile on her. "So you don't regret what we did – you know – on Thursday?"

She didn't feel embarrassed. She hadn't even felt awkward when he'd left her on Thursday or even when she'd seen him, fully clothed, on Friday. "No."

"Good." He nodded. "I'm glad."

And that was it.

The track was packed. "Big night, Saturday night," Jack explained. He handed her a race card. "There's a list of the races and the names of the dogs running." Pointing to a load of letters, he said, "That's the form. And their previous results." His eyes scanned the track. "It'll be brilliant; the weather's just right."

Meg smiled at his enthusiasm. It was like he was lit up from the inside. There was a restlessness about him that appealed to her. "So what do we do now?"

"We bet, is what we do." He dug his hand into his pocket and pulled out a twenty. "So what dog do you want?"

Meg bit her lip. "Oooh. I dunno." She giggled, feeling a bit nervous. "Whichever one I pick, it'll probably come last. I'll go with whatever one you think."

"Well, I'm going on number three," Jack pointed to an anorexic brown dog that was being paraded about by his owner. "I always think the colours a dog wears are important. That's the thing to look for."

"OK," Meg opened her purse. "Number three it is so." Taking out a pound, she said, "So what do I say? A pound on number three?"

"A pound?" He looked at her in amusement.

"Well . . . yeah."

"You'll have to bet out there so," Jack pointed to a row of guys that stood outside the enclosure they were currently in. "They take smaller bets."

She wished she'd done her research on betting before coming here. Now she felt like a thick. "Why, how much should I bet?" she asked.

"Whatever you like." He waved his twenty about. "I normally bet at least twenty. Makes the night more exciting."

Now he probably thought she was really scabby, but at the same time there was no way she was betting twenty quid on a dog. "A fiver so," she muttered. "Make it a fiver."

They placed their bets and Jack led her outside to view the race. "Much better than watching it behind glass," he said. "Better buzz."

They stood beside the fence and watched the dogs being put into their boxes. "Can you see?" Jack asked.

"Yeah."

He slung his arm around her shoulder and pulled her to him. "That's where the hare goes from," he explained, pointing. "First they let the hare out and then the dogs go after it."

She gained the courage to put her arm about his waist. He didn't seem to notice. He was bent forward, studying the dogs intently. "Any minute now," he said quietly. "Any minute now."

The hare went whizzing by them and the dogs were freed. Jack sprang towards the front of the fence almost wrenching Meg's arm from its socket. *"Come on, you beauty!"* he yelled at the dog as it went by them. *"Come on! Come on!"*

People turned to look at him and Meg felt slightly embarrassed. There was no way she was yelling out.

"Yes! Yes! Yes!" Jack's voice grew louder as the race neared its end.

Number three was slightly ahead.

"Come on," Meg's heart quickened in excitement. Her voice rose slightly. "Come on!"

Number three won by a nose.

"What did I tell ya!" Jack turned to her, his face beaming. "Beauty or what!"

A few people nearby laughed at his excitement. She laughed too. "Fluke!" she slagged.

"Naw, naw, naw," he grabbed her by the hand and led her back toward the bookies. "Now it's time to collect!" he announced.

He was almost making her run in his eagerness to get back inside.

"Oy, Jack!"

They turned. A small skinny fella with dark hair began to make his way toward them. "How's tricks? Haven't seen you here for a few weeks."

"Shane," Jack nodded to the guy, "how's it going?"

"Not a bother. Any luck?"

"A ton on the first race."

"Good man. Go for number four in the next. She's a flyer."

"Right so."

Shane looked with interest at Meg. "This the super-rich Vanny we've heard so much about?"

Meg squirmed and blushed.

Jack shifted uncomfortably. "Naw, eh, this is Meg. I, um, don't see Vanny any more."

Shane's eyebrows quirked. "Oh – since when? Since she paid your rent last month?"

Meg felt Jack stiffen.

Shane gave him a punch. "Done a runner, have you?" he chortled.

"Yep." He put his hand in Meg's and began to move her away. "See ya, thanks for the tip."

"No probs. And, eh, if you have super-rich-bitch Vanny's address, could you pass it on to me? I wouldn't mind . . ." The rest of his words were drowned out by the loudspeaker announcing the next race.

"Asshole," Jack muttered, smiling down into Meg's face.

She wanted to ask him what the guy meant about Vanny paying his rent. She wanted to ask who exactly Shane was, but she couldn't. And besides, there was no point. As Jack had said, Vanny wasn't on the scene any more.

"So," he gave her shoulder a squeeze, "will we go for number four?"

"Why not?" she tried her best to smile up at him.

Jack insisted on betting at the same bookies. It was important to keep things the same, he insisted, like doing a jigsaw. Piece slotting into piece. Like a ritual. He bet his whole hundred pounds on number four.

Meg felt sick. "But what if you lose?"

"What if I do?" he shrugged, not seeming to care. "It's the thrill of maybe winning that's the good part."

She admired him for not caring. So, she bet her whole winnings on number four too.

Jack laughed and told her she was brill.

And once again they went outside to view the race.

Number four lost.

"Christ," Jack threw his eyes skywards. "Didn't I tell you Shane was an asshole? Didn't I?"

Meg tried to smile. The fact that she'd just lost thirty quid on a race was all she could focus on. *Thirty quid.*

"I shouldn't have listened to him," Jack was scanning the race card. "He's cost me a bleedin' fortune. Still," he bit his lip, "number six in the third looks all right." Another twenty was dragged from his pocket. "Meg, what d'you think? Nice colours or what?"

"Lovely," she said lamely. There was no way she wanted to bet big again. Taking a pound from her bag, she said, feeling slightly ashamed, "I'll just go outside and put it on."

"Chicken," Jack's eyes met hers as he laughed. "Go on. Off you go and make your fortune." He pointed to the first booth in the bookies. "Meet you back here in five minutes?"

"Sure." Meg stood for a second watching him as he made his way back to the first bookie he'd bet with. He was acting strange, almost hyper. It was as if he couldn't quite keep still – one minute his arm would be around her shoulder, the next it was as if she didn't exist. And he was so *loud.* Jack had always been a bit mental, doing strange things, but he'd never been quite like the way he was tonight. She couldn't decide if she liked it or not. She watched him join the queue, shuffle from one foot to the next, rubbing his hands up and down his jeans, opening and closing his race card. And he must have felt her gazing over at him, because he turned and when he saw her he smiled. And it was like honey, the way it filled her up.

This guy loved her. He'd said so.

And he wanted her to have a good time.

So, what the hell if she lost a few quid? Taking another fiver from her bag, she joined the queue at the first bookie and decided to bet on number three – Gammy Danny.

"Fiver on number three," she said, when it came to her turn. She passed the money in through the slot and prepared to take her ticket.

"Aw, how are you, Peig!"

There was only one person who'd ever called her Peig. And though this person was not wearing his tight T-shirt or his soprano jeans, she recognised him. "Greg, hi," she muttered. She wanted to add 'bastard' just to appease Ciara, but she hadn't the nerve.

Greg looked beyond her. "On your own, are you?" he asked. He flicked his hair and smoothed it down with his hands.

"No," she said. "I'm with a friend."

"Ciara?"

"No. Someone else."

"Oh right, yeah." Greg took her money from her. "So, eh, how is Ciara? Is she telling anyone else to fuck off and die?" He scowled at Meg. "That's what she said to me, you know!"

Meg flinched. What did he expect her to do about it? "Yeah, well," she stammered, "I, eh, I reckon she's, eh, she's sorry about that." She grabbed her betting slip and prepared to leave.

"Is she?" Greg asked. "Is she *very* sorry?"

Oh *Jesus*. "Well . . . eh . . . I guess so." And then, without knowing why or wanting to know why, she blurted out, "I know she liked you a lot." And it wasn't a lie. Ciara had.

"Yeah, well . . ." Greg shrugged.

"And she misses you." And that wasn't a lie either, she told herself firmly. Ciara did.

"So," Greg said, "if I rang her, she'd be interested, yeah?" He smirked a bit, tossed his head, "I suppose the answer is obvious – huh?"

He was such a prick, Meg thought. Shame filled her up. What she'd just done was awful. How could she have said what she'd said? What was *happening* to her? She was on the verge of telling Greg that what she'd said was all wrong when Jack arrived beside her.

"Ready?" He kissed the top of her head.

"Eh Greg –" Meg said, but Greg was staring over her shoulder at Jack. His eyes widened in recognition. "Hi, Jock," he attempted a smile. "How's tricks? Any good tips?"

"A few." Jack nodded to Greg. He turned to Meg, "Coming?"

"Do you two know . . .?"

"So, making much money, Jock?" Greg got his question in first.

"A bit." Jack nodded curtly to him and began to pull Meg away. "Come on. Let's get to see the race."

"See you, Jock," Greg called. "And take it easy,

328

won't you! Don't be spending all Peig's money on her now!" Then, "Oy, Peig. Tell Ciara I said 'hi', won't you?"

"So how do you know Greg?" Meg asked.

"Aw, just, you know, placed a bet with him now and again." He stared beyond her to the track. "Come on. The race is starting."

"Now and again," Meg scoffed, as she ran to catch up with him. "But sure, he hardly remembers everyone who bets with him. He must know you from somewhere else."

"Yeah, yeah, maybe he does." He sounded impatient. "What does it matter anyhow?"

"It doesn't. I was just wondering –"

"*Come on, number six!*" His yell cut the conversation short.

Jack had no money left. "All gone," he turned out his pockets and laughed.

Meg giggled, feeling half-shocked at the same time. "So what about the last race?" she teased. "You'll have to sit it out."

"Yep." He sank into a table in the bar. "And I wouldn't mind, but I've a dead cert for that race too."

"Just like you had for all the others?"

"Even better." Mournful eyes gazed at her. "Now, if I just had twenty quid, just twenty quid, I'd shove it on number two."

"Why?" Meg sank into a seat beside him. "'Cause it's a load of shite?"

"Ohhh, very droll." He jabbed a finger at her. "But you'll see. You'll see."

She caught his finger and then stopped. She wasn't quite sure what to do with it. Should she kiss it? Let it go? Tweak it before letting it go?

God, she wished she hadn't caught it now.

Jack put his hand around hers and pulled it toward him. He kissed it, very softly and gazed at her at the same time. "Number two," he winked.

"Go on." Relieved that he'd solved the finger-kissing dilemma for her, she shoved a tenner at him. "I refuse to hand over twenty quid to Greg and his henchmen."

"Ta." Standing up, he looked down at her. "Get a celebratory pint in for us, will you?"

The pint wasn't celebratory. Number two limped out of the race. "Hard luck, Meg," Jack said as he lifted the pint to his lips. "Still, you took a chance. That's the main thing."

Meg paused. Slightly stunned. She thought she'd *lent* the money to him. She hadn't known she was placing the bet herself. But then, she hadn't asked, had she?

"Well, I won't be taking chances like that again," she tried to say jovially. "No way."

"Cheers," Jack clinked his pint glass to hers. He felt

like a heel, but he reasoned, if he'd won, he'd have given her some of the winnings, so it was only right that she should take the loss as well. Reaching across the table he took her hand. Lowering his voice, he said, "I vote we drink this and then head somewhere nice and quiet."

She couldn't get the drink down fast enough.

This had to be the best night of her whole life.

Chapter Twenty-eight

Meg was ten minutes late for work. Jack had stayed over for the first time and getting him up for work was like trying to get a corpse to rise from the dead. Especially as the corpse had a major hangover from drinking all the booze in their apartment the night before.

He'd come to escape from his flatmate, who was giving him major grief. He was always looking for money, Jack said, and it was terrible having to refuse him.

"What does he want money for?" Ciara asked as Jack downed another of their precious store of cans.

"Dunno," Jack shrugged. Then he launched into a detailed description of his flatmate's girlfriend that had both Meg and Ciara crying with laughter. "Serious," he nodded, looking bemused as the two girls ate themselves, "she wears earrings as big as high-rise flats and her hair keeps getting stuck in them. It takes Pead about an hour to liberate the bleeding things." He swirled his can about. "Still, that's about as near to foreplay as she'll let the poor bastard get."

It had been a great night.

But, Meg thought, as she swung open the door of the office, reality bites once again. Linda was sure to go off the deep end about her being late. To her surprise, Linda said nothing as she came in the door, just studied her through narrowed eyes. Though whether her eyes were really narrowed or it was just that her eyelids were struggling under the weight of the make-up, Meg wasn't quite sure. She decided that she'd ask Linda about her holidays, try and get on her good side.

"Good holiday?" she asked cheerily, as she switched on her computer.

"Was that Jack Daly's car I saw you arriving in?"

Meg flinched. She'd been dreading this, everyone finding out about her and Jack. She hated the thought of everyone talking about her. As calmly as she could, without looking at Linda, she said, "Yeah."

"How come?"

"How come what?"

"How come you were in his car?" Linda fired the question at her.

It reminded Meg of the way her mother went on when she'd done something she shouldn't. And maybe it was that that gave her the nerve to say, "Well, Linda, I don't think that's any of your business, is it?"

"Ooohhhh," Linda said. "Ooohhhh. Sorr-eeee."

Meg flushed and, finding herself unable to meet her

co-worker's gaze, she busied herself tidying up her selection of pens. They all rolled onto the floor. She dived onto the floor after them. She was vaguely aware of Linda coming towards her across the office. "Aidan was in earlier," Linda spat as she dumped some files onto Meg's desk. "He wants you to see him in his office."

"Why?" She stood back up and her gaze met Linda's sneer.

"How should I know – probably about some stupid mistake you made last week when I wasn't in." Linda rapped her nails on the desk. "Anyhow, I told him you were late, so he said to call in when you found the time to show for work."

She knew Aidan hadn't said that. It wasn't as if she was late all the time.

"I'll go now, so," she said, picking up a pen and notebook.

Linda didn't reply, just sniffed and muttered something about people not knowing the difference between a general inquiry and nosiness.

Aidan was sitting at his desk looking at some paperwork when she walked in. He shoved it into a folder as he indicated a chair.

"Sorry I was late in today," Meg said hastily as she sat down. "I just –"

"Not at all," Aidan waved her apology away. "A few minutes isn't late."

"Oh, right, thanks."

There was a slight pause before Aidan said slowly, "You're probably wondering why I wanted to see you?" As Meg nodded, he continued, "Well, two reasons actually." He leaned toward her and his voice grew serious. "The first is totally confidential and not to go beyond these walls, all right?"

"Sure."

"It's about Linda."

Oh God. She suddenly wanted to do a runner. Linda had probably said something about her or made Aidan think . . .

"Well, as you know she took last week off."

Meg nodded.

"Her son was up in court on Monday which is no big secret." Aidan gave a wry smile. "She's told just about everyone at this stage. Anyhow," he rolled his eyes, "he got three months. Apparently it's not the first time he's been up before a judge." His voice softened, "Linda's very upset. I had a job persuading her to even come to work today."

"You did?" She knew she was gawping but she couldn't help it.

"And if that wasn't bad enough, her husband has gone AWOL again. He didn't even show for the court case." He shook his head. "I dunno, I've worked here the past ten years and every time it's the same old story. Anyhow, when Linda arrived back from court on Monday, she discovered Leo had been in and taken everything – her jewellery mostly and some ornaments. He'd pawned the lot." He let it sink in before saying, "Linda's in pieces over it."

Meg felt slightly sickened. It was weird; she'd always felt sorry for Leo before but the way Aidan was talking, maybe she'd been wrong.

"And despite all that, she won't leave him." Aidan steepled his fingers and looked at her. "I've had that woman in to me month after month crying over everything that's happening and now, with Clive getting banged up, she's up the wall." He sighed. "Sure the kid hasn't a chance."

There was nothing Meg could say. Suddenly Linda didn't seem so terrifying. All that make-up and bitchiness and hardness wasn't for real. And some part of her felt sorry for Linda, clutching onto such a loser for so long in the hope he'd change. No wonder she came across as bitter and hard-done-by, 'cause she was.

"Now, Meg, I'm telling you this because I know you put up with a lot from her and anyone else would have told her to get lost long ago. I think, at this stage, it's only fair to fill you in." He tapped his nose, "But it's between us, right?"

His confidence in her made her feel great. "Sure."

"Thanks."

She got up to go but he held his hand up. "There's just one more thing," he said.

"Yeah?"

He turned to the paperwork he'd been looking at

when she came in. Pulling out a sheaf of invoices from the folder, he asked, "Those bills you gave me last week – have they all been paid?"

"Yeah."

"Mmm." Aidan studied them again. "It's just that the bills are massive. We seem to be ordering a lot of stuff."

Meg shrugged. "Well, all I do is pay when the invoices come in. You or the vice-principal sign the orders."

"I know." He chewed his lip. "If we don't watch ourselves we'll be over budget. I've told any of the teachers with large orders of stuff to come to me – that way I can keep track of things." He looked at her. "Just let me know if any more big bills arrive, will you?"

"Sure."

He smiled at her. "Thanks, Meg."

Just as she was closing the door, he said, "Keep up the good work."

The praise made her feel great. As if she could do anything.

"I heard that men with small cars have small dicks."

"What?"

"Well, Jack Daly has a small car."

And Leo hasn't got a car at all, Meg wanted to say. But couldn't. Even if she hadn't promised to be nice to Linda, she wouldn't have had the nerve. "I'm going on tea break," she said instead. "Back in about half an hour."

"So how on earth did you manage to get him to go out with you?" Linda gave a false high laugh. "I mean he's even *interesting!*"

She supposed the remark only hurt her because it was the truth. How on earth *had* she managed to get Jack to go out with her? Still, Linda had no business saying it. No business at all. She'd a good mind to ask Linda how her holiday had gone. She really had. Ask her how Clive was enjoying his three-month all-expenses-paid break.

But she couldn't. Instead, she did what she always used to do at home. She forgot about it. Pushed the hurt away and focused on meeting Jack in the staffroom.

Chapter Twenty-nine

"Round of applause for turning up," Dominic called out as Meg entered. He was sitting, his enormous bulk pouring out over the chair. The bright blue shirt and navy waistcoat he wore did nothing to slim him down. "So you decided to show, did you?"

"Hey, chill out, man," Alfonso called. He nodded to Meg. "Nice to see you."

"To see you, nice," Johnny supplied in a brilliant take of Bruce Forsythe.

Avril giggled and patted the chair beside her. "Over here, Meg," she called.

Delighted that she didn't have to choose a chair, she scurried down the room to sit beside Avril.

"Well, now that we've our full cast," Dominic stressed the word 'full' and glared at Meg, "we can actually get some work done."

"What's the story with Dymphna?" Tony asked. "Is she still on board or not?"

Dominic scowled. "Afterwards," he snapped.

"Which probably means she's been drowned at sea," Johnny said pleasantly. "Washed overboard from our sinking ship of a play."

"Don't you mean *stinking* ship?" Tony chortled.

Avril clapped her hands, "Oh, very good, Tone, that was very witty." She gave her habitual honk.

Meg wondered how Avril had the nerve to laugh when Dominic was going purple in the face. It looked like he was about to metamorphose into The Hulk or something.

"Derogatory quips over?" Dominic peered around at them all. No one said anything. "Are they all finished? Completed? Done with?"

Meg belched.

More giggles.

"Sorry," she floundered. "I, eh, always do that when I'm nervous."

Dominic didn't look convinced.

"Sorry," she said again.

"Right." He began to flick through his script. "I think we'll go from the very last scene today. Meg, up here please." He pointed to a spot on the floor.

"Excuse me," Sylvia put up her hand. "I thought we were doing my scene today."

"Meg, if you *wouldn't mind* standing here, please." Dominic indicated a place centre stage, talking really loudly so that Sylvia couldn't be heard.

Meg scuttled to where Dominic had pointed.

"Here?" she asked politely, knowing she was standing exactly where he'd indicated.

Dominic gave a curt nod and began to position Avril.

"You're looking great there, Meg." Alfonso gave her the thumbs up.

Beside her, she saw Dominic flinch so she just smiled over at Alfonso and didn't say anything.

"And Tony, stand here," Dominic pointed to where Tony had to stand.

"Ohh," Tony slithered up to Avril and, pinching her arm, said, "Don't get too excited now, I'm only acting."

"Arf, arf." Avril pushed him away as she honked with laughter.

Dominic was about to tell them to stop messing when Sylvia asked in a very loud, annoyed voice "When exactly are we going to get to *my* scenes."

"Scene," Tony whispered in an undertone.

Dominic walked down the room toward Sylvia. "Well now," he said weightily, "you're not exactly a major player in this drama, Sylvia. So perhaps, ummm," finger on chin he gave it deep thought.

Tony did an audio impression of his brain working.

Avril began to snigger.

Meg hoped Dominic wouldn't hear him.

"Ummm, next week, maybe."

"Well, in that case, I might as well go." Sylvia began to gather up her things. "I've been coming here for *weeks* and for what? To listen to you pontificate when I could have been doing something a lot more interesting."

"Like ironing," Johnny said.

Dominic gave him his usual glare before saying smoothly to Sylvia, "There are no small parts, Sylvia, only small actors."

"Well, if my part isn't small how come it's never been rehearsed yet?"

"I have my rehearsal schedule all worked out, Sylvia. You're down for next week."

"So call me next week."

Dominic looked shocked. "But it's *essential* you still turn up at every rehearsal to get a *flavour* of the piece."

"Yeah, and the taste of the thing is making me choke." She began to shove on her coat.

"Oh, come on," Dominic said patronisingly. "Don't do a Meg on it."

Meg gulped. The pig! It wasn't as if she'd ever let him down before. She had to say something. She had to. "I don't . . ." she stopped. She watched Sylvia struggling into her jacket and vowed that as soon as Sylvia had it on, she'd finish her sentence. As soon as her heart stopped hammering so hard.

Alfonso got there first. "Sure, we'll do Sylvia's piece tonight so," he said. He tossed his long hair back and looked defiantly at Dominic. "What's the big deal?"

It was too late to say anything now. What had stopped her? Why was she such a wimp? Sylvia could stand up to him. Johnny could. What the hell was wrong with her? Still, maybe it was better not to cause trouble. Keep her head down. But as she looked at

Dominic stomping across the floor, she felt slightly angry that he didn't seem to care that he'd hurt her. Then she felt angrier at herself.

Well, she vowed, the next time she wouldn't let him get away with it. And if it made her feel bad or guilty, well, then, so what?

It was better than feeling worthless.

Ciara was getting ready to go out. There was no point in moping over Greg any more, she'd decided. OK, so he'd been good-looking, good fun and loaded. But she was sure, if she looked hard enough she'd find another good-looking, loaded and funny guy somewhere else. There had to be at least one more out there. Preferably an unattached one, who wasn't gay. *And* who didn't spend his time looking at himself.

She had to admit it was a tall order.

But hadn't Meg found Jack? And wasn't Jack nice?

Well, she thought, he was nice *enough*. He was good-looking and funny, the most important things, but definitely not loaded. In fact, permanently broke would describe Jack. Or permanently tight. He'd arrived the night before and drunk all their booze.

Again.

Then after spending the night in Meg's room, he wouldn't get up. And when he had, he'd eaten piles of their biscuits for his breakfast and that wasn't counting the ones he'd taken for his lunch break.

But Meg seemed to be infatuated with him.

And when it came down to it, once Meg was happy, that's what mattered.

But there was no way he was drinking all their booze again.

No way.

Sylvia was marching about the stage and talking in her grand-actress voice.

"Isn't she crap?" Avril whispered to Meg.

"Sussh," Meg flapped her hand. Avril was liable to shout it out all over the room and then there'd be war.

Sylvia was a *serious* actress. She declaimed her lines and pulled monstrous faces. Her tragic speech about the death of the Onion Girl involved a lot of throwing herself about the stage and beating her chest with her fist whilst howling her lines skyward.

"Jaysus, me head," Tony gave a groan. "I think we'll have to supply a two-pack of Disprin for every member of the audience during that."

The others started to laugh.

"Or provide earplugs, whichever is the cheaper option," Johnny said.

"Quiet down there," Dominic interrupted Sylvia mid-flow. Then, once he'd satisfied himself that no one was talking, he nodded to her. "Keep going."

"Keep going!" Sylvia exclaimed. "I've lost all my emotion now." She took a breath. "I'll have to go again. From the top."

"Mmm," Dominic gave a shaky smile.

"Hey, Sylvia babe," Alfonso spoke up, "you're cool, you really are, but eh, this time could you try for more . . ." he frowned, "subtlety?"

"I was being subtle," Sylvia said indignantly. "You want me to be *more* subtle, right?"

"Sure thing, babe."

"Sylvia being subtle, this I have to see," Tony chortled.

"She's about as subtle as a cruise missile." Johnny lit a cigarette and lay back in his chair.

Sylvia started again. She lowered her voice and moaned out her words. *"And the Onion Girl will be in deep peril, if she –"*

"What's the story with Dymphna?" Meg whispered to Avril. "Did something happen last week when I wasn't there?"

"Did something happen?" Avril squealed. "Did – something – happen!"

"Avril – quiet!" Dominic boomed.

Avril made a face behind his back and lowered her voice. "You know the way she was meant to be designing the set for us?"

"Yeah."

"Well, her little fella had to go to hospital and all she had time to do was a rough sketch."

"So?"

"So," Avril gave Dominic the two fingers, "our esteemed director told her to get her act together and be more committed."

"What?"

345

"Yep. And so she left." Avril smirked. "So we've no one doing our set for us." She giggled. "I swear this is a gas group to be involved in."

"Gas group all right," Johnny nodded. "Especially when certain people are full of hot air."

"I can't concentrate," a shriek from Sylvia at the top of the room.

"That's the wrong line," Dominic began to flick the pages of his script.

"I refuse to say my lines with all the whispering going on down there."

"Lads, lads, quiet down there," Alfonso called out. Half-smiling, he added, "If yez don't, we could be here all night listening to Sylvia."

"*And* what's that supposed to mean?"

"Don't want you to ruin those vocals, honey," Alfonso bestowed a lazy smile on her. "Can't have that with just over six weeks to go."

"Oh." Appeased, Sylvia smiled slightly.

"Quiet, everyone." Tony stood up as if he was conducting an orchestra. "Contain your excitement please. After all, when Sylvia finishes, we all have to be informed about our new-fangled invisible set."

"Where were you, Sylvia?" Dominic asked, totally ignoring Tony and his barb.

"I'll have to start again," Sylvia glared at them all. "There's no point in going from where I was if I can't experience the emotion."

A communal groan went up.

"It's called professionalism," Sylvia took up her position. "It's what real actors do. Now, Dominic, throw me my first line."

"He should throw her onto a fucking line," Johnny hissed. "Preferably one that has a regular train service."

"Stop it! Stop it!" Sylvia screamed. *"Stop talking!"*

She knew she looked good. Her hair shone because she'd got it done that very day. Cropped tight and dyed blonde. Not peroxide but close enough. Meg had told her it was lovely, but then again, if she'd covered her hair in mucus, Meg would have told her it looked nice.

She made a point of putting on the clothes that Greg had liked on her. A shiny pair of silver combats and a black top. With her blonde hair, they looked mega.

She was meeting Laura in town at nine. In order to get to the bus stop, she had to pass the bookies where Greg sometimes worked. His dad owned it and in, order to give Greg experience, he made him work behind the counter during the weeknights. Other than that, Greg was normally sent to England or parts of Ireland to cover the race meets.

She was hoping he'd see her as she walked past. See her and puke at the chance he'd thrown away.

Just as she was going out the door, the phone rang. Shit!

"Yeah?" she snapped, hoping the caller would know she was in a hurry.

"Ciara, it's me. Not out tonight then?"

It was Greg. And he sounded amused about something.

"I'm just about to go out," she said back, her heart beginning to hammer.

"Sure." Now he sounded patronising. "I was just wondering if you wanted to meet up for a drink sometime next week." He paused. "Say next Sunday afternoon?"

He wanted her back. He was sorry. Despite all the names she'd called him, her heart lifted. She tried not to sound too happy about it. "Fine. All right."

"I'll ring you later in the week and we'll sort out a place – OK?"

He didn't wait for her to reply, just hung up the phone. She sat for a while, hardly able to believe it.

A solemn silence around the table as Dominic manoeuvred himself into his seat. His ears were ringing from Sylvia's high-decibel shrieks. Why, he wondered, did he have to work with such a shower of morons? The only one with any talent was Meg and she was the most irritating of the lot of them. She was great when she was performing but God, when she wasn't she was such a weirdo.

Even weirder than the rest of his cast.

He was in no mood for a battle. *No. Mood. At. All.*

"As you know," he began, lacing his fingers together, "we have a slight problem with our set."

"The slight problem being that we have no set," Alfonso contributed helpfully. "Isn't that what you mean, Domo, man?"

"I'm perfectly capable of framing my own sentences, Alfonso."

"Sure, sure, no sweat."

"Dymphna has let us down –"

"I don't think that's strictly true," Johnny sounded irritated. "Her young fella is *seriously* ill, Domo. Like as in 'at-death's-door' ill."

"Well, she *would* say that, wouldn't she?"

"I don't believe this," Johnny stared around at the rest of them. "Do yous?"

"I don't see how Dymphna can work on our play while she's so worried about her son," Sylvia spoke up.

"I don't think she's letting us down."

"Me neither."

"Nor me!"

Meg shook her head really quickly, not wanting to draw attention to herself but wanting to support the others.

"Can anyone here draw?"

"Well, you're drawing now, Domo," Johnny smiled. "Drawing a blank!"

"This is no joking matter," Dominic shouted over the laughter. "Now, come on, guys, let's work together on this."

Meg's heart began to hammer. It always did before she spoke up in a crowd. She tried to pretend she was on-stage, the only place she could actually talk without wanting to die. Taking a deep breath and hoping her voice wouldn't give the game away by shaking, she said, "Well, eh, I know a guy who might be able to help."

Dominic ignored her. "Anyone else?"

"Meg's just said that she —"

"Go on so." Dominic turned bored eyes upon Meg and asked patronisingly, "Who do you know?"

"Well, he's an art teacher." Her mind began to race in panic. "He's good."

"Has he done set design before?"

It was the way he asked it, sort of sneering, as if she was a thick. "Yep." She didn't add that it was in a school play a decade ago.

"So will he do it, do you think?" Alfonso asked.

"I dunno. I'll ask him."

"By next rehearsal?" Dominic snapped. "Will you see him by then?"

"Yeah." She was rewarded with a small tight smile from Dominic. She wondered what the hell she'd done. If Jack refused to get involved, it'd only make Dominic angrier at her.

Still, if on the other hand, Jack agreed, Dominic wouldn't dare pick on her any more for fear of losing another set designer.

It was worth the risk.

When she got back to the flat, she found a note on the table. *Greg rang. Wants to meet me. Brill or what?*

She smiled.

So now Ciara would have Greg and she'd have Jack.

There was no need to worry any more.

❧

NOVEMBER

Chapter Thirty

Jack arrived back at the flat, his head hammering. It had been a rotten day. He'd got a statement from the bookies that showed a five-grand deficit. Not that that bothered him, a few well-placed stakes and he'd be in the black again. But he needed money to do that. And he had no money. At least not until the following day.

And to top it all, he'd had the Second Years just before classes ended and they'd been their usual obnoxious selves. Brendan had made a rare appearance and had ended up totally pissing him off when he'd drawn a fella and a girl having it off. Jack tried to remain calm.

"It's an impressionist picture I wanted," he said. "Not explicit porn."

"It is impressionist," Brendan said. "I'm a virgin and it's an impression of what I think it's like."

Of course that had set them all off. And the class ended when Brendan, with a smirky smile on his face, said, "Maybe you and Miss Knott would have a better idea of it all, sir."

Wolf whistles and catcalls abounded.

Jack ended up going down the room and hauling Brendan out of the class by the collar of his shirt.

Jaysus, he hated kids sometimes.

Especially ones that acted the way he used to act.

He began to root around in the fridge for some grub. There was nothing, only a packet of ham slices. Peadar didn't seem to be buying much food lately. Taking the packet of ham he sat in front of the telly and flicked it on. He glanced idly across at the script he'd got from YH Theatre Group the previous Thursday and his heart sank. How she'd done it, he didn't know, but Meg had roped him into designing a set for her drama group.

Initially he'd refused, but the look on her face had made him relent. "Will I have to do much?" he demanded sourly.

"No." Then, "So you'll do it?" And when he nodded, she threw her arms about his neck and just as he hoped she was going to give him a snog, Linda had walked in. And passed some cryptic comment about the body size of Volkswagen Beetles.

He'd read the script of the play that night, much to Vanny's disgust. At least it got him out of going out with her to a corporate dinner.

"It's important," he said, waving the play in front of her. "School stuff, you know."

"But you're an art teacher!"

"Yeah, and I've to design the set for this thing."

"Well, it can't be so important that you can't come out with me. I told you about this dinner weeks ago." She folded her arms and scowled.

Vanny looked horrible when she got angry. Her face sort of scrunched up and big lines creased her forehead. Meg never looked at him like that. "Sorry," he reached out and took her hand. "No can do."

She pulled her hand from his grasp and flounced out.

"Bit rough that," Peadar commented from the doorway of his room.

"A bit rough?" Eileen poked her head out. "I think it's *awful* the way you treat her."

"I think it's awful the way you treat Peadar, but I keep me mouth shut about it," Jack said back.

"And what is that supposed to mean?"

"Eileen, love —"

"Well?"

Very softly, under his breath, Jack began to hum 'Come on, Eileen'.

"Shut it!" Peadar snapped.

Jack did. He couldn't really afford to fall out with Peadar. Lifting himself up from his seat he said calmly, "What Vanny and I do is none of your business."

"Well," Eileen scoffed, "the girl must be deranged to go out with you!"

"Eileen, love —"

"Deranged maybe, but she's got *taste.*"

"Taste, me arse!"

"Naw, thanks. I'll leave that to Peadar."

"Jesus!" Eileen glared at him. "You always have to drag everything down, don't you?"

"Only if she's good-looking." He got a thrill out of her furious face. Winking at her, he made his way into his room.

He managed to block out the sounds of Eileen yelling at Peadar as he read the play. It was a weird sort of story – reading it made him uncomfortable. It was set in some strange futuristic place and told the story of a girl who lost everything important to her. In the end, she was left, alone and exposed, on a sort of space-age mountain top where she died.

Seriously off-the-wall stuff.

For lack of anything else to do, Jack wandered into his room to search for some drawing paper. There was a pile of it under his bed, a bit dusty because it hadn't been touched in ages. There was also a fiver which must have fallen out of his jeans at some stage. Shoving it into his pocket, he began the hunt for his artist's pens. He located them in his drawer. Setting up his drawing board, he clipped a page to it.

And for the first time in months, he began to sketch.

It was pretty good, he had to admit. Maybe slightly ambitious for an amateur play but still good. He took some more pages and began to draw it from various angles. He could see it in his head, all silver and white. It'd look great with lights shining and reflecting off it. Maybe if he was finished in time, he could drop by Meg's and show it to her. He hadn't planned on seeing her that night because he had no money, but she'd be so thrilled with him for doing the set design, who knew where it would lead?

He took the risk of squinting out the window to make sure that Vanny's car hadn't arrived back from work. She was still in a huff with him for letting her down over the dinner. But it hadn't spurred her into getting rid of him. All she did instead was to make caustic comments about the sexuality of people who got involved in the theatre.

"And a lot of artists are bent too," she had sneered only last night.

That had hurt. For the first time ever, he had told her to shut up and walked out of the room.

He was in no mood to meet her that night.

There was no sign of her. Rolling up his artwork, he grabbed his combat jacket from a chair and sprinted out of the apartment. He took the stairs, because he knew Vanny would take the lift. Down the corridor to the front door.

And out.

Over to his car.

And in.

The engine fired first go and he thanked fuck. Whoever that was.

Meg was in. She buzzed him up. As he neared the apartment, he could hear a lot of hammering and belting going on. It must be the guy Meg had told him about, the slimy landlord who was fixing their shower and who wanted to bring her to a ball. Lucky for him, as it happened. It meant that Meg would be well out of the way when he went on his Christmas trip to Leopardstown. The highlight of his year. The buzz at that place was the best anywhere.

Meg opened the door to him on his first knock. "Oh, it's brill you're here," she whispered, dragging him in. "James is here and Ciara reckons he's wrecking our shower. She says he doesn't have a clue what he's doing."

Jack gulped. "And?"

"Well, you're a man. You know about stuff like that."

Jack grinned. "Meg," he bit his lip, "how can I put this? I know as much about showers as I know about nuclear fission."

"I didn't know you knew about nuclear fission." A very dusty, bedraggled Ciara emerged from the bathroom to join them. As Jack laughed, she thumbed towards the bathroom. "The guy is a moron," she said loudly. "He's trying to remove the tiles without breaking them. Recycling, he calls it."

"Aye, recycling!" James shouted from the bathroom.

"Fecking tight-arsedness!" Ciara snapped.

"My mam says that too about him," James Junior piped up from the telly room.

"Shut up there now, James Junior, and don't be letting me down in front of the girls!"

"Fuck off!"

Meg brought Jack into the telly room. "This is what's being going on all night," she said, massaging her head. She sank into a chair. "James hammering, Ciara yelling and him," she pointed to James Junior and her voice rose slightly, "wrecking my television."

"Fuck off, you!"

"Poor ould Meg." Ciara shot her a semi-exasperated look. "Not able for hassle."

Meg bristled. She hated when Ciara said stuff like that in front of Jack. Still, it was probably only a joke. Ciara had been in great form since Greg's phone call.

A particularly horrific-sounding bang came from the bathroom.

"Jesus Christ Almighty!" James came out, holding a rapidly swelling hand before him. "Water. Put a drop of water on this, will yez!"

To Jack's amusement neither Meg or Ciara rushed to help. Eventually, it was Meg who turned on the tap for him.

"Good girl," James gasped as the cold water hit his throbbing hand. *"Aaahhhhh!"*

"That's what he sounds like having an orgasm, Meg," Ciara whispered.

"Stop!"

Jack started to laugh. Meg looked disgusted.

"What's an orgasm?" James Junior looked up from the film *The Omen*.

Jack laughed again.

At Jack's laugh, James looked up. "And who's this?" he asked in a tone that suggested that if it was who he thought it was, he wasn't impressed.

"This is Jack," Meg said.

"Jack the boyfriend, is it?"

"Jack the boyfriend, it is," Ciara nodded emphatically.

"Well, how's it going, Jack? What's the *craic?*" James tittered at his wit.

"The *craic* is grand – sorry 'bout your hand."

Meg and Ciara laughed as James sneered, "Oh, very good." He paused and said in a nasty voice, "As a poet, you'll blow it."

"And as a plumber you're a bummer!" Ciara shrieked.

James, amid the grins and giggles, drew himself up. "I'll not stay and have my handiwork insulted." He marched into the bathroom and then there came the sounds of him flinging his tools into his bag. "I'll not be able to take them all with me," he shouted. "My hand is too sore."

More giggling.

"But I'll be back, Tuesday or one of the days."

"No rent unless you are," Ciara warned.

James ignored her. "Come on, James Junior," he ordered.

"What's an orgasm?"

"Aw, some class of a thing that lives in the earth." Picking his jacket off the hook on the door he let the two of them out.

"And that," Ciara chortled, "is Meg's admirer." She turned to Jack. "You're under fierce pressure there!"

Meg didn't think it was a bit funny. And it was even worse when Jack said, "I dunno. I think I'll have to opt for you, Ciara. I'm not up to fighting for my woman."

"Well, I'm ready when you are," Ciara laughed.

"I'm ready any time."

"Come on, Jack. Show me your drawings," Meg cut in on their laughter. Panicked, she tugged Jack's arm. "Come in my room. We can talk there."

"Talk? Aw, God, no wonder you're looking for a bit more action, Jack!" Ciara giggled.

Meg slammed the door on her.

His drawings were fab. "They'll love them," she said. "Oh, Jack, you're brilliant."

It was a long time since he'd done anything that had been admired. It felt good. Vanny hated his stuff. "It's all right," he said shrugging. "They're just first attempts. They'll probably change."

"No, they won't. YH hasn't had anything this good in ages. They'll love them." She paused. "Thanks."

"For what?"

"For doing the drawings and getting involved. I know you didn't want to."

"Naw, it's cool."

"Thanks anyhow."

"'S all right." He kissed her. "Any other way of thanking me?"

She'd been hoping he'd say something like that. Being with Jack was amazing. Having sex with him was something she couldn't get out of her head. Never in her life had she felt the way she did when he was close to her.

It had even stopped being scary.

Chapter Thirty-one

She legged it up Parnell Square, hauling her weekend bag with her. By the time she reached Mikey, her face was flushed and sweat was pouring off her.

"In training for the Olympics, are you?" he asked, as he handed her a ticket. "There wasn't any need to run, you know. I never pull off until I have at least one passenger." It seemed that she was *the* passenger he'd been waiting on because, before she'd even sat down, he'd revved up the engine until it was smoking and pulled out in front of a car, almost taking the side out of it. "And here we go now," he beamed, looking back at her.

Meg smiled and tried to get her Walkman out without him noticing.

"Long time no see," he shouted over the roar of the engine.

"Yeah."

"Business has been down one hundred percent since you abandoned me."

"I didn't aban –"

Mikey snorted. "But sure, these days it's the Celtic Lion and all that malarkey. So I suppose things should improve."

"They should." She had managed to get her Walkman out. Now it was just a matter of plugging it into her ears.

"And I believe the woman *herself* is back from her travels?"

She sighed. It looked as if Mikey was determined to talk all the way down. "Yeah, she's home," she answered. "Mam picked her up from the airport yesterday afternoon. I'm heading down to see her now."

"And I believe the Daisy wan didn't come home at all."

"What?"

He almost crashed the bus in his eagerness to tell her the gossip. "Did your mother not tell you? Aw sure, it's a great story. It's all over the place down home."

"What is?"

"The story about Daisy and her new man."

"Daisy has a new man?"

"Oh, aye. He lives out there – he's foreign, you know – and she couldn't bear to leave him. And what happened, only didn't she check in her luggage and then was nowhere to be found when the plane was taking off. Well, there was this major security alert, the plane was held up for hours, your Nan said, and the Daisy wan nowhere in sight. There was announcements calling for her and the divil knows what. Eventually, off went the plane." He pressed his foot on the accelerator to show what he meant. Meg was thrown backward and there was a jolt at the back of the bus as if someone had hit it. Mikey didn't seem to notice. "Anyhow, Daisy was left behind and later she rings your Nan and tells her she's in love."

"You're joking?"

"Not at all." Mikey smiled. "Sure isn't Daisy a gas woman? I'd have had her meself."

"Really?" she smiled.

"Good woman for working. Great on a farm, I'm told."

"And Nan?" she asked. "Did she have a good time?"

"Marvellous. She's like a black person, the colour of her. She's moving into Daisy's house until it sells."

"What?"

"Oh aye. Rumour has it your Nan might buy it herself. Leave room for the two lovebirds in your mother's place."

"Lovebirds?"

"Your mother and Danny McCarthy. Aw, sure they're like a boar and a sow in heat. They're mad about each other."

She didn't care if it was being rude. She began to assemble her Walkman. Her mother and Danny!

"And now that your father has done the dacent thing and dumped the two of you, what's holding them back?"

Music filled her head. Sound. It cut out everything he was trying to tell her. She stared out the window, avoiding his gaze until eventually he gave up talking and concentrated on driving.

Jack had five pounds and together with the money he'd collected for the gear he'd dropped into the pawn shop he reckoned he should be able to have a good afternoon in Byrne's. And maybe a good night in the pub later with Shane and a few of the lads.

He'd miss Meg but it was nice not to have to worry about turning up on time for her and all that shit. Plus, he figured, there was no point in heading back to his apartment as Vanny would be looking for explanations as to where he'd been the previous night. He'd have to get his head together and come up with something brilliant before he faced her. He'd grown to like the thrill of lying to Vanny – it was a bit like betting. One small move and she'd throw him off the thin line he was treading.

Feeling very positive, his heart thudding with anticipation, he parked his car in the small car park opposite Byrne's and made his way across the road.

Her mother's car wasn't in the driveway when Meg arrived home. Maybe her mother and Nan had gone shopping together or something. Still, she thought, at least she had a key to let herself in. Hoisting her bag onto her shoulder she began to trudge towards the house. Before she'd reached the porch, the front door opened and her Nan stood framed in the doorway.

"How's my girl?" she shouted.

Mikey had been right, Meg thought – her Nan's face was tanned and healthy-looking. Without thinking, she dropped her bag and ran towards her. "Welcome home!" She enfolded her Nan in a hug and then, realising suddenly what she was doing, she pulled away.

"Welcome home," she muttered, her face red. Her hands felt awkward, dangling by her sides.

"Come here," her Nan, beaming, took Meg's hands in hers and pulled her to her. "It's not often I get a hug from my only grandchild."

It felt nice, Meg had to admit. Alien, but sort of safe. She hadn't been cuddled by anyone in ages, except Jack. And he was different. After a few seconds though, the hug began to feel claustrophobic. Gently, she pulled away. "I'll just get my bag," she gestured to where she'd dumped her bag.

"You do that and I'll shove on the kettle. I've great news for you."

"Is it about Daisy?"

"Arrragh! And who told you?"

"Mikey."

"Well, the little shit. Trust him to get there first. The . . . the Internet wouldn't have as much information on it as that man carries around in his head." She flapped Meg away, looking slightly annoyed. "Go on, get your bag and you can fill me in on all your news. Your mother tells me you haven't been home for a few weeks?"

The minute he walked into Byrne's, he knew something was wrong. It was the way that feckin' poseur Greg came out from the back to ask him to step into the office.

"Just let me offload some cash first?" He produced some notes from his pocket.

"Yeah, in here," Greg ushered him forward.

Into the manager's office. Greg in his sprayed-on jeans and T-shirt sitting behind his dad's desk.

"You the manager here now or what?" Jack asked. He tried to smile but somehow it wouldn't come.

"My father's away this week." Greg did a bit of a swivel in his dad's chair. "He, eh, told me to talk to you if you happened to come in."

"Yeah, great. Nice talking to you, Greg. Now," Jack stood up and patted his shirt pocket, "I've some business to do."

"You owe us five grand, Jock."

"Jack," he corrected. He stayed standing. There was no way Greg was going to intimidate him. They must be the same age for Christ's sake.

"We can't take any more bets until you clear the deficit – *Jack.*"

"But I've cash here."

"So you can use it to pay off some of the money you owe us."

"Wha'?" Jack nearly laughed. "Will you get a grip! I'll pay when I've the money to pay."

"And when will that be?"

"When I'm allowed to place a few bets. That's when."

Greg shrugged. "Well, it won't be in here." He shrugged. "Sorry, mate."

"I'm not your fucking mate!"

Greg winced. "Look, Jack, I'm only telling you. It's the way we operate. Don't dig yourself in any deeper than you are already."

"If I need the Samaritans, I'll give 'em a call." Angrier than he'd been in years, Jack wrenched open the office door and, pushing past a few startled customers, he strode out into the street.

"So," her Nan leaned towards her, "I hear she told you about the divorce."

The gentle way she asked made Meg feel like snivelling. But she couldn't. It'd be stupid. And it would only upset her Nan. "She told me," she said flatly.

Her Nan reached across and patted her hand. "She said you took it very well. Didn't seem too upset over it."

Didn't seem too upset. *Jesus.* Who *wouldn't* be upset? Hot fury shot through her. How the hell would her mother know how she'd taken it? She hadn't seen her since and any telephone calls had been very brief and mainly concerned with telling her not to come and visit. *Upset.* Of *course* she was fucking upset.

But what was done was done. She swallowed the lump in her throat and it hurt.

"And it's for the best," her Nan went on gently. "Sure your dad hasn't been in touch in a long time. There's no point in hanging onto things when they go wrong."

Meg studied her nails. She picked a bit of fluff from her baggy jumper. Her Nan was talking a load of crap. If her mam and dad hadn't given up on each other, they'd still be together.

"And now, what with Danny on the scene, isn't it better that she's a free woman?"

"Any chance of a shower?" Jumping up from the table, she almost up-ended her cup. "Three hours on Mikey's bus and I need to be detoxified."

Her Nan looked startled, but just nodded and told her to go ahead.

She couldn't get out of the kitchen fast enough. Hauling her bag up the stairs, she banged it off every step, getting a sick satisfaction out of imagining it as Danny's head. She swore that if another person so much as mentioned his name, she'd scream.

Changing his bookies had been a brilliant idea. His luck was in. Three ton he'd made in the afternoon. He shoved half of it back on a race meet for the following day and decided to head down for a pint with a few lads that he'd met. They were a nicer crowd than in Byrne's. And none of them had wives that they had to run back to.

Jack knew it was going to be a great night.

Meg knew it was going to be an awful night.

Danny sat at the top of the table in his woolly jumper and woolly-looking trousers. Beaming around at Meg and her Nan and, of course with seriously nauseating glances in her mother's direction, he announced that he was taking them all out for dinner.

Her mother clapped her hands and said she thought

that was a great idea. Giving Meg a nudge, she said, "Isn't that lovely, Meg?"

"Depends on where he's taking us."

A collective gasp from all three.

She couldn't help it. It had been a shock. After she'd come down from her shower, she'd found Danny ensconced in the kitchen, laughing and joking with her Nan. Her mother had the kettle on and she was singing.

Singing!

In her whole life, Meg had never heard her mother sing. And she'd a nice voice.

But even more shocking than that had been the clothes her mother was wearing. Jeans and a shirt. No brown skirt and tights. No cream blouse and fitted jacket. No *shoes*. A pair of black boots.

Meg had slid into a chair and hadn't said a word until Danny mentioned dinner. And now they were all gawping at her. "Well," she said, "if it's McDonald's, it's hardly worth getting too excited about, is it?" Just as her mother was about to say something, she added, "Unless of course they're giving away free E tablets in the happy meals."

More stunned silence. She didn't care. It was one of the few times in her life when she hadn't cared what her mother would say.

"Well, it's not McDonald's," Danny broke the silence. "It's The Great Southern – how 'bout that now?"

"It sounds lovely," her mother said, standing beside Danny and glaring at Meg.

"It does," her Nan agreed.

There was no way she was going with them, playing happy families. And it wasn't as if Danny was even a part of the family. He was just an interloper trying his best to fit in. "I'm not that hungry," she stared at the tablecloth. A new one, she noticed then for the first time. "I think I'll have an early night."

No one protested, not even her Nan, which was quite hurtful.

Jack got bombed. It was like everyone in the pub was his friend. It was after twelve as he staggered back to his car. He managed to get inside and close the door before passing out.

Meg got drunk. Once they'd left, she took the whiskey bottle her mother kept hidden in the wardrobe. It didn't take long to polish it off. Feeling freer and slightly happier, she sat in front of the telly to welcome them all home.

Chapter Thirty-two

Vanny attacked him as soon as she set eyes on him. He wasn't in the mood for a row. His head was hammering, his clothes stinking and on top of that, he had to clean out his car. Sometime during the night, he'd been sick.

"What happened to you?" she demanded, barely giving him time to sit down.

Out of the corner of his very sore eyes, he saw Peadar sneaking out the door.

"Van, please," he held up his hands. "Later, all right?"

"You must be joking!" She poked her head into his and then recoiled. *"Jesus!"*

"I have to shower, sleep, change, you know."

"I know all that. What I don't know, and what you're going to tell me is, where the hell were you the last two nights?"

"Out." He managed to meet her eyes. "I got a call on Friday – one of me sisters had a new baby. And there was a bit of a session and well, I got locked."

Her eyes narrowed. "Boy or girl?"

"Boy."

"Name?"

Jack racked his brains for the last time he'd used this excuse. What name had he given his fictitious nephew then? "Eh, they haven't chosen one yet." Trying to look indignant, he asked, "Why? Don't you believe me?"

"Is there someone else?" She asked the question quietly, taking him by surprise. Walking away from him, she asked again, "Go on, tell me. Is there?"

"What do you mean?" It was the best he could come up with. A sort of cold fear seemed to be clearing his head for him. There was no way she could dump him now; he owed her too much. He needed her too much.

Jesus, he wished he'd never met her.

"Do I have to spell it out for you?" Vanny turned to him, her eyes wide. Slowly, her voice quivering, she asked, "Is there another woman?"

He was quite pleased at the laugh he gave. "So that's what you think!"

"What else am I supposed to think?" Her voice rose again. "You go out, don't tell me where, you let me down at the drop of a hat, you don't seem a bit interested in being with me . . ."

"I'm scared of commitment." He ran his hands through his hair, did the vulnerable, shy look that seemed to bring out the mothering instincts in all the women he'd ever known. "Me folks had a terrible marriage." And, then, his voice faltering and stumbling, he told the same story to Vanessa that he'd told to every other woman who had wanted to get too close to him.

And, as usual, it worked.

Ciara attacked her the minute she walked in the door. She wasn't in the mood for a row, her head was hammering and after the rotten day she'd had, all she wanted to do was bury her head under her bedcovers and forget all about it.

"How could you?" Ciara asked from her position at the table. "How could you, Meg?"

It was the hostile look in her eyes that frightened Meg more than the bewildered way she asked the question.

"How could I what?"

"How could I what?" Ciara mimicked. She stood up from the table and stared steadily at her. "Why didn't you tell me you met Greg at the racetrack last week?"

"Well, I . . ." she floundered as Ciara's face darkened. "I just forgot. Why, is it a big deal?"

"Apparently," Ciara said sounding ultra-polite, "he was under the impression that I desperately wanted him back."

"Was he?" She felt sick.

"Yes." Ciara nodded grimly. "He was."

She tried to laugh. It sounded crap. "All I said was –"

"All you said! All you fucking said! You as good as told him that I couldn't live without him. That I was so *sorry* for what I'd said!" Arms flailing everywhere, Ciara advanced on her. "Do you know, his fucking ego was so big he could hardly fit in the door of the pub!"

"Really?"

Even Ciara hated her now, Meg thought dully.

Ciara nodded furiously. "Really. Really. Really." Her voice was getting louder. "And he thought all he had to do was to click his fingers and I'd jump into bed with him. And all the time he talked, he was looking beyond me to the mirror behind my head. He never apologised, never said he was glad to see me, just thought, 'Oh, here's Ciara, she's *devastated* it's all off. She'll be an easy lay.'"

"Oh." Meg wondered when Ciara would stop the shouting. She'd had enough shouting that Sunday to last a lifetime.

"Oh!" Ciara nodded sarcastically. "Is that all you can say?"

"Sorry."

"Sorry. Is *that* all you can say."

"Well," she felt like a cornered rat, "I thought you *were* upset it was off."

"Not that fucking upset!"

"And you *did* miss him."

"Meg, are you a moron?"

She recoiled under Ciara's gaze. All she wanted to do was cry. And cry. And it wasn't just because of Ciara or her mother or –

"So why did you do it?" Ciara demanded. "How on earth could you *humiliate* me like that!"

"I didn't mean . . . I tried to tell him . . ." Meg gulped. "Well, I didn't *know* it would make you feel humiliated."

"And what way do you *think* it would make me feel? Having my friend tell my ex-boyfriend that I'm falling apart 'cause he's not around? How would you feel?"

"Dunno." Her voice was getting wobbly.

"If Greg wants me back, he apologises." Ciara folded her arms. "He stops eyeing himself up and starts acting interested in the rest of the world." She quirked her eyebrows. "Got it?"

Ciara was hard, Meg thought. She nodded. "Yeah."

"I don't need people telling him to phone me – right?"

"Right." She deserved all she was getting. Trying to be underhand had always blown up in her face. But it had seemed a great idea . . .

"So don't ever do that again, right?"

"Right."

Silence.

She began to fidget. There was no way she could live in the flat if Ciara was angry at her. The tension would kill her. "I'm really sorry, Ciara."

Ciara shrugged.

"Please believe me. Don't get any madder."

Ciara bit her lip. When Meg had walked in, she'd wanted to strangle her. All day, she'd fantasised about what she'd say to her, but Meg's refusal to get angry, her meek apology, her sad face made it impossible to say everything she wanted. It was frustrating. "It's not possible for me to get any madder," she said through gritted teeth.

"Oh."

"And don't start turning on the tears. It won't work this time, Meg."

"I'm not . . ." she stopped. Took another stab at it. "I'm not turning on the tears." Her voice came out in a rush and she wanted to die with shame. Rows always made her like this. It was like she was a kid and tons of emotions kept swamping her and she just couldn't get herself together. "All I said was sorry."

How was it, Ciara wondered, that whenever she confronted Meg about something, she *always* ended up feeling guilty? Her body sagged. What was the point of falling out with Meg? Knowing her, she'd only done what she'd done to help the situation. And Greg had got what he deserved, which was gratifying. "I dumped a pint over Greg and apparently I ruined his Lacoste shirt," she muttered.

"Oh." Meg didn't know what else to say.

"And he went mental and started shouting at me and slagging me off. He even dragged you and Jack into it."

"Jack?"

"Yeah, he met him with you last week. He said he knew him."

"Yeah, he does sort of. I think." She felt awkward. It was hard to talk naturally after a row; she always felt too self-conscious. "So, eh, what did he say?"

"Can't remember," Ciara shrugged. She did but there was no point in repeating it. Greg had only yelled it out of spite and she didn't want to hurt Meg's feelings. "Anyhow, it's well and truly all off now."

Meg wanted to say sorry again, but knew it would sound ridiculous. Instead she gave a sort of smile.

Ciara gave a sort of smile back.

That was all she could take. "'Night," she muttered as she bolted into her room leaving Ciara staring after her.

She dumped her weekend bag onto the ground and climbed into bed. Shoving her earphones into her ears, she closed her eyes and tried to sleep.

Big fat tears rolled down her face. And she didn't know why she was crying.

She woke up early. Well, it must've been early because it was still dark outside. She turned over and gazed at her alarm clock. Four o'clock. *Four o'clock.* She couldn't understand it, maybe it was wrong. She felt so awake. She located her watch on the bedside table. That too read four o'clock. It was weird, she thought, because she'd had trouble sleeping the night before and here she was, wide awake at some ungodly hour of the morning. She lay back down and that's when she noticed it. The way the darkness pressed in, all around her. Sort of like a blanket, over her head, over her mouth. Pressing in so that she couldn't breathe. She didn't know how the creeping terror that seemed to invade her from the chest and spread outwards, began. All she could remember was the panic. The way her mind slowly began to tumble into it. Like she was watching a kid cross the street in front of a car and she was too far away to do anything about it. The tumbling feeling of being alone. In the dark. Falling. Her arms wrapped themselves about herself, to stop pieces of her flying off into space. To keep herself together. To control the thoughts that were spiralling away from her. If she didn't move, she'd be OK. If she stayed where she was, nothing bad could happen.

DECEMBER

Chapter Thirty-three

Meg began to sort out the post. There was never that much in December. Most of the stuff was just brochures and junk mail from school-supply companies. Ripping open a brown envelope marked *Art Dept* she got ready to scrunch up yet another flash catalogue. There was a bill attached to the brochure. Pulling the bill off, she dumped the brochure in the bin. She put the bill at the top of her 'In' basket.

He'd meant to turn up for work, but the temptation had been too much. Yellow Halls Theatre Group had given him a cheque for one hundred pounds. It was to pay for the materials he needed to make his set design a reality. Domo, the weirdo director, had taken some convincing, but Jack had managed to persuade him, that only he, Jack, was able to get a knock-down price on the paints and sprays the group needed.

And it was true, he could.

And he'd meant to get the paints.

But then Shane had offered to cash the cheque for him. It had cost him twenty quid but it was worth it. Having eighty quid in his hand was just what he needed, especially as he knew exactly what horse to back to get a good return.

And then he could get the stuff for Meg's theatre group.

It was the afternoon by the time she began to sort out her in-tray. Normally she did it first thing, but she hadn't been able to concentrate. Her mind seemed to be all over the place these days. Waking very early in the morning didn't help. It was weird, she'd take ages to fall asleep and then, some mad dream would jerk her awake. And then it was impossible to get back asleep. Especially as all sorts of feelings seemed to pour themselves into her. It was like being an empty house where the wind rushed through all the broken windows.

It scared her.

The only thing that kept her afloat was Jack.

And he'd rung in sick earlier on. And now she was worried about him. Still, he'd told her not to worry, that he'd be fine. That he'd see her that night at rehearsals.

So, she thought, as she took the invoice from the basket, he couldn't be too bad.

The eighty quid was gone. All of it backed on one horse. He didn't care. It had been worth it, just for the

buzz. And it wasn't as if it was his fault. He never
should've bet on a horse wearing green colours. Green
colours never performed well on hard ground, everybody
knew that.

And, sure, when he got his next wages, he'd be able
to pay the money back. There were more races, more
horses.

And Meg'd understand.

He'd think up something to tell her.

That was the great thing about Meg; she seemed to
know exactly where he was coming from. Even when he
wasn't quite sure himself.

Meg studied the bill. Five hundred pounds. It wasn't
massive, but for art materials it was a bit on the steep
side. She scanned the bill for the school's requisition
order number. Finding it, she asked tentatively, "Linda,
have you the requisition book there?"

"Which one?" Linda was doing a lot of slamming
about. Trays and baskets were being viciously thrown
around her desk.

"For the Art Department."

Linda smirked. "So Jack rings in sick and now you're
pining so much, you need to see his handwriting?"

Meg ignored her. Ever since Linda had found out
about her and Jack, she'd chosen every opportunity to
sneer. She'd even declared Jack ugly. "The order book?"
she repeated.

"It's in my desk."

Linda made no attempt to get it, so Meg had to search through the desk herself.

"Not that drawer, this one!" Linda opened a drawer and, almost ripping the requisitions book apart, she shoved it at her. "Now take it and leave me alone!"

Stunned at the way Linda had nearly knocked her over, Meg opened her mouth to say something. Nothing came out.

The phone rang. Linda ignored it as she began slamming files about the place.

Sighing, Meg picked up the receiver. "Yellow Halls." She forced her voice to be chirpy.

"Is my bitch of a wife there?" a very slurred voice asked.

"Linda, it's for you – Leo." She held the phone towards her colleague.

"I don't want to talk to him."

"So, eh, tell him."

"You do it." Linda turned away. "Tell him to fuck off."

"I can't –"

"I heard that!" Leo roared down the phone. "I heard that. And you tell her I will if I could only get into my bloody house!"

"His house!" Linda screamed. "His house!" She wrenched the phone from Meg and began yelling down the line.

Meg slunk back to her desk, wishing she had somewhere to go.

" . . . my money that pays the mortgage . . . ha, when have you ever . . ."

Maybe she should go for a walk around the corridors.

" . . . don't you dare say it's all my fault! What?"

Or just have an early lunch. Sit in the staffroom on her own for the next half-hour. That was an inviting thought. She took her lunch box out of her drawer and made for the door.

" . . . well, of course I'd be there for you if you tried to stop . . ."

Hang on. This was looking promising. Linda always sounded like that just as she was about to tell Leo she loved him.

" . . . yes, yes I do. No, I can't." Giggle. "All right, I love you."

It was back to work.

When he got back to the flat, there was a letter for him. A big red bill from Byrne's. He didn't bother reading all the details, just scrunched it up and threw it in the bin. They'd be so sorry when he made it.

They really would.

Meg knocked on Aidan's door. It was the first time she'd ever called in on him without being invited and her knees were shaking. Still, he'd asked her to look out for any large invoices and to pass them on to him and that was what she was doing.

"Come in."

Pushing open the door, she peered around it. He had a stern look on his face which broke into a smile when he saw who it was. "Sorry, Meg," he stood up. "I was expecting that young lad, what's his name?" He frowned. "The second year lad that was in the car accident last year?"

"No." She shook her head.

"Oh, you know, the lad whose dad was convicted of drunk driving and whose little brother was seriously hurt?"

It had to be the fella Jack was always on about. "Brendan something?" she offered.

"That's it. Brendan Byrne." Aidan rolled his eyes. "Apparently he upended his table during religion and insulted Mrs Davis. She's very upset."

Mrs Davis was one of the TOFFs. Meg couldn't imagine her controlling a class of teenagers.

"Anyhow, if he arrives, he can wait outside." Aidan smiled at her. "So, what can I do for you?"

"Oh, it's nothing much." She put the order book and the invoice on the table. "It's just this. Well, you told me to look out for high bills and . . ."

To her surprise, Aidan snatched it off the table. Scanning it, he began to read. "Ten easels?" he exclaimed. "What the hell do we need those for?" His eyes dropped to the signature at the bottom. "John," he muttered. Pressing his intercom, he said, "John Dunne to Mr Gibbons' office please. John Dunne to Mr Gibbons' office please." He nodded at her. "Thanks."

She took it as her cue to leave. She wanted to leave before John got there because she was terrified he'd think she was trying to get him into trouble.

She'd just closed the door when she saw a sulky young lad walking towards the office. His school shirt hung out and his shoes were scuffed. Head down, he bumped into her. There was no apology.

Rubbing her arm, she glanced after him. The famous Brendan.

Well, there was a guy, she thought, half-annoyed, half-sadly, who, if he kept going in the direction he was heading, would more than likely get there.

Chapter Thirty-four

"So," Dominic asked, tapping his chest with his fingertips in a way that reminded Jack of Oliver Hardy, "you don't have anything for us tonight?"

"Nope."

Meg marvelled at how cool Jack seemed. He'd never given much of a toss about anything but with almost the whole cast of *The Onion Girl* aka *Naked* on his back he should have been a little flustered. Instead he lounged casually against the door, hands in the pockets of his denims as he stared them all down.

"See, Jack man," Alfonso said, "it's kinda hard to rehearse when we don't know the positioning of the set on the stage."

"Yes, for all we know, I could be standing *on* something instead of being positioned *against* something," Sylvia spoke up. "I know we're only amateurs, Jack, but really, I do think it might be nice to at least have a set."

"And you'll get a set," Jack nodded.

"Well, I don't see what the problem is," Avril said. "It's no big major deal as far as I can see."

"Ever think of investing in glasses?" Domo sneered.

"Huh?"

"Because you can't see very far at all, can you?"

Avril made a face and mouthed something that looked suspiciously like 'bollix'.

"Have you even *started* work on it?"

"Yep." Jack thumbed to Meg. "You've seen it, haven't you, Megs?"

"What – the set?" Puzzled, she looked at him.

"Yeah."

He was eyeing her encouragingly. Dumbly she nodded.

"And she thinks it looks great. Isn't that right, Megs?"

Another nod.

This seemed to satisfy them and, as Jack left, giving her the thumbs up, Domo started rehearsals.

Jack picked her up at ten. He didn't look at her as she climbed into the car beside him. Closing her door, she was jolted slightly as he abruptly started up the engine.

"Sorry," he muttered.

"It's fine." She did her best to sound cheery. But she failed. So much for being a good actress. But this was real life and in real life things were harder. She had to ask Jack why he'd wanted her to lie for him. Not that she minded. After all he probably had a good excuse, but still, she had to know. Only she didn't want to offend him. Maybe he would think that she wasn't being supportive and get angry. And she couldn't bear for him to think that she wouldn't support him 'cause she would. But it was hard to ask him.

And she didn't want a row.

"So how'd rehearsals go?" Jack broke the silence. He pulled the car into a lay-by and, switching the engine off, he turned and smiled at her.

"Fine." She tried to think of something funny that had happened, but her mind blanked.

"Good." He reached out and ran his hand down her hair, letting his fingers trail along her face. "I missed seeing you today."

"Missed you too." She was on autopilot. His face came towards her and his lips met hers. She kissed him.

He held her face in both his hands. Another soft kiss. He must have sensed her stiffen, because he pulled away. "Meg?"

"What?"

"What's the matter? Are you angry with me?"

"No." She'd said it too quickly. "Not really. Well . . . not *angry.*"

"So?"

The way he was staring at her made her feel guilty. "Just, just upset."

"Yeah?"

"About the set." She'd said it! Oh God, he'd hate her. "Well, I don't mind that it's not ready," she explained hastily, "not at all. But, it was just when you'd told everyone I'd seen it – well, I haven't." Jack said nothing. She touched him on the arm and smiled to show that she wasn't *angry*. "I think you made a mistake."

He shrugged her off. Turned and stared out the window. "So why did you say that you had seen it?" he asked.

She felt as if he'd hit her. "I thought . . . well, I thought that's what you wanted me to do."

"No."

"Oh. I see." Panicked, she wondered what the hell she'd done. "Well, I just got the impression that you hadn't started working on it and you wanted me to back you up. And so I did." She tried not to sound as desperate as she felt. "I only lied to help you out."

The words seemed to work. "So you'd lie for me?" He looked chuffed. "Really?"

"Yeah." All she wanted now was for him to hold her. To feel close to him again.

Jack debated whether to cuddle her or not. He decided to give it a few more minutes. He had to let his heart slow down first. Jesus, it'd been a close call. He'd been wondering how to broach the subject of the set but she'd done it herself.

There was only one thing remaining.

"I haven't been totally honest with you," he said, picking his words carefully. He had to come out the victim or else she'd dump him and he couldn't bear that. "I have started the set and I did think you'd seen it."

She wondered how he could have thought that when she'd never even seen the inside of his apartment. "And?"

He despised himself. "I spent a pile of cash on it and when I went to look for the cheque, it was gone. Some fecker must have stolen it."

"Oh Jack!" Deep sympathy. "Did you cancel the cheque?"

"It's been cashed. And I didn't want to tell your group because that director fella would only take it out on you."

He liked the way she hugged him. Meg wasn't spontaneous and, so far, he'd been doing all the running, which he didn't mind, but it was nice when she showed she cared by doing stuff like that. He hugged her back. "And Meg, I dunno what to do. I need that hundred quid."

"I'll give it to you."

"Naw, naw I can't –"

"It's worth it so Domo stays off my back." She gave him a smile so broad that he hated himself. "It's only money."

He loved her. He did.

He loved her so much that he hated himself.

But it was only money and, if she didn't mind, why should he?

⌒⌒

Chapter Thirty-five

Linda was really mad, Meg thought nervously, as Linda stormed into the office.

"The nerve," Linda fumed. "The bloody nerve." She wrenched her chair out from under her desk and sat down hard. Her hand shaking, she picked up her biro and pretended to start work.

Linda had been in Aidan's office the whole morning. Meg had thought that Linda had been doing more whingeing about Leo, but now she wasn't so sure. There had been no drunken phone calls from Leo or any abusive fax messages. He hadn't even come near the school with his offerings of flowers in the past few weeks. Things seemed to be going quite smoothly for Linda on that front at least.

"He wants to see you now," Linda said to her. The absence of hostility in her voice stunned Meg.

"Who? Aidan? Me?"

"Yeah, the guy that's trying to make out that I'm some sort of super-thief."

"What?"

Linda shook her head and waved her away. "He'll probably do the same to you," she muttered. "I always knew that he wasn't as nice as he made out." She stabbed her biro into her paper, causing it to rip. "I'm going to ring Leo," she announced. "We'll sue."

Meg left just as she was picking up the phone.

Aidan wanted to know the procedure for ordering equipment. He looked totally pissed off. Meg guessed that it was from being hemmed in with Linda all morning.

"Well," she licked her lips, hoping she could explain it to him without stumbling and making a fool of herself. "First, the department decides what stuff they need to order. Then a requisition form is filled out."

"An original and a duplicate?"

"Yeah. And this is signed by the department head and brought down to Linda and me. We price the goods, order from the cheapest suppliers and pay the bills when they arrive."

"Who brings the requisition forms down to you and Linda?"

"Anybody." Meg shrugged. "Sometimes the department head, sometimes just a teacher."

"And you and Linda hold on to the requisition books until someone needs them again?"

"Yeah."

"Fine." Aidan began tapping his pen on his desk.

"Great stuff." He thought for a second and then said, "See this order here, Meg." He shoved across the requisition order she'd brought to him a while ago. "See this order for ten easels. Do you remember ordering them?"

"Yeah, vaguely. I did part of that order and Linda did the rest."

Aidan rolled his eyes. "She says she can't remember."

"Well, I remember the ten easels."

"Good." It was the first time he smiled since she'd walked in. "That's all I need to know."

"So I can go?"

"Yeah, and Meg, bring me every personal file of every teacher in the Art Department, would you?"

"No problem."

"Thanks." Another smile.

When she got back to the office, Linda was gone on her tea break. She'd left a note on her desk saying that Meg's Nan had rung. Then underlined in red: *Don't you know personal calls are not allowed in work? Only for emergencies.*

She scrunched up the note and flung it at the bin. Linda, Personal Caller Supreme. Annoyed, she picked up the phone and began to dial. It was when she heard the numbers clicking through at the other end that she froze.

What, she wondered, if her mother answered?

Her Mam hadn't exactly been over-friendly since finding the empty whiskey bottle in her room. She'd been furious that her daughter could make such a show of herself in front of Danny. "It's lucky Danny is a discreet man," her mother had grumbled. "Otherwise, 'twould be all over the place."

"Loads of people get drunk," she'd said back. Of course she hadn't shouted it out, she'd sort of mumbled it, but still, her mother had dropped her gaze, sniffed and hadn't talked to her since. And even though she went down the following weekend, her mother had still been in a huff and she'd been deep-frozen by the atmosphere.

In desperation, she'd told Jack about it. Just about the getting drunk part and her Mam's attitude.

He'd laughed. "Don't bother going down," he advised. "That's what I do."

So she decided to give it a try. The guilt had killed her, so she'd rung home on the Sunday, only to be told that her mother wasn't in. The following day, she rang again, and her Nan had told her that her mother was not feeling great and couldn't come to the phone.

It had hurt.

And last week, she hadn't rung or gone down home at all. Jack told her she was finally cutting the tie that binds. "And fucking strangles," he finished, half-joking, half in earnest.

And now, her Nan was phoning.

And she loved her Nan.

She loved her mother too but her head couldn't take it any more.

And the strain of it all was making it almost

impossible to drag herself from the bed in the mornings and face the day. Only for the thought of seeing Jack, she wouldn't have bothered.

Meg decided not to take the risk of feeling worse by returning her Nan's call.

She turned from the phone and began half-heartedly to sort out the Art teacher files.

Her Nan rang again in the afternoon.

"Meg?"

A pull on her heart at the concerned voice. She glanced to where Linda was busy pretending to work, but really typing *Aidan Gibbons is a shit-head* over and over again onto her computer screen. Maybe rage would keep her from earwigging.

"Yeah, it's me."

"Just called to see how you are."

"I'm fine, Nan." She had to sound matter-of-fact. Anything else and she'd make a fool of herself.

"So – have you heard from your mother?"

"No." She didn't sound so composed now.

Her Nan was silent for a second. "I see." Then, "How did your weekend go? Your mother was convinced you'd been shot or something." She gave a small laugh.

It wasn't funny. She couldn't laugh. "Oh, so she noticed I wasn't there then."

"Meg! Of course she noticed. What's all this about? Is it about what happened with the whiskey bottle?"

"Well – she won't talk –"

Her Nan ignored her. "I know she can be hard. God knows, she's my daughter, but Meg, it was a shock for her, for all of us, seeing you in that state. Drinking a whole bottle of whiskey!"

"Well, it's not as if she's not used —"

"Now, now, let's not go over stony ground." Her Nan cut her short and continued in a softer voice, "What's the matter? Just tell me."

"Nothing," she said as firmly as she could. She began to knot the phone cord around her finger. "I just fancied a weekend up in Dublin. You're the one kept telling me to do it."

"Yeah, for yourself. Not to spite your mother or because —"

"I'm not spiting anyone."

"She'll get over it. You know your mother."

Meg said nothing.

"Is it because of Danny?"

"Listen, Nan," she muttered, "Linda's giving me dirty looks, I'd better go."

"Don't you like him? I know he's a bit of a gombeen but he's kind and he seems to love your mother and . . ."

She knew no one would ever understand. She didn't know if she understood herself. All she knew was that whenever Danny got mentioned, she felt hopeless. Empty. Worthless. "'Bye, Nan. Thanks for ringing."

"So we'll see you the weekend?"

She couldn't go down home. There was no point any more. "Maybe for Christmas."

If her Nan was disappointed, she didn't say. "All right so. Take care."

Alone in the flat that night, she had a drink. Just something to stop the terror invading her. And she deserved a drink because she'd cleaned the place from top to bottom.

Ciara, who hadn't been as friendly with her recently, had laughed and bunked off, delighted with what she was doing.

And now that the place was spotless, she was going to celebrate. Celebrate until she conked out.

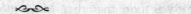

Chapter Thirty-six

She couldn't get up. Just couldn't. OK, so she'd a hangover and her mouth felt like the Sahara Desert, but it was more than that. Much more.

She'd woken at four and she'd decided that there was no way she was going to work that day. No way. And she didn't feel guilty about it. In fact, she didn't feel much of anything about it, except maybe the tiniest bit relieved.

She was going to have one day in bed.

Just one day buried under the covers with no one sniping or shouting at her.

Just one tension-free day.

At five to eight, Ciara knocked tentatively on her door. "Meg, are you awake in there?"

She wasn't going to answer. She didn't want to talk. She buried herself further under the covers, shutting out the chinks of lights that were attempting to coax her into the world.

She heard the door opening. "Meg, it's late. Are you not going into work today?"

"No – I don't feel well."

"I'm not surprised." Ciara sounded amused. "You were well on last night when I came in. Laura thought you were gas altogether."

Laura? Meg didn't remember seeing her. In fact, she could barely remember seeing Ciara. She pulled the blankets down from around her head and winced. The light hurt her eyes.

"And here was me thinking you were cleaning the flat and all the time you were planning to get locked." Ciara stopped. "And, Jesus, did you get locked!" she muttered.

Ciara's voice hurt her ears.

"Did Jack join you or something?"

"No." Down again under the covers. "Just felt like a drink."

"Oh."

"Bye, Ciara."

Ciara hovered hesitantly by the door. Meg didn't seem like Meg that morning. For one thing, she wasn't falling all over herself to apologise for puking up in the toilet the night before. Normally, she'd be down on bended knees begging forgiveness. And, despite hangovers, Meg normally never skipped work. And if she ever did, she'd beg Ciara to phone in sick for her, 'cause she was terrified of the girl she worked with. It really pissed Ciara off having to do her dirty work for her. And now, she wasn't being asked.

"Is Jack phoning in sick for you?"

"No."

"Will I do it?" She couldn't believe she'd asked.

She couldn't believe it when Meg shrugged slightly and muttered, "If you want."

Huh, if that's all the thanks she was going to get . . . "Naw," she snapped. "Maybe it'd be better off coming from you."

"Fine."

Stunned, Ciara gently closed the bedroom door.

She got up to get her latest book from the kitchen and to get a Disprin for her head. It wasn't every day she could stay in bed so she was making the most of it.

A good book, a cup of tea, warm bedclothes and she was set.

Before she climbed back into bed, she pulled the curtains tight so that no light could seep in from the street outside.

It was nice not to have to bother with anyone else. It was just her and the story in front of her.

Plunging herself into the book, she forgot about herself. Lost herself in its pages.

She only wished it could last.

At around four, the room grew darker. She put down her book and lay back in the bed. The good feelings were going. The day was ending.

Tomorrow she'd have to go back into work.

Tomorrow she'd have to start a whole new day, get through nine hours of being away from the flat. Nine hours of being with people and talking to people. Nine hours of tension and worry and making a fool out of herself.

And what made it worse was that Jack hadn't rung. Not even a phone call to find out how she was.

Life really was a load of crap.

She knew that as soon as the drink wore off, she'd be back to the rawness inside her. Back to the ache and the isolation.

Back to living.

He was living. This was life.

Fast.

Colourful.

Mental.

Athleague Guest was pounding home.

His voice and Shane's voice spiralled upwards on the air.

And when the horse crossed the line, it was over.

Over.

Until the next time.

∽

Chapter Thirty-seven

He had to pretend that everything was normal. Take it easy. Play it cool. It was unreal, history repeating itself like this. And he wouldn't mind, but he thought that Yellow Halls would be different. Have more vision or something. But, like the rest of the crummy world, Yellow Halls was a let-down.

Just as well *he* still believed in him.

She had to get up. It was the hardest thing she'd ever done, dragging herself from the bed. But, at least she'd see Jack and, if she'd the nerve, she'd ask him why he hadn't rung her the night before.

The day in bed had given her time to re-focus. To get things into perspective. Not that she'd *thought* about things, it was as if somehow they'd sunk into the background. And like a dying fire, if she didn't poke and prod at it, it would peter out – eventually.

He got up, washed, shaved, nodded to Peadar, who

must've been in good form, because he nodded back. At eight forty-five he left the flat, got into his car and drove in the direction of the school.

Oh God!

She hadn't phoned in sick yesterday!

Why – Hadn't – She – Phoned?

Meg's steps faltered as she neared the office. Things would have been all right if she'd only made that phone call. Now, she'd have Linda on her back the whole day, moaning on and on about responsibility, probably running to Aidan with all sorts of tales.

A couple of students passed her as she stood, frozen with indecision, in the middle of the corridor. They whispered and sniggered and she blushed. They were talking about her. She knew they were. And why not? There she was, twenty-seven and trembling like a kid. It was madness. She was mad. Taking a deep breath, pushing her hair behind her ears, clutching tightly onto her bag, she strode towards the office.

Her palms were sweating so much, it took two attempts before she got the door open.

Linda was there, head down, bent over a quiz in a magazine. It was something to do with finding out how compatible two people were. By the look on Linda's face, she guessed that what Linda had found out wasn't too favourable.

Great.

She wondered whether or not to say 'good

morning'. If she did, it would only draw attention to herself. But if she didn't, she might annoy Linda further.

Linda got there first. "You must have known," she said. Her voice came out through clamped teeth. Eyes narrowed, she studied Meg with a curled lip.

What was Linda on about? "Known what?" She strove for her usual upbeat voice. It made her sound unintimidated.

"About *him.*" The 'him' was spat out. "And all the time you let me think they thought it was me!"

"Sorry?" Totally confused, she stared at her workmate. "I don't get you."

Her confusion must have seemed genuine, because Linda's face cleared of its annoyance and took on another familiar expression. Triumph. Then that too went and a 'you-don't-seriously-expect-me-to-believe-you' look crossed it. "So how come you weren't in yesterday?" she snapped.

Here we go, Meg thought. "I was sick," she said. "I forgot to phone in." At least it was the truth.

"So why not get your flatmate to do it?" Linda asked. She was studying her curiously. Grinning almost.

"She . . . she . . ." Meg shrugged. "She forgot too." It was as if she was paralysed. A rabbit caught in headlights. There was something coming. She could feel it.

"Oh," Linda said. "I see." Briefly she turned away.

Meg took it as her opportunity to begin doing normal things like switching on her computer, checking her in-tray for important post, looking for a biro on her desk.

"I don't suppose Lover Boy was in contact?" The question was asked casually.

"What?"

"Well," Linda gave a laugh and turned back to her again. Eyes wide, she exclaimed, "If he had, sure you'd *never* have the *nerve* to show your face in here this morning."

"What?" She could barely get the word out. If something had happened to Jack . . .

"He was sacked yesterday."

Time stopped. She couldn't believe she'd heard right. "What?"

"What?" Linda mimicked. "You heard. Your fella got the sack yesterday."

"Fired?" She had to be dreaming. She had to. A sort of unreality was taking her over.

"Yep." Linda nodded smugly. "Turns out he was fleecing the Art Department. Changing the orders on the requisition books after John had signed them. Like, instead of one easel, he put a zero after it and thicko," she pointed to Meg, "ordered ten."

Linda sounded almost gleeful, Meg thought, her head spinning.

"And then, he took all the extra stuff and hocked it. Well, I suppose, he hocked it. I mean, what's a guy gonna do with nine easels?" Linda giggled. "Unless he indulges in some weird sexual practices!"

The thoughts of anybody sneering at Jack hurt her. This was the lovely gentle guy who adored her. Who made her laugh and told her she was beautiful. The only fella who'd ever understood her. Who made love to her and closed his eyes. "Don't," she whispered.

"Anyway, he's gone now and good riddance!" Linda picked up her magazine again. "We don't need people like that scum working here."

She sat, frozen.

"Now," Linda said, "let's see how compatible you were with him, Meg." She regarded her over the top of its pages. "Not *too* compatible, I hope."

"Fuck. Off." Through the numbness, anger began to push up. From the bottom of her toes, it seemed to surge up through her. How dare Linda laugh at Jack. How *dare* she!

"Ohhhh," Linda opened her eyes wide. "Nasty, nasty."

"You can talk," Meg said slowly. Her voice shook. "You can talk. What about all your gear that Leo stole? Or the gear your son stole?" She stood up. "Don't you ever, ever talk about Jack like that. Don't you dare."

Now it was Linda's turn to look shocked.

"And how's Clive getting on anyhow? Food nice in prison, is it?" She didn't care that Linda's eyes filled up. "'Cause the way he's going, he'll have to get used to it, won't he?"

"Stop!" Linda put her hands over her ears. "Stop it!"

"And how's Leo these days? Hanging around so he can rob more of your stuff?"

"Meg –" Linda was crying.

Linda's tears stopped Meg saying any more. Her whole body shook. It was a sickening feeling. The anger and the way she'd made someone cry. She'd never done that to anyone before.

She looked at Linda, at the way her make-up was smearing down all over her face.

Things began to close in.

She managed to grab her bag and escape the room before it came tumbling down on top of her.

He didn't drive for too long. Petrol was low and he didn't have enough money to refill the tank. After pulling into a lay-by for an hour, he made his way back to the flat. Both Peadar's and Vanny's cars were gone. Parking his own, he climbed out and gave the door a good hard slam. It trembled and he looked at it with distaste. Why the hell had he bought the stupid thing? Waste of good money. If it wasn't for his brother-in-law telling him . . .

"Jack?"

The voice made his stomach lurch. He was glad he hadn't eaten too much for breakfast. "That's me." He couldn't turn around and look at her. He couldn't bear to see the scorn in her eyes, even though he had nothing to be ashamed of.

Nothing.

A tug on his sleeve.

He gazed down at Meg. Big brown eyes, looking

as if they'd been crying not so long ago. Looking concerned.

"So you heard," he said, biting his lip.

"Not from you, I didn't."

Hope.

"D'you want to come inside?"

She nodded and put her hand in his. He squeezed hers and closed his eyes. She was just what he needed.

Hadn't he always known it?

She hadn't been inside his flat since they'd started seeing each other. It was a bit messy but bigger than hers and Ciara's. Some nice pictures hung on the walls.

"You do these?" she asked, as Jack plugged in the kettle.

"Yep. They're the ones I couldn't sell."

"Dunno why. I'd buy them."

"Naw," Jack laughed slightly. "I mean, I didn't *want* to sell them. They're some of me best work. That one there," he pointed to one of the sea and sunset, "is one I did last year. Out in Malahide."

"It's lovely."

"Yeah, it is." Jack didn't sound as if he was boasting. "I kinda like doing those ones. It's like taking a moment in time and keeping it forever." He shrugged. "Like, never again will the sky be exactly like that, not ever again."

Meg smiled. This was a different Jack to the one she'd seen in the car park. She'd been half-afraid to go near him, he looked so pissed off.

The kettle clicked off and Jack made them two mugs of tea. "Sorry," he said, as he dragged a packet of plain biscuits from a press. "There's never any food in this place. Peadar seems to have gone off eating or something."

Meg took one, though she didn't want it. Instead, she crumbled it up between her fingers. She watched Jack as he idly stirred his tea with his finger.

She wondered who'd broach the subject first.

He did. Without looking at her, he said quietly, "I was gonna pay it back."

She felt let down. So it was true then. He had fiddled the requisition orders. "But why?" she asked. "Why did you do it?"

He shrugged. "I'm not a thief, Meg. You know I'm not." She watched as he took a packet of fags from his shirt pocket. His hand shaking slightly, he lit up. "I needed extra cash. It was the only way I could get it." Eyes on her, he blew out a stream of smoke and asked, "What would you do if you'd a peach of an investment and no cash?"

She didn't think she'd fiddle requisition orders, that was for sure.

"I mean, I have the money to pay them back, but that bastard," he pointed the cigarette at her, "Aidan, he wouldn't hear of it. Just told me to go."

He was getting upset. She didn't want him to do that in front of her. "Jack —"

His head dropped. "I regret it, Megs, I really do."

414

"Stop, Jack."

"And, Jesus, the worst thing is, you must have such a crap opinion of me now."

He cared what she thought of him. A lovely warm feeling spread through her. She couldn't help the smile on her face or in her voice, though she tried to hide it. "No," she answered. "I mean, I mean, I was shocked when I heard, but, well, I know you, I know you're not a thief." Reaching across the table, she clasped his hand. "OK, so you made a mistake, but you've, well . . ." she laughed a bit self-consciously, "you've got me and I'll do whatever I can to put it right for you."

She loved the way his eyes seemed to light up. "Love you."

It was the first time he'd said it in ordinary conversation. This was too good to be true. She thought she'd die with happiness. And to think how rotten she'd been feeling just that morning. "Love you too."

Jack stood up. Still holding her hand, he pulled her to him. He looked at her for a while, his eyes searching her face. She was dying for him to kiss her, but all he did was look. And he looked sad. Or something. She had to cheer him up. "Kiss me," she ventured.

"Oh God, oh God, Meg . . ."

The rest of his words were lost in the hollow of her neck.

It was after three when he stopped loving her. When he stopped trying to prove to himself how much he loved her. He'd done stuff to Meg he'd never even thought of before. It was like the episode of *Friends*, he thought ruefully, when Joey couldn't make love so he was forced to consider the woman he was with instead of himself.

Well, his day had been like that. And it was the way he wanted it to be. He wanted Meg to *know* how much he'd loved her.

And it was the only way he could prove it.

Chapter Thirty-eight

It was the best night's sleep she had in ages. In fact, what should have been a horrible day yesterday had turned out brilliantly. She'd bought petrol for Jack's car and treated him to dinner and a few drinks. Both slightly merry, they came back to her flat and spent the night cuddled up on the couch. He'd messed about with the teletext, bored her with football results and made love to her on the floor.

She didn't care that Ciara was grumping about all the food he'd eaten. Ciara was turning into a right moan lately.

She was just jealous.

And, she thought, as she made her way to work in the pissing rain, even the fact that she'd to face Linda wasn't a big deal. Jack was still Jack and, no matter what Linda said, nothing would change that.

Linda wasn't in.

That was good.

Then Meg saw a note on her desk in Aidan's handwriting asking her to see him as soon as she arrived.

Oh God.

She read the note again. *Meg, see me as soon as you come in.*

There was no clue as to what it was about, but it had to be something bad.

Just when she'd thought she'd got everything straightened out in her head, this happened.

It wasn't fair.

She lowered herself into her chair and began to take deep breaths. *In. Out. In. Out.*

It helped steady her nerves before going on-stage, so surely it should do something for her now.

When she felt slightly more in control, she made her way to the principal's office.

"Come in."

Pen and notebook in hand, she entered. "You wanted to see me?"

"Sit down, Meg."

He didn't sound angry, that was good. Feeling slighter better, she perched herself on the edge of a chair. Her pen slipped out of her fingers and she bent down to retrieve it. Then her notebook fell. Aidan said nothing as she made a right eejit out of herself, trying to bend down without getting off the chair. In the end, she picked up her notebook and left the biro alone. Flattening down her hair, she tried a smile.

Aidan didn't smile back. "Meg, I'll get straight to the point. What happened with Linda yesterday?"

"Huh?"

"Did you let her know that you knew about Clive?"

"Well, yes, but –"

"I told you that in confidence."

He was annoyed.

"I know but –"

"You had no right to break it."

"I couldn't help it," she blurted. "She was slagging off Jack and I just . . ." her voice quivered and she had to stop for a second in case she was going to blubber, "I just flipped."

"Jack?" For a second he looked confused. Then, "Jack Daly? The teacher?"

"Yeah."

Aidan leaned back in his chair. He clasped his hands and began to rub them, one against the other. "So John was right," he murmured. "You were seeing Jack?"

It was none of his business. She badly wanted to say that. Instead she shrugged.

"That fella stole over two grand's worth of equipment from this school," he said. "He fiddled the requisition orders and then got *you* to order the stuff in."

She didn't want to hear that. "He was going to pay it back," she said. "I know him, Aidan. I know he's not a thief."

"Meg, the guy is bad news. D'you know how we caught him?"

She didn't have to listen to this. She didn't. But she couldn't just walk out. She tried to blank his voice out by concentrating on the way his mouth moved up and down when he talked.

"We double-checked the references of all our Art teachers. Any that had been validated by you, we didn't bother with." He leaned towards her. "It was because we trusted you."

She gulped. A vague memory was surfacing. Something about Jack having a personal file . . .

"But in the end, when we drew a blank on all the others, we started on the ones you'd checked."

She did not want to hear any more. Furiously she began to twist the spirals on the notebook spine.

". . . and the secretary at St. Enda's said that Jack had a personal file. It turned out, he'd been sacked for the same thing in his last place. The principal verified it."

"Jack's not like that," she said. "He's not."

"He got his reference from the principal long before he was caught on the fiddle."

"I know him. He's not like that."

Aidan shrugged. "It could've looked bad for you, Meg, you being his girlfriend and everything."

"What?" Stupefied, she stared at him.

"It's OK. I *know* you weren't involved. And besides, you were the one who brought me the invoice that helped track him down."

She'd never thought of that. That was *awful*.

"Plus, Jack went ballistic when we suggested it to him. It was the only thing that made him confess." He shook his head. "The guy is the most convincing liar." Then, "It wasn't that I thought for one second you had anything to do with it. It was John's idea – he figured if we dragged you into it, Jack would fold. Turned out he was right."

Jack had stood up for her. He'd dumped his job for her. It was the nicest thing she'd ever heard.

Aidan was silent for a second, studying her. She kept her face in neutral. Jack was not like he'd said. Everyone had him all wrong, just like years ago.

"Anyhow," Aidan said after a few moments, "that's not why I dragged you in here. I want to talk to you about Linda."

She couldn't have cared less about Linda. A small bubble of what *felt* like happiness was growing inside her.

"You upset Linda a lot, Meg. You've made me look bad."

"I didn't –"

"I know she's hard and I know she'd no right to slag off Jack in front of you, but neither had you any right to break a confidence. I think it would be better all around if you apologised to her."

She apologise to Linda? She must have heard wrong. "Me?"

Aidan nodded.

She *couldn't* do that. For the first time in her life,

she'd managed to stand up for herself. There was no way . . .

"So?" Aidan looked at her.

She was being sold down the river. All the work she'd done, all the times she'd covered for Linda and it was Linda getting the apology. She couldn't . . .

"Well?"

Her head dropped. What the hell was the point? "Yeah. Fine."

He looked relieved. "Thanks, Meg. It's better this way."

She stood up. She didn't return his smile. "Yeah."

She let herself out of the office and stood in the corridor. It was as if she was seeing it for the first time. It stretched out, miles in front of her. Miles and miles of hallway. Up and down. In and out.

Her legs felt tired as she walked it. The brown carpet was like desert.

And suddenly it hit her. Why she felt so bad most of the time.

It had to be the job.

It had to be Linda.

If she could just make a change in her life, things would start to improve.

All she needed was the nerve.

Chapter Thirty-nine

Peadar was hopping about, with a stupid manic grin on his face. He reminded Jack of Barney on speed.

"Tea?" he asked the minute Jack walked into the kitchen.

"Yeah, thanks."

Jack watched with growing suspicion as Peadar, still smiling, poured him a mug. He put it in front of him and asked, "Any chance you could not come back here this evening?"

Jack made a big deal of sipping his tea. "Dunno," he said innocently. "I'm on a day off work today. Got nothing much to do except hang around the place." He took a sick pleasure in watching the grin slip slightly from his flatmate's face.

"Well, I'll want the flat from around seven," Peadar said. "So could you maybe head over to Vanny's?"

"No can do."

The smile was gone. "Why?"

"She's going out with some friends tonight."

"So you'll be in all night?"

"Got nowhere else to go. I'd go for a pint, only funds are at an all-time low." He watched Peadar over the rim of his mug. "Anyhow, what do you want the place for?"

Peadar didn't answer. Instead he tipped some cash from the jar on the shelf. "Here." He shoved a couple of notes at him. "Use this. Go anywhere. Just don't be here at seven – right?"

Jack fingered the fivers. He wondered if ruining Peadar's night was worth a tenner. Still beggars couldn't be choosers. "I'll see what I can do." He picked his mug up and raised it. "Cheers." Then taking it into his room he shut the door and grinned.

It was like the time her mother had told her she was a disgrace. Her proudest moment and her mother had ruined it. She felt the same way now as she faced Linda across the office. Her coat dripping rain all over the carpet, the headphones of her Walkman dangling from around her neck, she knew she looked a sight. Looked like a loser.

Linda barely glanced at her. Just tossed her head and began to study the shine on her nails.

Meg clutched her coat about her, wrapping her arms around her body. She had to say it now, had to say it before she got sick with nerves over it.

"Sorry for what I said the other day." The words rushed over themselves. She dropped her eyes to the floor.

"What?" Linda flicked her a glance. "Did you *say* something?"

Meg felt disgust creep over her. Loathing. Might as well go the whole hog, she thought. "I said I'm sorry for what I said the other day." Hate filled her up.

"Mmm."

She began to make her way to her desk. It was funny, she didn't feel the way she thought she would. It was as if she was empty. Totally empty. The words she'd forced herself to say seemed to have drained everything out of her, except for the hatred.

"I suppose it'll have to do," Linda drawled.

She froze. This apology had kept her awake all last night, had woken her up at five that morning, had Ciara giving her weird looks at breakfast and asking her in a phoney concerned voice if she was all right and all Linda could say was '*It'll have to do*'! Without even thinking about it, she turned around and walked from the office.

"Hey –"

She closed the door on the rest of Linda's sentence.

Ten quid. It was better than nothing, he supposed. He decided to buy the paper, study form and then bet. Even the thoughts of it set his pulse racing; it was as if he was about to have it off with some gorgeous girl – though in that case the build-up was always better than the act itself.

Jack grinned at the comparison. Then stopped. Meg wasn't in that category. She was the one. The one he'd make into a queen when he got his big win.

And one day he would.

And they'd both be on top of the world.

She didn't remember the walk back to the flat. All she knew was that she was soaked. Drops of rain ran from her hair down the inside of her neck. More drops plopped from her nose onto the floor. Very slowly, almost as if she was too tired to do it, she peeled off her jacket. It fell on the floor and stepping over it she went into her bedroom.

She didn't bother to pull the curtains – the grey wet day was fine for looking at. Lying down in a foetal position on her bed, she pulled her blankets up around her.

Maybe if she left her job and started somewhere else, she could reinvent herself.

Maybe if she never went out, she wouldn't ever mess up again.

Surely if she stayed inside, nothing else could go wrong.

His money was gone, not that ten quid had got him very far, and he'd nowhere to go. He considered calling on Meg, but that Ciara one unnerved him. It was as if she was watching him all the time. Sure, she was nice, she was a good laugh, but behind it . . . there was something . . . Jack couldn't get a handle on it. Meg laughed when he'd told her. She just said to him that Ciara was jealous. And she'd looked up at him, with her brown earnest eyes and made him promise that he really did fancy her more than Ciara.

Meg was a bit weird like that.

Jack decided to leave it until the following night to see her. He'd meet her after rehearsals and bring her for a spin. That way it could just be the two of them.

So, being a complete prick and enjoying every minute of it, he looked at his watch. Half-eight.

Time to head home.

"Meg?"

She heard Ciara call but didn't bother answering. Just like the other day, being in bed was nice. Safe. She really didn't want to talk to anyone.

She heard Ciara switching on the lights, fiddling about with the heater and kicking the broken tiles around in the bathroom. She heard her heading into the kitchen and opening the presses.

"Got some chips, d'you want some?" Ciara yelled.

She didn't know what she wanted.

Without waiting for an answer, Ciara continued, shouting all the time, "That fella, what's his name, the blondy guy that works in the chipper?" She paused. "Jay or something. Anyhow, he gave me piles of chips. Told me to think of him when I was eating a long one." Plates were banged onto the table. "And I said, if he threw in some sweet and sour chicken balls I might get a clearer picture of what he was on about." A laugh. Then, her footsteps coming toward the bedroom.

Meg pulled the covers over her ears and closed her eyes.

"Meg? Meg? D'you hear me?" Ciara knocked and opened the door.

Meg could sense her standing in the doorway. She heard her approach the bed.

"Are you asleep?"

She knew she wouldn't be able to keep still. That her breathing would give her away. She turned to face Ciara. "Just tired," she muttered.

Ciara looked vibrant. So alive. The thought plunged her further into herself.

"Are you sick?" Ciara came in closer. Meg flinched at the concern on her face.

"No."

"But, but you're dressed!"

"Yeah."

"Did you leave work early? Or did you just go to bed when you came home?"

Her head wasn't able for all the questions. She wished Ciara would go and leave her alone.

"Meg," Ciara sounded cautious. She moved nearer the bed. To Meg's horror, she sat on it. There would be no getting rid of her now. "Meg, are things OK?"

Why did she have to ask the one question she didn't want to answer? The one question she didn't think she could answer. What *was* OK?

"With you and Jack, I mean?"

"Jack and me are fine." She spat the words out. She

428

knew what Ciara was up to. Trying to pinch Jack on her. But Jack had sworn he liked Meg better. He'd sworn it and she believed him. But Ciara was so beautiful, so funny. Maybe one day he'd go for her. "He loves me," she added.

"Good," Ciara looked relieved.

Meg closed her eyes.

"So, chips? D'you want some?"

Why did she have to make a decision? Everything she'd ever decided had been wrong in the past. "I don't know." She turned away and curled herself up.

"Meg, you have to eat. You hardly eat anything as it is!"

Ciara just wanted her to be fat. And spotty. So that Jack would hate her. "I'd eat if I was hungry."

"Yeah – right." Ciara didn't sound too convinced. Meg felt the mattress move as Ciara stood up. She heard her footsteps cross the room.

She heard the bedroom door close quietly.

Peadar was disgusted, Jack thought gleefully. His fancy dinner with Eileen all spoiled because he, Jack, had arrived home for nine.

Eileen said nothing. She merely folded her arms and quirked her eyes at Peadar in a 'I-told-you-it-was-too-good-to-be-true' manner.

"How's it going, folks?" Jack grinned amicably around. "Nice dinner there, Pead." He peered at their plates. "What was it, some kinda curry?"

"Shows how much you know," Eileen muttered.

"Aw, I knew you wouldn't be able to keep quiet

indefinitely," Jack winked at her. "You just love having a bit of ould *craic* with me, don't you?"

"Fecking crack your head open," Eileen answered.

"Ooouch!"

"I thought you were going out tonight," Peadar kept his voice calm.

"I did," Jack nodded. "But, come on, Pead, a tenner? To last all night? Anyhow, you only told me not to be here at seven."

"You knew fine well he didn't want you here at all."

"Now calm down, love –"

"In fact, if he'd his way, you'd be gone permanently, wouldn't he, Pead?"

"Aw, now, Eileen . . ."

"And what?" Jack asked, "Would you move in with him? You paragon of virtue?"

Eileen blushed and gulped.

Jack was so busy relishing her discomfort that the blow to his chin floored him.

"You shut your face and don't ever, ever talk to my fiancée like that again." Peadar wrapped his arm around Eileen and kissed her gently on the cheek. "Come on, love. Let's go."

Jack watched, stunned, as they left the flat. The shock of Peadar losing the cool paled into insignificance at the thought that the thick had actually got himself engaged.

He sat on the floor for ages rubbing his chin and wondering why he suddenly felt so hopeless.

⤜✦⤛

Chapter Forty

Ciara jumped as the door to Meg's room opened. It was like waiting for a monster to appear in a horror movie. All the previous night and, as far as Ciara knew, all that day, Meg had spent cooped up in her room. She hadn't gone to work, hadn't made dinner, hadn't done anything as far as Ciara could see. In fact, Meg was acting *really* weird, even weirder than normal. It was one thing never going out with mates and cleaning all the time, but quite another not even leaving the bedroom.

Ciara did her best to give a normal, natural smile as Meg shuffled out the bedroom door. Meg ignored her, just made a beeline for the mirror and began brushing her hair. She was still in the same clothes she'd worn yesterday.

"Are you going out?" Ciara asked, hoping her voice sounded natural.

"Yeah." Meg sounded bored. "Rehearsals."

"Good." Ciara smiled. "So, that means you're feeling better?"

"I feel fine," Meg answered defensively.

"Oh, right." Ciara racked her brains to think of what else to say. It was hard making conversation with someone who was so unresponsive. Normally behaviour like that would really piss her off, but hey, this was Meg, who was ultra-polite at the worst of times. She plumped for Meg's favourite subject choice. "Did Jack ring today to find out how you were? Betcha he missed you in work."

"He doesn't work in Yellow Halls any more."

"Oh." Bang went that subject.

"I'm leaving too."

Ciara's Coke fizzed everywhere. Down her nose it came and she started to cough.

Meg didn't bat an eyelid, just continued brushing her hair.

"*You're* leaving work?"

"Yep."

"Why? Have you another job? Are you going off with Jack?"

"No." Meg smiled slightly. "I just hate my job and I'm dumping it."

The casual way she said it stunned Ciara. "But . . . but . . . you just can't *leave* a job like that! Would you not wait until you get another one?"

"No." Meg turned to face her. "I've decided to go. Anyhow, with Jack not there, it's boring."

Ciara couldn't believe it. Over-cautious Meg dumping her job on a whim. "And why did Jack go? Has he another job?"

"No." Meg resumed her hair-brushing.

"So he just left Yellow Halls for no reason?"

"He had a reason."

"Which was?"

A slight hesitation before she said, "He just didn't like it much."

Ciara didn't believe that one. Despite the fact that Meg was acting strangely, she still wasn't a good liar. And, come to think of it, ever since Jack had come into her life, Meg had been different. At first she'd been happy, happier than Ciara had ever seen her before, but then, for some reason, over the past few weeks, it was like she was slowly shutting herself off from everyone. She didn't go down home any more, she seemed to avoid *her* at every opportunity – ever since the argument about Greg in fact – *and* the fact that she hadn't gone to work yet again and hadn't even bothered grovelling to Ciara to ring in sick for her, was *really* weird. The only things she seemed to want were Jack and the play. Idly, Ciara wondered if Jack was in some cult or other. Then she wondered if what Greg had told her was true. But it couldn't be . . . could it? Cautiously, she ventured, "Meg, can I ask you something?"

Meg didn't answer. Another thing Ciara had noticed recently. She seemed to drift off whenever conversation started.

"It's about Jack."

"Is it?" Interest brightened her face.

"Is he . . ." Ciara felt like a heel, "you know, in trouble at all?"

"In trouble?"

"Yeah . . . with money."

Meg went white. "Jack's not a thief," she said. "Who told you that?"

Ciara gulped, confused. "No one. That's not what I meant."

"What did you mean?"

Jesus, she wished she hadn't started. "Well, it's just, Greg said Jack owed money." Her voice faltered as she saw the dismay on Meg's face. "He said Jack owed money everywhere." Greg had also said that Jack was only going out with Meg to fleece her, but she didn't want to say that bit.

"Jack doesn't owe anybody anything." Meg bit her lip. "He's good. He loves me." Her eyes narrowed. "He loves *me*."

"I'm sure he does. It's just Greg said –"

"I tried to get you back with Greg, to keep you from taking Jack, but you wouldn't." Her voice was slow and deliberate. Her face seemed to shut down.

"What?"

"*Jack. Loves. Me.*"

"What?" Ciara laughed slightly, unsure if she'd heard right. "What was that you said about Greg?"

Meg shrugged. She shoved her brush into her bag and Ciara saw the way her hand shook as she zipped it closed.

"You think I'd want to steal Jack?"

"I'm going now."

Ciara opened her mouth to say more but Meg scurried from the room.

Despite her anger, Ciara was scared. Something was happening and she didn't know what.

There was silence as Meg entered the room. It seemed to her that everyone had arrived before her and had been talking about something, but as soon as she'd come in they'd all stopped. She smiled around, not wanting them to see how left out she felt.

"Hi," she ventured.

Avril nodded back and looked apologetically at her.

Dominic regarded her through narrowed eyes. "What's the story with your fella?" he spat.

"Now, Dom, we said it's nothing to do with Meg," Alfonso said uncomfortably. "She only . . ."

"Of course it's to do with her!" Dominic didn't even glance in Alfonso's direction. He kept his gaze fixed on Meg, as she stood awkwardly by the table. "You did recommend Jack to us after all!"

She flinched.

"And yet, despite this glowing recommendation, we still have no set."

"He said he'd have it today." All Meg's anger at Ciara drained away. She was left helpless again.

"Only he hasn't, has he?" Dominic opened his eyes wide in mock surprise. "Unless it's hiding somewhere . . .?"

"See here, Meg," Johnny's rich voice spoke up calmly, "we're not blaming you –"

"Huh!" Dominic made a face and folded his arms.

"We're not blaming you," Johnny said, ignoring

him. "But you've got to admit, Meg, it's pretty scary. We go on the week after Christmas and we've no way of knowing what the stage is to be like."

Meg shrugged hopelessly. What did they expect her to do about it? "Well, he *has* started it," she said. "He told me he had."

"So why hasn't he finished it?" Dominic sneered.

Everyone looked at her.

She looked down at her hands.

"We'll leave it at that, will we?" Avril chirped up. "Let's get on with rehearsing."

"Hell-o?" Dominic leaned across the table towards her. "Have you suddenly secured a promotion for yourself? Are you suddenly the *new* director of this play?"

"Jesus, no way!" Avril sniggered. "The less I have to do with this play the better!"

People laughed.

"I'll be seeing Jack later on," Meg said then. "I'll talk to him about it."

"Not if I see him first!" Dominic retorted.

They rehearsed the last scene. Meg alone on the stage. She imagined the set as Jack had drawn it. She let the feelings of being abandoned pour into her and the lines she'd learnt suddenly sprang to life. She stood, quite still, as she spoke. There didn't seem to be any need to move.

When she'd finished speaking, there was silence.

She thought she was going to throw up. Normally

doing a big emotional scene like that left her drained but on a high. But all she felt after she'd said the last word of the Onion's Girl's final speech was sickened. All she wanted to do was go home and forget about acting in this play. If only she'd the nerve to quit . . .

"Not bad," Dominic conceded.

"Not bad!" Alfonso jumped up. "Not bad, man? Are you for real? That was ex-sall-ant!" He gave Meg the thumbs up. "Just like I wanted it to be!"

"Are you the main director?" Dominic asked caustically.

"Well, not exactly, but come on, man, that was class."

"It was class if *I* say it was class," Dominic snapped.

"I think it was great too," Johnny said. He grinned at Meg. Then, "Hey, are you all right?"

"Fine." She got to her feet. She felt a bit shaky. It was probably because she hadn't eaten too much in the last few days.

"I loved it!" Avril said. "Look," she gave a big sniff. "I was *crying*. And I mean, the play is so strange that I didn't think I would cry."

Sylvia smiled stiffly. No doubt, Meg thought, she was under the impression that she'd be able to do the scene just as well. Still, the way the scene had made her feel, she would've let her, no probs.

Dominic decided that he wanted to run it again.

And again.

Every time Meg spoke her lines, Avril started to cry and sniff. She kept distracting Meg, who burped nervously every time Dominic glowered.

"Sorry," Avril apologised to him, during an extra-long blow of her nose. "It's just, well, she does it so *well.*"

"Oh for Christ's sake," Dominic snarled, "are you for real? It's only a bloody play for Christ's sake."

"Spoken like a professional!" Johnny sniggered. "A true lover of the theatre."

Dominic reddened but didn't reply. Instead he stood up, "Right," he said. "Let's call it a day for tonight."

"How apt!" Johnny clapped his hands. "An oxymoron spoken by a moron."

Only he and Alfonso laughed. The rest looked blankly at each other.

"Sure," Dominic smiled indulgently. "Whatever you say, Jon." Turning to Meg, he asked, "Is Jack outside?"

She had spotted the car through the window. "I think so," she mumbled. She hoped Jack wouldn't blame her for Dominic going off at him.

"Right, let's see what the story is." Dominic pulled his shiny PVC yellow and black mac around his large bulk and strode from the room.

"Poor Jack," Avril giggled. "He's about to be attacked by a bumble-bee."

Meg couldn't even raise a smile. Legging it as fast as she could, she followed the director out into the car park.

Someone was hammering on his window. Jack jumped and, flicking off the radio, he turned to see who it was.

That prick!

Dominic or whatever his name was.

Behind him he could see Meg's anxious face.

Giving her a grin, he reached over and opened the door. Dominic slid into the car with a speed that surprised Jack. Meg leaned against the door. Behind her, Jack could make out the other members of the group looking over across the yard.

"Hey, would you mind sitting in the back?" Jack asked, smiling easily. "It's just that Meg prefers to sit in the front. Don't ya, Megs?"

She smiled in at him. He noticed that she didn't look great. She was awful pale.

"I won't be long," Dominic said, not budging. "In a word, Jack, I'm here about the set."

"And in a word, Dom, I'm here for Meg. So if you wouldn't mind . . ."

"When are we going to get it?"

Jack tapped his fingers on the steering-wheel. He'd hoped to avoid this. There was no way he could produce the set on time at this stage. And that was even if he did have the money. "I'll let you know," he said. "Maybe later on in the week or something."

"That's not good enough!" Dominic's voice could be heard all over the car park. "I hope to Christ you haven't messed it up, Jack. I hope you *have* started it."

This was it. His opportunity. "Are you calling me a liar? Are you?"

"All I said was –"

"All you implied was that I've been feeding you a pack of bullshit about starting the set."

439

"Well, you've got to admit —"

"I'll admit nothing." He glared at him. "And I'll do nothing. No one shouts at me like that. No one accuses me of being a liar."

Meg gazed at Jack in admiration. Dominic's mouth was so far open he could have swallowed America. She wished she could make him squirm like that.

"I didn't accuse —"

"Let's get one thing straight. I'm the one doing you the favour, not the other way around."

"Yeah, yeah, I know but —"

"But not any more."

"What?" Dominic paled.

"Jack?" Meg wanted to die and celebrate at the same time.

"I don't like being treated or spoken to like that. Now, get outa me car and let Meg in."

"Now hang on here a minute —"

"You gonna get out?"

Dominic took a few furious breaths. He scowled at Meg as he got out. "You better make him change his mind," he warned. "Otherwise it'll be you —"

"It'll be her what?" Jack asked. He rubbed his finger along Meg's arm as she got in. "Well?"

Dominic went purple.

Meg gained courage from the angry set of Jack's face. She knew that no matter what she said, he'd stand up for her. And besides, suddenly, after tonight, she wasn't too sure that she wanted to be in the play. The feel of

Jack's arm on hers, gave her the impetus to blurt out, "I, I've decided to leave the play."

"What?" Dominic thundered. "You just can't –"

Jack gave a whoop of laughter and slammed the door on a horrified Dominic.

Meg tried to laugh too.

The car took off at speed.

She got in quite late. Jack had taken her to a pub, she didn't know which one. He'd met a few friends there and amid watching highlights of racing on the big screen, he'd told them all about his crazy girlfriend.

"Takes no shit from anyone," he'd boasted as he held the pint she bought him aloft. "That's why I love her."

And it was as if she glowed. And she fitted right in – they were all dead nice. That Shane guy was there and he'd been all over her like a rash. And for the first time it hadn't scared her. After all she'd been with Jack.

Still, the night had to come to an end. And as she lay in bed, the high went. The night pressed in and she thought her head would burst.

But she'd see him tomorrow.

Chapter Forty-one

She had the flat to herself. Ciara had gone out, thank God. It'd been hard work avoiding her for the last couple of days. She kept coming into her room and asking her if she was all right and telling her that she'd never take Jack. And then asking her what the matter was. And there was nothing the matter. Nothing. At. All. Just tiredness. And boredom. That was all. Nothing else.

Opening her bedroom door, she stole across to the fridge. As far as she could remember, there were a few cans still left. She'd had a couple last night, just to help her sleep and she badly needed a couple more.

Taking what was in the fridge in her arms, she scurried back to bed. If only she had Jack with her, she wouldn't need this. But she hadn't. He'd told her that his sister had a new baby boy and he had to go home for the christening.

She'd given him some money to buy the baby a

present. And he told her that he'd put his name and hers on the card.

Jack and Meg.

Sounded great.

She was just polishing off the third can when the phone rang. All week the phone had been ringing. And what was great about it was that most of the calls had been for her. Any other time, ever since she'd moved in here, the phone had only rung for Ciara.

And even better, she hadn't bothered answering the phone that week. Instead she listened to the calls on the answering machine and when the caller had said what they'd rung to say, she pressed the button and wiped them. It was a powerful feeling. Well, at the start it'd been powerful, now she didn't care.

Linda had rung. And rung. And rung. And cursed. And abused. And eventually given up. Her mother had rung, demanding to know why she wasn't in work. It was a 'how-dare-you-not-tell-me-that-you're-going-to-be-out-of-work' call. She had wiped that call before the end. And then everyone from the drama group had called. Begging, cajoling and asking her to come back to the play. Avril's call had actually made her smile. "Hi, Meg, it's me." Giggle. "Listen, Domo is after telling us all to ring you to get you to come back, sort of like a battle campaign. Anyhow, it's my turn." More giggles. "So please come back." Laughter. "But I don't blame you if you don't. He was such a shit to you. Well, he's just basically a shit anyhow. So, anyhow, my duty is done. Have a good Christmas if I don't see you." And then, "The only thing I will say is that Sylvia told Domo she'd do your part if you don't come back. Imagine! She's *so* crap. You'll be responsible for deaths as the audience stampede their way out of the hall." And just when Meg thought she'd finally finished, she added, "And guess what? I'll have to double up. Play my own part and Sylvia's. Can you think of *anything* worse?"

It was the first time Meg had laughed in days, but she still wasn't going back. Jack was so proud of her and anyway she knew she wouldn't be able to hack playing the *Onion Girl* for five nights.

And now, the phone was ringing again and, because she felt sort of relaxed and floating, she decided to answer it.

"Hello? Hello?"

"Hello."

"Aw, 'tis my favourite tenant!"

Could life get any worse she wondered. "No," she managed, "it's just me, Meg."

"Ohhh, very witty. Very witty. Now, I suppose you're wondering why I'm ringing you."

"No."

More laughter and snorting. "Well, 'tis about the shower. I can't get the part for it until after Christmas. Now, I've tried, I've worn me mouth out with asking everybody, but it's no go. So, you'll just have to make do with the ould bath until then."

"Oh. Right." Ciara would freak. Ciara cared about stuff like that.

"Well, aren't you a grand reasonable girl? That's why I like you. You understand. Anyhow, I'll be seeing you on the 27th. Righto! Happy Christmas."

He put down the phone and Meg wandered back into her room. The 27th? What was he on about? Maybe that's when he was going to do the shower.

Wearily, she pulled off her socks and climbed into bed. She drank the remainder of the cans and when they were gone, she lay down and felt the room spinning crazily. She hoped she'd sleep and sleep.

A furious hammering on her door woke her. Well, she wasn't too sure if the hammering was on the door or inside her head. Both probably.

Ciara, hands on hips, eyes glaring, stormed into the room. "Wake up!" She came towards her and shook her furiously. "Wake up!"

"What?" Blearily she focused on her flatmate. "I'm not going into work."

Ciara laughed and Meg winced at the scorn. "It's twelve in the bloody night," she spat. "That's of course if you're sober enough to read the time."

"I'm fine."

"Oh yeah," Ciara nodded her head. "Sure you are. You've just drank every single one of the cans in the fridge, haven't you?"

"I needed something to make me sleep."

"Cans I was saving for tonight!"

"Huh?"

"Oh, come back to my flat, girls, I've *loads* of booze there. Booze I paid for."

"I'll give you the money back."

"And what do we find. Nothing. Nada. Zippity-fuck-all."

"I'll give you the money for the cans."

"So they've all gone somewhere else, but not me, I couldn't stomach it. I had to have it out with you."

"I'll give you the money for them."

"Don't start whingeing, Meg. I've had it with your whingeing."

"I'm not. All I said was I'd give you the money for them."

"When? When you get another job?"

Ciara was really mad. Meg shrugged. "I've some money in my bag outside. Just get it."

"Just get it," Ciara mimicked. "Just get it." She fought for some control. "You drank a pile of my cans last night too, but did I say anything? Nope. I just went and bought more because, as usual, I didn't want to upset poor old Meg."

"Ciara –"

"But I'm done with it. You take and take, Meg, and never give one thing back."

"What?" Her head was spinning.

"I try and get you to go out, and do you? Nope. Fling it back in my face. And when you do, you drink and drink and ignore my friends. Or puke over a table and make a show of yourself."

Meg began to rock back and forward. Anything to shut the words out.

"I'm left baby-sitting you and then of course the next day, you're so remorseful, I feel sorry for you. And so, like a thick, I ask you out again and again. Well, not any more."

She tried to think of a tune she could hum in her head.

"And anytime we've problems with the rent, it's eejit here who tackles James. Oh yeah, Ciara is the tough one. She'll do it. Leave it to Meg and we'll get our rent doubled!"

A happy tune. Something to cut out Ciara's voice.

"Or the time the salesman sold you the encyclopaedias, I was the one who got you your four hundred quid back. Well, Meg, I'm sick of tiptoeing around you, of always being the one who fixes things. Last week you accused me of trying to take Jack from you, and after all I've done." Ciara's voice trembled. "You hurt me when you said that, but I ignored it 'cause I was worried about you. But it's just a ploy, isn't it? Be defenceless and no one can get angry at you, but it won't work any more. I've had it."

"Ciara –"

"I've been worried sick about you the last while, but now, now it's over. I know drinking all my cans mightn't be a big deal to you, but it's the last straw, Meg. If you want to stay in bed all day, do. If you want to live on cans and coffee, do. Jesus, if you want to hang yourself from the ceiling, go ahead. Just leave my cans alone and I promise," she gave a sour smile, "I'll leave your fella alone."

A slam of the door and she was gone.

Meg was glad. She didn't need her anyhow.

That's what she told herself.

Over and over.

Until she fell asleep.

It was a darkness or a brightness. She didn't know. But it was an escape. An escape from herself. The self that she hated. That she'd always hated from as far back as she could remember.

An escape from her body.

It was a tear in the fabric of her existence that allowed her to see the light.

Allowed her to reach for the thing that would bring her peace.

The quiet always came after the mental excitement. After the buzz. The quiet that allowed him to think toward the next race.

And the race after that.

And finally, when the races were over, he'd head home.

Drunk on victory.

Chapter Forty-two

He arrived back at the flat around noon on Christmas Eve. He'd driven Meg to her bus stop, given her her present and promised faithfully not to open his until Christmas day.

He hated Christmas. All that crap about goodwill to all men. When had anyone ever shown him a bit of goodwill? And he hated the way everyone cleared off home on Christmas as well. Look at Meg, a big long face on her, trying to convince herself that she really wanted to head home when he could see she didn't.

Not like him. He did what he pleased.

Another thing about Christmas that he hated was that it was so quiet. No sports fixtures. No racing. Not until Stephen's Day.

So he needed badly to cheer himself up.

And despite the promise he made to Meg, he was going to open her present the minute he got back to the flat. It'd be nice to see what she'd bought. And maybe it would be worth a few quid. Despite putting his car in the 'Buy and Sell', he'd had no offers for it yet, so he needed any spare cash he could lay his hands on.

Hiding the present in a plastic bag so no one else would see it, he closed the door of his car and made his way to the flat.

She didn't even bother replying to half of Mikey's questions as she sat on his bus. All she kept thinking was how the hell was she going to survive Christmas. She hated it. But this year it was worse than normal. For one thing Danny McCarthy was invited to Christmas dinner and for another her Nan had moved into Daisy's house until it sold, so it would just be her and her mother in the evenings. If even that.

It felt strange to be out in the world again. Alien. The only times she'd been out recently had been with Jack, in his car. And normally he turned up late so it was dark by the time she met him. It was nice being with him though, getting away from Ciara, away from her silence. But leaving the safety of her room was scary. And she felt scared now as she sat on the bus bringing her home. The only thing that stopped her freaking out was Jack's present which was wrapped in brown paper, with a handpainted picture of a big smily bear. Meg clutched it hard. It was comforting to feel the sharp edges digging into her hands.

And it smelt of Jack. Smoky and manly.

She couldn't wait to open it up on Christmas Day.

"Out!"

Peadar was standing in the doorway blocking him from getting in. His face was red and furious-looking. Nothing new for Peadar these days, Jack thought. He attempted to push past him but was surprised when Peadar gave him a hefty shove backwards.

"What the hell —"

"You are not staying here any more," Peadar said. "I've had it Jack. I've had enough."

"Will you get a grip? What's that girlfriend of yours saying about me now?"

"Eileen? Eileen hasn't said a thing. Eileen's gone home."

"So?" God, he hoped Vanny wouldn't witness this. He was due to call up to her in an hour's time before she too left to go home. Desperately, he tried to calm Peadar down. "What do you think I've done now?"

"What do I *think*?" Peadar gave a semi-hysterical laugh. "Think? By Jaysus, I more than think it."

"Well?" He tried to look innocent. Bewildered. And he was.

"I had two callers this morning."

"Yeah." He wished the guy would get to the point. There was no way he could stand in the corridor arguing with him all day.

"From Byrne's."

"Byrne's?" His heart skipped in his chest. "And?"

"Ooh, they were looking for you. A small matter of a debt you owe them."

"Yeah," Jack shrugged. "I know all about that. It's no big deal."

"No big deal!" Jack thought Peadar was going to have a seizure. "Five bloody grand is no big deal?"

"They'd no right to tell you my business." He tried to sound furious.

"Five grand!" Peadar repeated.

"Aw, grow up, Pead. It's nothing these days." Once again he tried to shove past him.

"You're the one who has the growing up to do!" Peadar began to poke him in the chest with his finger as he advanced on him. "I am not having two guys calling around here demanding money off me. God knows what they'd do."

Jack rolled his eyes and couldn't help the sneer in his voice as he retorted, "Pead, it's not the fuckin' Mafia we're dealing with."

"*You're* dealing with," Peadar corrected. He folded his arms and shook his head. "I dunno, Jack. I dunno what's happened you." His voice hardened. "You've an hour to get your stuff together and if you're not ready by then, I'll kill you."

He meant it. For the first time since Jack had known him, he knew that Peadar meant business. Talk about overreacting. Pushing past him, giving him an elbow in the ribs, he marched into his room and slammed the door.

"Happy bloody Christmas to you too," he muttered.

"Happy Christmas!" her Nan yelled from the front door.

Meg raised her hand in acknowledgement. It was such a relief to see her there. She didn't want to have to face her mother on her own. No doubt there'd be a question-and-answer session as to why she'd been missing from work.

As she neared the house, the look of concern on her Nan's face made her uncomfortable. "It's great to see you," her Nan said, her voice totally unconvincing. Then, "I hope you haven't been dieting again."

Meg smiled. Her? On a diet? No diet had ever managed to get rid of her huge hips and flabby thighs. "And what would be the point of that?" she said. "Sure it's Christmas."

"You're thinner," her Nan said. She looked her up and down, "Still, I suppose with all the baggy clothes you wear, it's hard to tell."

"I wear the baggy clothes to cover the flab."

"Well, it works." She smiled at her. "Come on inside. Your mother's gone off to buy Danny his Christmas present. She's letting him choose it himself."

"Why, what's he want? A pair of wellies?"

"Meg!" Her Nan gave her a mock slap and started to laugh. "Will you stop! The poor man!"

Meg bit her lip. It wasn't meant as a joke. Still, that was the problem with her. No one ever understood what she was trying to say. She changed the subject. The last thing she wanted to hear about was how happy Danny was making everybody. "So, any news about Daisy?"

Her Nan whooped and clapped her hands.

Motioning to a chair, she ordered, "Sit down there and we'll have a cuppa and then I'll tell you *all* about it."

"Can I move in here?" As Vanny's eyes lit up, he clarified hastily, "Well, it's just for a few days."

"Sure," she opened the door wide and he knew she was watching him as he dumped his plastic bags onto the floor.

"Got no case," he muttered, feeling ashamed.

"So what's happened?" She didn't sound sympathetic, only thrilled. "Did you finally see the light about scumbag Peadar or do you just want to be with me?"

He didn't want to have to answer. No matter what he said, he'd end up in deep shit. Instead he looked at his watch. "What time did you say you were leaving?" he asked.

"Anytime you want." She came towards him and placed her hands gently on his shoulders.

Closing his eyes, he tried to imagine it was Meg. "Love you," the words slipped out.

"Oh, Jack, I've been wanting you to say that to me for ages now." She rubbed herself against him. "I love you too."

Oh Christ.

To Meg's surprise, her mother never mentioned the un-returned phone calls. Instead she welcomed her home and asked how she was.

"Fine."

"You look pale." It sounded like an accusation.

"Aw, sure hasn't she spent three hours on Mikey's bus? No wonder she's pale," Danny winked at her. "Hey, Meg?"

"*Four* hours actually."

"Well, it's a wonder you can walk and talk at all then, isn't it?" he chortled.

Meg wondered if the man ever stopped smiling.

"So what wonderful present did Maureen buy you, Danny?" Her Nan began to poke around in the shopping bags.

"Arragh, just a jumper. Sure what more do I need. Haven't I got a great woman in my life now."

To Meg's revulsion, he pinched her mother on the backside.

And her mother *laughed*.

"I'm going to bed," she announced. "I'm tired." All this Christmas cheer was going to make her ill.

The three looked at her.

"OK," her mother said. "Off you go."

As she trudged up the stairs, she wished like anything that her mother had attacked her over not being down in weeks and over not returning her calls.

Anything rather than being semi-ignored.

He told Vanny that he'd be going home Christmas morning. She gave him her keys and told him to make himself at home. She'd see him the day after Stephen's Day. She gave him some money to get food in for himself for that night. Then, slipping out of bed, she showered, dressed, kissed him and left.

He tried to sleep but he couldn't.

He felt really bad inside himself.

He told himself it was just because it was Christmas.

Chapter Forty-three

He bought some cans and a giant packet of crisps for his Christmas dinner. Sitting in front of the telly watching the Christmas Day movies, he suddenly remembered Meg's present.

It was in one of his bags in Vanny's room. As he hauled himself up from the sofa, where he'd been sprawled out watching *Indiana Jones*, he started to pray that Meg hadn't bought him a watch. Vanny had already given him one and Jack knew he'd have to wear it all the time to prove he liked it. It'd take ages before it could be flogged.

If Meg had bought him the same, it'd be like musical watches.

On shaky feet he managed to manoeuvre himself across the dining-room and into the bedroom. Finding the bag, he tossed aside the card and proceeded to rip open the parcel.

She'd bought him a set of brushes.

Expensive ones by the look of them.

The thoughtfulness of the gift gave him a lump in his throat. Reverently he fingered them.

Then his heart sank. Christ, where'd he find a buyer for a load of artist's brushes? It'd been bad enough trying to get the pawn shop to take the artist's easels he'd borrowed from the school, but brushes . . .

Still, maybe Shane might oblige.

He put the brushes beside the phone to remind himself to ring Shane the following day.

There was so much food. Looking at it made her feel sick. The turkey was big enough to feed them for the next ten years; the ham looked like a full-size pig all on its own.

"Killed by me own hands," Danny stood up to cut the meat. He flexed his knuckles proudly.

"Will you get on with it," her mother said, "and don't be leaving us starving." Her normal sharp tone was missing – she looked tenderly at Danny and smiled around the table. "Isn't he awful teasing us like this?"

Meg gave an obligatory grimace and looked at the rest of the stuff on the table. Potatoes, sprouts, carrots, enough of each to rival the EU food mountains. Stuffing. Sauces. About three types. The only one she recognised was cranberry.

Danny cut the meat and put it on a big plate in the middle of the table. Everybody began to help themselves.

"Are you not having some, Meg?" her Nan asked.

She selected the smallest piece of ham she could find and laid it on her plate. "I don't really eat much meat," she mumbled. Damned if she was going to eat *his* meat anyway.

"Huh, must be that place you're living in," her mother sniffed. "All those fumes, turned you off decent food. I suppose you live on chips and pizzas?"

"No." Meg shifted uncomfortably. Now she'd gone and done it, made her mother angry. So just to appease her, she took some more ham.

"Well, I guess we'll see for ourselves next week," her Nan chuckled. "Sure won't we be up seeing you in your starring role."

The ham suddenly tasted very dry. She took a huge swig of wine to help it go down. The three were looking proudly at her. Even her mother. "Eh, the play's off," she said.

Her mother began to choke on her food. Danny stood up and began banging her on the back.

It was a distraction she was glad of. Time to think up some good excuse.

When her mother had recovered, she asked, "Are you saying that there is *no* play any more?"

She sounded annoyed.

Meg nodded. "Yeah, the director got sick." She didn't feel a bit guilty saying that.

"When?"

"Just a little while ago."

"So why didn't you let us know?" her mother demanded.

"Well, I –"

Her mother put down her knife and fork and leaned over towards her. Her voice was sharp and Meg flinched. *"Do – you – know* that I've booked Mikey to drive us up? He said he'd do a special deal and drive twenty of us up in his minibus for the night."

"Oh."

"Oh!"

"Calm down now, Maureen," her Nan said. "There's nothing so bad that it can't be fixed."

"Be quiet, mother!" Shaking her head, Mrs Knott continued furiously, *"Do – you – know*, I've the *whole* parish told. Every dog in the street knows that my daughter has got a starring role in a new play."

"Sorry."

"Sorry," she spat. She laughed bitterly and her voice rose, "But I suppose I should have known it'd fall through. I dunno, playing prostitutes seems to be the only thing you *can* do."

Meg winced.

"Now, Maureen, don't let's drag that ould chestnut up."

"Oh, that was a fine night. My own daughter up on stage playing a prostitute. It was the talk of the place."

"I got an award for it." Her voice shook. She hoped she wouldn't cry.

"An award! What good is an award when you made

a show of yourself? I've never lived that down. And now, here you go again. Letting me down in front of everyone. They'll all be laughing again, thinking I made the whole thing up!"

She wanted to leave, to go to her room but it was as if she was frozen to her place. She supposed she deserved the abuse. She *should* have told her mother the play was off.

"I dunno, you seem to make it your mission in life to disappoint me. Like father, like daughter, I suppose."

"Now, Maureen, you don't mean that." Danny gave a shaky smile over at Meg.

"I'm sorry, Mam." It was only because her mother was annoyed that she was saying these things. She didn't mean them.

"What use is sorry?"

Meg gulped. It hurt to have the word sorry flung back in your face. That's what use it was. It left you open if the other person didn't want to hear it.

She saw, through the foggy way her mind was closing up, Danny putting his arm on her mother's and asking her to calm down. For God's sake, to calm down.

Her mother shook him off.

Without thinking, Meg stood up from the table. Found herself walking out of the room.

Nobody seemed to notice.

Danny and her mother were yelling at each other.

When she closed and locked her bedroom door,

their voices became muffled. It was like years ago. Horrible but familiar and comforting.

He passed out around midnight. The telly stayed on.

Things seemed to have quietened down. No one had come near her since the row at dinner. Very quietly, she took Jack's present from her bag. She'd been saving it for when she was on her own. For when she needed cheering up.

Gently she unwrapped it. She wanted to keep the brown paper and the lovely picture he'd drawn.

Inside, was the picture she'd seen on the day she'd gone into his apartment. His favourite one, the one he'd said that had captured a moment in time. It was signed JD.

Holding it to her, wrapping her arms around it, she knew she'd treasure it always.

Chapter Forty-four

She dragged herself out of bed the next morning. She felt rotten but it was important that she talk to her mother, to apologise for letting her down over the play. She'd no idea her mam would take it so hard – it was just a sign of how proud of her she was.

Pulling on her dressinggown, she left her room and went downstairs.

Her mother was in the kitchen, her head down on the table. She too was in her dressinggown. A cup of tea was poured.

Slowly Meg ventured forward. "Mam," she said hesitantly.

"What?" Her mother still sounded angry, though she didn't lift her head.

"Sorry about the play."

"Fuck the play!"

She jumped. Her mother never cursed. Well, she hadn't cursed in a long time. Meg wondered if she'd been drinking. That sometimes had a bad effect on her . . .

Her mother turned her head sideways and asked through gritted teeth, "Do you *know* what happened last night after you swanned out of the kitchen? Have you any *idea* of the trouble you caused?"

"Trouble?" Meg asked faintly. She reached back and felt the sides of the door for support.

"Yes – trouble!" Mrs Knott sat up straight. Deliberately controlled fury spat the words from her mouth. "Danny only called off our engagement!"

"Engagement?"

"Yes, engagement!" She nodded her head so vigorously she nearly banged it off the table. Clutching her head in her hands, she closed her eyes.

She *had* been drinking.

"It was meant to be a surprise for after dinner, but you," she looked at Meg with such vehemence that Meg recoiled, *"you – spoilt – it – all!"*

She felt sick. Hopeless. There was no going back now.

"You with your –"

"You spoilt it yourself." Her Nan's voice cut through what was going to be a tirade from her mam. "You spoilt it yourself, Maureen," her Nan said again.

Her mother's hostility re-focused on her Nan. "You stay out of it!"

"No, no, I won't." Moving forward, she put her arm around Meg. "It's not Meg's fault and you know that as well as anybody."

"Oh, sure. Sure I do," her daughter said sarcastically. She glowered at the two of them. "Thick as thieves."

"I'm only trying to stop you blaming the girl for something you caused yourself."

"She's made a show of me."

"She hasn't!" Meg jumped at the anger in her Nan's voice. Advancing on her daughter, her Nan continued, "I've watched you for years blame that child for everything that goes wrong in your life. Your marriage, your drinking, everything. And I'm not going to stand by and watch it over again."

Her daughter stood up to face her. "Well, if you didn't spend all your time interfering in *my* life, I might actually have had one."

"Oh aye. Some life. Getting pregnant, getting married, getting stoned. Taking it out on the one person that actually managed to still love you through it all."

"You? Huh?" Mrs Knott threw back her head and laughed.

"No," her Nan shook her head. "Meg."

"Her?"

The way she said 'her' hurt Meg more than anything else her mother had ever said to her. Feeling ashamed, she stared hard at the floor.

"Her?" her mother repeated. "She's been nothing but trouble since the day she was born. Because of her, I had to marry that – that – gobshite John."

"No one forced you."

"And then she grew up and started mixing with crazies. Hanging out with the dregs of the neighbourhood and crashing neighbours' cars and never doing well in school." Her voice spiralled upwards. "And hiding about the house like some kind of a ghost. We couldn't get a word out of her. And then, acting being a prostitute. Making me the laughing-stock of the place. And after that moving away to Dublin and working in some crummy two-bit job and coming home at weekends and annoying me senseless!"

Her mother didn't mean it.

"She kept you together though. She stuck by you when you drank the pubs out of it after John left."

She'd scoured the pubs with Jack night after night and together they'd dragged her mother home. She'd wiped up puke. She'd cuddled, petted, wiped tears.

"I never drank that much! I didn't need her or you. In fact if I didn't have either of you, I probably would be better off now."

Her mother couldn't mean it.

"I only came to live here to give Meg a break. To get her out of the house and away where she could have her own life. Somewhere she could actually *laugh*. I think I could count the number of times I've heard that child laugh. And, you, you Maureen, you cling to her when it suits you."

She was still there. They were talking about her as if she was just a 'thing'.

"I didn't mind any of it, Mam," she said. She was startled at the sound of her own voice. Half-afraid, she glanced upwards as she continued, "I'd do it again."

"What?" Her mother laughed. "Do *what* again? Let me down, is it?"

"No –" She rubbed her hands over her face and moved towards her mother. "Please, Mam, I'm sorry about Danny."

"It's not your fault, Meg." Her Nan's voice was soft.

"Stay out of it, mother!"

"Meg, you did nothing wrong."

Meg didn't care. She didn't care who was to blame. All she wanted was her mother to forgive her. To take back everything she'd said. "Mam?"

"Danny was shocked at *you* last night, Maureen. Not at Meg."

"Mam?"

"Get – out – of – my – sight."

There was a blackness in her head. A refusal to acknowledge the rejection. "Mam?"

"Get out!"

"Leave it until later," her Nan put a hand on her shoulder, "until she's calmer."

The crashing of a cup onto the floor-tiles made both of them jump. Tea splashed everywhere.

"Just get out!" her mother shouted. "I'll never be calmer. Not ever again." Panting furiously, she advanced on Meg, *"Get out of my sight now!"*

And it was the way her mother looked at her, the

way she'd always looked at her, only she'd never seen it before, that suddenly Meg knew.

Knew that her mother didn't like her.

Didn't probably even want her.

It seemed like an eternity before she was able to turn away and start walking from the kitchen. Her Nan reached out and said something, she didn't know what, and then her Nan tried to touch her.

Why would she want to do that?

She shook her off.

He dialled Shane. His own mobile was cut off so he had to use Vanny's. Shane said he'd give him fifty quid for the paint brushes. They were worth more but Jack didn't argue, especially when Shane said, "I've a dead cert for tomorrow, Jack. Put your money on Athleague Guest in the Paddy Powers."

And Jack just knew, with a name like that, the horse couldn't falter.

It was all in the name.

Chapter Forty-five

"Now, Sylvia, this is the part where you meet your lover."

"Yes, yes, I know." Sylvia arranged her face to suit the scene.

"Hey, babe, what are you doing?" Alfonso, looking perplexed, peered at her.

"Don't call me babe," Sylvia snapped.

"Oohh, Pamela Anderson, eat your heart out!" Johnny yelled.

"Don't compare *me* to Pamela Anderson."

"Naw, naw, sorry!" Johnny held up his hands in a gesture of surrender. "Pamela can *act.*"

"Are you going to take this seriously or not?" Sylvia demanded. "And if so can we get on with it, please?"

"Tony, up here," Dominic pointed to a position on the floor. "Now, remember, for you it's lust at first sight."

"Hate that," Avril sniggered. "There's some acting to

be done there, Ton. Falling in lust with a fifty-year-old."

"Don't remind me." Tony got up and sauntered to the middle of the floor.

"Now, you really want her, Tony – right?"

She couldn't eat a thing at breakfast. Sixty quid a night and she couldn't eat a single thing. There had been only one room left in the hotel when she'd arrived yesterday. She guessed she'd been lucky to nab it, but for all the sleep she'd got, she might as well have bunked down on the street.

It was important that she stayed awake so that she could control her head. She'd watched TV, ordered drinks to her room, read the pile of women's magazines she found in the foyer. And now she was knackered.

A waiter in a Santa hat was serving her table and he couldn't understand for the life of him why she only wanted a cup of tea.

"I can't understand for the life of me why you only want a cup of tea," he chuckled.

Meg shrugged. "Hard night last night," she gave a rueful laugh.

"Oh, aye," he winked knowledgeably. "It's a raw egg you should be eating so."

"Naw, I'll just settle for tea, thanks."

She knew she looked a sight, a lone woman, staring morosely at the red and white tablecloth while all about her were people enjoying themselves.

Not that she cared what anyone thought.

She comforted herself with the idea that in a few hours' time she'd be back in Dublin. She could go to bed and stay there. She could ring Jack and get him to come over and he'd put his arms around her and tell her he loved her.

"Avril, it's your scene now."

Avril frowned. "Me?"

"Yes," Dominic said, in what for him was a patient voice. "You're playing the Nanny now, d'you remember?"

"Oh yes!" Avril made a face. "Oh God! Oh God!" She flapped her hands around and, standing up, did an agitated jig. "Oh *Gaaawwwwd*, I forgot to learn this scene." Flicking rapidly through the pages, she squealed, "And it's the *longest* scene in the play!" Big eyes looked at Dominic. "Oooohhh."

"How could you forget to learn it?" he thundered. "It's the most crucial bloody scene in the whole production."

"I know," Avril said meekly. "Oh God."

"You'll need more than God to help you," Dominic spat. "All the fecking saints and archangels will be on bloody overtime with your carry-on."

"I'll know them by . . ." Avril sought a realistic date, "by the time we go on?"

"Great."

"So, what? Will I, eh, read from the script now, or what?"

"Well, unless you think someone can transfer the lines telepathically to you?"

"No," Avril giggled a bit, unsure if he was joking. "No, I don't think that would be possible."

"Oh, technically it is possible," Johnny said. "All the scientific theories base their –"

"Read, Avril."

"Yeah, right." Avril stood up. "Now, I'm not great at reading aloud," she mumbled.

"Just do it," Dominic said, sounding totally pissed off. "And say it as if you were warning Sylvia, the Onion Girl, that all's not right."

Sylvia smiled graciously.

"Girl, me arse," Tony said. "Geriatric more like."

Avril exploded in laughter.

At least the bus was on time.

Meg put her bag on the overhead rack and sat down.

It was a far nicer bus than Mikey's, she thought. Padded seats, air-conditioning, piped music and most impressive of all, the fumes actually exited via the exhaust pipe.

It wasn't long before the motion of the bus caused her to drift asleep.

She jerked awake suddenly as her mother's face loomed in front of her. Fragments of strange thoughts that she couldn't quite catch vanished when she opened her eyes.

The guy beside her shifted slightly in his seat, looking embarrassed.

"Sorry," Meg muttered.

He shrugged.

She concentrated really hard on staying awake.

"OK, Sylvia. You are now making your decision on what to do," Dominic said. "It's kinda like the scene from *Romeo and Juliet* where she's wondering about killing herself. Did you ever see it?"

"See it?" Sylvia's voice dripped with scorn. "I *played* it."

"She didn't act it, that's for sure," Johnny whispered.

"Oh, stop!" Avril gave him a dig.

"Quiet down there," Dominic said imperiously. He gave a nod to Sylvia, "Right, off you go."

It was a spur-of-the-moment thing. Something to cheer her up. She bought a bottle of whiskey in O'Connell Street and, shoving it into her bag, she caught the bus that went towards Jack's apartment. He'd told her that he was only going home for Christmas Day and that he'd be there from Stephen's Day onwards. The thought of seeing him excited her.

It was no problem focusing on him instead of her mother.

And maybe the thing with her mother would all blow over? Maybe she just worried too much? In a few weeks everything would be forgotten, Danny would be history and her mother would be on the phone, annoying her like mad, asking her to come down for the weekend.

And one day she'd bring Jack down to Wexford to meet her mother. And they'd like each other.

And things would work out fine.

"Right Sylvia, here's the part where you discover the truth."

The bus stopped about ten minutes' walk away from Jack's place. Hoisting her bag onto her shoulder, Meg began to walk briskly along.

As Jack's apartment block loomed ahead, her head filled with doubts. What if he didn't want to see her? What if he was still in bed? What if he thought she was trying to crowd him? It was awful, but whenever she was meeting someone, which wasn't too often, she wondered why they would actually *want* her company.

Still, she told herself firmly, Jack loved her. Of course he'd want to see her.

As she reached the entrance to Jack's car park, her step wavered. Doing her best to look confident, she made her way across the car park. She had the uncanny feeling that she knew exactly how a soldier felt walking gunless in no-man's-land.

Jack's car was there and it cheered her slightly seeing the bright yellow flaking paint glinting in the sunshine. A big *For Sale* sign was plastered to the window. Meg stopped. Jack selling his car? He'd never mentioned it to her. Still maybe he'd only decided it over Christmas.

Maybe his brother-in-law, the mechanic, had found him a better deal.

She ran her hand across the bonnet and then, thinking how stupid she probably looked, she carried on.

The front door was closed. Pressing the buzzer for Jack's apartment, she waited.

There was no answer.

She pressed again.

Maybe he was out shopping or . . .

"Yeah?" A sleepy voice spoke. It wasn't Jack. Meg's heart sank. "Hello?"

"Oh, sorry," Meg stammered. "I hope I didn't get you up?"

"Well, I guess I should've been up by now anyhow." The voice sounded amused. "So, who is this?"

"Eh, I'm Meg. I'm looking for Jack."

There was a silence.

"Hello?" Meg said again. "Hello?"

"Jack's not here."

"Oh. Is he out?"

"Probably." The voice hesitated and then asked, "Is it a social call? You're not from Byrne's or anything?"

"Byrne's? Eh, no."

"He's moved into 4b if you want him. That's if he's there."

Meg guessed that the guy must be Peadar, the flatmate from hell. Jack had finally dumped him. "Eh, thanks," she muttered, scanning the bells for 4b. She found it and buzzed.

Answered first time. "Yes?"

The female voice threw her. "Eh, I'm looking for Jack? Jack Daly? I was told he might be there."

Another silence. "And you are . . ."

"Meg."

"Come up," slight hesitation, "Meg." The front door buzzed open and she went inside.

❧

Chapter Forty-six

She tried to dismiss the female voice from her head by admiring Jack's apartment block. It was much nicer than hers.

But who was the girl?

It didn't matter. She was there to see Jack.

She concentrated on the nice carpet in the foyer and on the fact that this apartment block had lifts and not woodworm-infested staircases. And the big containers of flowers that adorned the corridors were nice.

The only plant life in Yellow Halls was the fungus on the walls.

4b was situated in the middle of the second-floor corridor. Dumping her bag on the ground, Meg hastily flattened down her hair and peeked at her reflection in the brass handle on the door. The handle curved a bit, so it made her face look funny, but she looked as good as she could, she supposed.

Oh God, she hoped he'd be glad to see her. Heart hammering, she knocked.

There was movement inside. Footsteps. The door opened.

For an instant, her mind refused to believe who she saw in front of her. She'd only seen the girl once, waiting for Jack in the car park outside school, but there was no way she could ever forget that face and all that blonde hair. It couldn't be . . .

The two stared at each other.

The blonde girl, after eyeing her up and down, spoke first. "Meg." She had a saccharine smile plastered to her lips. "You're looking for Jack, are you?"

The smile confused her. Maybe it wasn't Vanny after all. Maybe it was just a friend that had called. She smiled back, "Yeah, yeah, I am."

"I see." The girl was quiet for a second. Then, "Well, Jack's not here at the moment. He's gone out with a friend." She paused. "I'm *Vanny*, by the way." She said Vanny as if it should mean something.

"Oh, right." Meg tried not to panic. What was *she* doing in Jack's apartment? "Hi."

"Hi." Pause. "Has Jack not mentioned me to you?"

"Well, yeah . . . I've heard of you."

"Oh really?"

"Yeah."

"Well, you know," Vanny said icily smooth, "that's *interesting*, because I haven't heard about you at *all.*"

"Oh," Meg tried to smile and when Vanny didn't smile back, she blushed. "Oh, have you not?" She wanted to kick herself for sounding so stupid. She knew what she should have said. She should have said that Jack was hardly going to tell his ex-girlfriend all about his current girlfriend, now was he? She bent down to pick up her bag and leave – there was no way she was going inside, Vanny was a bit too weird for her . . .

"So, what's the story?" Vanny barked. "Are you an ex-girlfriend?"

"An ex – ?" Meg shook her head. "No, I'm –"

"Did you give him this?" Vanny thrust something at her. "I found it on the floor of my bedroom. It's from you, isn't it?"

Meg looked at what Vanny had given her. A Christmas card depicting two snow people with their arms wrapped around each other. "It's my Christmas card to Jack," Meg said. "Yeah, I gave him it."

"Why?"

"Because . . ." She tried to make sense of Vanny's outraged face. "Because we're . . ."

"Going out together?" Vanny finished for her. Her voice was hard.

Meg nodded slowly, "Yeah."

Silence.

"You wagon," Vanny said slowly, "you *bitch*. You knew about me and still . . ." Her voice faltered.

What was her card doing in Vanny's bedroom? Vanny's? "Isn't this, is this Jack's new apartment?"

"Yeah. And mine." Vanny folded her arms and leaned toward Meg. "You've some nerve coming here, you really have!"

"Jack said it was over with you," Meg began to knead the card into her hand.

Vanny gave a slightly hysterical laugh. "Over?" she snorted. "Over?"

Meg gulped. This couldn't be happening. "It *is* all off, isn't it?" she asked.

"Off?" Vanny laughed harder. "That bastard moved in with *me* last week."

"But – but – I don't understand . . . he never said . . ."

"Oh, I understand all right!" Vanny sounded as if she was going to murder someone. Meg flinched but it was if her feet were frozen to the ground.

Vanny issued another furious, "I understand," before she slammed closed the door.

Through the numbness, Meg could hear Vanny stomping about inside the apartment. She stayed, staring at the white door for what seemed an eternity. At first, her head was totally numb, then the horrible voice that had lived with her all her life began its chant. *You should've known. How did you think he'd love you? Stupid cow. Ugly, stupid cow.*

Why would he be bothered with you when he could have anyone, when he could have Vanny?

The voice grew louder. Inside her head, things began to crumble. Thoughts began to tear through. It was like part of her was ripping itself open. The noise was unreal. Slowly, she bent down and picked up her bag.

There was so much noise inside her head.

There had to be some way of shutting it out.

"OK, Sylvia, this is it. The cruncher. You're alone, isolated, torn open, naked. Let's see it."

"Preferably not the naked bit," Johnny said. "I dunno if I could stomach it."

She got back to the flat. But it wasn't her. Not really. It was as if she was floating, flying, far above herself, looking down. Out of her body, feeling nothing. Only hearing the noise.

The bottle of whiskey that she'd bought looked inviting. Maybe with it she could shut out everything. Everything.

Chapter Forty-seven

Shane drove him back to the apartment block. He could have got a taxi but driving with Shane was better *craic*. They sang all the way home. Not only had they won on Athleague Guest but they'd won on the last race too. For the first time in months he was back. Back to form again. The guy with the magic touch.

Pulling up in the car park, Shane asked, "Are you heading for a jar tonight?"

"Bloody sure," Jack pulled on his jacket, "and I'm buying."

"Good man," Shane slapped him on the back. "See you in Foley's around eight."

"Sure." Jack climbed out of the car and waved Shane off. Patting the pocket of his jeans, he grinned to himself.

Life was brill.

He nearly made the mistake of getting off at the first floor. Old habits die hard. He remembered just as the lift was about to open. Pressing the button again, he impatiently waited for it to bring him onto the second landing. He wondered if Vanny had arrived back yet – in all the excitement, he'd forgotten to look for her car in the car park. He half-hoped that she hadn't because it would get him out of making up some excuse not to see her that night.

He jangled the keys in his pocket as he made his way toward 4b. A torn Christmas card was on the floor and Jack kicked it out of his way before unlocking the apartment door.

Vanny was sitting in front of the TV. She didn't even look at him as he came in. There were three plastic bags beside the door that he almost tripped over. Jaysus, he thought in exasperation, was there no end to the girl's efficiency. Out shopping already.

"How's it going?" he sauntered towards her and attempted to plant a kiss on her cheek. To his surprise, she pulled away.

"Your bags are over there," she said. "I want you out of here before I count to ten."

"What?" Stunned, he stared at her. "What have I done?"

"One."

"Come on, Van, tell me." He gave her a gentle puck. "Are you mad 'cause I wasn't here when you came back? Is that it?"

"Two."

"I didn't mess the place up on you. It can't be that."

484

"Three."

"You're lovely when you're angry, d'you know that?"

"And is Meg?" She twirled the remote control in her hand. "Four."

"Meg?" Jack repeated. "Meg?"

"Yes, Meg!" Vanny jumped out of the chair. All the calmness she'd promised to exercise vanished. "Or is she just one in a long line of extras?"

Jack felt sick. "How'd you know about her?" He tried not to sound panicky. "Well?"

"Oh, a Christmas card she sent, proclaiming her undying love for you was left in my bedroom."

He nearly died with relief. That wasn't too bad. At least Meg didn't know . . .

"Plus, the stupid bitch called around to see you today."

"No," Jack shook his head, "she couldn't have. She's meant to be going out tonight with –"

"Small, skinny, red hair?" Vanny walked towards him and he backed away. "Oh, it was her all right. A right little mouse."

"Don't say that about her."

"Ooohhhh, he cares, he cares!"

Jack felt sick. Ignoring Vanny's sneering tone, he asked, "And what happened?"

"What happened? What happened? *What. The. Fuck. Do. You. Think. Happened?*" She was almost eyeball to eyeball with him. The remote control in her hand suddenly looked like a dangerous weapon.

"Did you say anything to her?" Jack asked. He was backed up against the kitchen counter.

"Of course I did. I asked her who she was and what she wanted and then I told her who I was." Vanny began to poke him quite hard in the chest with the remote. "And her nice little smile vanished quick smart from her face, I can tell you."

"Oh Christ," Jack attempted to shove Vanny out of the way. He had to get out, to see Meg, to explain. His mind began racing. He could tell her that Vanny made everything up, that he'd only moved in with her because Peadar was annoying him and that he would have moved in with Meg only she was away for Christmas. That sounded good.

Vanny let him by. She watched him zipping up his jacket. "Oh, by the way," she said, "You owe me about five hundred quid."

Bitch!

Jack dug his hand into his pocket and pulled out a wad of notes. "Take what you want," he spat. He didn't care. He had to get to Meg.

To his surprise, Vanny didn't make a grab for them. Instead her shoulders slumped and she leaned against the counter. "Why?" she asked.

"What?" Christ, he wished she'd take the money.

"Why'd you do it to me, Jack?" Her head lifted and to his horror, he saw tears in her eyes. "I did everything you wanted, gave you everything."

"I, eh, gotta go."

"I never wanted anyone as much as I wanted you. I put up with all you did to me." She sniffed hard. "You even stood me up a few times and I accepted it."

He couldn't take this. "I'm going now. See you."

"Jack!"

He opened the door. He had to get away.

She followed him and tugged his sleeve. "Just tell me why? *Please?*"

He tried to shrug her off but she wouldn't let go. "Dunno," he said agitatedly. "I dunno." He tried to prise her hand off. "Just let me go, willya!"

"Where are you going? To her?"

"Yeah!"

Her eyes filled up. "Why?"

"'Cause I love her – right?" He had to say it, to get her off him.

That was it. She let him go. He saw the tears seep from her eyes. "Sorry," he muttered. "I'm awful sorry." Turning away, he let himself out.

The tablets lay smooth and white on the side of the bath. Fifteen white tablets all on a bath. *Fifteen white tablets all on a bath. If someone should take one, if someone should take one, there'd be fourteen white tables left on the bath.*

Giggling, smiling and crying, she sat cross-legged on the ground. The noise in her head was gone now, silenced. A beautiful calmness had descended. It was the best thing to do. She'd thought about it, and it was for the best. Living was so hard, living in her body was so hard that dying couldn't be any harder. And at least when she was dead, there'd be no noise or that horrible sad feeling she kept getting. Or any tension. And her mother would be happy and so would Ciara. And Jack . . .

She pushed him away.

Taking the tablets into her hand, she swallowed them, one by one. The remains of the whiskey was the ideal thing to wash them down with.

Why hadn't she thought of this long ago?

There was no petrol in his car, so he had to run all the way to Yellow Hall apartments. It seemed like an eternity before he arrived. It was like in his dreams, when he was trying to run away from something and his feet were moving like mad and he wasn't going anywhere. People stared at him as he pounded his way along but he never noticed. Arriving up to the door of Meg's place, he buzzed the bell.

No answer.

Jesus, he hoped she was there.

He buzzed again.

No answer.

He cupped his hands around his mouth. "Meg!" Then louder. "Meg! Open up if you're there! I can explain!"

Through the sleepiness she heard the buzzer. Well, she thought, whoever it was could go get lost. She didn't have to worry about stuff like that any more. There was shouting in the street. Yelling. Meg smiled. Soon there'd be no more shouting or fighting.

Her mind began to disconnect.

To free itself from her.

"Had a bit of a lover's tiff, did ye?"

Jack jumped, ready to belt whoever was making a laugh of him.

"Well, it won't be righted by tonight," James smiled up at Jack triumphantly. "She's off with me tonight. Dancing the light fantastic, don't you know."

"Have you a key?" Jack demanded.

"Amn't I the landlord?"

"Have you a fucking key?"

"Now, don't be taking that tone with me." James began to fooster about with his jacket pocket. "Don't be taking it out on me because you had a tiff with your lady friend."

Jack bit his lip. He had to keep quiet. There was no way James would let him near the place if he annoyed him. "Sorry," he apologised.

"'Tis fine." James buzzed the buzzer. "I'll ring and see if she's ready and sure, if not, I'll let meself in." He turned to Jack. "There's no point in you hanging around. You won't have time to talk to her."

"I need to see her," Jack said. "Just for five minutes."

James sniffed in disapproval. "Well, I suppose so," he said. "I suppose if she's fought with you, she'll be in no form for dancing with me tonight, so I suppose so."

Jack managed to look grateful. He couldn't help hopping from one foot to the other as James rang the bell again. She's not answering the bloody bell, he wanted to yell, but he couldn't.

"She's not answering the bell," James said eventually. "I suppose I'd better let meself up. I hope she won't mind. But sure she's quiet enough. She never says anything."

Laboriously, he began to unlock all the locks. "You're making me very uneasy," he chided as he banged into Jack on his way to open the last lock at the very top of the door. "Very uneasy indeed."

Someone was knocking on her door. At least that's what she thought it was. Knocking and calling out something. And she thought she heard Jack's voice. But that was only because she was getting drowsy.

Her eyes closed.

Bliss.

"She's not answering," James sounded worried. "I hope she hasn't forgotten. I mean, 'twould be *disastrous*. I'm after hiring out this suit and I've invested in tickets and everything. 'Twould be a terrible waste of money altogether." He knocked again. "Meg," he called, "I'm here!"

"Meg, open the door for Christ's sake." Jack began to pound on it. "I can explain. Honest."

"Hold on a second now," James put his hand up to

stop Jack. "Easily known you won't be paying for the door if you knock it asunder. Doors cost money, you know."

"Have you a key for it then?" Jack wished he could grab James, turn him upside down and make all the keys fall from his pockets.

"I have." James nodded. He knocked again.

"Well, use it, why don't you?"

"I'm not a snooping sort of a man. I only use it now and again." Another pious knock. "The girls need their privacy. Maybe Meg is in the shower."

"She hasn't got one."

James flushed. "Well, the bath then. And maybe she's this very minute rushing around, pulling on clothes, just getting ready to answer the door."

"If you don't open it, I'll knock it down."

James paled.

"Well?" Jack asked.

"Well, I suppose I'd better check that she's in there and that she hasn't forgotten," James grumbled. Taking out a bunch of keys from his pocket, he slowly began to sort through them. "I bring all my keys everywhere with me," he explained. "Never know who could rob them and break into the apartments." Eventually he seemed to find what he was looking for. Inserting it into the lock, he began a complex set of tweaking manoeuvres before the door clicked open.

Jack pushed past him and legged it into the hallway. "Meg," he called. "are you here?"

No answer.

James followed behind. "She's never forgotten," he muttered. "Holy Christ, I'll be the laughing-stock of the place."

Jack stood dumbly in the hall. The door to Meg's room was open and cautiously he peered inside. Her weekend bag was on the floor. The picture he'd given her for Christmas lay on the bed. Slowly he walked in.

"Hey, I don't think you should be doing that sort of thing," James chided, peering in himself.

Jack picked up the picture and held it. Where the hell was she?

The top of a whiskey bottle was on the bed.

Johnny Logan peered down. He looked slightly torn.

"Jack!"

The shout made him drop the painting, the glass frame shattering on the lino.

"Jack! Help!"

James' voice was calling from the bathroom. Jack got to the doorway of the bathroom just in time to see James slapping Meg across the face. "Wha'?"

"I think she's after taking some pills." James put his arms under Meg's armpits and tried to lift her. "Oh Jesus!" He looked at Jack. "Well don't just stand there. Gimme a hand."

Jack's head began to spin. She couldn't have . . . "Meg!" In two strides he was across the room and pulling her up. "Jesus, Meg?"

"Keep her upright," James ordered. "Keep her

walking. I'll ring for an ambulance." He looked at Jack. "James Junior's mother did this before."

Jack wrapped his arm around her. Her head lolled against his shoulder. He felt her hair on his face. He began to walk, her feet dragged behind, one of them bleeding slightly. "Meg, I swear, I swear, I'll make it up to you. Only please don't do this. Don't do this." He shook her slightly, "Please. Please." She didn't respond. He kissed her cheek. "Oh God, Meg. I love you. Don't do this."

He kept talking to her until the ambulance men came.

James spent his time pacing up and down the flat, saying over and over, "I know she didn't want to come tonight, but this is a bit drastic, isn't it?"

"It's not your fault," Jack said eventually, his stomach heaving with the admission. "I think it's mine." He kissed Meg, nuzzled her cheek. And felt something wet on his face.

For the first time in years, he was crying.

TWO DAYS LATER

Chapter Forty-eight

There was nowhere for him to go now. Nowhere except where he was heading. Jack sat on the bus, his face unshaven, his hair unwashed.

Meg didn't want to see him.

She'd told Ciara to tell him that she didn't want to see him.

He couldn't blame her.

When he'd arrived back at his apartments that awful day, he'd found his clothes scattered all over the car park. Vanny must have dumped them out. It was a relief, because he didn't want to have to face her and ask her for them.

He'd begged Peadar to take him back, told him he'd change, but Peadar hadn't bothered answering.

The guys from the bookies had found him and told him that unless he paid up soon, he'd regret it.

He was at rock-bottom.

He either had to keep digging to get himself out of

the hole he was in or give up and hand the spade to someone else.

They were going to discharge her the following day. Give her a pile of pills and let her off to live the rest of her horrible life. She didn't want to go. Ciara was beside the bed and was looking concerned. "Meg, why did you do it?"

She shrugged. Jesus, she couldn't even kill herself right. Her mother was sure to say that when she came in later. She'd probably made her mother the joke of Rosslare once again with her antics.

She didn't want to look at Ciara or answer her question. She pulled the bedclothes up and turned away from her.

"I told Jack you didn't want to see him."

"Good."

Ciara reached out and held Meg's hand. "I didn't know you were feeling so bad, Meg. I swear. I'm sorry for yelling at you." She squeezed her hand tighter. "If I'd known . . ."

"Nothing to do with you," Meg said. She pulled her hand from Ciara's grasp. "I just didn't want to live any more. My choice." Her throat felt like sandpaper.

"And now?" Ciara asked.

"Nothing's changed."

The bus dropped him off just around the corner from where he was going. He hadn't been near the place in about eight years and very little had changed. The bowling alley where he'd first met Peadar was now painted green instead of white but that was the only difference. Very slowly, he crossed the main road and began the walk down the lane.

Her mother stood at the end of the bed, unsure of what to do.

Her Nan came and looked down on her as she lay in the bed. "Meg, why?" she asked.

Meg closed her eyes. Why did everyone keep asking that? Wasn't it obvious?

"Why don't you buck yourself up?" her mother said. "God knows, I wish I'd time to be depressed." She gave a sort of laugh, as if it was all a big joke.

"Get out." Meg spoke softly, afraid that other people would hear. "Just get out, Mam."

"What?" Her mother's face dropped. "What do you mean, 'get out'?"

She didn't answer. It was as much as she had the strength or the nerve to say.

"I've travelled up here to see you. God knows, you gave us one awful fright. Didn't she, mother?"

"She did." Her Nan's fingers caressed her shoulders. "But thank God, it's all OK." Bending down, she placed a kiss on Meg's forehead. "We'll be here when you get out," she murmured.

That's what she was afraid of.

The house looked totally different. It sort of gleamed in the winter sunlight. Two of the top windows were open and all the blinds were up. A nearly new Fiesta was parked in the driveway. Jack stood at the pillar, unsure of what to do. Maybe he'd been mad to come? But he'd nothing left to lose. Not even, he thought bitterly, his self-respect.

His heart skipped about in his chest as he pressed the front doorbell. That chimed instead of buzzed. A happy sound.

Someone poked their head from the top window. "Down in a –" The voice trailed off. "Jack?"

He nodded. "Hi, Ma." His voice broke a bit. "I need help."

Her head disappeared from the window. He heard footsteps and the front door opened. She stood in front of him and held open her arms. "Come here. Come on."

Dropping his plastic bags onto the ground, he fell into her arms.

It was good to be home.

It was awful to be home.

Up in her old bedroom, dreaming horrible dreams, her Nan and her mother hovering about her like flies on shit.

Of course, she had to tell everyone that she had a virus. There was no mental illness in the family and there never had been.

Her Nan didn't approve of the lie, but her mother wanted it and she always did what her mother wanted.

But she couldn't any more.

So she slit her wrists.

∽

Chapter Forty-nine

"Meg, why are you here?"

She wanted to laugh. "'Cause my mother thinks I'm a mentaller?"

"And are you?"

"I just want to die."

The counsellor shook her head. "Most people who slit their wrists don't want to die," she said gently. "It's more a cry for help." She glanced at the anorexic-looking young woman sitting opposite her and asked, "Where are you now, Meg?"

Meg jerked. That was a weird one. "Here, in your office."

"No, in your head. Where are you?"

The question stunned her. It was something no one had ever asked her before. "I'm where I've always been," she said. She was afraid she'd cry. Afraid that this person would think she was mad too. And she was mad. She only had to look at her wrists to see that.

"And where is that?"

She wanted to say. She felt if she said it aloud, she might be free. But then again, it'd mark her out as weird.

"Go on," the counsellor pressed gently. "It'll be nothing I haven't heard before."

Her voice sounded like a scratched record as she began, very haltingly at first, to describe the place she'd lived in until she met Jack. But the look of acceptance on the other woman's face gave her courage. "I'm in a room," she said. "It's dark, but I can see into a bright street. People are going by and they can see me and I can see them." She gulped. "I can't talk to them though, 'cause they think I'm the same as them but I'm *not*. There's a huge sheet of glass between me and them, only they can't see it. And they wonder why I act weird . . ." her voice trailed away. Ashamed, she stopped. "My mother is right, isn't she? I am mad?"

"No. No, you're not mad. Plenty of people feel like that. They're anxious and depressed and when people feel that way, they can't connect."

In wonder and slight disbelief, Meg stared at her.

Gently the counsellor said, "I think you're ready for group therapy."

"No!" Meg jumped up. "I can't. I can't tell other people how I feel."

"Let them tell you and maybe one day you'll do it too."

He went back to GA. His mother said that if he didn't she wouldn't let him stay. She called it tough love. He called it tough luck. Week after week he listened to people telling their stories. Week after week he listened to advice.

Until one day, someone asked him his.

And he was ready to talk.

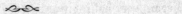

Chapter Fifty

"My name's Meg. I guess I've been depressed for years only I didn't know it. It was a way of life. Something I got used to. Then I met a guy and he made me happy." Her voice dropped. "For a while anyhow. And when it was over, I couldn't face life without the happy feeling and so . . ." she shrugged and held out her wrists, "*voilá*."

"How are yez? I'm Jack and," he bit his lip, "I'm a gambler." The admission brought a smattering of applause. "I've been one from," he screwed up his face, "well, since I was nineteen or so, only I thought I could control it." Someone laughed and Jack grinned. "I was different, you know. Anyhow, about eight months ago I met a girl, fell in love and wrecked her life." He was amazed that he could actually admit that in front of people. "And doing that to her made everything start tumbling down about me and . . .", he pointed to himself, "here I am."

"I guess I've always felt like an outsider, as if I didn't belong." Meg shrugged. "Which I didn't. My mother never wanted me." Someone sniffed and Meg was amazed it wasn't her. It was funny, now that she'd faced up to it, it wasn't half as bad. "She got pregnant with me at nineteen and married my dad. They weren't happy. And when my dad would leave after a row, I'd be the one to creep downstairs and start picking up the pieces. Telling my mother that I loved her and all that sort of stuff." Meg looked around the group. "My earliest memory is of being about three and trying to make my mother a cup of tea and she turning around and saying that everything was my fault." Rolling up her sleeve, she showed a small scar. "I spilled some hot water on my arm and my mother told me I was useless." She spent a bit of time covering up her arm, she didn't want them to see the tears that had come up out of nowhere. "But I loved them," she said, "my mother and father."

"I guess I always felt like an outsider," Jack said. "It was because me Dad was a bit," he rolled his eyes, "funny, I guess you could say." He looked down at his hands. He hadn't talked about his dad in years. "I suppose now he'd be diagnosed with depression or whatever, but the way my family dealt with it was by ignoring the whole thing. It was like," he laughed slightly, "like we had this massive elephant in the living-room and everyone pretended it wasn't really there." He looked back up. "Only I couldn't do that. I shouted and screamed and rebelled. Did mad things. And no one listened. No one except this girl I used to know." His voice faltered. "She was great. I was happy with her." He thought for a second. "My happiest memory of growing up is with her. I took me Dad's car – it was going to be repossessed as he wasn't going into work or doing anything so I said to myself, there is no bloody way anyone is getting their hands on our car. So I took it and brought Meg out with me. She didn't want to come but when she saw all the booze I'd brought, I guess she was afraid I'd kill meself or something. Anyhow she came and we both got a bit locked. And she ended up trying to drive me Dad's car home. She crashed it and while she worried herself sick, I laughed and laughed."

No one in the room laughed. Jack shrugged. "See. Shows how crap my life was."

"My happiest memory?" Meg smiled. "It's funny, most of my memories are pretty vague, but that's an easy one. It was nineteen-eighty. Johnny Logan won the Eurovision song contest. I thought he was gorgeous. So my Dad went and bought me a poster of him. It was probably the most thoughtful thing he ever did." She shrugged, "Just shows how crap my life was – huh? A Johnny Logan poster."

Someone laughed.

"My dad left the following week. Walked out without even saying goodbye. I never saw him again."

"My mam got a job in Dublin. I didn't want to leave. I liked Rosslare, everyone knew us there and I had friends. But it didn't matter what I said. My mother was going, my sisters wanted to go and my Dad was so out of it, he could have gone to the moon and not noticed." Jack's eyes narrowed. "In fact the only thing that bugged my Dad at all was the fact that I wanted to do Art. He kept saying that Art was for queers. He always picked on me." Jack stared glumly around. "It was the only thing that seemed to drag him back into the real world, me being a major disappointment to him." He shrugged. "Anyhow, the night before I was due to head to Dublin, I held this massive party in a field down home. It was brill, probably the second happiest memory I've got. I told Meg I'd write to her, and I meant to, but shit happened in Dublin and I couldn't tell her about it and I couldn't not tell her, so I just didn't write."

"My mother went to pieces after my Dad left. She drank herself stupid. I'd go looking for her every night with a guy I knew and we'd find her and drag her home."

Meg knew the next words she'd say would sound totally crazy, but everyone in the group had been so honest up to this. "I was happy in those days," she said. "My mother needed me and I was there for her. Somehow," she bit her lip, "somehow, I thought it'd make her love me."

"But it didn't?" someone said.

"She needed me, but that was it," Meg admitted. "I

was handy to have around. But it suited me. All I wanted was to make her happy. To get her to notice me." Big breath. "But she never did really, except when I made a show of her, which was pretty often so it seems. In fact, the only thing to have made a major difference to her was when she started seeing this guy Danny from down home. He made her happy and I was so jealous."

"Jealous?"

"Well," she licked her lips – she felt bad confessing how horrible she was, "he'd succeeded where I'd failed, you know. All my whole life had been for nothing."

"So it made you feel even more useless?"

Meg nodded slowly, "Yeah, I suppose."

"My worst memory?" Jack didn't need to think about it. "Finding my Dad dead in the garage. He'd killed himself with the exhaust fumes from the car." He ignored the gasps as he continued, hoping his voice wouldn't quiver. "We'd rowed quite badly. He'd slagged off my pictures, I'd told him he was a . . . was a . . . was a freak and it was the last thing we ever said to each other. Soon after that I had my first bet. My first big win."

"The most horrible thing that ever happened me besides my Dad leaving was when I played Rosie Redmond in a school play. She's a prostitute and," Meg hoped they wouldn't think she was boasting, "well, I really played her well. Really well." She kept her voice calm and unemotional. "We entered the play in a competition and it was the first time my mother had bothered to come and see it. I was so pleased that she was there. Thrilled. I acted my heart out. I won Best Actress and my mother freaked. She made a big deal of walking out. And when I met her outside, she started screaming at me. Telling me I was a disgrace to her, playing a whore. She made me pull out. Someone else got to play the part instead. Everyone in school thought it was a big joke."

She couldn't help it. Tears dripped from her eyes.

"The win made me feel big. Like a man. The man my Dad had always wanted me to be. The man I now wanted to be to make up for killing him. I sold stuff to get cash together to gamble. I," Jack gulped, "I stole. I stole to get money. And all the time I was being someone else. I wasn't Jack Daly, ordinary person, any more. And that suited me fine." He shrugged. "My family disowned me, me friends changed, I used everybody." He bit his lip, shook his head. "Jesus, I'm ashamed of the way I was."

To his surprise, people started to clap. Just a few at first and then everybody. Some woman patted him on the back.

For the first time, he felt accepted, understood.

And he knew, sooner or later, he'd be back to the person he'd lost touch with a long time ago.

"I kept up acting though," Meg said. "It was funny, being friends with Jack and acting were the only things I did that my mother didn't want me to do. But somehow I knew that if I didn't act, I'd curl up and die somewhere. I was careful of the parts I played though, nothing too offensive." She paused. "I was like a shell and acting made me forget who I was. Made me into someone else, filled me up. Made me into someone who wasn't afraid to talk or be funny or sad or whatever. But when I found Jack, I didn't need it as much any more. He made me feel as if I belonged." She gave a rueful laugh. "You should have seen the dregs I went out with before him. They were *bad*. I guess I thought they were so badly off they'd never dump me and plus, I could take care of them or whatever."

"But Jack was as bad?"

"Worse," Meg muttered. "He used me too. Or maybe I wanted him to use me, I dunno." She shrugged. "Anyhow, I gave up the play I was in. It was too close to the bone. I was playing myself in it and I didn't like that. I never wanted to be myself, not ever."

Someone told her they knew what she meant.

Meg looked at her amazed. "But you're lovely," she said.

"And so are you," someone else said.

Meg smiled, not too sure if she believed her or not. But she knew one thing: it was either find out who she was and live with it or be miserable, forever drifting.

Somehow, she knew that with this bunch of people she'd forged a connection. And that was a start in itself.

‿

EIGHTEEN MONTHS LATER

Chapter Fifty-one

There was only Meg left. And he'd eventually plucked up the nerve to see her. He'd rung up Yellow Halls and asked to speak to her. The person at the other end of the line had told him to hold, so he'd hung up. He knew she still worked there and that was all he needed to know. He'd already seen Peadar a few months ago – he and Eileen were now living in suburbia. Happily, blissfully married. They'd been dead nice. Eileen had even cooked him dinner. He wondered why he'd ever thought she was awful. Peadar had told him that there was no need to apologise but Jack knew that there was. He knew they'd never be the friends they once were but there was no bad feeling left and that was the best he could hope for. He'd stopped trying to turn the clock back on his life.

He'd tried also to track Vanny down, but she'd moved out of 4b and Jean said she didn't know where she'd gone. Just that she was happy to see the back of the bitch. Jack had felt bad about not being able to see her.

He looked at his watch. Ten minutes to lunchtime. He felt the pocket of his jeans for a fag and then remembered. No fags, no booze, no sex. Major danger of cross-addiction he'd been told. He was determined to give up the fags for good anyhow and maybe booze. And he knew that he'd never ever use sex to forget again. All he had to do was think of Vanny and he'd die with shame.

He spied some young fella sprinting across the yard, his head ducked low so that he couldn't be seen from the classrooms. He had his school-bag on his shoulder and he was so busy trying to avoid being seen that he bumped into Jack.

"Oy, watch it," Jack looked down, slightly amused. Then his eyes widened. "Brendan," he said, "bunking school, are you?"

"Nooo," Brendan said it as if Jack was stupid.

"Good," Jack nodded. "You don't want to waste yourself getting drunk for the afternoon, do you?"

Brendan's eyes narrowed and he stood up. "Naw," he said. "I'll just maybe take a pile of stuff from the school and try and flog it, will I, sir?" He said 'sir' with his lip curled up.

Jack flinched. He deserved it. "You don't want to do that either, Brendan," he muttered. "Look at what happened me."

Brendan didn't reply.

Jack took heart. "You don't want to blame your Dad for everything you do, you know," he said. "It's your choice too."

"With all due respect," Brendan hoisted his bag onto his shoulder, "just fuck off, sirrr."

Jack watched him saunter away. A few yards down the road, he took out a can of lager and raising it high, he turned to Jack and began drinking it. "Cheers," he yelled.

Jack began to wish he hadn't come.

The bell rang for lunchtime. Meg took out her lunchbox and turned to fill the kettle. Linda had spent the morning moaning on about how she was finding being single again after separating from her bollix of a husband.

"See, I realise now Leo being around was having a detrimental effect on Clive," she said. "You know, Meg, sort of making Clive *mental.*"

Meg nodded.

"I mean, you were a bit mental there for a while, so you'd understand, wouldn't you?"

"I wasn't mental," Meg said firmly.

"Yeah, right," Linda said as if she didn't believe her. "Of course not. Anyhow . . ."

And on and on she went.

Her mother had rung too, wanting her to come down for the weekend. So, because she hadn't made any other plans she agreed. She didn't feel sad going home any more. Sometimes she even looked forward to it.

And her mother, despite everything, was doing her best to try and understand why her daughter had suddenly gone mental and disgraced the family.

Meg smiled to herself as she filled the kettle up. It'd been scary at first, being herself, having an opinion, but it was nice when people looked at her and took her ideas on board. And she'd even managed to row with Ciara and still face her the next day. It'd been over the shower. James had installed the shower a year and a half ago, convinced that once she had a shower, she'd snap out of her depression. He'd asked her to pick what tiles she wanted and Ciara hadn't liked them one bit and they'd rowed. And compromised.

It was amazing how just saying what she wanted made her feel real.

There was a tap on the door.

Oh God, not at lunchtime. "We're on lunch," she called. "Come back at two."

"Meg?"

The cold water for the kettle splashed everywhere. She couldn't turn around.

"Can I come in?"

The water continued to splash into the sink as she tried to get herself together. "What do you want?" she asked, still unable to turn about. "You shouldn't be here."

"Yeah, yeah, I know, but I was too much of a yellow-belly to face you on home ground."

"So what do you want?" She made her voice hard.

She had to. This was the one person she hadn't liked thinking about. Even after all the time, the wound was still a bit raw. She heard him coming further into the office. "Well?"

"I need to say sorry," he said. His voice was firm. "I know it sounds crap after all I did to you, but it's all I *can* say."

Meg shrugged. She wanted to fling his apology back at him. To tell him that it was crap, but something held her back. Maybe it was all the apologies she'd had flung back in her face over the years. Nothing hurt quite so bad as that. "It's OK," she said. "Forget it."

There was a silence. She wondered if he'd gone, but he couldn't have because she'd have heard him. Slowly she risked turning around. He was standing opposite her, his head bowed, his arms dangling.

"Forget it," she said again.

"Thanks."

"No problem." She hoped he'd go. Seeing him brought it all back. She began to open her lunch box, trying to appear as if she had more important things to do.

"But, can I just say," Jack began, "can I just tell you that, well, I did love you. I loved you a lot." He ran his hand through his hair and looked straight at her.

"You don't have to say that."

"I'm not just saying it." The desperation in his voice startled her. "I mean it. I don't want you thinking that you didn't matter to me, 'cause you did. I came here to say that and now that I've said it I'll go."

"I suppose you said the same to Vanny?"

Meg sounded different, Jack thought. "Nope." He shook his head. "I was a bastard to her. I used her. I hated myself for it. But . . . but I loved you."

Jack's eyes looked older, Meg thought. The boyishness was gone. It suited him.

"I loved you to bits," he said softly.

"So why?" She didn't want to get into a debate – in fact she didn't want to talk to him at all – but now that he was here, in front of her, she had to know.

"I needed money. Vanny had money." His voice stalled and then started up again. "I had a gambling problem, Meg."

She wasn't surprised. It was as if she'd known inside somehow. "And now?" she asked.

He shrugged. "I don't gamble any more. I hope I won't ever do it again – but it's hard."

"Yeah, I bet it is."

"I'm looking for a job at the minute. Anything to do with Art."

"Oh, right."

"Is there anything going here, d'you know?"

The tongue-in-cheek way he said it made her smile slightly. "I'd say the only thing going would be you," she answered, "out the door."

"True enough," he nodded, glad that his horribly in-bad-taste joke had got a smile out of her. "Anyhow – I've said what I came to say. I'd better head." He held out his hand. "'Bye."

She hated that word, it sounded so final. "See you." She clasped his hand in hers. His was warm, his fingers long and slender. Artist's hands. "Take care."

"And you too."

He looked sad. But relieved.

"I'm glad you called," she said. "Thanks."

"Yeah." He let her hand go and turned to leave.

She watched the long length of him crossing the office. The bum that she'd found so sexy, the chinos, the new jacket that she hadn't seen before and probably wouldn't ever again. "Hey!"

Her voice made him turn around. He quirked his eyebrows.

Not knowing why she was doing it, she indicated her lunch box. "Seeing as you've come all this way, d'you – d'you want to share some egg and onion sambos?"

He didn't move. His hand tightened on the door jamb. His head bowed.

"Well?"

"I love them. They're me favourite."

The way he said it, sort of thrilled, made her glad she'd asked.

"Come over here so."

There was a slight pause. He wondered if he should. "I don't come in public."

Meg smiled. He smiled back.

He walked back towards her and she held out the foulest-smelling sandwich to him. Taking it from her, he couldn't help looking into her eyes.

He knew that he still loved her.

And from where he was standing she liked him a lot.

He could wait.

Even if it took forever.

THE END